# RIVER ᵒᶠSOULS

# RIVER OF SOULS

## A NOVEL OF THE AMERICAN MYTH

### Ivon B. Blum

SUNSTONE
PRESS
SANTA FE
New Mexico

This novel is fiction, entirely the product of the author's imagination, as are the characters and events which are used fictitiously without resemblance to actual ones, except purely by coincidence.

Sunstone books may be purchased for educational, business, or sales promotional use. For information please write: Special Markets Department, Sunstone Press, P.O. Box 2321, Santa Fe, New Mexico 87504-2321.

Library of Congress Cataloging in Publication Data:
Blum, Ivon., 1934–
    River of souls: a novel of the American myth / by Ivon B. Blum.—1st ed.
        p. cm.
    ISBN 0-86534-281-4 (hardcover)        ISBN 978-1-63293-148-1 (softcover)
        1. Mexican War, 1846–1848—New Mexico—Fiction.    I. Title.
PS3552. L8375R58    1999
813'.54—dc21                        98-46848
                                        CIP

Published by SUNSTONE PRESS
            Post Office Box 2321
            Santa Fe, NM 87504-2321 / USA
            (505) 988-4418 / orders only (800) 243-5644
            FAX (505) 988-1025
            www.sunstonepress.com

# DEDICATION

**The Memories**

Hon. Marvin A. Freemen  J. Everett Blum

with gratitude

**The ONE**

Beverly Krause Blum

with love

**The Partners**

Grant E. Propper

David W. Hardacre

with appreciation

**The Present**

Susan Burrell and Stephen Blum

with pride

**The Future**

Christina Allece

Savannah Marie

Sean Thomas

Jacob Ivon

with certain faith

# ACKNOWLEDGEMENTS

Barry Malsberg of the Scott Meredith Literary Agency said it was pretty good and agent Lisa Edwards has kept the faith with creative diligence.

The gals and guys at the Cambria Writers' Workshop sustain me.

# FOREWORD

By 1846, the American road to war with Mexico was a beaten path. For more than ten years, Americans from Missouri and parts east had been trading with the Mexicans of Santa Fe and beyond. The road of trade and of war was the Santa Fe Trail.

Along with the huge, ungainly freight wagons which rolled out of Independence in 1846, came an equally ungainly army of Americans with blood in their eyes and covet in their hearts. It was called the Army of the West under the command of Stephen Watts Kearny.

In August, the Army of the West took Santa Fe away from Mexico without firing a shot and with it virtually all of the vast area known as New Mexico.

In December 1846, Kearny headed his Army of the West toward California. He left Sterling Price, commander of the Second Missouri, as the military commandant of Santa Fe.

Price had just quelled an attempted uprising by a group of rich Mexicans who aroused the blood lust of the Pueblo Indians of the area to revolt. Thinking the lust of the Indians cooled and conspirators jailed, the new governor, Charles Bent, headed for Taos to spend the New Year 1847 with his Mexican, now American, family.

What Bent and Price did not understand was that Pueblo Indian blood, hot after two slave centuries, does not cool in a day.

In 1846, President Polk justified the war with Mexico by proclaiming that America's transcontinental destiny was manifest (plainly apparent for everyone to see and understand); but the war failed to prove that there was much of anything out west worth fighting for.

It took the discovery of gold in California, just as the Treaty of Guadalupe-Hidalgo of 1848 was being signed, to give sudden meaning to Polk's cry of Manifest Destiny. When the infant West joined it's little brother, Texas, it encompassed the desert lands of New Mexico, Arizona, Nevada, Utah, parts of Colorado and Wyoming—and California.

In 1847, Lieutenant E. Gould Buffum, New York Volunteers, arrived by ship at San Francisco, then called Yerba Buena (population 300 or so sleepy souls). He tells what he found there before the world rushed in.

"Prior to the discovery of the *placers* [surface gold easy to take] the country was thinly populated, the inhabitants being mostly native Californians [people of Spanish descent born in California], Mexicans [people of Spanish descent come from Mexico], and Indians [indigenous California Indians]. The better classes lived the indolent life of *rancheros;* their wealth consisting in immense herds of cattle and horses running wild upon the hills and plains. The Indians, with the exception of those living in a wholly savage state, were little better than serfs, and performed all the drudgery and labour. The great staples and principal articles of trade were hides and tallow, for which goods at enormous prices were taken in exchange.

"Money was the scarcest article on the coast, many persons never seeing a dollar from one year's end to another, ox hides having acquired the name and answering the purpose of 'California bank notes.'

"California with her delicious climate, her inexhaustible resources, and important geographical position, might to this day [January 1, 1850] have remained an almost unknown region, . . . had not a mysterious Providence ordained the discovery of the golden sands of the Rio Americano [American River in Sacramento].

"This event at once gave a tremendous impetus to commerce and imigration, and may be said to mark an important era in the history of the world."

Beginning in mid-1849, the world rushed into California. Attracted by gold and adventure in the new land, Mexicans from the Sonora mines, Californios from sleepy villages, Indians from the missions, Chinamen from an overcrowded homeland, other foreigners and gringos from the States all flocked like devouring locusts to the streams and ravines of the western Sierra Nevada mountains.

For the rest of the century and beyond, the trident magnet—gold, adventure and California—shifted whole populations westward and made a nation complete.

And so, the American West began in earnest. It grew up on the roll of wheels in the decade of the eighteen fifties (give or take a year or two).

As the decade opened, adventurers rode for gold on wooden wheels and dreams. Emigrants rolled across the plains and over mountains on iron wheels of determination. Goods and much-needed food followed tight behind on freight wagon wheels spoked with hard wood and rimed with perseverance.

By mid-decade passengers bounced into the west with the mails in leather-sprung coaches wheeled by six and eight horses and daring.

Wheels, weighed down with people and their things, plowed deep furrows in the new land. From 1841, when wheels first bent grass and tracked the snow, until 1848, perhaps 10,000 people made the crossing by wheel to the west coast. In 1849 alone, 22,500 or more people rolled into California; thousands more into Oregon. By 1857 a million animals had pulled more than 165,000 emigrants and at least that many wheels to California.

Like golden sands flowing through the rocker's sieve, people flowed into the new land, most spilling out the end, some, mostly nuggets, getting caught in the rifflers along the way. And where the people stopped, whether it was Sacramento, Portland, Salt Lake, Denver, Fort Kearny or Santa Fe, the people became markets for the goods and the news of the older east.

The goods came by the ton on wheels fueled by mules and oxen; and the news came by the thousands of letters on wheels, fast-moving, sprung wheels pulled by galloping mules and horses.

Wagon masters, missionaries, scouts, soldiers, scoundrels and settlers; bullwhackers, stock tenders, stage drivers and visionaries made the wheels roll to plow the long, deep furrows and plant the tall, everlasting people.

# I
# 1846
# THE TAOS WAR

# 1

Papa Cortez took the belt from the nail and, holding it in both hands, snapped it several times to clear the dust. The belt reflected gray and almost two generations of use in the slant of noon-day sun which lit it through the mica window of the adobe storage building. It had hung from a rusted horseshoe nail sunk into a piñon stud by Grandpa Cortez more than thirty years ago. Grandpa Cortez had died the year before. Now Papa Cortez was the Señor Cortez, known throughout the Valle de Taos as the Cortez.

"Assume the position, Pedro," he said in Spanish to the boy standing before him in the shadows of the large room.

"Si, Papa."

The boy, now sixteen, turned his back to his father and pulled down his deer-skin riding pants. He bent over and grabbed his ankles. Saddle calluses wrote of his boyhood across the pink of his rump.

The belt still looks big, he thought, but not as big as it used to look.

"In this country," his father said, "to risk the animal is to risk life itself. The animal must come first. You know it. Today you forgot. You raced her across the desert for foolish pride. Now the red mare is dead and with her, the many fine foals she would have dropped. Are you ready?"

The boy shut his eyes, not to the pain, but to the humiliation. Five times the belt flashed across the slanted streak of sun.

The thwack of the belt is still loud, he thought, but not as loud as before. The sharp sting was the same, and the shame which honed the sting with each stroke. The boy did not hate the beating. It was just. It was a work of love that would make him strong. This he knew. This he would remember.

"It is done," said Papa Cortez who smiled sadly but with pride in his eyes. He hung the belt on the rusted nail. "We will speak of it no more." Then he turned and walked from the room.

Pedro felt the sting deepen as the blood-welts began to rise on his backside. Slowly, he stood up. Pain wrinkled the desert lines already forming at the corners of his black eyes. I am sad for the red mare, he thought, and for the pain I have caused my father. Beneath the glowing rump and the shame, he felt a sense of joy which he did not understand, but accepted as natural, taking love for granted.

Pedro pulled his pants up slowly. Suddenly, he laughed with a groan, put his hand gently to his behind, felt the welts become ridges. He wrapped the red sash around his slim waist. The slant of sun through the gray dust of the mica-paned window lit the left side of his tanned face and bounced back from Spanish eyes.

He looked at the belt for the last time. Sweat dripped from the tip of his pointed nose and spilled into the black sheen of his carefully trimmed mustache. He bent over, picked up the wide brimmed leather hat from the dirt where it had fallen. Pedro ran a steady hand through satin black hair and crowned his broad shouldered, six foot frame. The laugh-groan had settled into a wry smile across firm lips.

It is tomorrow, he thought, that we move the horse herd from El Valle de Taos to the high mountains. To hide them from the American soldiers. Three days, maybe more, in the saddle. He imagined the all-day saddle hammer pounding the welt-ridges into rump-mountains and groaned again.

———

"It is done, then," said Mama Cortez as Papa Cortez walked into the cocina and tossed his flat crowned hat onto a hook against the wall. She spoke Spanish with a Missouri twang.

"Si." Papa looked at his wife and smiled. "It is not an easy thing to whip the boy who is almost a man."

"Man? Why he is still a child. My child," said Mama. She did not return the smile as she turned her back to stir the seasoned beef steaming in the large iron skillet.

"He is but a boy. He does foolish boy things. Sometimes wild things. You have hurt him for being a boy?" Her tone was not accusing; but a mother's sad voice.

"From the belt, a boy will grow, as I did, to manhood."

Papa Cortez put a hand on Mama's shoulder and gave her a gentle squeeze. She reached up and patted his hand.

"Not so soon," is all she said.

"I think, Mama, it is already too late. Today, I think I whipped a man. Pedro raced the mare against Montoya's Indian pony. The mare broke a leg in a snake hole. When I came upon him, he was standing over the mare. Montoya stood behind him with that Indian smirk on his face. When I rode up, the Indian stopped his sneering laugh, gave me a sullen look.

"The horse squealed with the pain of her broken leg. With only a moment's hesitation, Pedro slit the vein in her neck. I saw the sadness in his eyes; but there were no boyish tears. He had done what a man had to do, like a man."

———

As Pedro emerged from the adobe shed, he saw his younger sister, Anna, strike the iron triangle hanging from one of the vigas or roof beams which protruded from the adobe roof of the portal which shaded the entire front of the Cortez ranch house. It was dinner time.

Anna stood by the wide, solid piñon-log door with hands on hips and watched Pedro approach.

"Did the belt bite?" she asked with a toss of curly, auburn hair which framed a heart-face puffed by Spanish cheeks. A year younger than Pedro, she laughed a teen-woman laugh. Pedro saw feigned concern in the set of her soft lip line; but from the flash of black cat eyes flecked with green, he knew she was more than amused.

"You will know soon enough," he laughed. And they both laughed, knowing that Anna had never felt the sting of the belt. Its lesson was not for girls.

Pedro washed hands and face at the bucket which sat on a sideboard near the door and they went into the cool interior of the house. A large room served as both a living and eating space. Papa Cortez was already seated at the head of the long, oak table that, more than a hundred years before, had graced a room in the Cortez family home in Malaga, Spain.

"Sit, sit, children." The woman said this as she brought a steaming tray of food from the rear of the house, placed it on the table and took the high-backed wooden chair at the end of the table opposite her husband. The woman's hair was auburn, like the daughter's; but her eyes were Missouri blue.

When all were seated, Papa Cortez bowed his head. "Bless this food to our use and us to thy service. We ask in the name of Jesus Christ our Lord. Amen."

With a soft amen all around, Mama Cortez took a large tortilla of unbolted flour from the tray and spooned a helping of chili colorado over it. The tray was passed around the table. Papa filled a glass for each with wine. They ate in silence as was the custom for people whose meals were spanned by long hours of work in fields and on horseback.

Papa drained the last of the wine from his glass and picked up the clay pipe which lay on a sideboard. At the other end of the table, Mama rolled tobacco into a thin shuck of corn about three inches long. From a pocket in her skirt, she pulled a long, tin tube from the end of which hung a bit of cotton. She struck flint to steel and in a moment, the cotton tip was aflame. She lit her cigarillo and passed the tube to Papa who lit his pipe with the same flame. A sweet scented smoke soon rose above the table to greet the ceiling vigas.

"We Mexicans must be thought a singular people," said Papa Cortez through a wreath of smoke.

"Why, Papa?" said Pedro as he shifted his rump on the seat of the wooden chair.

"It has been only three months since the Americans came. Three months since Governor Armijo . . . ."

"That mountain of fat," said Mama quietly as she brushed ash from the front of her low-necked chemise.

" . . . demanded all of our horses, even those of our poor rancheros, those Indios who risk scalping and a parched or frozen death to safeguard our herds in the desert wilds, for the army to oppose the Americans. Only the rich Mexicans of Santa Fe favored war with the Americans. What care we, who must fight for a living from the land, that we are ruled and oppressed by a fat Mexican or a fat American. Yet, when Governor Armijo called for war, all New Mexicans shouted 'Viva!'"

"But Fat Armijo fled," said Pedro. "In August, he made a fort in Apache Canyon; but, at first sight of the Americans, he ran."

"Is still running, I think." Papa Cortez laughed.

"So," said Pedro, "the Americans took Santa Fe without firing a shot."

"And, in that way, they conquered all of New Mexico."

The pipe had gone out and Papa put it down.

"In the eyes of the Americans, we must appear a singular, cowardly people. Now, when we greet them in the street or at the fandango, we smile and call them amigos."

"Surely Govenrnor Bent will carry out the promise of the American general," said Mama. "The Bents have lived here in Taos for many years. His wife is one of us, you see.

"Last August in Santa Fe the American general stood on the roof top and said, 'yesterday you were Mexicans. Today you are all Americans.' And the people, the women, who had expected rape and branding, cheered."

"Then," said Papa wistfully, "the Mexican governor was after our horses. Now, in December, it is the American army which tries to take them."

"But, the Americans promise to pay for them," said Mama.

"In paper; not coin. Paper that may never be honored by the American government. That man who came here the other day."

"Sergeant Hess," said Anna. "Black Hess, he said his name was, his face peppered black. I did not like him."

"Nor did I," said Papa Cortez.

"He offered you ten dollars a head for the horses," said Mama. "Everyone knows the Americans offer to pay twenty dollars. 'Take the ten or your horses, we will just up and take; and you be damned.'"

Mama used English better to imitate the strange accent of the soldier.

"When you ordered him off the rancho, I thought this Hess would hit you or worse."

"Mama, for us, one oppressor is pretty much like another."

"This American oppressor will be back for the horses, I think," said Mama with a slight shudder of her shoulders.

Papa Cortez shot her a wise look and turned to Pedro.

"In the morning, we will take our horses to the high mountains where the soldiers will not find them. Go now, my son. Prepare the Indios for the long ride. Pick two good mules for yourself and for me. Until the horses are safe, it will be cold tortillas and cold beans for us."

"What of the Comanches, the Navajos?" said Pedro. "Since the conquest, they have become bolder, have raided many of the ranchos, killed, stolen."

"Our own riders can fight. They are Pueblo Indians. As fierce as any from the plains. Still, son, you are right. Nothing in this country is without risk. My hair is not so thick any more; but yours . . . ." They both laughed, then Papa grew serious. "In Santa Fe, the soldiers have just arrested many who would start an uprising against the American invaders. Mexicans—and many Pueblos."

"Our own mestizos would not . . . ."

"When the blood of a whole people is aroused, we must watch for sign. Watch." Papa paused in thought.

"Our backsides." said Pedro quietly.

Mama and Anna jumped up and, with quick movements, began to clear the table.

# 2

Montoya squatted in greasy buckskins and worn moccasins by the fire chewing a last piece of roasted antelope. He could tell from the night sounds that the horse herd was grazing peacefully. As he chewed, his hands rubbed the cutting edge of an arrowhead over and over across the thick piece of cowhide. This one was the last of some twenty arrows whose heads he had honed for war.

Of his five Indian companions, two were out with the horses, two slept and one picked between the small bones of the antelope carcass with a razor sharp knife for the last of the meat.

Montoya dropped the last honed arrow into his quiver and fingered the solid wood kachina which hung from a thong around his neck. It was his totem; and, with it, he saw the future in the rising puffs of smoke from the dying fire.

He stood as a new sound caught his ear from out of the night. The walk of a horse, not loose, but ridden. His small, black eyes pierced the darkness in the direction of the sound. His nostrils flared to the whiff of new dust.

"Hola! El rancheria," sang a voice from the night.

"Señor Pedro," called Montoya. "Venga."

Montoya's nostrils narrowed and so did the eyes. A quick sneer came and went with the purse of dark lips.

With a wave of the hand, Pedro entered the firelight.

Montoya stared back, expressionless. He did not return the wave.

The sleeping Indians were fully awake; but they did not move. Their bead-eyes watched Pedro dismount and warm his hands at the fire. The bead-eyes noted the two pistols in Pedro's sash and the musket on his saddle.

Pedro motioned with a shake of the head and a smile to the Indian by the fire to off-load the pack mule. Then Pedro turned to Montoya.

"How goes it?"

"Well."

"We move the herd in the morning, Montoya. Papa will be here with the sun. The pack mule has supplies for a week. See that the boys get some sleep. And yourself. You'll need it."

Pedro pulled the saddle from his horse and spread his blanket near the fire.

Montoya nodded; but stood his ground. He was a head taller than his Pueblo Indian companions and as tall as Pedro and thick in the shoulders and arms. The Navajos, who sometimes raided the Cortez rancho, knew him to be a fighter. So did Pedro. Although Montoya was only three years older, he had worked for Papa Cortez for as long as Pedro could remember.

In that time Pedro had seen him fight as a man; and, in the early years, Pedro had fought him knuckle and thumb, as boys will fight. Pedro had heard him sing and watched him dance in the firelight; but had never seen him smile, except for the quick sneer.

As Pedro settled down in his blanket, Montoya again squatted by the fire. He tossed several sticks on the fire and watched them catch the lingering fingers of flame and stretch them high into the dark. He caressed his kachina totem and saw the future in the rising sparks and smoke. He saw death in the rising sparks and smoke; and saw the killing. He saw horses prancing and biting writhing flanks and galloping up in the rising sparks and smoke. And, he saw lodges on a barren prairie and a Comanche woman, kneeling in the dust, chanting her death song in the rising sparks and smoke.

While Pedro slept, Montoya followed the smoke until it disappeared in the dawn; and they both awoke to the rattle of Papa Cortez coming into camp.

Pedro went to greet his father. Montoya watched the two white men, one his master for all of his life; the other his boyhood friend. He watched them embrace. His only expression was the quick sneer.

Then Montoya kicked the other Indians out of their blankets.

"It will be today," he signed with his hands. "I have seen it in the rising sparks and smoke."

"When you have eaten, Montoya," said Papa Cortez. "We will begin. We must move the herd fast; drive them to safety in the high mountains."

"Si, Señor Cortez," said Montoya.

The quick sneer flashed and vanished.

# 3

Billy Slade pushed at the coals of the fire with a burning stick as he talked.

"General Kearny, he says to Colonel Price, 'I need horses for the advance to California. Two hundred of these fine Spanish horses'll do. Pay twenty dollars a head' says the general."

Across the fire the large man with the blackened face listened.

"Well, the colonel, he tells the lieutenant. The lieutenant says, 'Cortez horses from up Taos way. They's the best in all of New Mexico.' I was there, Hess. I heard it all."

"In script of the government, the army pays," said the man called Hess, getting up and stretching his huge frame. "Cortez said he would not sell."

Slowly, Hess drew the saber from the scabbard he wore at his side, enjoying the sound of steel scraping on steel. He held the blade up to the firelight in a kind of salute.

"Maybe it was that funny accent of your'n," said Slade.

Instantly, Hess stepped through the fire and pinned Slade to the ground with the point of his curved saber.

"The accent is Prussian. Funny it is not." Hess glared down at Billy Slade.

"Ma-ma-manner of speakin," said Slade.

He tried to push the blade of the saber from his chest, cut his hand on the razor-sharp edge. He looked up at Hess. He could hardly see the face in the firelight. The face was nearly as black as the night. In the dark of the face, Slade saw the dull shine of ice-blue eyes, bleak with killing scorn.

" 'Course it aint a ha ha kinda fu-fu-funny," he said, trying to find a lifesaving word. "Di-di-different is all."

Slowly, Hess withdrew the blade from Slade's chest. He held the steel up to the light and watched the burn of reflected flame cut the dark like the burn of lightning skips across a night sky.

Still holding the saber up to the light, Hess said, "I come from the best. I am a Prussian. My father was a general. Napoleon, he fought. At Waterloo, he won. I was born with this blade in my hand."

Hess pulled his shirt sleeves up from hairless wrists and lowered his arms into the firelight.

"Look!"

Both thick forearms were ridged with scar tissue.

"It is how we played as children, young men, with the blade."

His face was in the light and Slade could see the ice of his eyes and the patches of gray over his cheeks, nose and forehead which made his face look black.

"If me and you are to work this thing of buying horses low and selling to the army at a profit, you must know of me, something." Hess slid the saber into the ornamented scabbard at his side and sat down beside Slade.

"No, Hess. I aint got to know nothin you don't . . . ."

"If you want to live, listen." Hess cut the Missouri man with a saber hand, chopping. "You have stared at the black of my face. No, do not deny. By the black of my face am I known. Schwarz Hess, Black Hess, am I called. When I was fifteen, a dog I had."

Hess let his arctic eyes wander into the fire of time.

"My dog had gotten old, like my father; but the dog was mine! One winter day, my old dog was lying in a spot of sun which sometimes warmed the cold stone floor of the great den in which my father spent his last years. Over the dog, my father stumbled. At my father, the dog growled.

"My father took a pistol from the many he kept loaded on the wall of the great den which was ornamented with his souvenirs of the wars. He cocked the pistol and handed it to me. 'The dog, shoot it so it will not growl at me,' he said. 'No!' I said. He struck me on the face. I pointed the pistol at my father and pulled the trigger. The pistol sprayed my face with burning powder."

"Did she blow up on you?" said Slade.

"At the time, I did not know. I could not see; the pain was nearly unbearable. Still, I heard my father fall. Even in the pain, I remember saying, 'you, no one, will slap Helmut Hess, ever.'" Hess rubbed his face. "Now, because of this, I am Black Hess."

"And your pa?"

"Shot through the heart. Dead. The pistol was just over primed."

"Your own pa, well, well. And over a slap in the face."

"An affront, a blow struck. My father knew. By him was I taught. A blow must be answered."

"All that 'cause of an old cur."

"The dog? Any other dog, I would have killed. But, this dog. He was mine!"

"Killed your own pa and got away with it?"

"Got away. From Prussia. Took ship in Holland. Jumped ship in New Orleans. Robbed my way up the river to Saint Louis. Killed many an innkeeper with this." Hess patted the saber. "Took what little they had, used their women. Them I also put out of the way; but more slowly."

He did not grin or smile, even; and yet, Slade thought, at least a smile was intended, though the black face seemed incapable of it.

"In Missouri, I stayed. Fought Mormons in '36 and until they moved on. When this war came up, the army I joined. The Second Missouri. I joined to carve Mexicans; but fight, they do not. This army, I am tired of."

"So we make us some money from government script and Mexican horses." Slade was smiling. He shoved another log on the dwindling fire.

"Now you understand," said Hess quietly. "I am, what shall I say, sensitive. Ja. A sensitive man. Not funny. Funny, not at all."

"Touchy," said Slade. "A mite touchy is all. Old Billy Slade'll remember."

"It is good. In the morning, we will buy horses at ten and, to the army, sell them at twenty."

"Or, just take 'um—for nothin. If'n the old Mex shuns us, we'll have to kill him."

"Ja."

"Two hundred horses. Fine Spanish blood."

Hess put a scared hand on the hilt of his saber. "Horses of Cortez!"

Billy Slade looked over at Hess.

"The woman and the girl. Handsome. Both handsome females."

# 4

A cold January dawn spilled gray light into the camp on the Rio de Las Animas, River of Souls. A piercing wind blew off the snows of Raton Pass.

Long John Hatcher crawled out from under the thick buffalo robe barely disturbing Louy Simonds, his sleeping companion. Hatcher sniffed the wind, circled the camp with sleep-crusted eyes, saw the picketed mules grazing where they should be and stood. He pulled a worn blanket from under the robe and, slipping his head through the hole in the middle, belted the square ends around his waist with elk hide. Then with charcoal blackened fingers, he combed the snarls out of his shoulder length, blond hair.

Hatcher knelt by last night's fire and arranged the surviving sticks into a small tepee above crumpled, dead leaves. Fluffing a tiny wad of cotton tinder next to the leaves, he extracted an extra flint from the leather pouch at his belt and a small file of steel. Flint hit steel several times until the sparks had ignited the cotton. The cold mountain wind did the rest and the fire blossomed.

Next, Hatcher took the sooted pot down to the river and filled it with water. Back at the fire, he took a handful of coffee beans from the pack and crushed them between two stones. A grimy hand brushed the ground coffee into the pot along with a bit of sand and a twig or two. Shoving the pot into the tepee of flaming sticks, Hatcher stood up and looked at the mounds of buffalo robes around the camp and smiled at the songs snored by dreaming men who slept into daylight.

Long John picked up his clay pipe, stuffed it with plug tobacco and lit it from a blazing twig. Indian style, he offered the first tendril of smoke to the east, the stem of the pipe to the west and inhaled a lung full of mountain man morning.

"This hoss is no bear to stick his nose under cover all the robe season," he exhaled. "Nor lay around camp like a damned Ned." His voice rose as he watched the mounds begin to stir. "There's two or three in this crowd aint had the greenhorn rubbed out even a little."

A head or two popped out from under the robes. From under Hatcher's robe, Louy Simonds grumbled, "Sacre damn hell. Holler when coffee, she is hot; till then, be shut about it."

Hatcher continued his morning song as if he had not heard.

"This child hates an American what aint seen any Indians scalped; or don't know a Ute moccasin from a Cheyenne. Sometimes he thinks of makin tracks for the white settlements; but, when he gets to Bent's Fort on the Arkansas River and sees the bourgeois and the fellers from the States."

Hatcher pulled on his pipe, let the smoke roll with the wind while his eyes watered from both.

"How them dandies roll their eyes at a Indian yell. Worse than if a village of Comanches was on 'um; or pick up a beaver trap to ask, 'what is this here contraption?' Just shows where the hellions had their bringin up.

"This child says, give him a little tobacco at a beaver plew for a pound plug, powder from Dupont and Galena lead, a Green River knife for eatin and scalpin, and this child leaves for the Bayou Salade. Damn the white diggins while there's buffalo in the mountains."

He stopped for a moment as several of the men slid from the warmth of sleep to wet the nearby brush.

"But old Charlie Bent's a friend of mine; and he's come up chief Mex of all New Mexico. He'll need men to side him." Hatcher looked all around the camp, blue eyes shinning with the fun of a fresh day.

"Are you for Taos?" shouted Hatcher, waving the stem of his pipe at the men. "This hoss is there in one sun!" And, he let out a whoop and slapped his thigh with his free hand.

Louy Simonds pulled up the front of his buckskin pants and jammed the wool cap down over his ears.

"The remuda's out pickin grass; and like me, too froze by half to travel."

He pulled a tin cup off the end of a forked stick which leaned near the fire and filled it with coffee. French eyes looked out at the small mule herd. With the first pull on the coffee cup he burnt his mouth, as he always did.

"Sacre damn coffee, why I do that each mornin?"

"With a whole day inbetwixt, it aint surprisin you'd forget, Louy," said Hatcher.

Long John Hatcher and Louy Simonds were middle age as the age of Rocky Mountain fur trappers goes—about thirty, going on thirteen. Hatcher was tall. Neither thick nor thin, he moved with the quiet and grace of a panther. His eyes of bright blue sky and billowy white cloud, never seemed to dance or dart. His look floated and drifted in the reflection of far off mountains; but never glanced back at his Virginia beginnings. Thick, dirty-blond hair hung to his shoulders and sometimes clung to the downy cheek-feathers which he had never shaved and which never seemed to grow past fuzz-curls.

Louy Simonds was short, not over five-six. He was olive and gray and French from Quebec. Hair and beard, which he sometimes trimmed in the spring, if he was drunk enough, were black—to match his teeth. Eyes the color of blue jay feathers mostly smiled and laughed, screeched and scolded in rhythm with the beat of talking hands. He wore a black, wool cap, which he never took off, except, sometimes, on a bet.

They had come to the Rockies in 1832 to trap beaver for the Rocky Mountain Fur Company with the likes of Jim Bridger, Joe Meek, Jed Smith, Tom Fitzpatrick and the Sublettes. Free trappers, they were, outfitted by the fur company; but free to trap and sell their plews as they saw fit and prices dictated.

They fed on the freedom of life in the Rockies. In times of starvation and plenty, they were sustained, like the free-soaring eagle, from within. When Indian arrow, snake bite or the high mountain snows of winter pushed a companion under, they laughed because they still lived in the face of death, free to soar on.

They laughed, too, because a tremor rippled in their blood. A tingle of fear overcome by a zest for adventure. To hesitate at the river's edge, to stop before the last snowy ridge was crossed, to dodge the fight, the hunger, the cold or the beaver saga was, for them, to miss life's all.

For them, to freeze, to thirst, to starve, to die meant a little; to live boundlessly meant everything.

· So, joyfully, in the ever constricting embrace of Fate's noose, heedlessly, they soared through life's treacherous hunt like the eagle.

For ten years, together they trapped beaver, fought and scalped Blackfeet and Crows. Starved on long treks over the unknown. Froze waist deep in rivers without end. Feasted on buffalo blood and broiled tongue and on nature's structured freedom. Their dead peopled every back trail. They sold their year's labor for just enough liquor to stay drunk for a week at rendezvous; and for just enough trade goods, powder, ball, beaver traps and tobacco to outfit them for the next year.

For ten years they soared like the eagle—until fate gave a yank on the noose—and the beaver ran out.

In the spring of 1842, Long John Hatcher and Louy Simonds left the beaver which had abandoned them; but they could not pull out of the noose of fate. With the youthful spirit of free trappers, they had worked off and on for Bent, Saint Vrain & Company as buffalo hunters, cattle drovers and Indian fighters, as the need arose along the Santa Fe Trail from Bent's Fort to Taos and Santa Fe.

Now, because they felt like going, they were headed down the trail again to lend a hand to Charles Bent, new governor of New Mexico.

In their camp this cold January morning were Captain Jackson, Company D of Colonel Price's Second Missouri with dispatches for Santa Fe, his lieutenant, a boy named Brown, to guard the dispatches and a private, called "private," to guard them both and all.

And there was Garrard, a seventeen year old boy from Saint Louis, out from the States for adventure. He, too, sought to dance in fate's noose—for a while, at least.

The neds, soldiers, so called because neds were pigs and salt pork formed the major part of Army rations and the mountain men, who carried dried strips of buffalo meat for food, mixed their rations in the pot for a warm and tasty breakfast awash with hot coffee. They ate quickly. When the last of the coffee was drained, the grounds were carefully saved. With full, warm guts, the men packed stiff legged mules ready to move out.

They headed south for Taos. Hatcher and Louy took the lead, with Garrard following them and leading the pack mules. The soldiers filed in behind Garrard and their own pack mules brought up the rear. Slivers of eastern sunlight cut among the turrets of gray and white cloud towers, the birthing day not yet decided between fair or storm.

As the small camp advanced out of the river bottom, the wind hit them with force from behind and before. It took the sharp dig of spurs to drive the animals into the face of the cold. Animals and men hunched over into the frozen knife of morning.

After several miles of undulating road, the trail began to climb. With the climb came some shelter as the trail cut along mountain sides and up a canyon into forests of naked aspen and piñon pine.

Suddenly, a rifle shot brought all heads up and a rush to the guts.

"Damn him, I miss," yelled Louy, his musket barrel pointing to a tall pine. A reddish squirrel scampered among the branches with a loud screech. Louy let his rifle rest again across the mule's neck and scratched his black beard with the free hand.

Then, turning in the saddle, he held up a hand. "It is many a time that this paw have held a forked stick with an old nor'west musket. She be one of Papa's guns—my papa who have long since gone under of the typhoid—when this child, his arm was no bigger than a beaver tail. This paw have propped this old musket for to shoot at such as that sacre damn squirrel.

"And when this old shootin iron would flash in the pan, I think, god damn old fusil. I am afraid to cuss out loud so my papa would hear. But pissed is pissed; and I be pissed; so, like an old bull buffalo still after a heifer, out come that 'god damn.' Then Papa would make me feel kinda like a sick beaver in a trap." Louy laughed. "But since then, this coon have raised hair so often he cares for nothin and nothin make him no more sick."

He pointed at the squirrel still scolding him from the tree and laughed again.

"What the hell's he talkin about," called the lieutenant. "The captain'd like to know."

Louy Simonds ignored the ned lieutenant.

"Garrard," Louy called back to the greenhorn. "Long John Hatcher, he will recollect the time me and him, we take Pawnee topknots away over on the Platte."

The boy, who had spent the morning quietly hauling on the leads of the pack mules and eating the leaders' dust, smiled, pleased to be paid a mind to.

"I can't believe you civilized white men scalped Pawnees, even if they were Indians," called Garrard into the wind.

"Tell him, Hatch," said Louy, turning his mule around an outcropping of rock which marked a sharp bend in the trail. Looking back he saw the soldiers pulling closer in an effort to hear the trappers' yarning.

"Tell, him." Louy disappeared around the bend.

Hatcher turned in the saddle. "Damned if we didn't."

He turned the bend in the trail and waited until Garrard had done the same.

"This child don't let no Indian count coup on his cavyard of horses and mules. But, this time, they come mighty nigh to rubbin us out. We wakes up in the mornin just before day, the devils yellin like mad. I grabs my knife and kills one and makes for the timber with four arrows in my meatbag."

Hatcher rubbed his stomach to impress the point.

"They have Louy. The Pawnees takes our beaver, five pack of the prettiest prime pelts in all the mountains and two mules. Lucky my traps is hid in the creek. But my rifle is in that beaver pack."

They had caught up with Louy again as the trail widened into a stream lined meadow of grama grass. They pulled up in a row along the narrow creek and dismounted to let the animals blow and drink. Hatcher squatted on his heels and scooped water into his mouth.

"Well, what happened then," asked Garrard.

"Was we killed, Hatch?" laughed Louy.

"Well, don't laugh." Hatcher's sky-blue eyes searched out each man's face. Smiles faded.

"'Here's a gone coon' says I to myself, 'if them Indians keep my rifle.' So I pulls the arrows out of my belly and follows their trail. At night I crawls into their camp and socks my big knife up to the Green River mark, first dig. I takes t'other Indians by hair and balls and makes dead meat of them too. Bein alone, still I count coup and dance over them. I gets my plews and the mules and this old bull thrower of a rifle. Then and there I make medicine over this here gun; and aint no damned hellion can draw a bead with it since, except me."

"Medicine or no, that old bull thrower and your bead is both blind as a tree," said Louy.

"Did you save Louy from that Indian camp?" asked Garrard.

"Best we get started," said Hatcher, eying the trail ahead and the back trail. He mounted.

"Louy? naw. He were scalped."

Hatcher looked at Garrard and the others with a dead serious face; then headed up the trail.

"It is truth," laughed Louy following Hatcher.

From the rear, Captain Jackson called out, "some tall tale. You from Missouri, Mister Hatcher?"

Hatcher reigned in his mule, looked back at Louy. The others closed up to them.

"Captain, I'm from the Rocky Mountains. I've took more beaver, hugged more squaws, drunk more mountain dew and told more lies than many another savvy old coon. But this aint no yarn. And to prove it, I'll put up all our buffalo meat against all your army ned—winner to feast, loser to hunger—till he finds game in these mountains or we get to Taos."

The captain laughed a sheepish grin. "No offense, but that isn't proof."

"Put up or shut up, Captain." Hatcher folded his arms across his chest.

"Our rations against yours, all of yours? We don't hardly have rations enough to keep hunger away as it is. Nor do you. But, cut a couple fellows out of the mess."

The captain hesitated, looked at the lieutenant who nodded slightly.

"Scalped? If you can prove . . . ."

He didn't get a chance to finish.

"Done!" said Hatcher. "Show him, Louy!"

Louy slowly pulled off his wool hat. His skull was bald. Around the crown ran a jagged, red halo. Within the halo, was a wrinkled, blackened scar-mass where scalp and hair once grew.

The captain inhaled audibly.

"Jesus!" said Garrard.

Louy ran his fingers over his head, scratching.

"When the winds blow, I think sometimes I still have the hair." He laughed.

"Put on that hat, Louy. Your scalp don't look right," said Hatcher. "Garrard. Cut out the army mule that's haulin the soldiers' rations."

Garrard looked at Hatcher. Then at Captain Jackson.

"Mister Hatcher," said Jackson. "You wouldn't take our food? Leave us to hunger?"

"Garrard, the mule," said Hatcher. "Captain, this hoss would and will." Then Hatcher smiled. "You aint got ought to worry you. By nightfall, you'll surely run across game. And tomorrow—Taos. Or, maybe day after."

That night, they camped at the top of the pass. Below them, many miles distant, El Valle De Taos. Hatcher, Louy and Garrard squatted around a roaring fire and scooped hunks of buffalo and salt pork from the pot into their mouths. The soldiers, at their own fire looked on, their only supper, army coffee.

Garrard looked over at the soldiers who were staring into their fire trying not to hear or see the two trappers smacking lips and licking fingers; but unable to avoid the alluring smell of the feast.

"Hatch," he said quietly, "it's time we gave some to them. The joke's been played out."

"Aint no joke. In the mountains, it's every man for himself. Louy forgot that first rule of survival and lost his hair to a Pawnee. Near come to dyin."

"Forgot?"

"At the first whoop, he comes up from the river; sees me a-pullin arrows from my gut and inchin toward the timber. He comes for me; but 'bout that time I jumps for the woods. Last I seen, an Indian lights on top of Louy and pulls his topknot slick as you please."

In spite of themselves, the soldiers were listening.

"After I regained the mules and my possibles, I found Louy sittin by the dead fire where our camp was, a-swayin and a singin the death chant of the Cheyenne. Right off, I could see his hair was gone and blood was fast spillin from the top of his head."

"This child knowed for true he was goin under," said Louy with a grin.

"I could see where the blood was mostly comin from so I sprinkles a little gun powder in the deepest cuts and lights her off. Well, with that Louy just stops his chantin and slumps back. I lays his head on the seat of his saddle and throws a robe over him. After a while, I gets wore out wavin my hat to keep the flies off of his crown; so I wets a quarter plug of tobacco and pastes it over the wound. It were two days before he wakes up and asks for coffee."

Hatcher stuck his Green River into the pot and tossed a hot hunk of salt pork at Louy who juggled it in his hands to let it cool. Then with a greasy smack of his lips, it was gone.

Hatcher found a piece of meat for himself. With strong white teeth, he tore off a chunk and chewed it down, lean and fat and all.

"Today Captain Jackson forgot. He gambled supper over a yarn. His own supper and that of his men. In these mountains meat is life."

He leaned back on his saddle and tamped tobacco into his pipe.

Captain Jackson got up from the fire and came over to Hatcher, his hand outstretched.

"You teach a hard lesson, Hatcher; but I'm obliged."

Hatch took the hand and gave it a shake. Jackson looked over at the steaming pot.

"Now that I've been educated somewhat, how about?" He nodded toward the pot. Hatcher picked up his big Green River knife and slowly wiped the grease from it onto his deerskin pants.

"Well, Ned, school aint out just yet. Not till you find game on your own." Hatch pointed the tip of the knife up at Jackson. "Like Louy will tell you, in these mountains, it's each man for his own self." The thick knife blade did not waver.

"A fat deer is better than army ned any day," said Garrard.

"Beats all save buffalo," said Louy laughing.

Jackson looked from Louy to Hatcher. After a moment he, too, laughed.

# 5

The boy, called Morning Light by his Pueblo family, sat on the dirt floor with his back to the adobe wall of the dark room. He was tired from the night long ride from Taos Pueblo to this lonely adobe ruin north of Santa Fe.

A slanting moon cast slivers of light and shadow through holes in the roof. On a rickety table a tiny candle flame mated with the moon to light the faces of five men.

The men stood or leaned on the table with their hands.

"Tomorrow night. Before the rise of the moon. You will kill Governor Bent. Kill all of the Americans."

The speaker wore the face and dress of a Spaniard, lace at the throat of a soft cotton shirt, a calf skin vest, leather pants, split down the sides and joined with silver buckles. A ruby colored sash held two pistols at his waist. A turquoise encrusted silver cross hung from the silver chain around his neck.

In a small village outside Santa Fe, he kept a woman who was mother to his four children. He had served the people of the village and of Santa Fe for many years.

He was their priest.

"It shall be done," said a tall Indian who stood at the edge of the table.

"We are the people of the pueblo. We have risen before to kill the Spaniards."

He did not seem to notice a slight hitch in the tall Spaniard's breath; or, did not care.

"The old people tell the old stories. Now, we will make a new story for our children to tell in the kivas. Never again will the Pueblo be the slaves of the Spanish, the Mexicans or these new Americanos."

The tall Indian said no more. The room was silent. His song of death had been sung.

"Muy bien," said the Spaniard after a moment. "Generalissimo Armijo will be well pleased with his Indian brothers."

Morning light stood up and approached the table. Although he was only a boy of sixteen, he carried the short, deadly bow of a warrior. Still, before the tall Indian and the others of his tribe, he had to speak with care.

"I am Morning Light, called Lopez by the Mexicans."

"You are but a boy," said the Spaniard.

·"I am chosen, Father, to carry the message of war back to my people in the pueblo at Taos.

"Bien, muy bien," said the Spaniard, dismissing Morning Light with a pass of his hand. "Go. Sit. When we have finished . . . ."

Morning Light put a hand on the table. The waving flicker of candlelight caught for a moment in his wet, black eyes.

"Generalissimo Armijo," said the boy in quiet Spanish, "is a coward."

The Spaniard flashed a hand to his pistol sash. The tall Indian's hand held it there in a grip of steel.

"The boy will speak."

"The coward, Armijo, fled before the Americanos, the Mexicans with him. I spit, my people, spit on his name."

All in the room felt the Spaniard stiffen like wet rawhide exposed to the sun. He said nothing. The boy continued.

"The Pueblo people do not fight for the Spaniards, the Mexicans, those who ran! We fight for our own place in this land which has been our life and our grave for a thousand years. We fight all oppressors. If we win tomorrow, if you Mexican Spaniards defeat the Americanos, even then, the Pueblo people will not join you. The valley of Taos will be ours. I have been told by the elders to say: It is the decision of the Pueblo."

"It is the decision of the Pueblo," said the tall Indian. Slowly, he released his iron grip on the Spaniard's wrist.

"I understand," said the Spaniard. He relaxed the hand on his pistol, felt the hand of the tall Indian withdraw. Fingering the silver cross with his newly freed hand, he looked around the small room at the shadow faces of the four older Indians. Each nodded. The boy called Morning Light stood tall and still.

"It shall be so," said the Spaniard. "If you win tomorrow. If you kill the governor, the Americanos."

The tall Indian waved a hand at Morning Light.

"It is war!"

The boy turned and vanished from the abandoned adobe. In an instant, the men in the small room heard the sudden thud of his running horse. In another instant, silence.

The remaining Indians walked from the hut to a string of mules laden with weapons supplied by the Spaniard. Rifles, powder, lead, knives. They checked the loads. Satisfied, they mounted their ponies and slowly led the train of mules across the barren land down a north-sloping moonstreak.

"It is war!" whispered the Spaniard although now alone. A sly smile cut the corner of his mouth.

"Praise God!" he sighed up at the night-streaking moon.

# 6

Pedro Cortez stood tall in the stirrups and put the Arabian headed, gray horse into a lope around the grazing herd. When he reached the front, he pulled the horse to a walk. Papa Cortez sat an identical Arabian gray and watched the huge ramuda file past him along the narrow mountain trail. They were hazing the horses away from the Americans to a wide, grassy canyon high in the mountains.

"I count one hundred and twenty four head, Papa."

He still stood in the stirrups, remembering the pain with each pat of his rump on the saddle.

"Nearer to one fifty, I make it," said Papa Cortez. "Most all the loose stock in the valley, for sure. Some, maybe, are not even ours. But, we have no time to sort them now."

Father and son looked out over the herd being pushed slowly by Montoya and his five Pueblos. The Indians rode Cortez horses. Pedro watched them circle the herd, now and then jumping a horse back into the line of march. Pedro noted that, as usual, each Indian was fully armed with bow, a full quiver and a belt knife. Usually, the bow was carried in the quiver—unstrung. But, now each bow was in hand. Each was tautly strung.

Once, he locked eyes with Montoya; saw the quick sneer quickly pass.

"The Indians do not shout and sing," said Papa Cortez. "They are riding very quiet. It is not like them."

He watched Pedro settle carefully back into the saddle; noted the straight back and broad shoulders with pride; and the way Pedro checked the pan of his musket to make sure the priming powder was there.

"Regain the point, my son. When you are out of sight of the Indians, check your loads and re-prime the pistols." He pointed to the two single shot flintlocks in Pedro's red sash. "Have much care."

Pedro flashed a broad smile and, again up on his toes, he cantered along the edge of the herd toward their leaders and the canyon of refuge.

The trail was all in shade now. High rock walls rose to meet the sun's descent and push it down the other side of the mountain. Pedro rode far ahead of the herd leaning to the side with each twist in the trail or forward as the gray Arab scrambled up over rocky steps. Soon the trail plateaued and widened slightly. Ahead Pedro saw the ridge which formed the lip of the canyon. He spurred the gray away from the trail and through the trees.

Quickly he met the trail again at the top of the ridge, ready to turn the herd into the sloping canyon mouth. He looked into the deep canyon, saw several antelope feeding in belly-high grass, watched evening's shadow wash down jagged rock columns splashing vermilion and mauve with steepening purple.

Pedro measured the canyon with his eyes. A little over a mile long; maybe a half wide. Grass, water from the spring at the far end. Most of a day's sun in summer; almost none in winter. In winter, mostly sheltered from the deep snow. This will support the herd for maybe a month, a little longer. Then we will have to move them. This is not my valley, he thought. Not the valley of my dream. Too high, this one. Too small for a permanent rancho. And, yet, like this one, is the valley of my dream.

Abruptly, Pedro turned his head, made a quick jab with the spurs, turned the gray to face down the trail. He saw the coming horse herd.

But that was not what had made him jump. He heard it again. A gun shot! Two shots, maybe another he had not heard. Papa!

Sensing his master's anxiety, the gray danced and threw its head, spume coming from its mouth. Pedro sat the saddle hard; but did not feel the pain. He reined the horse in tight. What to do? If I go to Papa, the horse herd will not turn into the canyon, he thought. In an hour they will be spread all over these mountains. But, if I stay?

Suddenly, three inch rowels dug into the gray's ribs. Instantly, he jumped into a dash down the trail toward the oncoming horses. At the last minute, Pedro turned the gray up the mountain side to climb and slip and slide along the flank of heaving, sweaty horse flesh now stampeding past him. The gray lunged down toward the flying herd compelled by panic to panic with its own kind.

Trembling legs stiffened into a slide as the steep slope gave way. On its knees now, hind legs flying out behind, the horse rolled over onto its head and tumbled into the heaving mass of pounding hooves and slashing shoulders and undulating death.

Just before the lunge, Pedro had felt the panic surging through the gray, taking control. He fought the sudden jerk of reigns in his hands, hauled the horse's jaws with all of his strength, spurred for control. Lost his hat. Lost his musket. Lost control.

The horse rolled forward into the stampede. Pedro rolled sideways into a tree trunk.

He lay where he had fallen at the root of the tree for a long time. The herd was gone. Its dust had settled into the dark of night; but he still smelled the raging fear.

Pedro listened to the quiet. The clacking of naked aspen branches, the scurrying of small feet, a sharp squeaking, a flapping of wings, rocks clicking with night's cooling. Mountain quiet.

As Pedro's head cleared, he remembered. With effort, he pulled himself up by the tree trunk. Even in the dark, he could see the body of the gray horse lying across the trail below. Letting go of the tree, he took a step on quaking legs, slumped to his knees and rolled down the mountainside to the trail.

After a dizzy moment, he got to his feet and stood waiting for the wobbles to leave his legs. Slowly, he limped over to the dead horse. With effort, he pulled off the saddle and bridle and lugged them to the side of the trail. He felt the cold. From the saddle bag, he took out a serape and pulled it over his head. He fumbled in the bags for anything else that might save him from the mountain. Food. A knife. Flint and steel for a fire. Powder and . . . .

It was then that he felt for the pistols in his sash. They were not there.

Although Pedro climbed the mountain to the place where he thought he had fallen, he found nothing. The pistols, his musket—gone.

Back on the canyon trail, he pushed the saddle and tack behind a tree and into the low brush, hoping he, but no one else, could find it.

Pedro reckoned that he had come about five miles since he had last seen Papa. He began to walk back down the dark trail to find Papa and the Pueblos, a camp, a warm fire and food. Although he hurt all over, he quickened his pace, careful to miss the roots and loose rocks, stumbling anyway.

A wolf's siren echoed against canyon walls. How close? Pedro could not tell. He could see the rocks and ruts in the trail better now. Last night's moon, even bigger and brighter tonight, he thought.

In the hours till dawn, Pedro walked, stumbled, rested, shivered under his serape and walked on. He did not find a warm camp or fire or food.

But, in the pale light of dawn, he found Papa Cortez.

From up the trail, Pedro first noticed a lump, meaningless, except that it looked out of place. As he approached, the lump took on shape and sudden meaning. Then Pedro saw the arrows. He counted seven sticking out at odd angles from his father's back. Papa Cortez lay on his left side, legs and arms drawn into his chest, the way he must have lain just before his primal scream at life.

Up close, Pedro saw that his father had struggled for a long time. The left leg had dug a deep circular trench as it swung back and forth in the trail dirt, like a pendulum swinging until the clock stopped. The outstretched left hand had clawed the sand and pebbles until the nails had torn. The right hand was a clenched fist against his chest.

The black hair shot with gray—thinner than Pedro's—was gone—except for a halo tinged with red around the scalp-line.

Pedro looked up to the paling sky, up the trail over which he had walked the night away, down the trail to the valley below from which they had come. But, he could see nothing else in the new-dawn except the lump which had been his father and the seven Pueblo arrows sticking out.

Young Pedro knelt at the lump's drawn up feet as if to pray. He reached a hand out to touch the dead shoulder. His hand recoiled from cold and stiffened texture. Death smelled like dust. He yanked at the arrows, as if to withdraw them would restore warmth to the lump. They would not come lose. One broke off in his hand. He looked at it for a moment; then dropped it in the sand. He clasped the right handed fist; felt something in it; pulled. A kachina totem fell to the ground.

"Montoya!" he screamed at the dawn. "Montoya!"

The dawn answered. A splinter of light danced across the lump's dead face only to fade away at the whim of the marionette sun.

Pedro began to shake; and he knelt there in the deserted morn and shook; but tears did not come to his eyes—only to his heart. It took Pedro until midmorning to dig a burial slot in the mountainside. He used sticks and pieces of rock; and finally, the hole was big enough. Still, Pedro had to break off the arrow shafts before the corpse would fit far enough into the slot to keep out the wolves. He said no words over the burial mound; thought of Papa Cortez only as he had lived.

He was my strength, prayed Pedro. Until now, always outside me, a man-tit upon which I suckled a little at a time while I grew. He felt the transfer of strength flow into him. Now his heart is my heart, his strength is my strength, mine, inside me. Pedro looked up through the trees and into the sky where all men search when there is no place else.

"Wherever you are, Papa," he prayed aloud, "I will make you proud. I will care for Mama and Anna. I will reclaim the horses—and your scalp! I will, I will, I . . . ."

He gripped the kachina totem in his fist, felt something break. Now the tears came—and the shame for them.

Pedro wiped his cheek, crossed himself and turned from the grave. He tied the kachina totem around his neck. He did not notice the right arm was broken and missing.

Montoya will know, he thought. He will know I come.

Involuntarily, Pedro looked all around him. Maybe, even now he waits—for the first shot.

He looked down the steep trail toward the Valle de Taos and home. He looked up the trail where his horses and his Indians, and Montoya, had gone. He was tired and hungry and hurt; but he headed up the trail.

Sadly, he whispered into the night, "now, I am the Señor Cortez! I must be the Cortez!"

# 7

The morning sun hung in the sky like winter, light without warmth. Black Hess and Billy Slade rode into the yard of the Cortez rancho and pulled up at the hitching rail in front of the log front door to the adobe ranch house. Billy Slade slipped from the saddle to the dry ground. Hess sat his saddle. He looked across the yard to the corral, saw three young horses nosing the dust for bits of straw. One of the horses raised his head and looked back at Hess. The young horse trumpeted a greeting and trotted to the pole fence of the corral and flared his nostrils at the newcomers.

Hess turned his powder burned face to the door and called out, "the house, hello!"

There was no immediate response. Billy Slade pulled his musket from the saddle scabbard and moved to the left of the door.

The curious horse whinnied again from the corral. As if in response this time, Mama Cortez came around the end of the long adobe. In her arms she carried a gaggle of women's things, chemises, cotton skirts, undergarments, the morning laundry.

As she saw the riders, she stopped, pressed the ball of clothing closer to her bosom. She hesitated only a moment, then stepped along the veranda to the door.

"Buenas días, Señores," she said, but did not smile.

Hess stared at her, saw past the bundle of washing, saw the mature woman, saw the handsome face framed by auburn hair, saw full lips, now hard set, saw her narrowed, blue eyes squeeze the laugh lines at the corners, saw no fear.

Hess fisted the hilt of his saber. Mama Cortez' expression did not change.

"Cortez, he is here?" he said. "The horses. We have come to take the horses for the army."

Hess looked off to the west into the grassy plain which only last week had held the large herd. Now, he could see it was empty. He pointed.

Mama Cortez put the clothing down on the long bench by the door, glanced at Billy Slade leaning on the muzzle of his musket, faced Hess. With a bounce of her ample bosom, she placed hands on hips.

"The Cortez horses are not for sale to the Americano army. My husband told you that. You have had a long ride for nothing." She crossed her arms in front of her chest. "You may have water from the well," she pointed to the well next to the corral, "for yourselves and your horses, before you go."

"From a woman, I do not buy horses."

"Not from this woman," Mama Cortez slipped from Spanish to Missouri. "That's for damn sure."

"Call your husband; or aint he here?" said Billy Slade with a leer to his voice.

Hess got down from his horse. "We will see," he said.

Mama Cortez moved to block the door. Hess walked right through her; her back slapped hard against the log door; the door swung open. Backward motion exceeded Mama Cortez' foot speed and she slammed rump first onto the floor. Hess stepped over her and froze. Billy Slade, who had followed close on Hess' heels, jammed the barrel of his musket into the Prussian's stiff back. The impact did not move Hess. He stood over Mama Cortez and stared into the dark room of the ranch house.

"Mama slide to your right," said a girlish voice. "Out of the way."

Hess watched the older woman roll over and crawl to a table to his left, watched her pull herself up. Then he looked deep into the room. He saw a dim outline of the girl as his eyes adjusted from outside to inside.

Her feet and ankles were covered by a large wooden washtub in which she stood. From the covered ankles up to the thatch of red hair piled on her head, she emerged from outline to fullness in the new light from the wide open door, wet, soapy, naked.

"Aint she somethin," said Billy Slade, peeking around Hess' shoulder.

"Anna! Cover yourself!" said Mama Cortez from the table where she now stood. The girl reached to the floor and gathered a cotton robe which she put on; but not in haste.

"What do these men want, Mama?" she said.

"Horses," said Mama Cortez.

Anna laughed. "They are gone with Papa and Pedro."

Mama shot a hard look at Anna. "Leave us," she ordered. "Get dressed. Stay in your room."

"Stay here," said Hess. His voice, like a bugle call to order, ordered it. "The horses, they are where?" Again the bugle call, the order. "Tell!" Hess pulled the saber until the steel blade grated on the scabbard; then he jammed the blade to the hilt with a crack. In spite of herself, Mama Cortez jumped to the crack of hard steel on steel.

"The horses are gone," said Anna.

"Anna, be quiet," said Mama Cortez as she moved away from the table to face the two men who now stood side by side in the large room. Billy Slade still leered at Anna, still saw her naked in spite of the robe. Anna stepped from the wooden tub. As she did so, the robe split from ankle to crotch. Billy Slade laughed.

"The horses, I will have," said Hess. He spoke quietly. Even in the quiet way, his voice held the timber of the bugle. "For you, her, I care not."

"Awe," moaned Billy Slade. "Ouch!" he moaned as Hess' elbow found his wind.

"If tell me, you do not, I will carve my name into your face. H-e-s-s." He made the mark of each letter with his finger in the air. "Your husband will like? No. I do not think he will." Hess again wrote his name in the air. Then he looked over at Anna. "And the girl I give to my friend. See how he hungers for her. Think how happy they would be."

Billy Slade laughed his leering laugh.

"Where are the horses!"

"Gone," said Mama Cortez. Her voice was quiet, steady. "You touch me or her; my men will see you dead for your trouble."

"Where gone?"

Hess ignored the threat. He reached his right hand across his middle and put it on the hilt of the saber.

"To Santa Fe."

Hess saw the lie in Mama's eyes as soon as she had spoken. Slowly, so as to make the steel grind on steel, he pulled the saber from its home. He raised the blade to the light.

Involuntarily, Mama Cortez took a step back, then another.

"The horses. Where!" This time the bugle voice called out hard and mean.

⸻

Anna put a hand to her mouth and backed away from the wash tub to the far wall. When her buttock hit the wall she put her other hand out for balance and felt the cool steel of the shotgun's barrel where it lay in hooks bored deep into the adobe. She jumped away from the touch of cool steel and exhaled so all in the room could hear her. No one, she knew, except Mama, heard.

"Now it is the time. Tell me where are the horses. I will not ask again."

The room was close and silent. Mama Cortez thrust her breasts out at the gray faced man but said nothing. In the moment that followed, they heard the stamp of a horse outside, the hum of morning flies, the hiss of intense breathing.

Suddenly, the beam of light from the open door was cut for a bare instant, like a flash of lightning seen only from the corner of the eye. Anna heard Mama Cortez cry out; saw her collapse to the floor. The blade dangled from Hess' taught wrist. The diamond edge winked bright and clean in the slant of light.

Blood did not soil the blade as it cut through Mama Cortez's left cheek from eye to jowl. The blade cut fast and keen; a flash, there and gone before blood could begin to flow. The cut was deep; but delivered so quick that the severed skin re-joined as the blade slid down her cheek. Only when Mama put her hand to her face

did the skin separate and Anna saw the blood begin to seep into her mother's probing fingers.

"Mama!" cried Anna, frozen to the far wall.

Hess pointed the blade; tweaked a bit of flesh from the end of Mama's nose.
"The horses!"

Before Mama could reply, the room filled with the clack—clack of cocking
gun hammers. Hess looked to the new sound, saw two huge round holes pointed at
his belly from the long barrels of a great shotgun held in the tiny, trembling hands of
the girl backed against the far wall of the room. He saw the huge holes sway back
and forth; knew that no matter the sway, if the girl pulled either trigger, he'd be cut
in half. Slowly, he raised the blade and took a step toward the shaking girl and the
swaying, gaping holes.

As he took his step, the holes steadied. He saw the shining eyes of the girl;
knew fear and death lived together behind those eyes.

Anna did not speak. Hess felt the shotgun steady on his belly as if the barrels
touched him cold and hard.

From the floor, Mama Cortez said, "I am all right and out of the way. If they
do not leave, Anna, kill them. One barrel for each. If they do not leave now!"

Hess felt Billy Slade already backing out the door, saw his musket was held
vertically in one hand, the other raised in a sign of surrender.

Anna raised the shotgun and took a step toward Hess. Hess put a booted
foot behind him while he held the bright blade up in front of his chest and waved it
back and forth.

"That knife won't stop buckshot," said Anna. It was the first thing she had
said. "Now, vamoos! Or die!"

"C'mon, Hess," called Billy Slade from the back of the horse he had quickly
scrambled aboard. "This aint our time," he pleaded.

Hess took another step back, felt the wood of the veranda. Slowly, he raised
his saber in salute. He clicked his heels and bowed slightly and plunged the blade
into the scabbard. He held Anna's eyes for just a moment more, found the same
menace. Then he turned and mounted his horse. With a brutal jab of spurs, he felt
the horse spin around and he rode out of the yard.

He looked back to see that Billy Slade followed. As Billy passed the door,
he tipped his hat to Anna who stood rock steady with the huge shotgun at her
shoulder.

As soon as the two men were out of sight and sound, Anna dropped the shotgun to the floor and, with a sob, ran to her mother.

Mama Cortez' cheek and face were now red with blood. She lay still. Anna gently shook her. She did not move, except for a slight quiver of her breasts.

Anna went to the open door and recovered the shotgun. Before she let the cocked hammers down, she looked across the yard to the corral and the sloping fields of the plain beyond. She saw nothing except the shimmer of mid-day heat playing above the still grass and fading dust.

She closed and bolted the door.

# 8

Moonlight speckled the trail with gauze light and unnatural shadow. Pedro sat beside a small stream, his boots off and bare feet soaking in the cold water. His empty stomach rumbled a hunger he had never felt before. In spite of the chilling night, he bathed his sore head with hand scoops of water from the stream. Far down his backtrail, a she wolf called her mate to supper.

Pedro had trudged the day away, climbing steep ridges and sliding into lush vales, as he searched along the side of the mountain. In mid-afternoon, he had passed the leg-stiff gray lying in the trail where it had met the stampede. Its gut, torn by the butchering knives of a pack of wolves, gaped, open and empty of entrails. A turkey buzzard flapped its wings as Pedro stumbled up to the carcass, landed a few feet from its interrupted supper, content to out wait the man. Pedro stared sadly at the dark rib cave, thick with blowing flies which fed away the day on bits of wet flesh left by the wolves.

In a small meadow, he had seen three of the horses; but, each time he coaxed and whistled, the horses cropped and moved just out of reach. Finally, he gave up and moved on, each moment expecting the rush of an Indian attack.

Now it was late and dark and growing cold. He put boots on over wet feet, wrapped the serape tighter around his shoulders and clambered on through the night looking for a safe place to sleep.

Suddenly, he stopped. He sniffed at the night. Wood smoke! There is a camp nearby, he thought, but whose? His head still reeled from the fall against the tree trunk. I must think. Whose camp? The Pueblos? Montoya? Who else? Unconsciously, he fingered the kachina totem hanging at his throat.

He crept along, slowly now, careful not to dislodge a rock or snap a stick. The smell grew stronger. There through the trees, the glow. Fire. Warmth, food—or death.

He had no weapon. He felt on the ground for a stick. He found a long rock that fit his large hand with six inches of blade to spare. He swung the rock hatchet several times and wondered if it would shatter on impact. He thought ahead to the camp. Quietly, one at a time as they sleep. Six blows and it's done. If they are awake, I'll rush them. Swing while I'm able.

Excitement increased the lightness he felt in his head. He trembled but crept on. Closer. Through the trees, he saw men in robes sprawled by the dying fire. He counted six mounds. There had been six Indians.

Beyond the fire he heard the sounds of animals quietly feeding. Closer he crawled, closer, until he was kneeling at the edge of the small camp. Outside his body, he made no sound. Inside he felt the blood pounding; so loud, he thought, it must wake the whole camp.

Suddenly, one of the mounds moved ever so slightly. Pedro shrunk back into the shadow of the low standing brush. He saw the mound move again; heard the click, click of metal on metal. His eyes froze to the glint of dancing firelight on steel. A rifle barrel reflected moon beams into his eyes.

As Pedro tried to back away from the edge of the camp, he saw the rifle barrel swing his way. Suddenly, smoke puffed into the frozen moment.

The small band of Pueblo Indians walked silently from their ancient village and headed south toward the town of Taos. Behind them, the moon crept over the great breast of the Mother Mountain just north of the village and beamed a misty light between the block houses which had sheltered this steadfast people for as long as the songs of the old men could recall.

Morning Light had delivered his message of war to the elders gathered in the underground kiva. As dawn crept over the Mother Mountain to cast ever decreasing shadows on the pueblo, the old men had chanted old songs in the rising smoke and sparks of the kiva fire. The old songs echoed the Pueblo soul.

The echo told the story of a thousand years of life in the Taos valley; the time before time when the people were free and the gods were their own; the time of the coming of the white gods wrapped in steel shirts and a slaving faith; the time of whips and chains and starvation.

They sang of that other time so long past that no man living can count the snows. That other time when the Pueblo had erupted from the earth. That other time of uprising when it was learned that the white gods, like men, die from the knife and the arrowhead. That other time when all of the land had been washed with oppressors' blood; when the Spaniards had been slaughtered in their sleep; cut down as they fought behind village walls; chased and herded from all of the villages, from Santa Fe even, from the entire country.

In the rising smoke and sparks, the elders saw the uprising people of the songs of that time when, countless snows ago, the Pueblo had been freed and free, as the God of their Mother Mountain had intended for her people.

The elders saw, too, that other time, from then to now, when the Pueblo again were yoked to cruel oppression by men who were not gods—by men who would die this night.

In the smoke and the sparks of the underground kiva, the old songs echoed the Pueblo soul.

Morning Light had spent the day in the smoke and songs of the kiva and wondered why his once free people had, again, become slaves of the swarthy white invaders and their cross. Wondering, he slept through the last of the songs and into the beginning of the killing night.

Now, Morning Light walked a little faster to keep up with the others. His short bow, tautly strung, swung in his hand to the meter of his rapid stride. His eyes glistened with excitement and the songs of the old men echoed in his soul.

As he walked through the night with his tribesmen, Morning Light, called Lopez by the Mexicans, held his head high. At sixteen he was not on his first hunt; but tonight, he went silently along the side of the gentle stream to the town of Taos, on his first great hunt.

As his moccasined feet sensed each pebble and root along the path he knew so well, he wondered at the path he was taking on his great hunt. Tonight, he thought, I am but a boy, a slave in my own land. Tomorrow I will stand a true man. Tomorrow I will wash my hands in the blood of my masters.

For a moment, a sliver of moon reflected from a man's eyes that seldom cried.

In the town of Taos, Governor Charles Bent sat in a leather chair before the fire. His Spanish wife knelt by his side, her head on his lap. Neither spoke. Each felt the longing heartbeat of the other. The pulse signaled contented reunion.

Bent had just returned from Santa Fe where he and the American army had dealt the death blow to the last of the stubborn Mexican rebels who would not take Governor Armijo's cowardice for their own. These rebels had schemed and been caught before a shot could be fired in reaction to the American conquest of New Mexico.

Bent patted his wife's head fondly. He sighed. "It is so good to be home."

His wife looked up into the firelight dancing in his eyes. "Yes," she whispered, "it is good."

Suddenly, Bent laughed. "Weren't much of a war. Armijo ran. The people, Mexican and Indian alike seem satisfied. General Kearny's off for California. Now we can rest for a spell."

"It is good."

"Garrard! What in sacre hell are you shooting at?" Louy Simonds yelled from the tree line.

As soon as the shot was fired, Louy rolled right over Hatcher, out the side of their communal buffalo robe and into the woods. Hatcher was nearly as quick. They squatted together in the dark, long scalping knives drawn and ready.

"Indians," said Garrard. "There. Mexicans, maybe. Next to the fallen tree."

There was no reply from the tree line. Hatcher went in one direction and Louy took the other to scout all around the camp. Where there was one Indian, or Mex for that matter, there would be others. Time seemed to stop in the camp.

The Neds sat in their blankets, muskets ready; themselves ready targets in the moon-laced fire light. Garrard had learned enough by now to jump for dark's shelter at the first cry or shot. The second jump landed him on top of his target at the edge of the woods by the fallen tree. As suddenly as he landed on soft, warm flesh, he rolled off and steadied his rifle at the body, forgetting what he had already forgotten—to reload.

"Here! Here he is. I got him dead center!"

The soldiers came running. They stood with Garrard looking down at the body that did not move. In a moment, Hatcher slid into the camp from the opposite side, then Louy.

"Cap Jackson. You soldier boys. See to the stock." Hatcher whispered quietly, which scared the soldiers even more. "Louy? Sign?"

"None but his and yours."

Louy walked over to the body and squatted down seizing the thick, black hair in his left hand. The Green River gleamed in his right hand. The knife went to the hair line. Hesitated. Louy looked up at Garrard.

"Your kill. You scalp him!"

Louy couldn't see Garrard turn sick-green in the dark; but he did. He coughed. Then spit. He saw Louy pull the head up by the black hair. Garrard jumped into the woods at the same time that the body moaned.

While Garrard puked; Louy rolled the body over on its back. It moaned again.

"Sacre! The ball, she dance on the side of the head. This critter aint kilt."

"Aint scalped a live Indian yet. Aint about to, Louy."

Hatcher walked over to the tree line to look at the body.

"This child's seen a mess of Indians and many a Mex. He aint none of them. That there is a Spaniard. Garrard! Throw sticks on the fire so's we can see him proper-like."

———

Pain-thumps in the head woke Pedro. Eyes blurred in the bright light under the overcast morning. He could smell coffee and frying salt pork. He sniffed carefully; but his head hurt no worse for the effort. So, he inhaled a nose full of the food smells and sat up. The inside of his head halved and quartered like a log split with an ax and split again. But, he was up; and between the ax blows, he could smell the coffee and the frying pork. Spit ran out the side of his mouth. He moved toward the fire, grabbed a piece of pork from the hot pan, bit a hunk off and began to chew and burn. As he chewed, he sucked in mouthfuls of cold air. Within minutes the chunk of salt pork was gone. Pedro reached for another; but a huge knife blade got in the way of his outstretched fingers.

A hand, stained by sun and soot, reached toward him. Its fingers held a cup. Pedro took the cup and a large swallow from it; then looked from the hand, along the greasy, buckskin arm to the dirt-splotched face set hard beneath curly blond fuzz.

"Who the hell are you, boy?" the face said. Pedro just stared.

"Well, you do howsomever you like; but this child can remember a hungry time on the Snake. Three men come into camp, said they was a week without a morsel in their meatbag. Went to wolfin our buffalo the way you're tearin at the pork. Well, they ate their fill. Two died—from eatin when they wasn't used to it."

Hatcher squinted as smoke from the fire blew into his eyes with a gust of cold morning wind. "But, like them, do as you please. Same to us."

Pedro drank the hot coffee more slowly; but still in gulps. He handed the cup back to the blond-bearded man and looked at the others standing around the fire.

"American soldiers?" he said in perfect English.

The men were packing the mules. Jackson turned from the pack tree he had just cinched to the back of an army mule and squinted at Pedro.

"Captain Jackson, Second Missouri."

"Me and Louy and the boy here," Hatcher pointed to Garrard, "him that shot you, we aint army."

Hatcher picked up a pack and slung it onto a mule's back.

"We're for Taos to help Governor Bent," said Garrard. He squatted in front of Pedro. "You all right? I thought you were an Indian, the way you were sneakin up on the camp." Garrard smiled, showing an overbite of prematurely yellow teeth. His bright, blue eyes reflected honest guilt.

"Guess you missed most of my head," Pedro said. "Hurts. But I aint dead."

He gently touched the swollen place on his head where Garrard's bullet had bounced off.

"I'm Pedro Cortez of the Valle de Taos where my father has . . . ." He hesitated in a flash of memory. "We have a rancho. Horses. Two days ago, Pueblos—our own Indians—killed my father and stole our herd. Last night, I was sneakin on your camp because I thought you was my Pueblos."

"Your Pueblos?" Hatcher laughed. "Aint no Indian ever been any white man's Indian. I don't wonder." He laughed again, then sobered. "Killed your pa and took your horses?"

Pedro told the story. He looked defiance at Captain Jackson when he told why they were taking the horses to the high valley. Unknowingly, he switched to Spanish and had to be prompted by Garrard as he finished the burial of his father.

"By now your herd is nigh to the Canadian and the Comanches," Hatcher spat in disgust. "Them Pueblos and your herd aint comin back. They'll sell your horses or trade them with the Comanches for wives and a place with the tribe."

He looked over at Louy who was pouring out the last of the coffee into his tin cup. Louy drank the coffee off in a gulp and nodded.

"Cortez," Hatcher continued, "you've seen the last of that Montoya feller. By and by, he'll hunker down with them Comanches—or they'll scalp him for his horses—your horses. There aint nothin in these mountains for you now. Better come down the mountain to Taos with us. We'll stake you to a mule to get you home to your rancho."

Now Pedro nodded. "You are right about my father's—my horses. Montoya? He will—must—live, until we meet again." Pedro put a hand to the bloody gash on the side of his head. "I will come with you. Maybe we will find some strays along the way." He smiled in spite of the pain. "Gracias."

The loads for the mules, now much lighter after the long trek from Bent's Fort, were distributed so that one mule was made free for Pedro to ride. There was not an extra saddle. Pedro rode bare back. With each lurch of the animal, his head hurt with an alternating dull ache and sharp bite.

The rump welts inflicted by the belt were forgotten. The belt and Papa Cortez were no longer a memory. They were embedded in the new man, Pedro Cortez.

Still on the back side of the pass to Taos, they climbed the morning away, never, it seemed to Pedro, coming nearer to the high top that marked the entrance to the Valle de Taos. Just before noon, they came over the lip of the trail into a sloping meadow.

A small herd of antelope was grazing in the knee-high grass. Captain Jackson pulled out of line and ran his mule at the herd. Heads came up with ears pointed. Just as quickly, the antelope began to leap for the nearby trees. Jackson fired from the saddle on the dead run. A doe, not as quick as the others, disappeared in the grass.

Antelope roasted over the fire at nooning. Jackson, his lieutenant and the private had already cut nearly raw chunks from the now steaming carcass. Jackson chewed hard, bit off more before he had swallowed the first and squinted at Hatcher. Hatcher smiled back. The soldiers had not eaten in more than a day.

They climbed above nine thousand feet to Palo Flechado, the summit of Raton Pass. The pass was almost bare of trees which for decades had been cut by the Indians for arrow shafts and by the Mexicans for fire wood. On the down-slope, they saw a line of walking brush heaps, burros loaded with the dry, resinous pine brush and led by peónes, swaying down the trail.

Their eyes bounced from the wood train toward the circular valley below, guarded to the right and ahead in the distance by the high mountains and to the left by the gorge of the Rio Grande River twenty miles to the west. At the foot of their trail lay a small village, to the west, another and to the northwest, the town of San

Fernandez de Taos—Taos. The level plain far below looked cultivated, civilized, peaceful.

Then, like thunder in the far off mountains, they heard thunder in the valley.

"Cannon, sounds like," said Louy.

"Artillery, by God," said Captain Jackson. "We got us a war down there after all. C'mon!" He spurred his mule and, followed by the lieutenant and the private, began the long slip and slide to the valley floor below.

"Cortez," Hatcher said. The muzzle of his rifle swung slightly toward Pedro. "What I'd like to know . . . ."

"The Sacre damn fuss. It is about what?" finished Louy.

Pedro looked from one to the other and then to Garrard. Then he looked out on the valley. Northeast of the town of Taos, he could see smoke.

"The fight is at the Pueblo. The Red Willow tribe. They've fought us before." He hesitated for a moment. "Cannon fire means the Americanos. Your soldiers attack the Pueblo.

"The Gachupines, Spanish-born ricos, will not soil their hands with fightin. They stir the Indios with strong drink and false hopes. There is much shame in this, I think."

Pedro felt surprised and embarrassed. He had never really thought about the recent upheaval; only listened to his father's talk. Pedro spurred his mule down the steep trail.

"Pueblos from the same tribe, my Indios, killed my father and stole our horses," he called over his shoulder.

"Hold up there, son," said Hatcher. "Just where do you fit in this if its Americans against Mexicans and Indians down there? This old hoss wants to keep his hair."

Pedro pulled the mule up sharp and turned to look at Hatcher. "I stand with my family. My Papa is—was a Spaniard. My mother was a Texan from Missouri before she married Papa. The Indios betrayed our trust. Now your soldiers punish them."

Pedro turned and jumped the mule down the trail with a jab of his long-roweled spurs. Hatcher and Louy laughed.

"This child aint been to a cannon shootin war," said Hatcher, "since the Sublettes drug a cannon clear to the Green and scared hell out'n the Blackfeet with it."

And, with a whoop, he lit out after Pedro with Louy close behind and Garrard bringing up the rear.

It was dark when they reached the town of San Fernandez de Taos. All was quiet, except for the here and there cry of a town dog and a distant coyote, answering from the mountains. American soldiers sat in the streets in small groups, cooking over impromptu fires, talking in low voices or sleeping.

Pedro stopped on the edge of town. To avoid sentries, he led Hatcher and the others around the town and out to the northeast toward the Pueblo de Taos, the village home of the Red Willow Indians.

"Halt. Halt or I'll shoot and don't give a damn!" said a loud, shaky voice out of the dark. Pedro pulled up the tired mule; but Hatcher rode right around him.

"Here rides Long John Hatcher; he's a Bent an' Saint Vrain man; he can see in the dark; an' his rifle is pointed right at your middle, sonny boy, an' hammer's eared back."

The challenger cried out as Hatcher's mule hit him square in the chest; his musket fired into the air; and, instantly, they were surrounded by angry men pointing loaded muskets up at them.

"Hatch? That you?" The voice was loud and the words bent slightly to a French accent.

"Captain Saint Vrain. Sacre! Sacre! It is I, Louy Simonds. With me is Hatcher and friends. To help you fight these sacre Indians."

The soldiers backed off as a short, thick man in powder and sweat stained clothes came into the center of the ring and shook hands all around until he came to Pedro. "A Mex . . . ."

"As is your wife, Señor," said Pedro. "I am Pedro Cortez. My father . . . ."

"I know him. Even now, my company of mountain men and freighters ride Cortez horses. Come. To my camp. Come."

As they walked with Saint Vrain, they could see the Pueblo village about a quarter of a mile to the northwest. Its three principal buildings were bathed in a ring of flickering light from the fires of the soldiers which surrounded the village. In the foreground was the long, rectangular church, its bell tower breaking the plane of the flat roof in its reach toward heaven. Beyond the church stood a huge stack of adobe rectangles and shadows piled one on top of the other to the height of seven stories. Across a bubbling stream, another pueblo seemed to match the great mountain guarding its rear in the distance.

"The rebels, mostly Indians, a few Mexicans," said Saint Vrain, "are hold up in the pueblos yonder. Some are in the church. We pounded them with cannon this afternoon; but, mostly, the balls go right through the walls or just bounce off the adobe and do not tear them down. We'll finish them in the morning. Muskets have never been a match for twelve pound mountain howitzers."

They sat around the camp fire of Saint Vrain's company. Hatcher and Louy knew many of the men. Garrard, who had been on the frontier since the previous spring, knew some of them.

"Come mornin, them as scalped Charlie Bent will get theirs lifted," said one of the men.

"Bent scalped?" said Hatcher. "This hoss be damned. Another good man gone under."

"It weren't just Charlie. Narcisse Beaubien, just in from Bent's Fort, got scalped in an out house," said another man of the company.

"I knew him," whispered Garrard to Pedro. "We were of the same age and education."

"And next off, they hit Simeon Turley's place," said another. "Kilt him right off. We aint a-gonna take shit like that there. Turley used to make the best Taos Lightnin to be had. Aged it sometimes most of a week. Them Indians and Mex's drank Turley's whiskey and smashed what they couldn't drink; spoilt my whole winter."

They all laughed.

"Spoilt Turley's too." said another.

"Then the rebels head for Santa Fe. Another bunch kills Americans on the trail home to Missouri. Them Indians along with some Mexicans meet Colonel Price at Embuda Canyon. Price whips 'um; but they don't quit. Price an' his boys chase 'um over the snow clear back to this pueblo. I give 'um credit. Them Indians fight like hell, and the Mexs too; but tomorrow . . . ."

Heads nodded; but no one laughed.

The crack of a baby howitzer shook Pedro from his blankets. He rubbed the gray dawn into his sleepy eyes and looked around. Garrard was by the stream splashing water on his face. Hatcher and Louy were gone.

Pedro felt the side of his head where Garrard's ball had bounced off. The lump was sore to the touch; but his head was clear.

The cannon fired again. Pedro watched as the ball stuck in the soft adobe of the church's wall some four or five hundred yards away. Suddenly, the wall of the church erupted with puffs of smoke as the rebels returned fire. A ball hit the ground and rolled to Pedro's feet, its force spent.

"We're too far for the rebels to reach us with their fire," said Garrard wiping his wet face with his sleeve.

"Where are Hatcher and Louy?" said Pedro.

"Gone with Saint Vrain to block a retreat from the church. Pulled out early."

The cannon was firing steadily now; but with little effect against the thick adobe. Near one of the guns, a soldier fell, rolled over and sat up. Pedro watched the soldier rub his chest.

"Damn," Pedro heard him say. "Got me plum center."

Then, the soldier reached inside his shirt and pulled out a lead ball covered with blood. "Hardly scratched me," the soldier shouted to his companions around one of the cannons.

Suddenly, a group of Indians, firing as they ran, dashed from the deep shadows of the Hlauuma, the north pueblo house. Some took cover in the stream bed to reload rusty muskets or notch an arrow. Others jumped the stream and headed for the huge log door of the church which had opened to receive them.

Three Indians fell at the door. The last to enter was a young brave with the light of morning in his eyes.

"Charge!" echoed against the gun-shot dawn. A young officer, waving his sword in the air, led a group of about thirty soldiers toward the stream.

The Indians lying there fired a volley and jumped for the church. The soldiers returned fire. Two Indians fell. Then it was knife and knuckle in the open area between the stream and the church.

The young officer cut and slashed. Indians fell, only to rise and make the church. It was over in a minute. Four soldiers down and wounded. Six Indians lay dead or dying.

"That was Captain Burgwin and his dragoons," said Garrard. "I met him at Bent's last spring."

He ran to the young officer who was sitting on the ground, his bloody sword by his side. Pedro followed. He and Garrard dragged the young officer to cover. A knife stuck out from his ribs.

"Why, Garrard. Nice to see you," said Burgwin through pinched, white lips.

Just then one of the dragoons bent over the officer and picked him up. "We'll care for him and thanks," the soldier said.

The Indians poured a galling fire from the church, shooting through loopholes cut in the adobe. The cannon moved to within a hundred yards of the church walls. Now, some of the balls pierced the tough adobe to splatter flesh and bone inside. Still, most of the shot caromed away or stuck, half in, half out of the thick adobe vestment of the church.

Pedro turned as a bunch of men filed past him. At their head was Burgwin, clutching his side with one hand and waving the sword with the other.

"To the door," he yelled. "Breach the door and at them."

The men stormed the church door. It gave for a moment. The entry was filled with the smoke of exploding muskets. Then the door closed. Burgwin slumped against it and slid to the ground—dead.

The men retreated under withering fire. None was hit.

"Axes, men. Axes will breach the wall. Follow me." Another young officer was shouting and directing the dragoons to a cart.

The men seized axes and raced toward the west wall of the church.

"Cannon. Cease your fire," yelled the officer. "We'll chop our way in."

Two men fell to rebel fire. Several others reached the wall. Ax heads flew against the soft adobe. In half an hour, the breach was made. The men stood aside.

The cannon was run up to the opening. Its fuse was touched. Agony howled from inside the church. The cannon fired again and again into the crowded mass within. Suddenly, the gun fell silent. Soldiers pushed into the breach, yelling, firing—some dying—they entered the Indian stronghold.

Indians poured out the church doors and ran between the huge pueblo houses toward the mountains. Above the din of final battle rose the Blackfeet war cry as Saint Vrain and his mountain men met the fleeing Indians. Few escaped to reach the safety of their traditional, mother mountain.

Morning Light was one of the last to leave the church. As he ran between the Hlauuma to the north and the Hlaukwima, the south house, he reached to his back for an arrow. His quiver was empty. He dropped the useless bow and pulled the thin-bladed knife from his belt. Just as quickly, he felt a blow to his chest. One of the mounted men of Saint Vrain's company had run him down. He lay stunned in the dust as the last of the battle—and his boyish dream of the great hunt—died out.

Everywhere, swirling dust and powder smoke blinded the light of morning. It was over in an hour. Pedro and Garrard walked to the church door as Hatcher and Louy rode up. Hatcher gave an Indian yell and jumped from his mule. He beamed amid rivers of sweat which ran down his powder-blackened face.

"Many a sorry Indian gone under this day," he said, shaking his rifle in the air. Suddenly, he frowned as he came up to the church door and stood beside Pedro.

"This coon," he said quietly, "has made many an Indian go down. But not like that."

They stared in disbelief at the carnage inside the church. Body parts lay everywhere—dismembered. Flies were already sucking at bloody bits flesh.

"Must be near a hundred," said Hatcher. The blood in his eye drained. He swallowed. "Maybe more."

"An hour ago they were yellin and fightin," said Pedro softly, "the best of the Red Willow tribe. I see some I knew. Some I rode with as a boy. Now they're as nothin." Involuntarily, he crossed himself.

Louy still sat his saddle. "Look," he pointed a black finger. "The soldiers bring the captured ones."

A roped string of about twenty Indians shuffled by the church, eyes down, surrounded by soldiers. Morning Light stumbled at the end of the line. His arms thrust out and then back as the man ahead of him jerked on the rope that bound him to tight hopelessness just as the spirit bonds of the night before had made him one with all Pueblo, before him and to come.

"What will happen to them?" whispered Garrard.

"Hang 'um sure," said Louy.

"I go home now," said Pedro. "My family must be told of my father's death. The loss of our horses. Our ruin—and this."

He turned to go and find his mule. Then he stopped.

"Gracias, señores. For my life—and the mule. I shall return it."

Pedro rubbed the lump on the side of his head. He looked at Garrard.

"Your musket shoots some to the left," he said through a wistful smile. "Adios."

# 9

Mama Cortez wept quietly into the edge of her green, cotton reboza. The saber scar on her left cheek from her eye to her jowl, usually a thin white streak, was now a wet, red line. Anna clutched her shoulders and nuzzled her mother's breasts.

"Papa, Papa," she breathed.

Pedro stood at the door to let them cry it out alone. He looked to the north and the east at the bowl of mountains formed by the Sangre De Cristos. He thought not about Papa Cortez but about the man, Black Hess, who had dared to mark his mother. He imagined the fight, as Mama and Anna had described it, and tried to picture the powder darkened face of the brute who had been so cruel to his Cortez women. I will know that face, he thought, when I see it.

He saw little Anna, near naked and shaking, as she had said, standing up to the man, shotgun waving in her bare arms. He laughed at the picture; then sobered. I must find this Hess and kill him, he thought.

Suddenly, his mother was standing beside him. "Papa is up there?" she asked, following Pedro's eyes across the valley to rest on the mountain breast. She wiped her cheek with a bare arm and the scar paled, then flushed red again.

"I buried him in the mountain, along the trail to the high valley."

"We must bring him home to lie out there with his father and with his babies, my babies who did not live."

Pedro shuddered. Without even a blanket in which to bury Papa, he thought, the corpse will be putrid by now. Besides, it aint Papa out there. Just a lump.

His mother read his thought. "Anna and I will bring him home. Just show us . . . ."

"It is a long way up the mountain, Mama. I may not be able to find the place."

He hesitated at the pleading look in his mother's eyes. Then he said, "I must find my saddle, my musket and the pistols. There may still be some of our horses in the high valley. If I find Papa's grave, I will bring him home."

His mother smiled and hugged him. He hugged her back. "But first I must bathe and eat," he said finally. Mama put soft fingers to the wound at the side of Pedro's head. "Yes," she said. "Anna!"

Anna was walking toward them. She stopped and turned to the kitchen. "I will heat water," she sighed.

Pedro's belly was full for the first time in many days. He felt clean because he could no longer smell the sweat, the dirt, the blood. He pulled at the bandage wrapped around his head. His mother had washed the wound. Although Pedro protested, she insisted on the bandage.

"You will carry a deep scar," she said.

"Like you," he said.

Mama Cortez smiled. The thin white scar half-mooned across her cheek. She sat opposite Pedro now, his strong hands in hers. She smoked a cigarillo, her third in the last hour.

"In the spring we will plant corn," she said. "The larder holds enough till then. We have many cattle. You will find some of the horses. I know you will. A mare or two and a stallion. We will survive."

"It will not be easy without," he paused a moment, "without Papa."

And without—me, he thought. The idea scared him; but it was there, had been there for a long time.

"You know, son," she spoke English. "I come from Missouri. The hollars of the Ozarks. My folks didn't have much. My first husband took me out to Texas. He traded with the Mexicans of Texas, Texicans, we called them, Spanish or American, alike. Didn't do much better than stay about even—for a lot of hard work and rough travel.

"Your father was one of many Mexican traders we met, trading his horses for our stateside goods. Señior Cortez and his father were men to behold. Your papa was there when Will died of the cholera. Eighteen twenty eight, it was.

"Guess Papa had his eye on me because he began courtin me soon's it was proper. He told me of the beauty of this Taos valley, and it is that, and of the rancho his father had started and he was building.

"Well, it sounded fine and I came. Turned out Papa, his father, a couple of Indians, some chickens and a pig all lived in the adobe shed. I flat refused to live in that mess. Lived in the wagon for a month till this house, or this part of it anyway, was built. There was no acequias to irrigate the land, no corn or wheat except some scrawny maize the Indians growed dry. Only horses."

She rose and went to the door and swept the outdoors with her hand.

"Only horses."

"But now, as long as I can remember," said Pedro, "there have been hectares of wheat, corn, sweet melons, a vegetable garden, fruit trees, grapes for the wine."

"My doin," his mother said, hitching her shoulders square and placing hands on hips.

"While Papa was building my house, I found an old forked-branch tree trunk. Cut it down myself into a stout plow. Then with one of the gentler horses, I rode four miles to the nearest acequia ditch with water in it. That horse pulled me and that forked-tree plow all the way back here. Seein what I was doin, Papa got some Indians—yeah, later on, Montoya was among 'um—to do the heavy work. Me and them Indians plowed all the land back of the house, plowed the ditches to water that land, and planted corn and wheat, all in the first year. I done it before. We'll get us some Indians and do her again."

Pedro smiled, then frowned. "It will not be safe to hire Indians after what has happened."

"Indians got to eat—now more than ever. We always fed them good and treated them like people. They'll do fine; and I still have that old two-holer shot gun."

She laughed out loud for the first time since the death of her husband had hit her.

"I'll help, Mama," said Anna. "There is nothin I don't know about makin a horse work." She thought a moment. "'Cept pullin a plow, maybe. You did it. So can I—and any damn horse," she finished with a stamp of her small foot. The heart of her lips puckered up. Mama laughed again.

"I am sure you can, and will, my child."

"If she can find a real smart horse," said Pedro, smiling fondly at his sister, "maybe she can learn from it."

After a moment, he frowned.

"I'll leave for the mountain valley and—what you asked—in the mornin."

⁂

Pedro climbed the same mountain trail searching for his father's grave. He still rode the mule bareback in the hope that he would find his own rig. He probed trail sign and his own confused memory; but the more he studied the less sense he made of either. He had been careful to hide the grave from scavengers. Too careful.

By late afternoon, he knew he had missed the grave site. The pale, winter sun was off the trail and half way up the mountain side when he found the remains of the gray horse, a mere skeleton, picked and re-picked, white bones gleaming clean beside the trail.

He found his saddle where he had hidden it. He saddled the mule. The musket and the pistols he found on the slope of the mountain where they had fallen when his gray horse had bolted into the stampeding herd. He cleaned and re-loaded the weapons. Then, he climbed the last few miles to the mountain valley.

At the narrow entrance to the high valley, he saw a dozen horses, all mares, grazing contentedly in the tall grass. He squeezed past the high rock cliffs on both sides and into the valley.

Suddenly, an arrow hit the rounded pommel of his saddle. He lifted the musket from where it lay across his saddle and fired high and to the left. An Indian fell from the rocks and lay still. Pedro spurred the mule deeper into the valley's high grass.

The echo of the gunshot came back to him from off the steep walls. He reached for his powder horn; but too late. Two Indians rose from the grass like ghosts of their dead brother. They rushed at him on foot, knives drawn, knowing his one shot was spent.

Pedro dropped the musket and drew the two pistols from his sash and let them come. He knew them both; had worked with them for most of the years of his life. He yelled their names.

"Chollo, Jiminez. It is I, Pedro."

The Indian called Jiminez, the younger of the two, hesitated; saw Chollo raise his knife; heard him cry an ancient, killing cry. Jiminez, too, raised his own knife and his own cry for blood. He sprinted to catch up with Chollo.

"Stop!" shouted Pedro. "It is over in Taos. Many have died. The killin must stop."

Chollo and Jiminez ran side by side. Pedro heard their cry; knew its meaning; shuddered. He saw the swinging blades; saw the stain of blood on the swinging blades; saw savage blood in the eyes of his former companions. He knew its meaning too; had seen it long ago as they played at war as children. Rabid blood.

Now, Papa's blood, he thought. "Papa!"

Pedro's cry fused with the ancient cry of the onrushing Indians. Twenty feet and running. Ten feet and knives flashing.

Chollo and Jiminez ran side by side—and surprised—when Pedro shot one and then the other.

The Indians fell not five feet from his stirrup. The mule stood his ground in spite of the shots and that surprised Pedro. Death, more death, did not.

One of the Indians moaned and sighed, "Pedro!"

Pedro reloaded the pistols and got down. He approached the Indian whose chest heaved in short bursts of dying breath.

"Chollo." Pedro said the boy's name softly. "Montoya? Where?"

"Comanches," said the boy.

Blood and spittle spilled over his lips. Pedro watched the spittle bubbles burst. The chest was still.

The three Indians he had killed were—had been—his friends. He rode with them, shared mushy, unbolted flour called atole with them and beans and cold and rain and snow. Papa Cortez had treated them well; but the threat of a new oppressor had made them warriors. They had responded with death arrows. And, in turn, Pedro paid them in kind. They were like him—boys suddenly flipped into men by circumstance. Except they were dead.

So he buried them. As he turned the earth, he felt neither satisfaction nor remorse. When he put down the last stone and crossed himself, he knew that growing up had ended.

Easily, he rounded up the dozen horses from the lull and lure of rich valley grass.

On the way back down the trail from the high valley, the horses moved willingly with bellies full of easy mountain living and spring water. Knowing the horses would be rank from the long stay in the valley, Pedro still rode the mule. He studied the trail ahead, trying to make out where his father's grave might lie.

Suddenly, the lead horse stopped and snorted, ears bent forward. Then she carefully circled around the up-slope and dashed ahead. Each of the other horses did the same.

Papa Cortez' own horses had found him. They recognized the smell of death.

The mule didn't seem to catch the smell or didn't care. As Pedro dismounted, the mule stood, legs braced against the down-slope of the trail. Pedro wrapped his father's remains in the blanket from his own saddle bag. Then, he tied the blanket-bundle across the rear of the mule.

To this, the mule objected. He kicked out and bucked. The bundle jumped and bumped, but stayed put. Pedro, cussing and laughing, got the mule to stand still for a moment. He mounted and sat through a few slips and slides and crow-hops until the mule decided the extra lump wasn't worth the effort. No longer interested, he settled down to a lazy, swaying walk.

The smell and the bump, bump of decayed remains followed them all the way home.

⁓⌁⌁⁓

A brother of the Penitentes said the mass under the fruit trees behind the house, his mumbling a mix of Latin and Spanish. Papa Cortez was buried in the blanket inside a pine box next to the grave of his father.

The women wept. Tears cleansed their cheeks. The crying inside cleansed their souls of selfish pain and seeded the soil there with nurturing to feed empty hunger which would come to them in the lonely night, to cover irrational blame and loss beyond reason.

Pedro did not cry. His father was not there in the ground. Pedro felt his father's living strength inside himself. The boyhood challenges, his failures and the strong hand that kept him from falling too far; the thrill of riding after crawling; of breaking a mean horse after so many falls; and the teaching, growing, knowing, understanding—the belt and the loving eyes.

The grass of my soul was sown at my birth. It has been nurtured with pride and love during all of my growing up. Upon its richness will I feed for the rest of my life. The soul of my father is in me. Now, in sorrow, I am complete.

I can not explain it; so I search the sky while the brother mumbles of God and the women weep.

The gray mare, one of the dozen horses Pedro had driven from the high mountain valley, was not just gray. The hair across her back was light, almost white; but from the ground up, her legs, belly and flanks were a smoky pearl as if in forming, she had risen from the dying embers of a green-wood fire. She ducked and danced among the other horses as Pedro approached the wide corral.

He spoke quietly to the horses as he opened the gate, lariat in hand.

"Which of you will be my perfect horse? The one which can carry me safely to the perfect valley of my dream? You have been allowed to grow fast and strong and fat on the grass of our rancho. None of you has felt the hand of man."

He walked toward the horses which began to bunch nervously at the far side of the corral. He swung the lariat in his hand. The horses jumped and tumbled against each other.

Then the gray stepped out of the herd with a prance of her dainty feet and a toss of her head. She snorted at Pedro, her eyes a-blaze. He laughed at her.

"Come. I am here. Can you trample me?"

He swung the lariat over his head making a loop which grew wider as it whooshed through the air. With a slight lunge of his arm, Pedro snaked the leather over the gray's tossing head.

As the riata bit into her neck, the gray sunk her haunches and rose on hind legs, flailing the cool morning air with her fore feet. Pedro gave her slack and cinched the lariat to a snubbing post in the center of the corral.

The mare fought the braided leather of the rope, dancing from side to side, rearing, ducking, pulling; until, with a mighty twist of her head, she hit the end of the rope and fell on her side. In an instant, she was up. She stood spraddle-legged, head down, body a-quiver, staring at Pedro.

Pedro pulled a sack of corn from the fence post and walked slowly down the lariat to face the horse. He held out a hand full of corn. She sniffed his hand, then nipped at it. He pulled his hand back; then tried the corn again. He spoke to her. "You will like the corn. It is sweet." He opened his hand and reached for her mouth. Eyes flaring, she sniffed the corn again. With a lunge of her head she snapped it up; then backed away. Pedro took more corn from the sack and held it out.

"Come. Papa and I have gentled many a fine horse with corn and soft talk. Come. We will be friends. You must trust the gentle man who brings you sweet corn to eat."

She took more of the corn from Pedro's hand. He reached up and stroked her firm neck. Soon, with the corn sack in one hand and the lariat in the other, Pedro walked the gray horse around the corral. The other horses looked on but kept their distance.

For the rest of the morning, he walked the horse around and around, talking to her and filling her with small handfuls of corn. He felt her relax a little, pull and dance back less frequently on the end of the lasso.

The dinner bell clanged. Pedro looked toward the veranda and waved at Anna.

"My turn for some food," he said to the gray.

He stripped the rope from her neck and walked a few paces away from her. She did not move; but watched him all the way to the gate. Then she shook her great neck and pranced back to the other horses.

"I'll be back, smoky horse," Pedro called over his shoulder.

By the end of the day, Pedro had slipped the bridle on and off the gray many times. Each time he did it, he fed her some corn.

The next morning started as the first; but by supper time, the mare had taken the blanket and saddle. She did not like the saddle; but she liked the corn and the soft talk and the caressing hand.

The third day Pedro repeated each step in order. Bridled and saddled, the gray stood munching corn.

"Easy, smoky horse, easy," Pedro whispered. Then he put a moccasined foot in the wide, wooden stirrup and lightly swung aboard.

For an instant, the gray froze. Then her body electrified. She shrieked, bent double, head and tail to the ground. Pedro felt like he was on the top of a dust devil. The smoky horse spun and lunged and jumped and bucked at the strange, plunging weight wrapped around her spine.

Pedro tried to talk to the horse; but heaving breath pushed the words into grunts through chattering teeth. Still she bucked and he stayed with her. Finally, she stood stiff-legged in the middle of the corral, her flesh shuddering. Her breath came in short gasps.

Instantly, Pedro leaped off. He took her head in his hands and rubbed and she felt the strong, sure hands. He fed her corn and walked her to cool her. In a few minutes, he stepped again to her side. This time, he gently pulled the horse's head around so she could watch him mount. Then he slowly climbed into the saddle, felt her tense, felt the quiver of flesh ripple under the saddle. He turned her head with the reins and spoke to her.

"Come. This way."

She followed his lead with a jump; then settled into a lope around the corral. Each time she came up to the other horses, she hopped or twisted or bucked a little, as if to show off. Soon, she smoothed out as she ran around the corral. For the rest of the day, he practiced mounting and dismounting until she didn't seem even to notice.

"A day or so more and you'll know all the signs. When to go, to stop, turn, all you need to know for now."

He patted her neck. She nuzzled him for corn.

"Smoky horse, you're gettin fat on corn," he called from the gate. He smiled as he looked at the mare, her ears pointed at him, the smoke-gray sides bathed in sweat and shinny.

"Smoky horse. Smokey!"

Pedro found Hatcher and Louy and Garrard at Estis' tavern on the main street of Fernandez de Taos. It was near noon. The light wind, cold off the mountains, hardly noticed any warmth from the pale, late winter sun. Pedro had ridden the smoky horse all morning, leading Hatcher's mule.

From the beginning the horse and mule didn't like each other. Each time the mule crowded the hind end of the horse, she kicked back at the mule, which, in turn nipped at her rump. Each time Smokey lunged out with her hind feet, Pedro yelled and laughed and spurred her flanks with bare heels. At the spurring she still bucked a little before starting her run with a jump. It was a bumpy, hard ride; and Pedro was glad to tie off the mule in front of the tavern.

"I brought your mule, Mister Hatcher," said Pedro smiling. "Gracias."

He looked around the large room. He saw mountain men in greasy buckskin, Yankee traders and freighters in homespun wool, Mexicans in leather pants, split down the sides, the flaps tied with fancy buttons. And the señoritas. Short cotton skirts showing ankles and more, white, low-necked blouses showing more of unbound breasts, gaily colored rebozas covering shapely shoulders and the ever-present cigarillo between puckered, smiling lips.

He saw no man with powder darkened face or wearing a saber at his side.

"Pedro, amigo," shouted Hatcher. He stood up, weaved from side to side and sat down again with a plop.

"Sacre liqueur, ce tres bon. Oui, tres bon," shouted Louy raising a clay cup toward the rafters and then taking a gulp.

"Yeah," said Hatcher also waving a cup. "This nog knocks the hind tits off old Taos Lightning. This child has drunk a heap of liquor in his chargin lifetime. There's such as makes drunk come mighty quick; but burns up the innards; and a feller feels like a gut-shot coyote. Then there's Taos aguardiente. Damned poor stuff, can taste the corn in it. Makes me think I'm a horse a-feedin away after plowin deep furrows."

He drained the clay cup and refilled it with a dipper from the bowl on the table. His weed patch mustache was soaked and he licked it with a thick tongue and smacked his lips. His wide-set, mountain-seeing, blue eyes sparkled.

"Plowin deep furrows. This hoss always squeals an raises his hind foot to kick hell out of any man comes near his heels."

He kicked out his moccasined feet and slid from the chair.

"Then there's this here State brandy," he said from the floor, "with eggs and nutmeg swimmin in milk. That's good! Can drink on it all day and night; but this coon wants to dance Indian when he hides this in his meatbag."

Hatcher rolled over to his knees and pulled himself up to his feet. He turned to Pedro.

"Grab you a squaw."

He reached across the room for one of the young women and took her hand in his paw. She resisted and almost pulled him over.

"Here's luck, boys," and, taking a hitch around the girl's waist, he began to twist her this way and that, shouting an Indian chant.

"Whee, this coon is drunk, muy boracho, as you damned Spaniards say." He breathed the words into the young girl's smiling face as he whirled her around the room to no music but his own.

Louy laughed and clapped. Hatcher and the girl pranced and spun. Suddenly, Hatcher sank to his knees, sliding his hands down the girls hips and legs. Then, with a loud groan, he fell on his face. He didn't move. Soon he was snoring, his finger of a nose buried in the loose dirt of the floor.

"Come, mon ami," Louy shouted to Pedro. "Eggnog spiked with sacre American brandy." He handed Pedro a cup and raised his. "Bon Sante!"

"Salud!" said Pedro. Both downed the nog in one gulp. A chorus of salud! rang through the room.

"Death to the Pueblos," shouted a Mexican, spilling nog on his shirt and yellow sash. "Mañana, they will be tried by the court," he sang.

"Then we'll hang them bastards," said an American soldier sitting quietly, his chair slanted against the adobe wall of the room.

Pedro saw Garrard push through the door. The boy swayed when he walked, using each successive chair back as a crutch. He slumped into the chair from which Hatcher had slid only moments ago.

"Couldn't make her to the outhouse," slurred Garrard. He laughed and slapped his side while spittle ran from his lips as if to hide from the liquor breath.

"Pedro! How's the head?"

"Fine. My mother makes me wear the bandage; says it'll scar some. I see you're doin fine your ownself."

"Fine indeed," Garrard laughed again and drained the last of the nog from Hatcher's cup.

"Garrard, Louy," said Pedro, his voice low and quiet. "I'm lookin for a man with a powder burned face. Name of Hess, Black Hess. Was a soldier. Wears a long sword by his side. Seen him?" Pedro's dark, serious eyes stopped the grin on Garrard's face from becoming a laugh.

"Been here," said Garrard.

"Where's he now," said Pedro. The words fell on the room like musket balls.

"Why? Why the sacre damn hell you want that bastard?" said Louy. "And that little Billy Slade that licks his butt behind? You want him too?"

"Both!"

Pedro told Louy and Garrard what he had found on returning home. He told them Mama's story and Anna's.

"Little girl should-a shot them when she had the chance," said Garrard. "She sounds like a mighty fine young woman, your Anna. I'd like to meet her."

"Now," said Louy quietly, "you look for these men? When you find them?"

"I will do the killin," said Pedro. "When I find them." He put one hand on each of the pistols in his sash.

"Ah!" said Louy. He smiled. "They are gone from Taos. Cap Jackson says they're headed after Kearny to California. I am glad. Black Hess, he is a sacre damn German. A Prussian. A killer is this Hess. Not for need. Not for hire. For fun, he kills. For fun!"

"Gone to California? Damn," said Pedro. "That's not a ride I was expectin to take, until now."

"You will follow Hess and Slade to California?" Louy smiled. "Perhaps you will wait for the trial of the Indians."

"And the hanging," chirped Garrard. "Here's to the hanging!" He raised his cup and shouted.

"The hanging!"

The room full of men shouted back.

"Salud! Salud!"

# 10

One by one the words thundered into Pedro's head.

"Hangin's—too—good—for—the—bastards!"

Each word was like Garrard's musket ball; but this time, they bounced off the inside of his skull. A sharp pain answered each impact of a word-ball. He could taste the vomit still in his mouth; but he did not remember throwing up, or anything else of the previous afternoon and evening.

He sat up, bumping his head on the under side of a table, and tried to orient himself. He sat on the dirt floor of the tavern. Several of the previous day's revelers still sat or lay where they, too, had passed out.

Pedro turned his head slowly, looking around the room. Each turn of his head sent the musket-ball words pounding against his skull.

"Bastards! Bastards! Bastards!"

He caught the stale smell of curdled nog, sweat and vomit. His own stomach lurched, then settled. In a few minutes, the spinning in his brain slowed, focusing the pain just behind his eyes.

Garrard helped Pedro to his feet. Each could see the other's pain. They headed out back for the outhouse and the bucket of cool wash water.

"Don't want to miss the trial of the Indians," said Garrard as he splashed water from the bucket on his face and chest.

"What was in that drink," asked Pedro in a shaky voice.

"Brandy, eggs, milk and nutmeg. A regular Spanish fiesta."

Garrard tried to laugh; but stopped suddenly and gripped his head in his hands.

"I've had wine with dinner since I can remember," said Pedro. "And, I've tasted aguardiente, felt my belly burn. But, this!"

He looked at Garrard with a wry smile and spit several times. Then he drank a dipper of water from the wash bucket and spit again.

Garrard took Pedro by the arm.

"The trial of the captured Indians is about to begin. C'mon."

Unsteadily, the two young men walked around the tavern and up the street to an adobe house on the edge of town. Mexicans, arrayed in many colors, as if for a celebration, milled outside the house. Some Indians, dressed as always, for labor, stood or squatted by the walls. A small troop of uniformed soldiers stood guard over sixteen Indians, who sat in the street, hands tied behind their backs.

Pedro and Garrard squeezed into the court room. The room, already filled with spectators, was small, oblong and dimly lighted by two narrow, mica-filled windows. A thin railing, newly constructed, kept the audience separated from the lawyers, witnesses and the judges.

Beyond the railing sat three women. Missus Bent, widow of the slain governor, was a handsome woman with a good figure for her age. Pedro stared at her for a moment. A few years past she must have been truly beautiful. Missus Boggs, though younger, was plump and plain.

"That one," whispered Garrard, "is the wife of the famous Kit Carson. Pedro saw a tall woman with down-cast shoulders. Her expression was haughty in an otherwise beautiful face whose intelligence shown through lustrous, black eyes.

All three women were dressed for the kill. Each had been an eye witness to the massacre.

There were two judges. Judge Beaubien was the presiding judge of the Taos District and the father of one of those killed in the uprising. Because of Judge Beaubien's obvious feelings in the matter, Judge Houghton had been brought up from Santa Fe for the trial. They sat at the end of the room behind a tavern table. A pistol lay near to the hand of each.

Along the right side of the room opposite the female witnesses sat a dozen men, some Mexican, most American: the jury. Chad Chadwick, an American trader, was foreman. He smiled at the crowd of spectators and shook his fist in the air.

The crowd hushed as six Indians were brought into the room under guard. Pedro saw that their hands were securely tied behind them. They stood sullenly at the rail while the charges were read by F. P. Blair, Jr., the district prosecutor.

"These five, your honor, is charged with murder in the first degree."

The lawyer pointed to five of the six Indians.

"And this one for treason against the United States of America."

He pointed at Morning Light. The Indian boy stood with his fellows, head down, face expressionless.

"We all know what happened out at the pueblo. We know these rascals was among the Indians captured just after the battle. These ladies here will tell us if any of these Indians killed any of the peaceful citizens of Fernandez de Taos in the uprising that took the life of Governor Bent and—your son, Judge Beaubien—and thirteen others, American and Mexican alike. These ladies seen it all or most of it anyways."

Morning Light, singled out for treason, shuffled his feet. Slowly he raised his head. His eyes looked over the judges and through the adobe wall. His look reflected the great mountain that shaded the town and his own kachina. His Indian name meant Morning Light; but no one except his mother called him that. He was called Lopez because of his light skin and a question about his father.

His look did not acknowledge the proceedings. He understood no English. Morning Light was just sixteen.

"Proceed, Mister Blair." Judge Beaubien's eyes shown with wet.

Missus Bent kissed the Bible and swore to tell the truth. Her eyes were dry, her mouth turned down at the corners.

"Tell the jury what you saw on the day in question, January 19, 1847."

"Supper was over. It was a cold night, snow was on the ground. Charles— Governor Bent—had just built up the fire.

"I heard a shout outside. No. More like a scream."

She looked at the judges, cleared her throat and raised her chin. The lawyer started to ask a question; but she held up a hand. Her voice was clear and hard.

"Sudden-like, there was a poundin on our door. In an instant, it burst open and a hoard of Indians flooded into the room. Charles picked up the ax and ran to the back of the house. The Indians poured after him. They paid no mind to me. I followed. I saw Charles, his back to the wall, facing the Indians.

"A shot came through the window and struck him down. I cried out and tried to reach him; but the Indians held me back. I could see Charles lying on the floor. Seein me, he raised up on an arm and said, 'vaya con Dios' and 'my brothers will care for you and the children.'

"At that moment, I managed to break through the Indians and fell to his side. He took a paper from his pocket and tried to write; but he had not the strength. 'God bless.' He died in my arms." She paused and looked around the room, daring any there to exceed her grief.

"I was shoved aside and they scalped him. One Indian ran to the door and held up the scalp for all of his companions in the street to see. Then they picked up my husband's body and bore it above them and handed him from man to man until he was gone from my sight."

The prosecutor turned toward the Indians and pointed. "Did you see any of these Indians in the room at the time your husband was shot and scalped?"

"Yes."

"Which ones?"

"All of them!"

"All?"

"That one shot him from outside and crawled through the window shaking his smoking gun and screeching."

Missus Bent pointed a small but sharp finger at the tall Indian standing next to Morning Light. The prosecutor pulled him out of the line.

"This one?"

"Yes," she pointed and shouted. "Yes, yes!" The Indian stared back at her outstretched finger. No movement flickered in his body or face. The prosecutor pushed the Indian back into line.

"And that one scalped him. With one swipe of his knife."

Missus Bent was still shouting and pointing. There was fire in her dry eyes. "That one helped. And that one. All were there. They all touched Charles. Lifted him, lifted, carried him from the room."

"And this boy, called Lopez, accused of treason, did you see him kill . . . ?"

"All of them. Well, the boy? I don't know. They was all there. He must-a been there."

"When you followed them outside, what else did you see?"

"I saw Liel, district attorney Liel. They were dragging him by his heels."

"Who was dragging?"

"He was," pointing again. "And some of the others. Those outside now, waiting for trial."

"With respect to this one," said the prosecutor, pulling another Indian from the six in line. "You saw this one dragging Mr. Liel?"

"Through the street. It was lined with Indians and not a few Mexicans. Many of them were pricking him with their lances."

"Was he alive?"

"Yes. Alive. But—scalped! Scalped alive!"

Now she began to break. Her voice broke first, then her dammed up eyes. Through an occasional sob she continued.

"He begged them to kill him. They laughed and poked him the more. He cried out for death for more than an hour. Finally, a merciful shot rang out and he slumped to glory and peace."

"Who shot?"

"A kind Mexican. I do not know him and would not recognize him, except in my prayers.

"Stephen Lee was killed on his own house top. Narcisse Beaubien," she looked at the judge who nodded a grim face, "killed and scalped when he tried to hide in the outhouse. He had almost escaped the crowd when a Mexican woman screamed from the roof of a nearby house, 'kill the young ones and they will never become men to trouble us.' The enraged hoard returned and found Narcisse."

"Did you see any of these men kill young Beaubien?"

Missus Bent hesitated. She had stopped crying. She opened her mouth as if to bite, then snapped it shut.

"No."

Missus Boggs and several others testified to the killing they had seen. All of the six Indians in the room had been identified as a killer by at least one witness.

The defense counsel, although a lawyer back home, was a private in the army, assigned by the army to defend these Indians against charges of murder and treason, at age twenty-two. In spite of his tender years, he asked no questions of the witnesses. Perhaps he sensed that more testimony would only further infuriate the jury.

He argued that these simple, oppressed Indians should not be held account-
able for the crimes planned and instigated by rich Mexicans in Santa Fe and farther
south. He pointed at Lopez.

"How in justice can this boy be guilty of treason. He is but sixteen years old;
has always lived in the Taos Pueblo, grubbin out some parched corn with his mother
and sisters. He has no allegiance to the United States just as he had none to Mexico.
He doesn't know what allegiance means, what it is. He has no country; has never
had a country. How can you find him guilty of treason. He is not charged in the
killins. Let him go."

The jury adjourned to a separate room. In less than five minutes they were
back.

"Have you got a verdict, boys?" asked Judge Houghton.

"Guilty in the first degree," said Chadwick, smiling. He raised a clenched fist
again to the crowd. Many clapped and shouted.

Judge Beaubien looked down at the six Indians who stared passively back at
him. He raised the pistol and slammed it down butt first on the table.

"Muerto! Muerto! Muerto!"

Morning Light drew his serape more closely around himself as the guard led
him and the other five Indians out of the courtroom to await hanging.

"I saw that boy at the church the morning of the fight," whispered Pedro to
Garrard. "He did nothin more than all the other Indians that day."

"Missus Bent did not seem so sure that he was among the Indians who killed
her husband."

"He'll hang with the rest." Pedro shook his head.

In the next two days the rest of the prisoners went on trial. The witnesses
changed. The verdicts did not.

A bright Friday morning hung over Taos. The sun, hooded by a few fleeting
clouds, loomed over the rim of the Eastern mountain. The mud and adobe houses
glistened in the new day's light, some freshly white washed, others yellowed by ne-
glect.

Pedro stood with Garrard, Hatcher and Louy in the almost deserted plaza of
Fernandez de Taos. Here and there, they saw a señora in her night dress, hair di-
sheveled, throw open a window or a door to let out the pungent smell of breakfast
chili colorado.

"It is a perversion of justice," said Garrard. "To hang them for resisting inva-
sion, even if the invaders are Americans. To hang the boy for treason. Shameful."
He stamped the butt of his musket to the ground to mark the point.

"This child," said Hatcher, cradling his rifle in his arm, "don't savvy perver-
sions. This child has made many an Indian go under and took a top knot or two."

"Or two? Sacra two," laughed Louy. "How come you brag so much, Long John?"

"Well, a few more'n two. But this coon has never, never scalped 'um live, like they done to poor Liel. This child's no hellion and he says it's unhuman, agin nature. Them Indians ought to choke."

"They will," said Pedro. "Here come the soldiers to the jail."

A troop of eighteen soldiers marched up to the prison which stood alone on the far edge of the town, an officer on horse back at their head. Pedro and the rest walked the short distance and greeted Lieutenant Colonel Willock.

Beyond the jail by about a hundred and fifty yards two upright posts linked by a stout cross beam framed the distant fields. Some two hundred American troops were paraded to the side of the gallows.

"Hatcher, I see you boys is armed. You can form part of the guard," Lieutenant Colonel Willock called to them from his horse. He smiled grimly. "Bring them out boys."

One by one the Indians were led from the jail to blink in the bright sunlight. The soldiers formed a square, six abreast in front, six on each side. The prisoners were herded into the square. Pedro, Hatcher, Garrard, Louy, jury foreman Chadwick and two others closed the square at the rear. All carried muskets or rifles in bent elbow, except Pedro, who fingered the butt ends of his father's two pistols tucked into his red sash.

Willock gave the order. "Forward march." The troop stepped out toward the gallows. As if on the same signal the roof tops of the houses filled with spectators, women, children, few men. They emerged quietly; stood in silence to watch the first official American hanging in the Valle de Taos.

Pedro looked back at the silent throng; saw the soldiers on the roof of the jail swing the muzzle of one of the mountain howitzers to bear on the gallows. An officer lit a cigarillo with the lighted match.

"A touch of that match and that cannon will blow us all to hell," whispered Garrard, following Pedro's gaze.

Within fifteen paces of the gallows, the square of soldiers opened. The Indians stopped. Some stared at the gibbet, others kept eyes down. Many seemed to Pedro to be shivering in spite of the warm sun.

At a signal from Willock, Pedro's group urged the prisoners up to a government wagon which sat under the cross beam. The sheriff of Taos and his assistant stood at the head of the docile team of mules harnessed to the wagon. A wide board was balanced across the rear of the wagon between the two posts. Six Indians were pushed and pulled up into the wagon and ranged on the board, two in the center to balance and a pair on each end. The space between the posts was so narrow, the doomed touched shoulders. The board shook with them.

"They've soaped them riatas to soften the leather," whispered Garrard to Pedro.

"Look stiff as them posts," said Hatcher.

The six leather nooses stabbed sharp angles down from the cross beam at the bent heads just below. The sheriff and his assistant struggled to adjust the loops around flexing necks. A black cap was placed over the head of each Indian.

Suddenly, the mere boy, called Morning Light by his Pueblo family and Lopez by the gringos, who had been convicted of treason shouted, "Caraho, los Americanos, los asesinos—assassins!"

At a word from the sheriff, the mules pulled the wagon from under the cross beam.

"Adios," shouted one of the prisoners.

"Vaya con . . . ."

Lopez hung from the stiff leather noose with the others, legs kicking, body convulsing. A loud hiss, hiss, hiss came from the dancing sextet as each tried to suck in air. Two of them swung together and grabbed hands with a firm grasp. There had been no drop. No broken neck and instant release. Slowly, soap-greased riata bit into bulging neck muscles. Slowly, the air-ways constricted as quaking tendons stretched and sagged.

The two gripping hands hung together for almost a quarter of an hour before their impulsive brotherhood relaxed.

At the end of one rope, Morning Light choked and croaked and his eyeballs bulged and split and the pulp ran down his cheeks. A sliver of wispy cloud crossed the morning sun and light went out of the morning.

After forty minutes, the next six were hung. Another forty minutes—ample time to die. Then the last four Indians.

Following a similar interval, the soldiers were dismissed.

The cannon was removed from the jail's roof. The women and children came down from their high perches. Some went in to a hot breakfast of beef and beans or chili colorado. Most ate nothing.

Pedro's group was drafted to help in the removal of the bodies of the last to hang.

Hatcher was removing the riata from the neck of one unfortunate when a teamster approached. The leather was too stiff to untie, so Hatcher pulled out his Green River.

"Hi, there, hi! Them's my riatas," the teamster yelled. "Don't cut my lassos. I won't have nothin to tie my mules with."

Hatcher turned and pointed the Green River at the man.

"You damned fool. The redskins' ghosts'll cling to these noose-ropes sure, like raw flesh does to a blood-wet hide. Make meat of you certain."

"Damn me if they do," said the teamster. "I'm a government hauler. Them's government ropes. I lose them, I lose a dollar apiece."

"Work for 'um," said Hatcher pointing at the four bodies, each with a leather rope squeezed tightly around his neck. He put the knife back in his belt.

"C'mon," he gestured to the others. "We need a fill-up on that special nog."

They walked toward Estis' tavern, leaving the teamster to try to untie the stiff knots to reclaim his ropes. Pedro looked back at the gallows field. He saw the dead piled into the wagon to be hauled back to the pueblo for sacred burial by waiting families.

"I have sometimes wondered how long a man can hang without him a-dyin from the air, when she is cut off," mused Louy. "Now I know."

"About as long as it takes this child to get drunk on that brandy-nog," said Hatcher. "Some longer than it takes you."

Hatcher slapped Louy on the shoulder as they entered the tavern, already filling with laughing soldiers and pouty Mexicans.

"The Mexicans don't look pleased," said Garrard to Pedro. "Only a few of them was caught and hanged."

He gave Estis a negative nod and pushed a cup of nog away.

"How do you feel, Pedro? You're Mexican, though when I parted your skull, I christened you part Yankee anyhow." He laughed to cover his fluster at asking the question.

Pedro laughed for the same reason. "My mother is Missouri born and raised. My father and his father have always lived in the Taos valley. They were Mexicans; but of pure Spanish blood. There was always much cruelty in the Spanish, and later the Mexican rule of this remote land. The Indios have suffered for centuries. The Spanish enslaved them. The raiding Comanches, Navajos, Utes, Apaches kill them and steal their food and their women. My father always treated the Pueblo Indians well. They killed him for his horses." Pedro paused to think, to remember.

"In the mountains, I killed three Indians who were my playmates as a boy, my compañeros on many a trail. They had my horses. They attacked me; may have killed Papa. I am not sorry I killed them. But, I am sorry they are dead. Like those today. I am sorry they are dead."

"And, of the American conquest? How do you feel?" Garrard had filled a bowl with the spicy colorado and was eating.

"I have no feelin. They've made promises. We are to be free. Like all Americans. The army will protect us, our families from the Indians raidin from the plains and the north. I am as white as you. But, I was a Mexican. Will I be free? Will the army protect my mother, my sister, their rancho against men like Black Hess? We will see. Then, I may have a feelin."

Pedro refused a bowl of chili. His stomach still felt raw. He ate a tortilla with some goat cheese.

Hatcher and Louy came up to them. Each held a cup of the brandy egg nog; but today they were sipping, not gulping. The four men sat around a table.

"This coon is for the Bent's rancho on the Purgatoire," Hatcher said, raising his cup. "Try my hand at farmin, split share and share alike with the Bents."

"You, a farmer?" Louy laughed and slapped his thigh, then the table. "Long John Hatcher, a, a, sacre—a plow-mother." He laughed again.

"Aint like the damned Frenchies to understand a man," said Hatcher. His face was expressionless, except for a glint in the far-mountain blue of his eyes. His hand crept to the hilt of the Green River. He looked at Louy.

"Plow-mother, plow-mother," Louy chanted, just a little loose from the fresh nog.

"If this coon be the mother," said Hatcher quietly. "Then, Louy Simonds be the father. And the father does the pullin." Hatcher was still looking at Louy.

"Louy, he aint no sacre father to any damn no-good plow. Hatch! Your meatbag is full of nog. Same as that bag under your sacre top knot."

"Maybe," said Hatcher, still quiet. "Maybe so. But the Bents hired me on for plow-mother. And, I hired you on as the papa. The plow-pullin papa."

Louy stared. His face fell from shock to anger. He spluttered in French.

"No use to argue, Louy. You signed the book."

"Book? Book?" Louy spit 'book' out like the egg nog had suddenly turned sour. "I sign no damn book. I do not write. Do not sign."

"Knowin you couldn't write, like the friend that he is, this coon signed 'Louy Simonds.'" Hatcher wrote the signature in the air with his finger. "Clear as the writin of a school marm, too. 'Louy Simonds.'" Again, he wrote in the air.

"Don't mean I'll plow sacre damned ground. Don't mean nothin."

Hatcher turned away from Louy. "And, Garrard's goin back home to Missouri. Pedro stays to rebuild. How you goin to rebuild a horse ranch in one lifetime with just twelve mares?"

Pedro looked around the table. "I have not told Mama. I do not wish to stay. First, I must find this Hess. Then . . . ."

He looked at the far wall for a moment; turned and settled dark, Spanish eyes on Hatcher.

"Since a little boy, I have had a dream of my own. A valley of many hectares. Good, deep grass. High in the mountains but not too high. And water. Year-around spring water. My valley! Someday, filled with my horses. Cortez horses."

He stopped, a blush on his face. Then, quietly, as if he were alone with his dream. "The smoky horse, maybe. And a woman I have never seen."

"Perfect valley, good horse, dream woman. Don't seem likely. Oh, that smoke horse is all right. But, the rest?"

Hatcher looked down at his hands. With one long fingernail, he pulled a wad of dirt from under another.

"This child has had him a dream or two. Plenty beaver. Bein a free man astride virgin lands. Hoorayin at life. Dreams? They trick you. Suck you in. Then shuck you like a rank mule. Dreams? In the end, they come to nothin." He looked at Pedro; but his eyes were far away, mountain blue.

"Your dream, Hatch," Louy said. "It has come true. You goin to be plow-mother, grow plow-tits!"

Louy bent double, then dodged off the chair just out of the reach of the flashing tip of the big Green River. Standing out of range, Louy cackled with laughter.

"Plow-tits. Old Plow-Tits to his compañeros."

They all laughed, each with one leg squared to leap, if need be, away from the flash of the huge knife.

Hatcher put the knife away and said something in a low voice.

"What?" said Garrard. Hatcher looked up at Louy who still stood a safe distance away from the table.

"Plow-balls!"

"Plow-balls?"

"Louy'll be draggin his plow-balls from here to the Purgatoire." Hatcher boomed out a laugh. "Nog, Señor Estis. Nog all around."

Even Pedro took a cup. "I will go home only to say good by," he said, feeling the brandy-heat. Then I will go to California—for Hess."

"A far piece just to kill a man," said Hatcher.

"The rancho was of my father and his father. This is my time. A new time when a man can be free to build his own rancho. I will kill this Hess—or him me." Pedro shook his head. "No. I will see him dead. I will build my own rancho, señores. If it is there, I will find it. Maybe, in California."

"What of your mother, your sister?" said Garrard.

"Ah! My sister. Young. You would like her, Garrard. And she would like you, I think." Pedro smiled a brandy smile at his friend.

"I'd like to meet her," said Garrard.

"No. You go home to Missouri. She stays, will always stay in this valley. It is her home. My mother and Anna will do well. Instead of horses, corn, wheat for the aguardiente" he shouted. "And to feed the horses of others. The army. The Yankee traders. The new settlers who will come to this valley of America. They will do well."

"Pedro," said Hatcher. "On the way to your valley, would you want to work with this child, Old Plow-Tits, and his plow-balled side kick. Earn some cash, a share of the crops."

Pedro looked over at Hatcher to see if he was funning or serious.

"This child don't tell any hellion what trail to ride, though he's rid a-many. Do as you please. Louy here's a-goin to need a hand with his plow-balls."

"And Hatch's sacre damn plow-tits'll drag just as low."

Pedro looked from one to the other to Garrard who winked at him and nodded. "I've been with them for more'n a year. Aint been bored. Barely kept alive. Learned a lot. Maybe enough to stay alive a while longer." He did not wink this time.

"This child kin ride like a Comanche," said Pedro, mimicking. "Kin shoot these here pistols and hit any hellion he points 'um at." He looked Hatcher in the eye. "I got no tits." Then he turned to Louy. "This coon's sacre damn balls be his own affair." Pedro smiled. Louy laughed.

"I have farmed," Pedro said. "Don't like it much; but, it is true. California'll take an outfit and that takes cash which I aint got." Then he held out his hand. "When do we leave?"

Hatcher took the outstretched hand. "Expect you got some goodbyin to do first. We'll leave from your rancho."

# 11

Hatcher and Louy were out by the corral looking over Pedro's mares. "It's long past sun up," said Hatcher, looking at the distant shadow of high mountains wearing a fresh sky-cap of morning blue.

A week earlier, they had provisioned at Fernandez de Taos. Now the mules were loaded with fresh produce and seed corn from the Cortez rancho. It was past time to go; but Pedro was still in the house with his family and Garrard.

"The women do not give up the boy without a fight, I think," said Louy.

"That Garrard, now. He is surely taken by Sister Anna."

Hatcher smiled. "Aint nothin for sure, 'cept them mountains."

Garrard, already packed for the trip home to Missouri, sat at the table in the cool of the house shadows and sipped coffee.

Mama Cortez did not cry. Anna was crying for them both. Pedro tried to make them understand his need. He described his dream valley. The clear, everlasting water, the tall grass, strong horses. The gut burning urgency to search out, to find, to build his own rancho. He did not speak of the woman. He could not have described her. He would know her if he ever found her.

He did not mention Hess.

Garrard tried to help by explaining his own urgent need to wander the new lands. With one look, Anna cut him to embarrassed silence.

Mama sat quietly and listened. Anna raged. Rouge flooded her cheeks and sparks lit her eyes.

"You are too stupid to be the son of my father. Here is your rancho. Your home. As it has always been. But, no. This, we, are not enough."

Pedro put his arms around her.

"A sister is not a wife," he whispered.

Anna pulled back and looked at Pedro. It was finally clear to her that Pedro was determined. She snuffed the sparks with tears. She turned to Garrard.

"It is you! You have turned him from us, from his home, his family."

"No ma'am," replied Garrard. "It's the itch."

"What is this itch of which you speak." Anna looked Garrard in the eye; and, suddenly saw his itch and that she might scratch it, if she wanted.

"It's a need. A need to," Garrard searched his own need, before and then. "A need pullin at a man's gut to see, to feel this new land, feel the wind of it in his face. Taste of its sweet water. Tangle with it. Conquer or be conquered. It's the need to be a part of the birth of it, watch it grow and grow with it. It's a young man's itch." Garrard looked at Pedro for help.

"Mama, Anna. He is right; but, for me, it is something more. This rancho is, was, Papa's and Grand Papa's. Now it is yours. My rancho is in another valley."

"A dream valley," said Anna, stamping her foot.

"Yes, it is so. But, the valley is real. I will find it. It will be mine. My rancho to start, to build, to grow and to grow with, or to lose. Truly, as Garrard says, I have a young man's itch. And, it itches somethin fierce."

"And, you, Señor Garrard," said Mama Cortez. "You have this young man's malady, too?"

"I had it for sure. Been on the wild plains and mountains for more than a year. Scratchin that itch."

"Now you go home satisfied, all scratched out." Mama Cortez arched a brow as she looked at Garrard.

"Yes, ma'am—and no. On the one hand, I've done my wild roamin. On the other," he flashed a quick glance at Anna. "I feel another itch comin on."

"Oh!" said Anna. Fire lit her eyes. "You men never outgrow the boy. Itchin and scratchin."

"Anna," said Mama, sternly. "Apologize. You are rude to a guest in our hacienda."

"Yes, Mama. I am sorry, Señor."

"No need for apology, Miss Anna. I reckon you were right. I was fixin to go home to Missouri, go to farmin like my pa. But this new feelin. Well, now, if you folks will have me, I'm fixin to stay. Right here. Help out while Pedro looks for that dream valley of his. I like this valley just fine."

Garrard smiled at Anna. Anna tossed her head, leaving her pert nose high in the air. But, the tears had stopped.

"See if you can find some scratchin for that new itch of yours?" said Pedro.

"Maybe," said Garrard, still smiling at Anna.

"Of course, you may stay." Mama Cortez smiled at Garrard. "Your help will be most welcome."

Then she looked at Anna who stood with legs apart and arms folded against the rapid rise and fall of her breasts.

"More than welcome, I think."

The sun was past nooning and parting time. Pedro led out on Smokey, followed by Louy, leading the pack mules.

"We'll send your possibles soon's we can get word over to Bent's Fort," Hatcher said to Garrard, as he leaned down from the saddle to shake the young man's hand.

Then, all three riders turned the heads of their animals to face the trail to the high mountain pass. Garrard, standing next to Anna, shouted, "Keep your hair under your hats, boys." Then, suddenly inspired, he yelled, "Hey, wait along."

Garrard ran to the corral and threw down the gate poll. He jumped to the bare back of one of the newly broken mares and grabbed a handful of shaggy mane. The horse side-stepped and threw her head.

"I'll ride a ways with them," he said to Anna. "But, I'll be back."

She dropped her eyes. "As with any friend of Pedro's, you will be welcome, Señor," she said softly.

Garrard bent down and planted a wet kiss squarely on Anna's pouty lips. He waved at her and spurred the horse into a gallop to catch up with his parting friends.

Anna raised her eyes and smiled.

"Vaya con Dios, Pedro," called Mama. She looked across the yard at Anna and saw the girl brush her lips with shaking fingers.

"And Anna, my child, God be with you," she whispered.

She turned to the dark, empty doorway. Out of sight and sound, she wept and wept.

⁓

They were eight days out of Taos and heading down to the Purgatoire River just below them when they saw the dust cloud to the east. It rose from the flat of the plains to blot out a part of the blue sky.

"Buffalo?" said Pedro.

"Maybe," said Hatcher. Quickly, he looked over their back trail and their own dust cloud. "Riders, more like. About the same number of animals as we got, judgin by our own dust."

"Indians," said Louy. "Comanches, and that aint no sacre damn good." Louy rubbed his scalp with a handful of hat.

"There's cover along the river bank. Let's head for it, slow-like to keep the dust down. Maybe they aint seen us just yet."

Hatcher eased his mule in among the low growing junipers and slowly walked it toward the deep cut of the river. The others followed. It took a half hour to cover the mile to the river. Finally, they ducked off the plain and into the river bed. They dismounted and tied off the stock. Then they scrambled up the steep river bank to watch the dust cloud.

"About five mile, I'd judge," said Hatcher.

"Turned some." Louy spat. "Lookin to meet up with us?"

"Looks like," said Hatcher. "Louy. You and Pedro take the stock upstream to them cottonwoods." He pointed to a stand of large trees about a half mile upstream. "If we got to face Comanches, we might as well do it from cover. Walk the stock in the river. Indians may not follow if it aint easy for 'um."

Pedro crawled down the embankment followed by Louy. Each took a hand-ful of reins and headed the animals into the river. Hatcher came after them wiping out their tracks as best he could. Then he followed.

Hatcher squatted behind a tree facing downstream, his Hawkin rifle resting across one knee. Louy nestled among the twisted bones of a dead-fall, his father's trade musket sighted on a large boulder sixty yards above his position at the edge of the embankment. Pedro had crawled to the top of the river bank where he could see out over the plains, Papa Cortez' own long rifle, now his, in hand.

"They have turned this way. I can see them now. Indians. Comanche!"

Pedro checked the pan of his Kentuck and lay the gun on the flat ground atop the bank. He pulled the pistols from his red sash and checked the priming on each. He lay the pistols next to the musket. Then he felt his belt pouch for extra balls and patches. The powder horn, cut from a Cortez bull by his grandfather many years ago, hung by a thong from his neck. As he prepared for battle, he felt his father deep within and the teaching.

Pedro watched the coming dust ball which haloed a half a dozen riders and twice as many horses. As the cloud closed with the river bank, the riders emerged, recognizable people. Suddenly, Pedro sucked in breath.

"Montoya!" shouted Pedro. "Montoya!"

"What the sacre. They hear you," hissed Louy. "Damn! They find our scalps for sure."

"Leastways, you needn't worry your French topknot on it," whispered Hatcher to Louy. "You give up yours long ago."

"Who the sacre hell is Montoya?" said Louy ignoring Hatcher's reminder.

"One of my father's Pueblos." Pedro turned his head to look into the dead-fall, then at Hatcher behind his tree. "He was like our foreman. He killed Papa!"

He looked back out on the plains. The coming dust cloud trailed behind the riders. Six Indians, naked except for the leather at their loins. All but one carried a strung bow in one hand and a full quiver of arrows across his back. One, a head shorter than the others, held a musket across his horse's neck. A powder horn and possibles bag hung from a rawhide thong down over his chest. This one had a hank of hair—human hair—tied to the horse's mane.

"The horses, por Dios. Cortez horses! My horses!"

Suddenly, Pedro jumped up on the flat in plain view of the six Indians, each riding an Arabian-headed horse and leading another. Pedro's weapons still lay on the ground where he had placed them. He did not think of weapons; but of betrayal.

"Montoya! Aqui tiene Pedro Cortez."

He tore the kachina totem with the broken right arm from his neck and held it up.

"You know me. You kill my father; steal my horses; hide in fear among the Comanches. Ladron! Sin verguenza!" Pedro shouted the challenge at the band of Indians.

They jerked reins and wrestled prancing mounts startled by the words rising from the earth. Then, the Indians saw the man and stopped about a hundred yards from the river bank where Pedro stood.

The Indians stared at Pedro for a moment. Then the short Indian slowly raised the musket. As if by magic, five arrows notched in taught bowstrings.

"Center their hearts, boys," yelled Hatcher from behind his tree. "One Indian moves, kill them all!"

"We hear you, Long John Hatcher! Kill every sacre damn one."

Louy spoke loud enough for the Indians to hear. Then, he tossed a stick across the deadfall toward the river bank; and another up stream. As each stick landed, six Indian heads pointed toward the new noise, black eyes sparkling. The musket froze in mid salute.

"Montoya! Whose hair hangs from your saddle?"

Pedro took several steps toward the Indians. The short one spurred his horse to a fast walk, the musket resting again across the horse's neck. At thirty yards, the Indian stopped the horse with a jerk of the reins.

"Cortez hair," said the Indian. The quick sneer quickened his lips and was in his voice. "The hair of your father hangs from my saddle. Soon yours will join it, Pedro Cortez."

The other Indians took this opportunity to walk their horses closer to the river bank where Pedro now faced Montoya. A tall Comanche with eagle feathers in his hair rode up beside Montoya.

"Long John Hatcher?" the tall Indian said. Pedro glanced back and slightly down stream. "I know him," continued the Indian in broken Spanish.

"This child be Long John Hatcher; and, if you know me, you know I've put many an Indian under; but never a Comanche. Not yet."

Hatcher emerged from behind the tree and slowly climbed the steep river bank. At the top he stood his rifle butt on the ground.

"Do you know me?" He looked the Indian in the eye.

"I know you of the yellow hair. I have seen you at Bent's. There you are known as a great warrior. We shall see!"

The tall Indian moved his left hand away from his body. The Indians behind began to spread out.

"Pararse! One sacre damn Indian move and we open the sacre ball!" Louy almost sang the challenge.

The Indians pulled up their horses. The tall one smiled. His eyes flickered from log to stump to tree trying to see and count his enemies. He saw no one.

Hatcher walked past Pedro and stopped in front of the tall Indian. Pedro still faced Montoya, fire in his eyes.

"The boy here says this one," Hatcher jerked a thumb at Montoya, "killed his pa and stole his horses. Weren't no coup. T'was coward's work. He scalped the old man and stole his cavey whilst sharing the old man's lodge and fire." Hatcher looked around at Pedro. "That the way of it, boy?"

"Si, it is so," said Pedro finding the tall Indian's eyes and holding. "I claim my horses and my father's hair for burial," said Pedro quietly. Then louder, "and, my enemy's hair for my lodge!" He looked at Montoya. "Coward. You and I will fight. You will die. It is my right to avenge mine." Again, he held the kachina high in the air for all to see.

Montoya did not reply; but Pedro saw a mesh of hate and fear in the black eyes.

"It is true," said Hatcher. "It is true with the Blackfeet, the Crows, Flatheads, even. It is the law of all of the brave tribes of the mountains. It is his right."

Hatcher raised his rifle and cradled it in his arms; but the meaning of the movement was not lost on the tall Indian.

"Even with the Comanche," said the tall Indian. "The challenge to single combat must be answered. So it shall be." He looked over at Montoya.

"You will fight!"

Montoya's black eyes darted from the tall Indian to Hatcher, then settled on Pedro. The sneer bent the face for an instant; then the face was without expression. Only the eyelids blinked.

"As boys we fought," said Montoya. "As boys, Pedro, you could never beat me. How can . . . ."

"We are no longer boys!"

Pedro stared at the short, thick-bodied Indian. He thought he would feel hatred, pure and simple, for this back shooting Indian. But, instead, his hate was mixed with the idols of youthful companionship. Rivalry filled with boyish serious-ness which ended, sometimes with a little blood, always with laughter. Even in the work, the wet, the cold, the heat, Montoya meant friend and teacher.

Still, idols of boyhood shatter with age and betrayal. Now, he is just a man, the killer of my father. And yet, this man I must kill was my boyhood.

"If Montoya wins?" said Hatcher.

"We go. You go," said the tall Indian. "We take horses and the boy's rifle and pistols—and scalp."

The tall Indian pointed in turn at the far trees where the stock was hidden, at Pedro's weapons lying at the edge of the embankment and at Pedro.

Then, he looked down at Hatcher and said, "if the boy wins?"

Montoya interrupted with a low, guttural laugh like a growl. Hatcher seized the interruption.

"We'll take all your spare horses, Montoya's horse and musket—and his scalp."

Hatcher looked over at Montoya and smiled. Then, he took a step toward the tall Indian. He waved a palm at each of the other Comanches, one by one.

"The rest of you can ride off or fight as you see fit."

The tall Indian grunted.

They traded lives like they traded horses. It was the Indian way.

Hatcher turned toward the trees and called, "ease down on your hammers, boys, but keep a sharp eye on them bucks. If they move to fight, kill 'um!"

Then he turned to Pedro.

"Since you jumped up like a fool and left your weapons lyin in the dirt, take this Green River. Knives on the end of rawhide?" he said to the tall Indian.

Again, the Indian grunted and smiled. Then he motioned Montoya to dismount.

Montoya glanced around at the other Indians, at the trees, up at the sky. Then he slipped off the horse and handed the musket, powder horn and possibles bag to the tall Indian. The tall Indian got down and laid the equipment at the edge of the embankment next to Pedro's weapons. Winner take all.

Pedro walked over to Montoya's horse and ripped at the scalp, his papa's scalp, tied to the horse's mane. It would not yield. He turned to the tall Indian and pointed at the scalplock.

"Mine!" he shouted.

The tall Indian passed one palm over the other.

"Fight!" he said.

Pedro walked on slightly rubbery legs to the field of battle. Montoya and Pedro stood facing each other. Pedro had removed his serape and cotton shirt. Long, sinewy muscles rolled across his broad shoulders and coursed down his arms. He was a head taller than the thick, squat Indian; but of about the same weight.

Pedro stood very still as the tall Indian knotted one end of the rawhide riata around his right ankle. Hatcher tied the other end around Montoya's right ankle. They could fight with knuckles, feet, knives and the lasso, itself; but always bound within a rawhide radius of about ten feet. Winner take all.

Without a word, Hatcher and the tall Indian backed away.

"Let the ball begin!"

Pedro and Montoya squared off at the end of the rawhide radius. Each was right handed. From each right hand the glint of steel flashed in the sunlight. As if at a signal, each moved to his right, circling, circling, circling.

Suddenly, Montoya lunged back with his rawhided leg. The leather pulled Pedro's leg out from under him and he staggered forward. Like lightning, Montoya leaped across the rawhide gap, the knife slashing, slashing, slashing. Pedro felt a bite to the bone across his upper arm. Then he was on his butt and swinging a tethered leg against the back of the Indian's leg. Montoya fell back. Now, both were butt-down in the dust.

Pedro sat up on Montoya's left and thrust the Green River at a flailing leg; felt the point slide among sinew; but not deep as the leg pulled away from the knife point.

Instantly, both were on their feet, panting like dogs after running a coon.

Pedro glanced at his left shoulder. The gash was hidden under blood and dirt. He moved the arm up and down. It hurt; but it worked. He looked over at the Indian. Blood flowed from his left thigh.

Behind the Indian, a horse whinnied and jumped and caught Pedro's eye with the toss of a Cortez head. Pedro caught the dance of the scalplock tied to the horse's mane.

And, so, he almost missed the Indian's sudden lunge. He tore his eyes back to the fight; saw the flash of steel pass his ear. He twisted away to the end of the rawhide. Lunged with the Green River. Missed. The Indian came at him straight up. Steel clashed on steel as they met.

Prance back. Lunge. Prance back. They danced a struggling dance under the killing sun.

Pedro held the Green River in an under hand grip with the cutting blade poised upward. Montoya griped his knife overhand. As each grabbed the other's knife hand wrist, he felt the sting of surgery on his own wrist. They separated. Gripped wrists again with opposite hands.

Pedro sliced up, felt the strong Indian arm holding his; still, he cut flesh. Still, the Indian grasped and held while he peeled skin with his own knife hand. Pedro's left forearm bled; but he too stopped the descending arc of Montoya's blade. Each pulled the other from side to side. Neither could wrestle the other to the ground. Again, they separated, gasping, gasping, gasping until . . . .

Suddenly, Montoya bent to the ground, grasped the rawhide with both hands and pulled its length to him. At the same time he jerked up. Pedro's feet came out from under him. As he rolled away from Montoya's flying body, Pedro dropped the Green River and landed on hands and knees.

Montoya fell partly on top of Pedro and partly to his left. He let go of the rawhide and raised the knife for the final death plunge.

Pedro rolled onto his back; saw the hate-squeezed face of the poised Indian. With his left hand, Pedro slowed the fall of death. With his right, fingers flying, he probed and probed for the Green River.

Instead of the knife, the probing fingers found loose rawhide; gripped it; held it up for other fingers to grab; stretched a length with both hands across the death-arc of descending steel; blocked the first thrust.

Montoya rose up to thrust again. Pedro saw the sneer on barely parted lips.

Pedro twisted his hip and slipped out from under the Indian. The rawhide was still in his hands. He jumped to his feet and behind Montoya. The Indian tried to turn his trunk and swing the knife around.

Pedro wrapped the lasso around Montoya's neck. He took another turn and pulled and pulled and pulled.

The Indian's knife flashed in the sun, stabbed the air, dangled in twitching fingers and fell to the dirt, followed by a limp arm. Still, Pedro pulled the leather garrote. He did not stop pulling until Hatcher gripped his arms.

"It's done old son. Now, you can bury your pappy's topknot. You've hung another Pueblo."

From the riverbed dead-fall, Louy's voice boomed. "All right, boys! Them sacre Indians so much as chose to fight, bounce a ball or two against their red skinned heads."

Pedro lay on the ground sucking wind. Hatcher stood up and looked at the tall Indian, his rifle held loosely at the port, thumb taut on the hammer. He said nothing. The tall Indian held an empty bow and could see it was a long way to pull an arrow from quiver to bow string. Still, he faced Hatcher. Neither flinched.

Slowly, Pedro pushed himself up onto his knees, then his feet. He staggered between the tall Indian and Hatcher. He still pumped for air; but easier than before. He picked the Green River out of the dirt.

"You can kill each other in just a minute," Pedro panted, "but first, let me get my papa's scalp and my horses."

He limped toward Montoya's horse, took it by the bridle and reached for the scalp. With a rip of the knife, he cut the topknot from the horse's mane and held it up above his head. He turned slowly so all could see. Then he stuffed the scalp into his red sash.

The Indians sat their horses watching Pedro and not moving. When he gathered the lead ropes of the other horses, still they did not move. He passed the leads to Hatcher.

Next, Pedro walked back to Montoya's limp, contorted form. He looked down on his own dead idol. Kneeling, he ran the sharp Green River blade around Montoya's skull. He tore at thick, black hair, heard the skin-rip of it coming loose and the suck of clinging blood.

From behind the river deadfall, Louy moaned. Pedro remembered the wrinkled skin of Louy's scalped scalp.

Silently, he held up Montoya's dripping scalp. The Indians all watched and nodded as drops of blood fell into the dead Indian's naked face.

Suddenly, the tall Indian turned and mounted his horse.

"It is as it should be," he said.

Without another word, he turned the horse away from the river toward the endless, empty plains. The others followed.

The extra horses were left for the victors.

In the soft sand of the river bottom, they buried the dead Montoya and his scalp.

In a separate grave, Pedro buried the dried scalp of Papa Cortez. He said no words over the grave; but he ran a gritty hand through his own black hair, felt the thickness of it and a new strength.

"Now your papa can climb the stairs of heaven," said Hatcher, "with a full head of hair and all."

"That there Indian," said Louy. "He must ride the sky through eternity lookin for his topknot."

"And lookin for his kachina totem with a broken right arm," said Pedro. He tossed the doll out onto the plain. As Montoya's body would decay in the sand and sun and wind and water of desert time, so would his kachina spirit.

"His kachina, his soul, betrayed him—and us."

"You got some of yours back this day," said Hatcher.

"Did I?"

They spent the night along the river near the battleground so Pedro could rest. His cuts were dressed in a boiled mixture of tobacco and wild onion. Louy boiled more onions and some dried beef in the same pot.

Hatcher and Louy smacked lips as the stew went down.

"Must be them wild onions makes this stew so tasty," said Louy.

"Tastes like you left some of that plug of tobacco in it," said Hatcher, licking grease from his blond mustache. "Pedro, eat some of Louy's slumgullion. Aint half bad, tobacco or no."

He looked over at Pedro for an answer; but Pedro, wrapped in his serape, had lost to sleep long before the stew was done.

Nine Arab-headed horses were tightly hobbled with the mules and Smokey on a patch of lush river-bottom grass. Bull frogs beat a bass drum roll as Hatcher and Louy lit pipes and smoked in silence. The dying fire flickered against the cave of night.

"That boy, he can fight," said Louy.

"Sleeps good, too," said Hatcher smiling through a wreath of thick tobacco smoke.

# 12

They rode through a hundred acres of last year's and the year before's dead corn stalks toward the squat log cabin nestled against the pine bluff above the river bank. Pedro drove the Cortez horses taken from the Comanches into a broken down corral at the foot of the bluff. He got down from Smokey and quickly put up the fallen fence rails.

It had been two days of riding up stream since the fight. Pedro's left arm still hurt where Montoya's knife had cut the deep gash; but the cut was responding to daily applications of chewed tobacco poultices.

The Bent's farm was nothing more than a wide spot in the bed of the Purgatoire River. Still, the soil was rich. Corn grew tall and bore sweet, thick ears by the bushel. When the corn could be harvested, it was a valuable resource for the fort, particularly in winter when the grass was sparse and the animals grew thin. In the spring and summer, corn brought a good price as animal feed and for bread and tortillas for the freighters passing down the trail to Santa Fe.

"Can get two good crops, maybe three, afore snowfall," said Hatcher.

He and Pedro and Louy sat on the front porch of the small cabin waiting for tortillas and spicy beans to settle enough so they could sleep.

"We can make more'n a hundred dollars apiece. That is, if'n . . . ."

He sniffed the air and looked down from the cabin porch across the dead rows. Bats flew in and out of the broken stalks in the purple evening light.

"What sacre damn 'if'n?'" Louy took the hot pipe from his mouth and spit.

Pedro sat with his back against the rough log wall of the cabin. He wondered what Hatcher was stumbling over while he watched his horses strain against tight hobbles to feed in the tall grama grass along the river. Two of them stallions, he thought. The start of my herd.

Across the river, he watched pastel time pull purple shades down the steep mountainside which formed the far bank. He could smell the straw smell of sun dried corn stalks mixed with the moldy gas of rotting fibers along the river bank.

"Well," said Hatcher finally. "It's the bears."

"Bears," said Louy. "Only bears? What they do we can't handle?"

"If'n the bears don't eat the sweet corn," said Hatcher. "Last time we tried to farm this bottom, bears ate the ears as fast as they grew. Faster, seemed like."

"Then why the sacre hell do you bring us here to grow corn for the bears to eat?"

"This coon hates to give in to a bear. Besides, I figure we can build some scaffolds in the field. We'll keep a fire or two going all night. That'll help keep 'um out. And, from the high perch we can see any bear, day or night, and shoot him afore he harms the corn. Give us plenty of meat too. And skins we can sell."

"We'll be up day and night." Louy got up from the ground waving his pipe in the air. "Keepin the fire lit and shootin bears. Not to mention plowin, plantin, waterin and weedin all that acreage. Mother plow-tit, Papa plow-balls and little bearass," he thumbed at Pedro. "Crazy. Sacre damn!"

Louy went into the cabin and pulled a burning stick from the fire. He lit his pipe, tossed the stick back into the fire and turned toward the door.

"What sacre damn bear cause all this trouble?"

"Grizz," said Hatcher quietly.

"Grizz? The grizzly bear? Damn! Long John Hatcher, I've chased you in and out of some sacre damn fool hunts; hungered and froze across high mountains; fried and died of thirst in the sacre damn desert; trapped the beaver in ice water up to my armpits; kilt Indians, buffalo; and, mais oui! not a few grizzly. But, growin corn for them same bears?"

"Now, Louy. We can stand 'um off; and come fall we'll have us a cash crop of corn and bearskins. Won't be no trouble."

Hatcher looked down at Pedro and winked.

"What do you say, Pedro? You goin to let a few grizz scare you off of more'n a hundred dollars cash? Why, hell. It'll be more like huntin than farmin. And who don't like a bear hunt now and again?"

Pedro glanced down at his horses. He watched one of the stallions toss his head and nip at a mare which grazed too close for his comfort. Come fall, he'd have four foals. And cash money for Mama and some to set him on his way to hunt for Hess and his valley. He looked out at the night. The hook of a new moon seemed to pull the distant mountain tops with it as it rose to fight off the starlight.

"We will start in the morning," he said. He stood up and entered the cabin.

"Let the great bear hunt begin mañana. Buenas noches."

———

Hatcher and Louy finished their pipes and, they too, went inside. By the light of the dying fire, Hatcher carefully checked the priming of his Hawkin rifle, Pedro's Kentuck, Louy's musket and the musket Pedro had claimed from the dead Montoya. He leaned the weapons against the cabin wall. Before he was finished, he could hear Louy snoring in French.

"Sacre, sacre damn. Sacre damn grizz. Grizzz. Grizzzz."

Down by the river he heard cicadas put bow to string, crickets play their thimbles on a thousand wash boards and bull frogs sing barump, barump. An owl whoood and whoood. Small feet and furry bodies tap-tapped on dry stalks. From the mountain across the river, coyotes yip-yiped and yipeed. The purgatory night danced along the Purgatoire River.

"Burnt powder and hot barrels afore this fandango is done," he whispered to the night sounds.

In the days that followed, they repaired the cabin with a stout door. They added thin branches packed with mud to the roof to keep some of the spring rains out. And, Pedro added new corral rails and posts to keep the horses in at night.

As spring pushed winter back into cold memory, they plowed about fifty acres and planted the seed corn they had brought from Taos. Along the river, vast patches of berries began to turn from green to red in anticipation of the sweet purple of summer. The river rose with the swell of spring rains in the mountains and the seeping snow melt. Each day was brighter, filled with bird-song ballads of new life along the Purgatoire.

They saw no bears; but there was sign from the fall before. So they built three stands among the corn. Long tree trunks were hauled by the mules from the dead-falls and slopes along the river. Steps were notched in the logs and a cross member for a seat was strapped to the top. Then each trunk was raised until the foot sank into its deep post hole. A man, perched on the cross member twenty or so feet in the air, could see over the new corn. No bear would be safe from the corn guard unless the man went to sleep and fell off his perch.

Upstream from the corn patch, they cut an acequia in from the river to irrigate the corn. By the end of May, green shoots sprang from the earth to cover the planted acres. As the green shoots became stalks, deer and antelope began to feed on them. A guard was mounted throughout the night to tend the fire and shoo the animals away from the corn.

One late June night, Louy had the guard. Down the slope from the cabin, he kept a small fire burning. Occasionally, he would circle the corn patch singing a loud French bawdy song to the night.

Almost at the end of one circuit, Louy sang out—and the night sang back.

"What the sacre damn hell."

The answering chorus was not an echo, but a growl and heavy breathing and close. One of the stands was nearby and Louy made for it. The heavy breathing followed close behind and the growling voice. Louy hit the log pole on the run and climbed to the top.

"Now we see about . . . ."

He looked over toward the cabin which he could not see in the dark; but he visualized his musket leaning against the cabin wall.

"Damn!"

The growl and the heavy breathing was at the foot of the pole. Louy looked down. Beady eyes looked up at him and long fingered claws reached for his moccasins but missed by about six feet.

"Grizzly!" whispered Louy. The bear was a dark growling mass in the night, standing up at the foot of the pole. Suddenly, the pole began to rock and sway. Claws thundered against the thick trunk of the perch.

"Hatcher!" yelled Louy. "Hatcher! Sacre damn bear. Grizzly!"

The bear clawed the pole; lunged at Louy's feet; tried to climb; slipped back; tried to climb; clawed; growled through slavering lips; bit the pole; bit again. The pole rocked back and forth.

Back and forth Louy rocked on the cross member and rocked and rocked. He felt his perch slip once, again; then with each lunge, with each huge bite, he felt the slipping perch slip more and more.

"Hatcher! The bear, he is just now biting at my toes. Hatcher!"

The cabin door squeaked on stiff, leather hinges and scrapped across the dirt floor as it opened.

"This child has napped through scalpins, buffalo stampedes, thunder and lightnin; but that French squallin, aint man nor beast can sleep with that a-humpin and a-bumpin the night air like logs poundin a hollow tree."

"The bear. He is knockin me off your sacre bear post. Shoot him."

"Shoot him your own self so a body can get his sleep."

Hatcher was out of the cabin now with Pedro following close behind. They ran toward the bear stand, weapons in hand.

"Can't shoot him, damn your eyes. Left my sacre fusil at the cabin. Oh! Merde! The seat!"

As Hatcher and Pedro approached the stand they began yelling. The bear heard them and dropped down from the post to face them. Firelight flickered in his eyes. He rose again to full height, his great bulk no more than a darker darkness in the night. There was a loud thud and the bear squealed in pain and anger. The cross beam hit the ground.

"Louy! What'r you throwin at that bear? You'll just make him mad; and we aint got no pole to climb."

"Not throwin," panted Louy. "Hangin by one sacre fingernail. The damn seat, she fall off; and me, I almost go with her. If you don't shoot him, I'll fall on his head too. I'm slippin down this greasy damn pole."

"Now just hang on, Louy. Can't see that bear in the dark."

Hatcher grabbed Pedro by the arm.

"Get a burnin end from that fire we can see by."

He pushed Pedro back toward the dying flames. In a minute, Pedro was back with a flaring branch. Slowly, Pedro advanced toward the pole, the burning faggot in one hand and his Kentuck in the other. Hatcher was right behind, Hawkin at the ready.

"Hey, Louy," yelled Hatcher. "You crazy? Aint no bear down here. This corn patch is as quiet as a cemetery. C'mon down."

Pedro held the light high; but there was no bear to be seen. He lowered the light to the ground.

"Look," he said softly to Hatcher.

"Big fellow," whispered Hatcher as he felt around in the paw print. "Big as I ever seen."

Hatcher stood up and looked all around to the end of the light-circle and beyond.

"Now, Louy. Aint no bear down here. You been holdin out on the Taos Lightnin? C'mon down and go sleep it off."

"But, Hatch," said Pedro. "You seen the tracks . . . ."

"Shush, Pedro. Louy aint seen 'um." He began to snuff out the tracks with his moccasins.

"Long John Hatcher," yelled Louy. "There was a sacre damn bear, and you know it. You hear him. Why you do not shoot him, damn you?"

"Why, Louy. Can't shoot a bear that aint there."

Louy slid down the pole and stood shaking in the dying light of the faggot in Pedro's hand.

"There," said Louy. "The cross beam. The bear shook it loose. Look. The pole. Claw marks. Feel 'um. See 'um. Pedro hold the fire close."

The post was slashed with deep ridges and gouges made by claw and tooth.

"Well, I'll be," said Hatcher. "What do you suppose done that?"

"Damn you," Louy yelled as he jumped at Hatcher and wrestled him to the ground. Hatcher laughed.

"Damned if you aint a bear your ownself, Louy."

Then they were both laughing and rolling on the ground.

Soon after first light, they were back at the bear stand.

"Look at that," said Hatcher. He knelt down and placed his palm over a bear track splashed in the wet furrow. "At least twice the size of my hand."

"Tracks come from the river," said Pedro, following the prints in that direction. "Lead back the same way. C'mon."

They were fully armed, with bullet pouches and powder horns swinging as they walked toward the river.

"Fresh bear meat. Just the thought makes my meat bag rumble after these weeks of eatin atole and skinny deer. Lead on, boy." Hatcher pointed toward the river and followed Pedro.

"C'mon Louy. Guess you might-a seen a bear last night."

"Sacre damn right."

"He crossed the river. I see his tracks goin up the slope." Pedro pointed across the river.

They stripped naked and held clothes, weapons and possibles high above their heads as they forded the river, still swollen and cold with spring run-off.

On the other side, they lay in the weak warm of the early morning sun and shivered in brittle air to dry off. Within minutes the desert air drank them dry. Quickly, they dressed and climbed out of the river bottom.

On this side of the river, the bluff, cut here and there by a game trail, rose steeply to become a mountainside of a thousand feet or more. The bear's track feathered into the dust of a million passings across the mountain's face. They took the game trail, noting the deep scratches which appeared from time to time to cross-hatch the sand as if a bear, fresh with the fear of man, had clawed his way up and up.

About half way, the hill plateaued for a space of a few hundred yards then climbed again. Pedro was still in the lead.

"Look, a cave," he said.

After the climb, his breath still came easy. Hatcher panted up beside him.

"Them same tracks cross there on that loamy spot. Headin for the mouth of that cave. Louy, c'mon up here. This coon sees your bear, for sure."

Louy stood behind Hatcher and looked at the dark opening.

"My bear? Much yours as mine, Hatch. I found him. It was you as lost him."

They crept up to the cave, weapons at the ready, trying to see inside, expecting any moment to see the huge grizzly charge out at them. At the opening the ground was a mass of tracks and donuts. The opening blew at them with animal breath. They saw nothing but shadows slip under the overhang and deepen into yawning blackness. Above the cave, the mountain, humped with boulders, sloped away and up to the sky.

"I'll climb up above the mouth," said Louy. "In those rocks. Shoot her behind the ear when she comes out of her den."

Louy started to work away from the cave and up the slope.

"What makes you think she'll come on out any time soon?" said Hatcher. "Why call it a 'her,' anyhow?"

"That bear, she growl like mama growled at papa; and, if'n you want bear meat, you're goin to have to run her out here where I can shoot her." Louy kept climbing.

Hatcher looked up at Louy and licked his lips. Louy looked back down at Hatcher, smiling.

"You afraid of my bear?" said Louy. "You are, you can let Pedro go in and flush her."

"I'm your man," said Pedro, smiling up at Louy.

"Aint no hellion of a Frenchie can call this child afeared of no bear," bellowed Hatcher. "Pedro. You take that side. I'll take this'n."

They stalked the cave mouth and ducked into its low entrance. Once inside, they waited to let their eyes adjust to the shadow. Soon, they could see that the cave had a high ceiling, tall enough so that a man could stand. From just inside, they could not see the back of the cave or the bear.

But, the cave crawled with the pungent smells of unseen hair still wet from a river crossing, fresh bear sign, the dried stain of old vapor from centuries of gentle winter breathing, birth and after birth, death and afterwards—grizzly smell.

"Louy's mama's in here, boy. I can feel her," whispered Hatcher.

They crept deeper and deeper into the den. Suddenly, they heard a growl, another growl. Then another.

"Jesus," said Hatcher. "They's more'n one bear."

"I, I count three," said Pedro, feeling an awful lot like backing out of that cave. "Look at the one in the middle. Tall as a house."

In the far back of the cave, three bears stood on hind legs and shoulder to shoulder like a choir in church. Noses sniffed and questioned. Yellow light from the entrance caught in their eyes as they searched for the hunters. A low, steady growl came in unison from the grizzly trio.

Hatcher was on one side of the cave and Pedro on the other. Each sank into the stone wall out of the light.

"Hold there, boy. I'll see if I can move them."

Pedro froze to the wall. Hatcher eased forward. The bears sniffed the air, growled quietly, did not move. Soon, Hatcher was within touching distance of the bear on his side.

"Cover the others. I'm after this one."

With that, Hatcher thrust the muzzle of his long rifle into the bears groin and laid back flat against the wall. The bear gave a deep grunt and bolted for the entrance.

"He's a boy bear," laughed Hatcher.

The bear disappeared out of the cave. A shot sounded from outside and a grizzly squeal. Abruptly, the outside squeal screeched at the cave mouth. In it came, screech, squeal, screech, right in the middle of them, all of them, men and bears, bears and men.

"Wounded grizzly! Damn, Louy! Shoot him Pedro! Shoot!"

Hatcher's rifle sounded with the word, 'shoot.' Pedro's Kentuck fired a half a second later. The whirling bear stumbled against the others, bounced off the far wall and toppled to the floor of the cave—right on top of Long John Hatcher.

The remaining bears seemed not to notice death. The huge bear still growled thunder from hind legs. He cast his head in the air, this way and that, his nose blinded by the acrid pall of burnt gun powder. Neither bear moved.

Pedro leaned his empty rifle against the wall and pulled his pistols. He pointed one at the gleaming eye of the huge bear and fired. Without waiting for the effect, he fired the other pistol at the smaller bear's head.

"One bear on the way out," he shouted.

The huge bear fell in his tracks, dead before he hit the rocky floor of the cave. The smaller bear let out a squeal of its own and dashed for the entrance. Pedro's ears were ringing; but he heard the shot and the squeal and heard the squeal die.

Amid the bells in his head, Pedro heard a small, unfamiliar voice.

"Uh, bein squished. Get me out from under this bear squaw. Pedro!"

It took both Pedro and Louy to pull the bear off Hatcher. It took all three of them to catch Hatcher's breath. He sat at the mouth of the cave huffing and puffing.

"Shame aint the half of her," said Louy. "Crawlin under that there bear skin to hide while Pedro does battle with them fierce and deadly animals to save your sacre damn ass."

Louy stood over the panting Hatcher wagging a powder stained finger in his face.

"Now look at you, all over slobber and blood and shit. Take a heap of Purgatoire scrubbin afore you'll be fit to share my blanket—if'n ever you are."

"Now Louy," Hatcher puffed. "Yo-yo-you're just glad, I know, glad that bear didn't put me under."

"Glad? hell. That bear, she put you under all right. That's where we found you. Shame is, she didn't kill you, for all the sacre damn trouble you cause on this here bear hunt."

With that Louy started down the mountain and back to the cabin for a couple of mules.

"Damn shame, damn," he mumbled as he stumbled down the steep mountainside.

"Louy gets kinda, ah, sentimental, you might say, when it comes to my safety, him countin on me like he has all these years."

"I've noticed," said Pedro, smiling.

"I'm not surprised," said Hatcher, pointing toward the deep inside of the cave. "I recollect some scripture about Daniel in the lions' den."

Getting up with a grunt, he pulled the Green River from his belt and began to skin the huge bear.

"Made that Daniel sound like some kinda man. 'Course it were winter and them lions was probably a-suckin fresh killed blood from their paws. Maybe he didn't know them lions just wasn't hungry. Anyhow, from this day, tell me no more of Daniel or lions. We are his equal in this here den; good as he ever dared to be."

It took them the rest of the day to skin out the three grizzlies, lay the choice cuts in thick bearskin robes and pack the meat down the mountain to the mules.

That night they roasted bear meat and gorged themselves with the lean and the fat of it. They spent the next two days cutting the lean into long strips and smoking them over a slow-burning fire. While the meat smoked, they dug a deep hole near the cabin. The floor and walls of the hole were lined with green cottonwood limbs. They covered the hole with a roof of thin branches and thick river bottom mud. At the end of the hole facing the river, they cut steps down into the hole, closed off at the bottom by a log door.

When the meat was smoked, it was wrapped in a bearskin. In the cool depths of La Cave, as Louy called the cellar, they stored the great pack of smoked meat.

"It'll last the summer and the bugs and worms don't get at it," said Hatcher, smiling.

"Or the bears," said Louy.

The perfume of spring faded in the pulse of summer heat. The heat ripened miles of blackberries along the river and acres of sweet ears of corn in the first patch. They had plowed and planted the second fifty acres and the young stalks now showed green above the ground. But the young weeds beat the young stalks by a mile.

Louy was the fastest weed chopper; and he liked it as much as any of them liked any of this farming—which wasn't much.

"Sacre damn weed tops, they grow faster'n anythin. Faster'n corn for sure. Only thing that beats them a-growin is blisters on my hands."

Pedro's hands too were blistered. The river had dropped below the mouth of the acequia and he had to dig a deeper ditch to bring water to the corn.

"This is the work of Indians on my father's rancho, not the work of a va-quero," he said, smiling at the thought of his mother behind a mule plowing her own acequia to the rancho in her early days.

"Do you good. Make you strong and one with the mother earth," said Hatcher who was sitting on the ground in the shade of a cottonwood just finishing a hat full of blackberries. "One with the earth, like this coon." He leaned back against the tree, scrunched his hips into the soft soil and pulled the hat over his eyes.

"That bear watch of nights sure tuckers a man or I'd help you out with that water ditch, Pedro."

"Tonight I will sit up on that perch and watch for bears," said Pedro, mop-ping his face with the back of his hand. "Tomorrow, after you're all rested up, you can finish this acequia. Aint fittin work for a horseman, anyhow."

"Now, boy." Hatcher lifted the hat just off his lips so he could talk. "I appreci-ate your willingness to spell me at the chore, the all night job, of protectin our corn crop; but it aint necessary. After a little nap, I'll be fit as ever."

He dropped the hat brim down on his lips again; then spoke through it. "'Sides. A horseman like your ownself will want to stay ready to help out them mares of yours. They're about ready to drop their foals. Any time now. That's horseman work, for sure."

Pedro's four mares each dropped a foal. Three of them lived, a filly and two colts. In the dark of night amid the frantic screams of the mares, a grizzly broke into the corral and killed the infant filly and carried it off. The next morning, Pedro found the carcass of the foal a mile down stream, its guts eaten out. He saw wolf tracks among those of the grizzly. From then on, he, too, stood bear guard at night.

Attracted by the miles of sweet, ripe berries along the river, the bears came to the corn as it ripened. They trampled as much as they ate. Hatcher and Pedro and Louy shot at the dim shapes and the marauding night sounds; but, come the dawn, they found no dead bears. Nothing but the prints, the crushed stalks of corn, ears stripped, chewed and spit out and an occasional splotch of blood.

By August, the first corn crop had gone to the bears; the second was going under to the searing heat.

"This aint workin the way Saint Vrain said," Hatcher complained one night. "We got little corn and will make little more come fall. We've worked this near half year for the god damn bears."

"We have the horses, eight mares and the two studs and two male foals," said Pedro.

"No mares like that Smokey horse of yours," said Hatcher. "She's a princess of horse flesh, if I ever seen one. And I have."

"The other mares will produce fine stock," said Pedro. "Cortez stock!" He smiled at the show of family pride in his voice. "Cortez horses," he said quietly. "Papa's horses."

"Speakin of mares reminds me of the time I was winterin with the Blackfeet on Squaw Creek." Hatcher re-lit his pipe.

"Louy and some of the other Sublette boys had gone off for supplies to Saint Louis. It had snowed for two weeks, game was scarcer'n hot, young squaws in that village. The head shaman spent day and night wavin his do-dads and singin for sign of game."

Hatcher waved his pipe around the room like the shaman.

"We was near starved when in rides a mountain man, Cobb by name, with a fresh-killed elk buck across the saddle of his horse."

"A Cobb," said Louy, "left his scalp tied to a Crow lance. Summer of '42, it was."

"Same Cobb; but that was later, Louy. Years later. Well, sir. This Cobb, he dumps that elk at the shaman's feet. 'I bring you what for to eat; and you grant this child a warm lodge out of the snow and a warm squaw to winter with,' says Cobb.

"The shaman's eyes light up and he whirls in the snow wavin his gee-gaws to the four corners of mother earth. Then he stops and says to Cobb, 'you have blessed this village with life. I will grant you more than a bed and a woman. I will grant you one great wish.'

"Cobb scratches his beard skeptical like. 'Grant away, old man,' says Cobb.

"'What is your greatest wish, my son?' says the shaman.

Cobb looks at the Indian medicine man. Then, thinkin of that squaw, he looks at his horse.

"'You promisin a warm bed and a squaw for the winter?' he asks, still lookin at his horse.

"The shaman nods. 'What is your wish?'

"'Make my manhood as big between my legs as the one on my horse,' says Cobb, not believin; but knowin he's got to play along or get scalped.

"I'm watchin and laughin. Oh, not so's the Indians could tell.

"Not seein the humor in it, the shaman waves his eagle claw and his bones over Cobb and chants some sing-song words. In spite of himself, I can see Cobb is about to break out laughin.

"Suddenly Cobb doubles over and grabs himself between the legs. His horse snorts and crow hops a might.

"'It is so,' says the Shaman.

"Well, by this time Cobb is on his knees in the snow and groanin somethin awful to hear. I jumps up and grabs his arm. He looks up at me and there's pure anguish all over his face.

"'My god, Hatcher,' says Cobb. 'He done it.' All the time he's got hold of his crotch.

"I says, 'congratulations.'

"He says, 'congratulations, hell! I was ridin old Bessie, the mare!'

"From that time until Cobb died, the boys at rendezvous would fight and die over who was to winter with him."

"The tale, she is tall," said Louy.

"Tail is what them boys was after—and you along with 'um, Louy Simonds."

Hatcher chuckled. Louy cast his eyes down, but smiled. Pedro laughed and slapped his thigh with his hat.

Outside in the corral the Smokey horse snorted. Several of the other mares joined in.

Hatcher plucked a hot chunk of bear meat from the black pot slung over the fire.

"Even the bear meat eats poorly after a summer of it, steady-like."

He looked at Louy and Pedro seated Indian fashion on the floor of the cabin. Pedro was still smiling.

"Don't get a ball into his pea brain, grizz don't die," said Hatcher. "More you shoot into his thick hide, madder he gets; but he don't die."

"What you think," said Louy. "Louy, he tell you. He tell you in Taos. Plow-tit. Plow-balls. All for sacre damn grizz."

"I'll take the stallion that matches the markins of my Smokey," said Pedro. "You split the rest. Show somethin for your half-a year."

"That's mighty generous, boy," said Hatcher. "But, we'd just trade them horses for whiskey and tobacco, powder and lead and a few goo-gaws or a squaw for the cold of winter, maybe fixed like old Bessie." Hatcher smiled through a wreath of tobacco smoke.

"That sounds very good to this Frenchman." Louy waved a hand at Hatcher. "He could keep warm and fed for most of a winter on what four of those fine horses will bring." Louy smiled at Pedro and poked the fire with a stick to stir up the coals.

"Now just you hold up a minute, Louy."

Hatcher pulled a twig from the fire and held it over the bowl of his pipe until smoke-curls mixed with his curly, blond hair. Unconsciously, he offered the pipe stem to the directions of the compass before he spoke.

"We'll just trade the horses away; and some Indians or Mexs—pardon, boy. No offense—will ride them to death."

"Horses is for ridin," said Louy.

"Now, Louy. Pedro, here, will take them horses and grow him a herd. Them are the seed stock. Horses too good just to use up. In a couple or three years, when this bunch has maybe tripled, then we'll cut us a colt or two for tradin, and in the years after that, for ridin as need be." Hatcher blew a smoke ring Pedro's way. "Well?"

"They'll be at my father's rancho, until I find my valley. You will always be welcome to cut out a horse as need be. Both of you."

"It is clear to this Frenchman that we have done with farmin. What now?"

"I reckon," said Hatcher. "We can sack up the rest of what ears we can find with what we got and take 'um to Bent's Fort. Bring a few dollars in trade. Too late to hunt beaver. If there was any left to hunt."

"I will take the horses home to my mother. Then, I will begin the search for Hess and my valley."

Pedro stood up and walked the few steps to the door of the cabin. He looked out at the corral, at his, their, horses.

"Where will you search for that Prussian and your valley?" said Louy, smiling. "This close to winter?"

Pedro stood for a long moment at the cabin door still watching the horses. Then he turned back into the cabin.

"Well, Louy. While I was diggin ditches, choppin weeds and chasin bears, I was thinkin on that. Thinkin hard. I learned real quick that you don't grow corn from the back of a horse." He smiled.

"So I aint goin to grow corn again. This, or any other desert river bottom, won't make one hectare of my valley. I learned that too. Oh, it aint the bears. Wherever my valley is, there'll be bears, wolves, Indians. No, it aint high up where the air is clear and you can see till Sunday. I must find my valley in the mountains. Not too high; but up where a man can breath."

Pedro stopped talking. His dark face reddened a bit. He turned away again to look at where the horses would be. It was now too dark to see them in the corral; but he could hear them and smell the dust of their stirring.

"But, where?" said Louy.

"Hess is rumored gone to California. With winter so close on, maybe California." Pedro said it low and slow. "California."

"Damn long way to ride," said Hatcher, "just to shoot a man. Jed Smith went out there in '29 or '30. Trip damned near killed him. Though, when he got back, he spoke of no prettier land on earth. No beaver to speak of.

"Horses? Great herds. Wild for the takin. Many like your Spaniards. Brought over from the same Moorish stock. He called California as near to paradise as man would get. 'Cept for the Mexicans. Said they don't want Americans comin into their land. Kept Smith and some of his boys prisoner. Then threw them clear out of the territory."

"Like New Mexico, I think California will soon be Americano," said Pedro. His color had faded a little.

"If not, well, to a Mexican, I am Mexican like one of them!"

He forgot himself in the seriousness of the subject.

"Last winter, after he took Santa Fe, General Kearny headed for California. To capture it, too, for America."

Pedro hesitated for a moment, listening to the night. "I think my valley is in California; and, except for the high mountains, I hear there aint no winter in California, even in winter. And there's horses, like your man Smith says, for the takin in California."

"This child's heard a heap of talk about that place; but never been there his ownself. Time. High time. Louy, you aint been there neither."

"You're welcome. Both of you." Pedro smiled broadly, his dark eyes catching the glow of the fire. "If you'd care to ride along to California. Maybe earn your share of the horses by catchin a few more."

"Sacre damn dry trip. In winter, hot by the day, freeze by night. No water across miles of desert. No game. Hunger. Damn."

"Hell's fire, Louy," laughed Hatcher. "We got plenty of bear meat—and corn on the cob."

# 13

It was a cold mountain morning in Taos; but Estis' Tavern was open as usual, serving tortillas stuffed with beef and beans to the early eaters and coffee or nog to the few drinkers who still lingered from the fandango of the night before, and to those few weary travelers just arrived in Taos.

Long John Hatcher walked stiffly over to the bar to talk to Estis.

"Nog," Hatcher said without so much as a howdy. "Since it's mornin, heat the milk for breakfast."

"Si, Señor Hatcher," said Estis, "and a good mornin to you too."

The tavern owner smiled to show he did not mean to offend by politely pointing out Hatcher's rudeness.

"Rode most of the night just for some of your nog," said Hatcher. Estis put a pitcher of milk on the fire.

"I am pleased, Señor, that you remember," said Estis.

Louy Simonds plopped down in a wooden chair and put face to hands and rubbed dust stained eyes.

"Oh! Oh!," he moaned. "All night, we ride so Hatcher can have the sacre damn nog for breakfast. I need the sleep, not the nog."

Pedro Cortez started to sit down at the table with Louy. Suddenly, something at the far end of the long room caught his eye. He stared at two men sitting at a table by the wall. They were talking and did not look up from their coffee. Even in the shadow, Pedro could see the tall man's face was scared black. But that is not what had attracted Pedro's attention. At the tall man's side a long, curved scabbard bumped and scraped the floor as the man moved restlessly in his chair.

The other man was shorter and thinner and his eyes danced in the shadows. They danced over at Louy and Pedro; but didn't seem to notice them or care.

"Brung eleven fresh horses into Taos this mornin," said the man with dancing eyes.

Pedro heard the two men now in the nearly empty room. Neither seemed bent on hiding their talk.

"Young Cortez and some friends," said the smaller man. "Good stock by the looks."

"By rights, ours," said the man with the sword. "Our horses. Cortez horses."

The man with the powder burned face looked up then and locked eyes with Pedro.

At Bent's Fort on the Arkansas River, Pedro, Hatcher and Louy had traded a load of corn and bear hides for fifty dollars apiece and an outfit and supplies enough to get them most of the way to California. They moved fast over Raton Pass to Taos to take the Cortez horses to Mama Cortez for safekeeping while Pedro went after Hess and his valley dream.

Before reaching the Cortez Rancho, they stopped in Taos to complete the supplies they would need for the long, winter trip.

The lure of Estis and his nog was great after the long spring and summer on the Purgatoire.

"Estis!" Hatcher reached over the bar and stuck a thick, black finger in the milk pitcher. "This milk is hot enough. A nog for me and my pardners there." Hatcher fisted a coin down on the long table that served as a bar. "Cigarillos all around. Music."

It was only ten in the morning; no musicians were in the place. Four Mexicans drank coffee at a table across from the bar. Three American soldiers sipped hot coffee and ate tortillas filled with beef and beans at another table.

The two men at the far end of the long room still talked over coffee. They didn't look up at Hatcher's cry. Hatcher didn't seem to notice them either. He was filled with the need for nog.

"It's Estis' strong brew that's had this old dog a-bayin at the moon on many a fine night."

Hatcher stood, palms down, shoulders squared to the bar. He looked at Estis from a serious, dusty face. His voice was loud and gravely. He put a hand to his throat.

"This old dog has surely been treed like a coon a time or two, his throat so raw from bein dry, he couldn't cry out the name of that there brew to save himself. It's been like that this whole hot summer. His throat's so dry; his noggin's so fried by sun and wind, he has plumb forgot the name."

"Nog!" said Estis, laughing. "It's called Nog!"

"Nog! That's a name fit for a brew to cool a man's fried noggin."

Estis poured Hatcher a cup.

"Thank you, Estis."

Hatcher raised the cup and saluted the room. "Salude to my pardners, Louy Simonds and Pedro Cortez."

Hatcher drained the cup and smacked his lips.

"Nog, I says. All around."

Estis refilled Hatcher's cup and brought one to Louy who sat in a tired ball at the table and to Pedro who stood by his side.

At the far end of the long room a chair scraped.

Pedro ignored the cup in Estis' outstretched hand. He watched the tall, black faced man get up from his chair and walk over to stand in his face.

"You," said the black faced man, "are the young Cortez?"

Pedro leveled his hard, black eyes at the ice-blue eyes of the man.

"Hess? Black Hess? The coward with the saber who cuts women and runs from children!" Pedro spit out the death challenge. "I am Pedro Cortez!"

Behind Hess, another chair scraped the floor. Billy Slade pushed his way to the far wall, his musket in hand and pointed at Hatcher.

The four Mexicans drinking coffee put down their cups and smiled at each other. The three American soldiers kept on eating. One held out several dollars to the others and pointed at Hess.

"I am Pedro Cortez!"

Black Hess took one step back and reached for the hilt of the saber.

"Quickly, I shall carve you as I did the old woman, your mother!" Hess' voice was like the ice of his eyes.

Faster than the hand could draw the saber while the words still hung between Hess and Pedro, Pedro pinned the sword hand to the big man's side and drove the hilt deep into the scabbard.

As the words hit, so did Pedro. His left hand, balled by hate, smashed into the black nose, smashed again. The nose exploded with bloody pulp; sprayed the black face red.

Hess doubled over with the pain. In doing so, he wrenched his sword hand from Pedro's grip. Instantly, the saber gleamed in the morning light.

Too late, Pedro spun away from the long knife. The blade flashed in the air; it nicked Pedro's ear as he turned; then cut his shoulder, deep to the bone. Pedro reached for the back of a chair, for a shield; felt it ripped from his hand; heard the crack of the heavy blade splinter wood.

In an instant, Hess was on him with the blade; but, instead of thrusting home, Black Hess toyed with Pedro. He rested the tip of the blade on Pedro's chest; flicked tiny cuts in his deerskin shirt. Blood soon appeared although Pedro did not feel the nicks. Pedro backed into the wall; but could not get away from the saber blade.

"Not unless you want my musket ball in your belly," said Billy Slade. Hatcher froze with his hand on the Green River, his eyes on the ample muzzle of Billy Slade's musket. "Let them fight." Billy Slade smiled.

Suddenly, Billy Slade's smile twisted, bent, broke. The room filled with smoke just as the loud gunshot pounded eardrums. The four Mexicans lit out for the door. The three Americans stopped eating for a moment.

"Pedro," yelled Hatcher.

They saw the bright flash of the Green River cross the room. Now each hand held money. One man pointed his money at Hess and smiled. The Americans ignored their food. This was serious fun.

Billy Slade slipped down the wall to sit on the floor in his own blood.

Louy Simonds bit a paper cartridge and spit away the end as he filled the smoking barrel of his trade musket with a new powder charge.

Hess turned his head at the shot; saw Billy Slade slump down the blood-washed wall; caught the flash of the Green River out of the corner of his eye.

He turned back to Pedro ready to end the play. He gripped the saber's hilt for the final thrust; saw Pedro catch the big knife; saw the blade of the Green River flash against the sword hilt; winced at the surprise pain in his fingers; saw a finger jump from his hand to the dirt floor; saw another—and a spurt of blood.

Hess jumped back, hardly able to hold the sword in his blood-slippery, two-fingered hand. He raised the blade so it would not fall from his hand.

Pedro locked the heavy blade of the huge knife against the saber blade and pushed upward. The push unlocked the hilt from Hess' blood-wet hand. The saber clattered to the floor. Hess' black face was ashen now; but ice was in the eyes.

Pedro extended his arm until the point of the knife was at Hess' cheek. Then, he flicked the blade. A wide gash smiled red on Black Hess' black face from left eye to jowl. Pedro waved the tip of the Green River in Hess' face slowly backing him to the bar.

Pedro's left shoulder was red with blood; but the flow had stopped. He felt nothing but the need to kill this man.

Across the room, the three Americans clapped hands. One of them held all of the money and smiled. He was not the man who had smiled before and pointed at Hess.

"Kill him, boy," he said, voice low and slow and deadly. "Kill him!"

Hess' back hit the bar. He tried to blow the snot and blood from his flattened nose; sprayed his shirt. He stared at the tip of the Green River. For an instant, his eyes crossed; then he looked at Pedro. He gripped his bleeding right hand with his left. From the sockets where his fingers had been, blood poured down his hand into his sleeve.

"Afraid?" Hess challenged Pedro. "Is it that you are afraid to kill a man!?" A thin crescent of blood marked the deep cut on his powder burned cheek.

"Black Hess," said Hatcher suddenly in a loud voice. "This here is Pedro Cortez. He aint afraid of anythin, man or beast."

Hatcher moved up to Hess and Pedro; put a hand on Pedro's chest and shoved him back a foot or so. Hatcher pointed at Louy.

"That there is fearless Louy Simonds. Black Hess, you move and he'll gut shoot you like he done your pal."

"Hatch?" Pedro resisted the shove.

"Kill the German bastard," said the smiling soldier.

"You've cut him good, boy," said Hatcher talking just to Pedro. "Just like he deserves. You've got him at your mercy. We can string his severed fingers for a necklace for your mama. It's been a good fight. Kill him if'n you've a mind." Hatcher looked at Pedro.

"You kill him, though; and he won't have to go through the rest of his life, a two fingered swordsman."

Hatcher laughed; turned to Black Hess, laughed in his face.

"That'd be too bad. And folks wouldn't get to see that half-moon you carved on his black face; so's they could laugh, knowin how he got it. Cut by Pedro Cortez for the wrong done to his mama. That'd be a shame."

"Kill him," said the three American soldiers in chorus.

Pedro stood stiff-legged in front of Hess, the Green River still extended. He looked at Hatcher.

I kill him now, Pedro thought, and it's kinda cold-blooded. He's finished for now. His side kick is all shot up, probably dead. His face is marked for life. His right hand empty of fingers.

Pedro flexed his own fingers around the handle of the big knife. He felt his own blood cold in his veins. Not as cold as it needs to be, he thought.

Pedro handed the Green River to Hatcher.

Hess smiled, tipped his head ever so slightly. "Feigling," he said. "Coward!"

"Kill the German bastard, Cortez," said the American soldier again.

"Coward!" said Hess, waiting to die.

Pedro did not look at Hess or the American. He walked across the room and picked up the saber where Hess had dropped it. He raised the blade high over head, caught the slant of sun, brought the sword down hard over the back of a heavy chair, dodged as the severed blade flew past his ear to bury itself into the wall. Then he threw the hilt end of the broken saber at Hess' feet.

"If I see you again, I'll kill you, Hess." Pedro motioned toward the door. "For now, when they laugh at your scarred up face, tell 'um about the coward, Pedro Cortez."

Hess, still gripping his crippled right hand in his left, stared icey fangs at Pedro.

"Hess you will not see again!" Hess murmured.

He took a step toward the door. Almost to the door, he stopped. Without looking at Pedro, he turned back into the room. Slowly, he walked to the wall and fumbled in the dirt of the floor with his left hand. In a minute he stood. He held up his left hand—and two extra fingers, already beginning to shrivel. Blue-ice eyes froze the room.

"Fool, Cortez!" he called out. "Hess, you will not see again—before Hess sees you—first!"

And, he was gone out the door.

In a minute, they saw Hess pass the window on his way down the street; and, soon, they heard the slow, heavy foot falls of a horse bearing wounded weight, west, out of Taos.

Estis called an Indio to haul Billy Slade out the back door for burial among the unmarked graves of Taos.

A Mexican woman came with warm water and muslin. She cleansed and wrapped Pedro's shoulder. With a whip of her wrist, she sewed a dangling piece of ear to its former place of adornment.

The Indio brought a pair of spurs, a musket, powder horn and pouch and two dollars to Estis. Estis gave the spurs to the Indio.

"This here is all that's left of Billy Slade," said Estis and pocketed the money. He handed the musket, horn and pouch to Louy. "Your shot, Señor."

"Merci," said Louy. He took the plunder as if by rights.

"A nog all around," said the American soldier waving the money he had won from his friends.

"This hellion's for that," said Hatcher. "C'mon Louy, Pedro. Step up to the bar. It's a long, dry and mournful ride to California."

"Better we get to it, I'm thinkin," said Louy.

"This hellion don't tell another what for to do. But, Louy, today he's a-goin to drink nog. Tomorrow's soon enough for him to ride for California."

Hatcher filled clay cups for each of them. He raised his.

"Tomorrow!"

"Demain!" said Louy. "Sacre, damn. Always, tomorrow." He drank the cup dry.

"Mañana!" said Pedro. He too emptied the cup.

"Mañana and California!"

# II
# 1848
# BEFORE THE WORLD
# RUSHED IN

# 14

From somewhere high up the piney slope, gun thunder rumbled across the deep river canyon.

The first shot caught a man in the middle of his wide sombrero. Slowly, the man knelt down on the sand bar in the middle of the river below. He put callused palms together on his breast and pitched from prayer to prone, half in and half out of the water. His face was buried in the rush of the river as it slid around the sandy bar.

The other three men looked up from the bar they had been placer mining. One, a chubby American dressed in a wool shirt and army britches, shaded his eyes with his hand. He looked up the steep slope trying to pierce the piney woods from which the rolling thunder had come; not able to believe that it was gunfire or aimed at him.

As he hunted for sign, it was given to him. He saw a puff of smoke billow from the trees; felt lightning strike his ample gut; vaguely heard the thunder roll as he tumbled on his butt in shock. There he sat hunched over, motionless in the morning sun.

The other two men, both Mexicans like the first man to fall, began to run down the bar. Thunder pounded the bar once more and the leader tripped, fell, dug a furrow in the sand with his nose and lay still.

The last man went for the tent camp on the bar and his own rifle. He reached the tent, saw his rifle lying by; but reached his hand instead to grasp at the new hole in his arching back. For a moment he posed arched and reaching. Abruptly, he melted into the tent. An empty flour box clattered in the pebbly sand, lay still.

A mournful silence followed the thunder. The deep river canyon sighed in the slight breeze of morning. The breeze, like the river, flowed soft and gentle, fast and roily, down from the high mountains to embrace the bar and rush on. The giggle of silly water murmured up the sheer cliffs and narrow ravines to meet the drumbeat clicking of aspen leaves.

A red headed woodpecker played mountain taps.

On the piney mountain slope, high up, a blue jay suddenly screeched a territorial complaint at the bright morning. A tall wire of a man walked out of the trees at the top of the slope. His homespun shirt was tattered. Where the skin showed through, it was gray with dirt and sweat. He wore no hat. He carried a Sharps rifle at the port as he slipped and slid down the steep incline to the edge of the river. The blue jay canceled its complaint with a final shriek.

The man easily forded the near fork of the river. He came out at the spot where the first Mexican lay with his face awash in the gentle flow of the river. The man did not look down. He walked directly to the tent; kicked aside the remains of the back-shot Mexican and stooped to crawl under the collapsed canvas and India rubber. In a moment, he ducked out from under the tent. He held a large, leather sack in his hand.

His hand quivered with the weight of the full bag.

"Gold easier to dig than take?" he questioned the corpses around him. "So say you now?"

"For you, seems the takin is the easier," responded the chubby corpse still sitting hunched over in the sand where the bullet had sat him down.

The man with the rifle and the sack jumped and turned and dropped the sack. He held the Sharps steady on the talking corpse.

"You alive?" he said and pulled the hammer back.

The chubby man slowly turned his head and looked into the muzzle of the rifle.

"No need of that," he said softly. "You've done for me sure."

He pulled his bunched fist away from his ample belly; and the blood gushed free like the rushing river.

The man lowered the rifle and, without a word, picked up the heavy leather sack.

"Help me to the tent where I can die out of the sun."

The man with the rifle stared down at the chubby man. Then he lay down the rifle and the sack; and, taking the bleeding corpse-to-be under the arm pits, dragged him to the topple-down tent. He pulled a section of the gray canvas over the chubby man.

"Reckon that'll have to do."

"What come over you?" said the chubby man through clenched teeth. "We was share and share alike. Why this?"

A hint of smile flickered across the wiry man's lips. Without a look or a word, he picked up his rifle and his sack and re-forded the river. He stepped out where the miners had picketed their mules in the river bottom grass.

In a minute, the man saddled the nearest mule and turned the mule to climb the steep grade.

The gut-shot man watched his killer mount the hill.

"Son of a bitch," he mumbled to himself as he felt the pain claw at his soul. "Man I trusted. Got my gold, taken my life. Now the bastard rides out of my death sittin atop my very own saddle.

"I surely seen the elephant," he coughed. "Or, maybe—he seen me!"

# 15

On September 14, 1847 the first American flag that ever waved over the capital of a conquered nation was hoisted at seven in the morning in the Plaza de Armas of Mexico City; and on the same date, about an hour later, Sylvio Escobar was kicked in the head by a mule at a gold mine deep in the Sonoran desert of Mexico.

From that time on, Sylvio never spoke, always hung his head, worked just as hard for the patron—and heard everything.

When Juan Escobar spoke to his wife, Maria, about the new gold discoveries in California, Sylvio heard his brother. His other brother, Luis, always whispered about the new gold, as though the patron might hear of their plan to escape the serfdom of the Mexican mines to become rich in California. He heard his brothers' quiet whispers in the dark of night.

Sylvio bounced his chin off his chest with each stroke of the shovel. While he worked shoveling chunks of ore onto the conveyer that ran ore up to the great, loud stamper to be crushed, he wondered what a California tree looked like. Juan had spoken of California trees and endless cool shade. Except for scrub oak and juniper, Sylvio had never seen a tree.

What does a California tree look like? That simple question to which he could not now know the answer occupied his scrambling mind all through the hot morning.

Sylvio heard the ore truck even before it reached the mouth of the long tunnel that slanted down, deep inside the tell-tale outcropping of rock more than eight hundred feet above.

Juan Escobar pushed the ore truck up the ribbon of narrow track toward the opening of the long, hot tunnel. His brother, Luis, limped behind him, a pick and shovel over one shoulder. It was a walk from Hell into the blinding light of the midday Sonoran desert. Juan halted the heavy ore truck to let his eyes adjust to the heat of the searing light. Luis stumbled into Juan's back.

"Lo siento, Hermano," Luis said.

A sudden whish! cut the still, hot air. The lash, like sharp teeth, slit Luis' thin, cotton shirt and bit deeply into his back. Luis sank to his knees; quickly recovered; stood.

"Clumsy fool," said Obregon, the overseer, from the high back of his Spanish horse.

"Move! Move!" Obregon coiled his bull whip. "It is not Sunday. It is a day of work."

"Si! Si, Jefe." Luis jumped to help Juan.

Head bowed, Juan pushed the ore truck up the steepening grade to the dump site a quarter of a mile into the blistering sun and sand. With Luis' help, he upended the truck and dumped the chunks of raw quartz onto the growing pile of gold ore in front of the huge stamp mill. Sylvio never missed a beat with his shovel as he threw load after load of ore onto the stamp's mule-powered conveyor tongue to feed its clamorous jaws. Juan's ears nearly collapsed to the thunder of the stamp as it ground the endless stream of ore with iron teeth.

Obregon cracked his whip above Juan's head.

"Slow! Too slowly do you Escobars work; except for the dumb one."

He pointed his whip at Sylvio. Then the whip cracked again, closer to Juan's ear this time.

Luis tossed the pick and shovel into the ore truck and joined Juan at the rear to return the truck to the bowels of the deep mine for another load. They pushed together; but the empty ore truck seemed no lighter. As Juan pushed, he saw the blood seep from the gash in Luis' back to stain white cotton crimson and his own soul with the nourishment of hope.

"It will be tonight," whispered Juan. "With Sylvio, we will go to the sea. There we will take the ship to California. To the new gold."

"There we will work, but for ourselves," whispered Luis wincing as sweat salt-washed his wounded back. "There we will be free men. What we mine will be ours. If the stories are true, we will become rich in weeks instead of this. Poor men, slaves to the patron, for all our lives."

Luis grunted against the weight of the truck.

"If the stories are true."

"I know the stories are true," panted Juan, his shoulder pushing against the hot iron of the heavy ore truck.

"I know it!"

⁕

That night Juan hugged his wife and their three children in a long-armed embrace. Maria wept; and the children, seeing their mother shake with fear, cried too. Luis stood by the single burro which would carry their meager possessions from deep in the Sonoran desert of Old Mexico to the Gulf of California.

Next to Luis, Sylvio Escobar stood, head down. He was the youngest of the Escobar brothers. One side of his head was flat and still bore the unmistakable imprint of the iron shoe of the kicking mule. Sylvio said nothing, heard everything.

"Come Juan," whispered Luis. "It is time. Soon the patron's men will pass through the camp on patrol. Come!"

"We have carefully saved some gold . . . ."

"Stolen, Juan. From the patron." Maria's fear lit even the dark of the black night.

"Earned!" said Juan. "Earned with our blood from the whip and callouses so rough my children cry when I touch them. Earned!"

Juan reached out a hand to her face, saw her wince at the rough finger tips which he wanted so much to be gentle.

"There will be enough to last you and the children until I return. Obregon will ask questions. Tell him nothing. We have just gone. You do not know where. I will see you in the spring."

"Juanito, do not go," cried Maria. "Do not go, Papa," chorused the children.

"I must," was all Juan said.

He hugged the children again and kissed Maria. Then, he turned and followed Luis and Sylvio to walk to the Gulf and California gold.

As the Escobar brothers pushed and pulled the reluctant burro into the melting black of desert night, they heard the soft tread of horses enter the camp they had just left behind. They heard the bit chomping and horses breathing hard. A man laughed at the night.

"All is well," they heard the man say.

"All is well," whispered Luis as he pushed the rump of the burro. "All will be well," he hissed. "In the spring we will return rich with California gold."

"Si," said Juan. "If it is God's will."

Unconsciously, he made the sign of the cross and kissed the tip of his thumb.

"If it is God's will," whispered Luis into the hot desert night.

Sylvio walked in the lead, pulling the burro. His head was bowed as usual; except now, tears streamed down his dusty cheeks. He cried, like the children, because Maria had cried.

He cried too for the California tree. Soon he would know it. Juan had spoken of endless, cool shade.

Sylvio heard everything.

# 16

The woman called Millie was young but not pretty. Her cotton bonnet was bent back over the top of her head and dull brown hair fell in wet strings into her red, tear-swept face. She stood ankle deep in mud-soup on the wagon track that served as a road to the placers through the camp at Buff's Bar on the Bear River.

On either side of the sliding track stood round tepees and bedraggled square tents, leaning plank hovels, log sided cabins with canvas covers, even an A frame of pine limbs draped with old calico shirts and gray underwear.

Millie was the only woman in Buff's Bar; maybe the only woman within fifty miles.

She had sailed around the Horn with her father. On a windless day off the coast of Chile, he coughed up blood and died. Her passage was paid to California; so on she sailed. Finding herself alone on a deserted ship in San Francisco, she helped herself to the ship's stores of sugar, flours, molasses and lard. These she loaded aboard six mules and came by sail with the wind and against the current up the Sacramento River to the American.

She walked the mules for a ways with the first rush up the American, then back down with the rush to new diggings. Again, she and her laden mules went with the human flow up a winding trail for a few miles to the north; and, along the rushing Bear River, she climbed to Buff's Bar.

Millie and her mules carried the only supplies for miles around. She planned to mine the miners by cooking and baking for gold they dug out of the river's edges and sandbars.

Her plan worked out well and she accumulated almost four hundred dollars in the first few weeks—until, two men, one called Jed and the other named Sam, long-time friends and partners in a rich claim, sampled of her baking. Jed ate her sourdough biscuits. Sam ate her corn bread muffins.

Both fell in love with Millie.

"Millie. That there nugget is mine and . . . ."

"I can not take this," Millie wailed, stamping her boots in the mud. "Not from either one of you."

She held her two dirt stained hands out in front of her. In her hands she clutched a huge nugget of gold-laced quartz weighing more than six pounds.

She looked to her left at a tall, very thin man who stood in the mud, with legs apart, his gray-bearded face pocked with hate. He held a cocked pistol in his hand.

This was Jed of the sourdough biscuits.

She swung her pleading, porcelain eyes to the right and looked into the muzzle of another pistol. The man behind the muzzle was also tall; but thick bodied, with a beardless, round face. He smiled his hate for the man in front of him as a store-keeper smiles his thanks.

This was Sam of the corn bread muffins.

"That there nugget is mine," said the round faced Sam, "and I give it to you as a sign of my love."

"Taint his nugget to offer," said thin-faced Jed. "And he don't know true love from the calf kind." The thin-faced Jed squealed his reply as if he could hardly get breath past his hate.

"It's my gold," said Sam. "Mine! Marry up with me and it's yours, Millie."

"Now, Sam," cried Millie. "You and Jed stop this conbobberation. You both come on the nugget in the same hole at the same time. You're partners, friends; have been since you come to Buff's Bar. Share and share alike. It's half your gold, Sam, and half yours, Jed. I won't take any of it from either of you; nor marry you, one or both."

Jed and Sam glared and waggled their pistols at each other and Millie cried and the rain-gray light sank in the western sky.

Suddenly, Millie hunched her small shoulders, shook her head and dropped the nugget into the mud where it sank from sight.

"Here's your damned gold nugget. Kill each other for it or for me or, for all I care, the Devil hisself. Men!"

Then, with a deep sob, she fled inside her clapboard shack.

"Reach for it and be damned to Hell," yelled Sam, cocking his pistol and gesturing with the muzzle at the spot in the mud where the nugget had sunk.

"Don't think I'm goin to leave that gold for the likes of you, do you?" Jed pointed his cocked pistol at Sam's head.

The two men stood like that while the last of the day painted the gray light black and a dark night brought the November rain sloshing down on Buff's Bar and the placer mines in the river bed below.

———

Long John Hatcher sat hunched in his saddle looking down the wagon track into the camp at Buff's Bar.

"This coon's been wetter'n he is now, but not by more'n a drop or two."

The rain alternately slanted in torrents or misted across the gray, dawn sky. Mud stewed and swirled around the horses fetlocks before it rushed into the plain of scattered oaks behind the camp.

"Sacre damn snow be better than this rain," said Louy Simonds as he wiggled his neck in response to the flow of cold rain that ran under his greasy collar.

"I've never seen a picture like that," said Pete Cortez. "Two men, either dead or asleep, sittin out in the rain in a river of mud."

"Well, looky yonder," said Hatcher.

Pete edged his smoky horse toward the nearest man. The man sat with head slumped on his chest and rain-driven mud sloshing around his middle. Farther up the track another man sat with one arm extended into the mud behind him, his head cocked to one side as if trying to find shelter in an arm pit.

Suddenly, the near man started, turned with a creaky motion to face Pete's horse and raised a pistol from the goo in his lap.

"One step more toward my nugget," he said, "and I blow your head off."

Sam was awake now. Pete watched him feel in the mud as if he'd lost something he wanted real bad.

"Where the hell? Where? It's gone. My gold."

Frantically, he splashed around in the flowing mud with one hand and waved the mud-plugged pistol at Pete with the other.

"Gone!"

Pete pulled the smoky horse up and leaned across the pommel. "Mister. You shoot that thing and you'll blow your own head off."

"And if you don't, this child will."

Hatcher said it quietly; but the cocking click of the hammer rang atop his Hawkin rifle like a come-and-get-it gong in the early morning silence.

"What are you so all fired upset about," said Pete. The smoky horse jumped a little to avoid some pebbles running under her hooves with the stream of mud.

Suddenly, the other sitting man cried out. "Don't shoot him boys, he's mine!"

Stiffly, Jed pulled himself up to his feet, his own mud-packed pistol barrel pointed at Sam. Jed shivered and shook. His thin face twitched so hard the mud slid down his whiskers like hot syrup running off the flapjacks.

"Now, mister. You're shakin so hard, if you shoot, you're liable to kill a horse or one of your neighbors."

Pete began to circle Sam who followed him with the muzzle of his pistol.

Behind Pete a woman's voice cried out. "All night. They been there at each other's throats all night."

The smoky horse spooked at the voice. Pete grabbed rein and turned in the saddle and looked down at Millie.

"Let 'um kill each other and get it over and done with," she said.

A scattered cheer went up from several men standing along the mud track in front of their tents and log and canvas shacks.

"Holdin a Hawkin rifle like this, with the hammer eared back, gives an ache to my thumb." Hatcher leaned toward Sam. "You don't lower your gun, my thumb's a-gonna slip. Then we'll see if I kept my powder dry in all this mornin's California rain."

"I'll kill him for you, by God," yelled Jed and he pulled the trigger. Sam pivoted and dropped his own hammer.

Click! And then, Click!

Neither gun fired. For an instant Jed and Sam stood staring at each other. They clicked another cylinder and another. Jed threw his useless pistol at Sam. In spite of rain and mud and the sleepless night, Jed's pistol bounced off Sam's skull and disappeared in the mud. Jed stumbled at Sam with balled fists.

Sam didn't seem to notice the growing mound at the front of his head and waded in the mud to meet Jed, his own pistol still to hand. Sam slammed the barrel of his pistol down hard onto Jed's skull. Sam raised the gun barrel high again as Jed sagged into his chest; but the mud won. Sam's pistol slipped from his hand and disappeared in the brown flow.

Entwined, both men slid into the brown soup and lay still.

In a flash, Millie waded into the track and tugged at their collars.

"Help me," she cried. "They'll drown. Help."

Several of the men came to her rescue and that of Jed and Sam. They carried both men to a log shack down the street and lay them on their bunks. One man stayed and started a fire in the iron cook stove.

Millie looked deep-sunk eyes up at Hatcher as he stuck his rifle back into his saddle scabbard.

"They been crazy, fightin over me for more'n a week now."

She stood in the mud of the track, her hem pulled high over bare ankles, her loose hair stranding over shoulders left naked by the soft, cotton night shift.

"Each offerin to kill the other. To marry me. Give me all their gold."

"What a beautiful love," said Louy Simonds softly. "She touch the heart." The short Frenchman rested a hand across his chest.

"Nice to see, says I." Hatcher grinned at the girl. "It aint confined to mountain men."

"What aint?" said Pete.

"Squaw nuts."

"What?" Millie squinted her question up at Hatcher.

"Insanity. Men packed away in a wilderness. Go crazy over a woman."

Hatcher's grin wrinkled the corners of his eyes.

" 'Course. Never happened to this child."

Louy laughed out loud. "Remind me of the time over on the Musselshell . . . ."

"Now Louy. We're wastin time we could be diggin for gold. Ma'am. Maybe you could show us the way to the mines." Hatcher tipped his broad brimmed, beaver hat.

"Up river. Anywhere up river that aint claimed. In the rock crevices. On the sand bars. On the banks of the river."

Millie stepped into her shack and emerged with a heavy, wool serape which she pulled down over her head to shield her from the cold rain and her tempting white shoulders from the squaw-nut eyes of the miners in the street. She turned her bare feet in the mud and began a duck-walk over to the log shack where the men had taken Jed and Sam.

"Obliged," said Hatcher.

He motioned to Pete and Louy to follow and headed up the sliding stream of mud between the tents and shacks of the camp toward the river. Here and there along the way, a miner waved or tipped a cascade of water from his hat.

At the top of the slight grade, they looked down on the Bear River, brown and bucking from the rains.

# 17

It had taken Pedro Cortez, Long John Hatcher and Louy Simonds almost six months to haul what corn they could salvage from the rage of the grizzly bears to Bent's Fort, take the Cortez horses home to Mama Cortez and Pedro's sister, Anna, and outfit for the trek to California.

It had taken Pedro a few seconds out of a finger-slicing morning to rid New Mexico Territory of Black Hess. It took days for Pedro's wounds to heal.

They had tried to talk Garrard into joining them for California; but, Anna had smiled a woman's smile at him. He begged off, saying that the rancho needed so much work. The new horses needed breaking. Cattle, some belonging to the family and some of his own, needed to be driven to market in Santa Fe. So much work. Maybe in the spring. He would join them in the spring.

Anna had smiled; and Pedro knew Garrard would never leave.

"Pedro is Mex for Peter, aint it?" Garrard asked Pedro as they squatted by the corral fence eying the next horse to be cut out for breaking.

"Yes. Peter of the Bible."

"In California. In America, you'd do better callin yourself Peter or, maybe Pete, for short. You don't look Mexican. With the war just over, folks may not take kindly to the Mexicans for a spell. An American with a Spanish surname and a Missouri mama is different."

"Peter? Pete? Pete! Not so bad," said Pedro. "Sounds American."

Mama Cortez had cried. All the rest agreed with Garrard. From then on, except for Mama and Anna, Pedro was Pete. Pete Cortez, partly from Missouri, partly from Malaga, by way of Taos. Pete Cortez, former-day Mexican. Pete Cortez—American.

When they had started up the Old Spanish Trail from Santa Fe, each had sat a prime horse or favorite mule. Possibles and supplies were packed on a mule apiece. Each led an extra mule or horse for riding, trading or eating, as need be.

They followed the footsteps of Father Escalante through Colorado, west across the Green River, into the Uinta Basin, south down the long Utah Valley. The

Old Spanish Trail. Where Father Escalante and his starved expedition turned back for Santa Fe, Pete Cortez, Long John Hatcher and Louy Simonds headed southwest down the Virgin River.

During the long trip, game was scarce; provisions dwindled. Some rotted but was eaten anyway. Some was lost to the sun, the fall rains and the rivers they crossed.

They stayed at the lodges and villages of the Navajo, the Ute and the Mojave Indians. They traded tobacco, lead and powder for a few more days of life.

The Virgin River ran into the Colorado; and they went down the Colorado a ways to the Mojave Indian village where Jed Smith lost ten good men to an Indian ambush. Many in the village remembered the fight only twenty years before; and the victory against the white intruders was sung by the fires. The Mojaves fed Pete, Hatcher and Louy from a good harvest that summer of 1848. Songs by the fire and time had cooled blood lust; and they did not have to trade their scalps. But when they left, a mule, once called Mandy, was smoking over a number of fires. In exchange, one of the Indians agreed to guide them across the Mojave desert.

From the Mojave Indian village they swung across mauve sand and volcanic rock, daytime hot and nighttime cold. They drank at hidden springs; traveled mostly by night across iridescent salt flats agleam in silver moonlight.

During the trip, they ate two of the spare mules, one in Colorado and Utah and the other in crossing the desert.

"This coon had as rather eat mule upon mule as eat any of that damn snake," complained Hatcher as their Indian guide roasted a five foot rattler over the twilight fire. Before they reached Los Angeles, Hatcher ate snake a time or two. "Better than bein dead of an empty meatbag," he said, as he chewed snake in puckered cheeks.

After almost two dry, lip-cracked weeks, their Indian guide left them at the desert bottom of Cajon Pass. In two more days they rode into the sleepy Californio village of Los Angeles; and, right away, ordered a couple of pounds apiece of manzanita-broiled beefsteak.

Their possibles were mostly in tact. They had extra tobacco to trade with the Californios. It was in Los Angeles that Pete traded one of his father's flintlock pistols and a pound of good Virginia for one of the new Colt Army issue cap-and-cartridge six shot pistols fresh from the belt of an American soldier who had played monte once too often with a wily vaquero. The heavy, .44 caliber six shooter had been designed by Captain Walker for the Mexican War. Pete threw in some flints and a powder horn for the flintlock; and the vaquero handed him a box of almost a hundred of the new caps and about thirty of the cartridges made up with a measure of powder and a ball wrapped in paper ready to slide, slick as you please, into one of the six chambers of the pistol's revolving cylinder.

In Los Angeles, the talk was of the gold mines in the north. Just that May, Sam Brannan, storekeeper and recent member of the Mormon Battalion, had walked the newly named Montgomery Street in the newly named San Francisco waving a glass bottle of chunky nuggets. "Gold! gold! Gold in the American River!" he'd cried. Brannan had kept the news quiet for almost a month while he hoarded all of the shovels, shoes and frying pans he could lay hands on.

Now, it was October 1848. Still, there was no rush for gold. A handful of men swept north and south from the American River where, in January, Marshall had first discovered his fateful nugget in the tail race of Sutter's Mill. Mister Reading went up along the Trinity in the north. Bidwell was on the Feather. Jacob Leese and John Marsh and a few others washed thousands from the Yuba around Park's Bar.

Others, with their Indians doing most of the work for a pittance, sloshed sand on the Coloma and Weber Creek down to the Stanislaus, Tuolumne and the Mariposa in the south. In all, a few Americans, many Californios, some Mexicans from the Sonora mines, some muscled by Indian labor, were spilling flakes and nuggets of surface gold from their pans and rockers.

On the trip up to the mines from Los Angeles, Pete had met several opportunities to trade Smokey for horses, cattle, gold dust and, even, a woman; but he passed on all of them. Still, he sat a little taller in the saddle on his Cortez mare. And, Smokey seemed to raise her pearly gray fetlocks just a little higher as they rode through each small town.

Pete marveled at the seemingly endless flows of wild horses and milling cattle which ranged over Southern California.

"Here are all of the horses a man could ever want," Pete sighed.

"And hardly worth the effort to catch 'um," said Hatcher. "No man could want so damn many."

"Still, in Taos there are not so many. Here, I can round up a herd for the askin and take it back home to sell or hold until I find my valley."

"Maybe your sacre damn valley is here in California," said Louy.

"Maybe," said Pete.

They re-outfitted in Los Angeles and headed up the coast following the call of gold. Just above Santa Barbara, they rode through a narrow canyon in the steep coastal mountains, cut across the Sisquoc and Cuyama Rivers of the Sierra Madre mountains and entered the dry, desert valley of the lower San Joaquin River.

They kept to the eastern edge of the coastal mountain ranges because there was better water and more game. Finally, after a month's hard travel they came up to the junction of the Sacramento and American Rivers.

At the junction there was nothing but a few oak trees upon a vast plain of wild grains, now dried out and brown from the heat of summer. An old store-ship beached on the shore of the Sacramento was the only habitation. Yet, parties were daily arriving, headed for Sutter's Fort and the gold mines beyond or leaving with pockets full of dust and nuggets.

Pete and Hatcher and Louy camped under oak trees at the river confluence to let their stock recruit from the long trek north.

One night, a man helloed their camp and was invited in for coffee and talk. He rode a mangy mule to the edge of the firelight, dismounted and threw the saddle to the ground. He covered the saddle with a blanket and left it in the dark. Then picking up a Sharps rifle from his light saddle pack, he came to the fire.

"Set and yarn some," said Hatcher while Louy poured the man a cup of coffee.

"Frank Potts, by name, recent of the Mexican War."

He was a tall wire of a man. His face was a tear drop just ready to fall, skin glassy, eyes round and black like bullet holes. He was dressed in dirt-soaked tatters stained with recent blood. He drank boiling coffee from a tin cup without noticing the burning.

"Aint had coffee in a while," he said through lips turning red. "Aint had much of anything, come to think on it."

"Welcome to share some beef and biscuits," said Hatcher. "Beef runnin wild. Had no brand. So I shot it yesterday."

"The day before yesterday," said Louy. He cut a steak from a fresh rump and put it in the frying pan with some tallow.

"Gamy. Wild tastin beef. But you're welcome." Hatcher motioned to Pete to get the flour for some biscuits. "Can't say Louy's cookin has ruint it much, though."

While Pete mixed flour with water and some of the melted tallow, Hatcher introduced himself and the others.

"Pleased to meet you," said Frank Potts, coffee spilling from the corner of his smile. "I'm from Missouri by way of Mormonism at Navoo City. Come south to fight Mexicans. Give my army pay to John D. Lee in Santa Fe to take back to Brigham Young. Just about starved since. Come on to California with Kearny. Aint shot ary a Mexican. Still hungry. So I and some of the boys went into the mountains for gold. Found it too."

He pulled a large, leather sack from inside his torn shirt, spilled a handful of coarse, yellow gravel into his hand.

"Maybe five, six thousand dollars. More, hell's more, where we found this."

Pete and Hatcher and Louy each inspected the grainy, yellow pebbles in the black hand.

"So that's gold," said Hatcher.

"Pure nuggets," said Potts, carefully spilling the gold back into his sack. He put the sack inside his shirt and wiped his hands over the fire sprinkling twenty dollars of dust into the coals.

"Be I you, Mister Potts," said Hatcher, "I'd fight shy of showing off that much wealth so casual-like."

The bullet hole eyes swept the camp. "Man can gather this much and more; easier than he can steal it." Potts patted the shinny walnut stock of the Sharps rifle which lay across his knee.

Hatcher smiled. "I reckon," he said.

Pete put the biscuit dough in the frying pan alongside the steak which Louy had just turned.

"With all that gold, why are you headin out? If you don't mind me askin?" said Pete, smiling.

"Blood," said Potts. "That steak looks about right," he added and reached for the pan. "If you don't mind, I'll just help myself." He pulled a long knife from his boot. "You boys goin to eat?"

Hatcher shook his head and began to stuff tobacco into his pipe. "Already et." He pulled a flaming stick from the fire and lit the fresh tobacco. "Blood, you say?"

"This here gold is stained with blood."

Potts stabbed the steak in the middle, held it up on the point of his knife and began to tear large chunks of it with yellow, used-up teeth, hardly chewing. He talked as piece after piece slid directly from the point of his knife past his sharply heaving adam's apple.

"Me and Ed Buff and three apostates from the Mormon Battalion was outfitted by Mister Brannan for a fifth of the gold. June it was; and we set out to discover our own mines away from the American River and the Mexicans. Went north. Turned up the Bear River. Nothin at first. Not in the Bear or in the small streams runnin into it. More'n a month we worked up the river. In a couple-a weeks, color began to show in our pans. Oh, not much; but more each day. Them Mormons finally quit and went back; but me'n Buff kept on."

Potts stopped long enough to scrape the burnt biscuits from the bottom of the frying pan with his knife. He made sure each biscuit was soaked in hot grease; blew on them for a moment and popped them, one after the other, in his mouth. He didn't swallow at first, just chewed. His cheeks had giant mumps. When the spit ran out, he drew on the tin coffee cup and chewed some more.

Suddenly, he gulped. The onion shaped adam's apple jumped once; and half-a-dozen well munched biscuits followed the unchewed steak. When he caught his breath, he said, "Obliged," and rolled a long belch across the dark plain. Then he held the cup out for more coffee.

Pete poured coffee for all of them.

"Well?" said Hatcher.

"Well, one day we come on some locals, Mexs, diggin in a long, wide sand bar which split the river. Fact is, them Mexs, three they were, wasn't doin any work to speak of. They had a dozen or so Indians doin the diggin and such.

"By the looks of their camp, they'd been there a spell. Had three or four rockers workin. One or the other of them Mexs was always standin by or walkin around the Indians as they worked. And whichever Mex he was, he carried a shot gun in hand, like them Indians was slaves or somethin.

"They'd found gold, all right. But, they hadn't hardly begun to cover that sand bar. So, me and Buff set up camp and went to diggin and pannin; and each pan held an ounce, some two or more. We'd struck it rich. Them Mexs never said a word; just sat around their camp, guns close to hand, while their Indians worked the placers. Time to time, they'd give us the evil eye and jabber Mex among themselves.

"After a couple-a days—and we could see this bar was rich pickins—why, old Buff went over to talk to them Mexs; see how they was doin; see if they had any more Indians we could buy, rent or steal. Our hands was bleedin from diggin in the sand and rocks; and we was froze most of the time from workin in that river water."

Potts held out his hands. The nails were split, broken back, a couple torn off; and the flesh was a mass of cuts and scabs.

"I am workin the lower end of the bar when Buff goes over to talk. Next thing, I hear whoopin and yellin and I look up in time to see the three Mexicans up and jump Buff. Sun on steel is all I see—and gunsmoke. Buff is down and them Mexs is comin on me like stampedin mules. I grab my possibles and jump plumb into the middle of that river. I hear a shot; but directly, I'm around a bend and into a rock slide. I stay in the river for a couple-a miles, then get out. They didn't follow."

"Seems queer," said Hatcher. "Them attackin you thataway without warnin you off or somethin."

Hatcher could not help looking at the man's near-new Sharps breech loading rifle and noticing that the rifle was the only clean thing about him.

"Guess them Mexs just didn't want us diggin on their bar. You're right, though. They could have warned us. Funny thing. As I was scramblin into the water, I seen them Indians as was workin the claim, I seen them runnin in all directions, like they was escapin while the iron was hot; while the Mexicans was a-scalpin old Buff."

Pete looked hard into the man's bullet hole eyes, shinning black and bottomless in the fire flicker; thought he saw something in the eyes that was not right. Guilty eyes? Lyin eyes? Just rememberin, maybe? He looked away quickly.

"Goin back?" Pete said.

Potts held out his hands and studied the cuts and scabs in the glimmer of the fire. He shivered. "No," he said slowly. "I seen the elephant!"

"Mind given us careful directions on how to get there?" said Hatcher. "Guess we can take care of a pack of lazy Mexicans. No offense, Pete."

"None taken," said Pete. "If'n the bar pans out and we don't get killed, we could give Mister Potts some gold for his trouble. Say, a tenth of what we mine."

"Before this year, she is end," said Louy.

Hatcher laughed. Potts joined in.

"Hell, for another steak in the mornin and some hot coffee, you can have the bar and them killers all to yourselves. I'll direct you boys for a tenth of your find . . . ."

"Till the end of this year," said Louy.

"And gladly. Till year's end is better'n I got now."

Potts hesitated for a moment, nudged the frying pan with the toe of his worn boot.

"No mornin steak and coffee, no deal," he said and looked around the fire.

"I'll be damned," said Hatcher getting up and looking down at Potts.

"This hoss has seen traders. The Nez Perce. Give a squaw for a horse. Then steal the squaw back next day and all your horses with her. The Crows. Prime beaver for Green River knives; then stick the knives in your blankets at night. If you was in 'um, too bad; but bless the vinegar and piss that's in me, boys, I aint never seen such a trader as this Mister Potts."

Hatcher laughed and laughed at the man's tear-drop face that was all cry.

"A tenth of the gold and vittles to boot, by god . . . ."

"Well, Mister Hatcher. If it ruffles you some," Potts hesitated only a moment. "Forget the gold. Just . . . ."

"Forget the gold? Hell, I can't forget the gold. You'll get that and breakfast. Aint that so, Louy." Hatcher laughed and winked.

"Till the end of the year," said Louy. "Gold till then. And a breakfast steak, sacre damn right. That and meat for your pack."

"Meat?"

"Hell, yes. To keep you from starvin while you float down to San Francisco. Hell! We'll just go out and shoot us another one of them wild steers."

They all laughed then.

Potts said, "obliged," and laughed some more. But, Pete noticed, the eyes did not laugh.

In the flicker of the dying fire, Potts drew a map in the sand. "Can't miss it, boys."

Dawn found Pete and Hatcher loading the mules. Louy fried three steaks, only, in last nights grease.

"Just up and sneaks off," said Louy. "Sacre damn funny man. Forgot his mornin steak."

"Left that map plain to see in the sand," said Hatcher.

"Potts aint a feller I'd much trust," said Pete. "Don't know as I trust that there map of his'n."

"Where else you got to go?" laughed Hatcher.

# 18

And so it was that Pete Cortez, Long John Hatcher and Louy Simonds came to Buff's Bar on the Bear River—looking for the elephant! They found a plain girl ankled in running mud.

"I got me six brothers. I've seen the shinny ass of man."

Millie's voice, though slightly muffled from inside the partners' thin-walled shack, spiked the soft sound of the rain on pine needles like an extra shot of whiskey in a plain beer.

Pete swung around in his saddle and glanced back down the track between the tent and log shanties of Buff's Bar. He smiled as he picked out the tent shack where Sam and Jed had been carried.

"Strip, I say," came the spike of Millie's voice. "Sam, you're near froze. Jed is drowned in mud. It's a warm fire and blankets for the both of you."

Pete turned back and bent down over the pommel to study the river below, Louy and Hatcher sitting their horses beside him.

"There," said Hatcher. "Must be the bar where Potts' friend was killed." Hatcher pointed up river to a long, wide patch of sand which forked the tumbling stream.

"Much more rain and she sink under the river till spring," said Louy, hunching his shoulders against the downpour.

"Still, men are working it. I count fifteen. Workin single or in twos and fours. I don't see no Mexican outfit workin any dozen Indians."

The miners were working the upstream end of the long bar. Most stood in holes several yards square, some just started, others so deep, only the tip of the shovel could be seen as it pitched wet sand and gravel onto a blanket or hide. Four rockers were working the sand and gravel, one man shoveling from the blanket mounds, another pouring pans full of water into the rocker and a third moving the machine back and forth by the handle to wash the sand and gravel over the rifflers to catch the cascading gold. Every now and then, the men rotated jobs.

"She look to me like the diggers have the hell of a time to keep up with them other fellers rockin the cradle," said Louy.

Pete sat up in the saddle ready for the slip and slide down to the river.

"Across the river," he said and pointed. "There's a meadow ringed with trees. Good wood. Might make a passable camp."

"That there sandbar," said Hatcher, "looks big enough for three more gold miners."

He started the descent over the worn crest of the hill and into a rain-packed gully already stripped bare by the ups and downs of miners' feet. His horse began to slip. Behind, the pack mule fell to its knees and drifted into the backside of Hatcher's horse. He pulled up on the reins hard and glued his butt to the saddle. The two animals slid haunch-down and back to front, freight train style to the river bank two hundred feet below. Pete and Louy were no more graceful; but none of the animals fell or spilled a pack.

"Better talk to some of the boys over on the bar. See what rules they follow. What the hell that cradle thing does. We'll introduce ourselves first; then set up camp in Pete's meadow." Hatcher headed along the sandy river bank toward the sandbar.

When they got to a likely place to cross over, Hatcher stopped. "Check your primin, boys. Pete, you hang back a little ways with that six shooter handy—just in case."

"You think . . . ."

"Just in case Potts was tellin the truth."

Pete waited until Louy and Hatcher had crossed. Then he urged Smokey into the rush of cold, deep water; felt the push against the horse's belly and his boots take water. Smokey quartered upstream and gave a lunge and they were across.

Hatcher was talking to one of the crews working the nearest rocker.

"There's gold a-plenty, stranger," said one of the men pointing to the downstream end of the bar.

"Hatcher's the name. Long John Hatcher. This child's been ten years with Sublette trappin beaver and killin Indians in the Rocky Mountains." Hatcher waited for a moment to let the name sink in. "This here is Louy Simonds. A Frenchman. Killer of grizzly bears in summer. A two-squaw man in winter."

Louy nodded his head slightly and raised the muzzle of his musket just enough. Pete smiled at the mention of Louy and grizzly bears.

"That there is Pete Cortez from Taos way. Killed and scalped the mighty Comanche Chief, Montoya, knuckle and skull, down to the Purgatoire."

Pete sat Smokey a few yards off, his coat pulled back, hand on the butt of the Colt in his red sash. Still he smiled.

"Boys," he said.

The miner looked at all three of them. "Bill Higgins, recently from Massachusetts. I'm a sailor by trade. I have not killed anyone; but, please, do not hold that against me."

Higgins smiled and held out his hand. The other miners crowded around. Some also shook hands; others just nodded. All looked cold and soaked to the skin. Many shivered and that made them stutter when they talked.

"Thought we'd try our luck," said Hatcher. "Start downstream and work our way up."

"Ba-Ba-Bailey's the name," said a young miner. "You ca-ca-can claim what you clear, provided you work it regular."

He smiled and hugged his body with both arms.

"It's work or fr-fr-freeze for me," he stuttered and turned back to the river from which he dipped pan after pan of cold water to wash the dirt shoveled into the rocker. The others went back to work.

"Say, Mister Higgins. How does that cradle contraption work?" asked Pete as he got down from Smokey to take a closer look. Higgins was rocking the cradle back and forth.

The rocker was about five feet long made from logs split lengthwise and nailed together to form a three-sided box. Bars of wood, called rifflers, were nailed across the bottom about a foot apart. Near the closed end, a sheet of rawhide with large holes punched in it was slanted to form a strainer across the width of the box. Rounded cradles were nailed sideways under the box so that the cradleman could rock the box back and forth.

"Henry, here throws in the gravel from that hole we dug in the bar. Down about eight feet now, aren't we Henry? The sand and rock hits against this rawhide screen."

Henry tossed in a shovel full of dirt.

"The screen keeps the big rocks out of the box."

Higgins picked the larger stones from in front of the sieve and threw them away.

"Bailey sloshes water on the sand and it washes through the holes in the screen and onto the bottom of the box. See? I rock the box like this and them rifflers catch the heavier sands and the gold. The rest washes out the tail end."

Henry shoveled, Bailey sloshed and Higgins rocked and the sand and water sailed through the screen, along the bottom of the box, across the rifflers and out the open end. As he rocked, Higgins constantly cleaned out the larger rocks from in front of the rawhide screen.

"At the end of each washing, about sixty shovels full of dirt, the gold mixed with that heavy black sand is scraped from the rifflers and put in a pan to be washed again until most of the black sand is gone."

Higgins stopped the rocking and the whole process halted. He took a spoon and carefully scraped the black sand from the rifflers and put it in a large, deep-sided tin plate. Just as carefully, and in spite of his shivering, Bailey poured in water until the sand was covered. Higgins rotated the pan first one way and then the other. Slowly, the water spilled from the edge of the pan carrying with it the loose, black sand. Occasionally, he picked a larger pebble from the pan and tossed it aside. When the water was gone, Pete saw a pile of black silt mixed with chunks and flakes of gold shinning yellow in the bottom of the pan.

"This remaining gold and residual silt is stored in a tin cup or bottle until the end of the day." Bailey held the cup while Higgins gently swept in the wet harvest with the tip of his finger.

"In the evening back at camp, the remaining mixture is dried over the fire and the silt carefully blown away. What is left is just about pure gold. We divide the day's take among us. After that it's each man for himself. I've filled more tobacco sacks with gold than I can smoke. Keep the tobacco in a can. Anyone is welcome to it."

"Seems kinda unnatural," said Pete. "Havin all that gold to hide and worry over."

"No need to hide it. There's plenty here for all." Higgins waved his hand across the long, wide sand bar. "No one steals gold here."

"In the early da-da-days," said Bailey, "before I got here. There was a claim robbed. Some men killed. Since we got here, it's tr-tr-trust and be trusted."

"Man named Buff was killed. Right over there." Higgins pointed to the upriver end of the bar. "Came out in '47 with the Army. Everybody knew him. Named this bar after him.

"Before he died, he was able to write some of what happened. He wrote in his diary that he'd been shot from on high and left for dead. His Mex partners also killed. For their gold. Killers took their gold, almost a month's worth, and left them for dead. His diary ends two days after he was shot. Pencil just trails past a blood spot and off the page."

"He had others with him who were killed?" said Pete.

"Found him and three rancheros. All dead. They were friends from Monterey. Came up to the Bear together after the American River commenced to fill up with people."

"Did they have Indians with them?" said Pete.

"Not that I heard anyone tell of."

"Well I'll be pa to a hunnard squaws!" said Hatcher.

"Potts!" said Pete.

"What? What was that name?" said Higgins, putting his face close to Pete's.

"Potts. Frank Potts. Man we met on the Sacramento."

"Potts. Damn," sighed Higgins. "He was the only survivor."

"You know him?" asked Hatcher.

"No. But the last thing Buff wrote was hard to make out. Looked like 'p-a-t-t-t' or 'p-o-t-t-t.' Three tees. Potts would fit. Like he was tellin us Potts got away."

Pete told the story of their meeting with Potts and his version of the affair.

"A man chased by killers down a river. Still, he had him some gold in his pack. A new Sharps rifle. And, funny lookin eyes."

"Don't say," said Higgins turning back to the rocker. Henry threw in a shovel of dirt.

"Bailey, you rock and I will slosh. The work will keep you warm."

Higgins and Bailey switched places and the process began again.

"Good luck," called Higgins as Pete got up on Smokey.

Pete waved and headed Smokey into the other fork of the river to cross to the meadow. Hatcher and Louy followed with the pack animals.

The Bear River rushed from northeast to southwest, in a serpentine fashion between almost vertical, pine clad hills, laced with outcroppings of huge boulders.

The meadow was merely the open fan of one of the sheer side ravines which regularly cut down the mountainside into the river gorge. About one hundred fifty yards wide at the river, the meadow narrowed to a steeply rising gully three hundred yards or so inland. The upstream side of the meadow was a perpendicular cliff face made up of a single boulder which rose sixty or seventy feet in the air before sloping into the rising forest above.

It was on a sand flat against this huge boulder that the boys decided to build their shelter for the winter.

The first night, they slept under a lean-to of slender pine tree trunks laid up against the rock face and covered with their buffalo robes to keep out the rain. The next morning sunshine replaced the rain. They set out to cut and haul tree trunks sufficient to put up a small cabin of logs chinked with smaller trunks and branches and mud.

By evening they had erected a six foot high, eight foot long wall of logs which ran from the rock face and tied at right angles to a ten foot wall of equal height parallel to the rock. Their fireplace lay against the rock face which formed the third side of their cabin. The fourth side was left until the next day. The floor was damp sand.

It stayed dry that night. The next day they enclosed the cabin with a log wall to match the one opposite.

For a roof they placed long thin branches across the log walls and covered them with pine boughs and mud. Working hard, they had finished just after noon. Pete and Louy stood back to admire the work with pride. Hatcher lit his pipe and let blue smoke out into the new afternoon.

"This coon has crawled into caves and tepees, brush huts and log cabins. High on the hog and without no hog a-tall."

Hatcher stood outside the cabin, hands on hips, looking at the small end of the cabin and up at the rock face beyond.

"Never did live in such as this, though. Come here, boys."

Hatcher waited for Pete and Louy to come around to the small end of the cabin.

"Look all you want. Aint no door!"

Louy and Pete looked all around the cabin. The logs fit snugly up against the rock cliff and against each other. There was no opening, door or window.

"Seems you forgot somethin, Louy," said Hatcher. "We climbed out over the wall to put the roof on. Now there aint no way to get back in."

Hatcher wrinkled his forehead and sniffed the wind. "And, it smells like rain."

"Now, Hatch. You was just as much builder of this house as me or Pete an' just as sacre damn blind."

"Well, just a minute there, Louy. I was in charge of cuttin and haulin. Pete here was the roof man. It was you as laid out the walls. You was in charge of walls— and doors."

Hatcher pointed with a dirty finger at the doorless walls of the tightly roofed cabin.

"I was so busy settin the logs and chinkin and layin on the roof poles, I really didn't notice," said Pete.

"Even a Frenchman should know a cabin needs a door, seems like to me."

"Hatcher? You aint goin blind, are you?"

Louy walked over to where Hatcher was standing and put his nose up into Hatcher's face.

"Blind? Why, hell no. I saw it right off."

"Then why not tell."

"Didn't want to interfere with your work, Louy."

"Sacre damn hell. And, you Cortez. What you laugh at?"

"We were all blind," laughed Pete. "And I don't believe Hatcher for a minute. Now, let's cut a doorway into this here hacienda grande. Besides, if we don't get over to that bar and make our mark, we'll lose out. I seen more men comin onto the bar this mornin."

They cut a doorway four feet high and three feet wide and hung it with a deer skin. Inside they spread their buffalo robes on the sand, piled as much dry wood as they could find next to the fireplace and picked the driest spots for their flour, smoked beef, salt pork and beans. Then they took shovels and crow bar and waded over to the sand bar to mark their gold mine claim.

# 19

By the end of the day they had cleared a large area across the lower end of the bar. They drove a stake deep into the sand at each corner to mark their diggings. Before leaving their claim to the night, Pete scraped some surface sand into his pan and slowly held the pan in the river to let it fill with water. Then he sloshed the water around in the pan, first one way, and then the other. He picked out some larger pebbles. Finally he held out the pan to Louy. It was nearly dark and bats flew low over the river.

Louy looked closely at the bottom of the pan and stirred the residue with his finger.

"Black sand. And some lighter chunks." Louy almost put his nose in the pan. "Gold!"

Louy jumped up and down.

"Lemme see," said Hatcher, pushing Louy aside.

"Gold!" he yelled.

That night they dried the black sand over the fire and carefully blew it away. Left in the bottom of the pan were several pieces of yellow metal, peppercorns of pure gold.

"Weigh a couple of ounces, I reckon," said Hatcher. He dropped the nuggets into an empty tobacco pouch. "Boys. We're goin to be rich; or this coon aint never skinned a beaver."

The next day was warm and sunny. By noon, their deerskin shirts, which had been soaked by rain and river for more than a week, were almost dry. Still, their leather pants, and long johns underneath, stayed wet from wading the river to the bar.

And their hands stayed cold as if the bones had frozen below the flesh making the warmth of the sun more irritant than comfort.

Pete moved to a big boulder which marked the downstream end of the bar while Hatch and Louy began to pan the previous night's surface sand.

"Need to make one of them rockers," said Hatcher. He winced as the icy cold water numbed his fingers.

"We'll prospect for a spell," said Pete as he kneeled in the wet sand at the base of the large rock. "Dig here and there around the claim. Pan as much of the diggins as we can until we find the richest sand. That'll be the time for the rocker."

"Dig, pan, rocker. Sacre damn. Whatever I do, she smell like work."

Louy was knee deep in a hole he was digging.

"Them fellers was gettin the gold from diggin holes in this bar. So, I dig; but I do not like her."

Pete looked up from his rock. The long, wide bar was now covered with men. Some were digging like Louy. Others were panning the surface gravel like Hatcher. One was trying to nail a rocker box together.

From the top of the bar, Bailey waved at Pete. "Yo-yo-you boys settled in?" he called.

Pete nodded. "Snug as three bears for the winter."

Pete noticed a string of five riders sliding down the steep gully from the town above. Mexicans by the saddle trappings and heavy serapes. Only three pack mules between them. A-fore long, there'll be some hungry Mexicans on this bar, he thought. Pete turned back to his rock. Time to get to work.

He jammed the bar into the sand at the base of the boulder to loosen the sand and thick clay that lay a few inches underneath. He scraped off the surface sand and began digging. Soon he had exposed the base of the large rock to a depth of about three feet. He got down in the excavation and studied the clay clad face of the rock. Scraping here and there, he found a long, slanting crevice which disappeared at the bottom of his hole. The crevice was from one to three inches wide and contained a hard, bluish clay.

Pete searched the furrow with the point of his Green River knife carefully removing the blue clay. Underneath the clay, all along the bottom, he saw bright, yellow peas of gold.

"Madre de Dios," he breathed, feeling the breath come short as his heart raced by. He looked over at Louy who was digging a few feet away.

"Look at this," he whispered, glancing up the bar at the other men to see if they heard him. "Look!"

Louy dropped his shovel and leaned over Pete's boulder. "Sacre merde! It is more gold than the world has ever seen, I think."

Hatcher put his pan down and stuck his hands under armpits to warm them as he walked over to Pete's rock. He didn't say anything; just stood and looked down at the crevice lined with yellow nuggets. While Louy and Hatcher watched, Pete carefully removed the golden peas with his spoon and piled them in his pan. Louy whistled quietly under his breath. Hatcher shook his head and jumped like a kid back to his own pan.

During the rest of the day, Pete dug deeper at the base of his rock. He followed his first crevice to its end and several more, all sprinkled with the golden pebbles.

By the time of blind dark, he had filled his pan with nuggets and part of his cartridge pouch. Hatcher and Louy had already crossed the river to the cabin.

My luck, Pete thought, I'll fall in the river and feed all this here gold to the salmon. He stepped into the torrent holding the heavy pan and his pistol and cartridge pouch high above his head. It was the first time crossing the river that he noticed how very slippery the underwater rocks were.

He sighed with relief as he stepped out of the river and headed up the meadow to the cabin. That night, he needed to blow no sand; his nuggets were clean and pure and weighed about three pounds!

"Almost four hundred dollars. In one day."

They worked a mostly dry December 1848. Each day saw new arrivals on the bar until there was no more room for a new man to dig or wash his sand. Pete had cleaned almost two thousand dollars from his rock in the first few days. Then, with Bailey's help, he built a rocker and washed the huge quantities of sand and clay dug by Louy and Hatcher. In the few weeks they had mined the bar, among them, they had washed nearly five thousand dollars.

The five Mexicans Pete had seen ride in on the third day had settled at the other end of the meadow. They had pitched a large canvas tent. As a group, they claimed an oversize section in the middle of the sand bar and began diligently to work with shovel, pick and a new contrivance. The one who could speak English called it a Long Tom.

He called himself Juan Escobar. Two of the Mexicans were his brothers, Luis and Sylvio. The other two were Indios picked up on the way from Sonora.

The Long Tom was a box like the rocker, only about twelve feet long with many more rifflers. Instead of dipping water into it with a pan, the Escobar brothers built a small flume which diverted river water at high speed into a wooden trough which in turn fed the water into the Long Tom. This meant no one was needed to dip water. The twelve foot trough could handle a lot more sand much faster with its many more rifflers and three shoveling Mexicans and their two shoveling Indios. The flume-fed water rushed over the rifflers so fast that rocking was not necessary to separate the heavier sands and gold from the chaff.

Not a few American miners on the bar felt sand in their craw as well as in their rockers as they watched the Mexicans strip and wash huge quantities of gravel from deep holes. Many an envious eye coveted the fast gold from this much improved operation.

"Call themselves Escobar by name," said Bailey. "From the Sonora mines. Mexicans! Aint even Americans. Damn Mexicans! Takin our go-go-gold. What'd we fight the da-da-damned war for, anyhow?"

Bailey said it; but it was what they were all thinking as the weeks of bone crushing labor and chattering cold wore on the men. And, many pans and rifflers which held nuggets a few weeks ago now washed only flakes and dust.

"An-an-and there aint hardly enough for us that is true born Americans," said Bailey, again echoing the thoughts of all of the miners.

"Th-th-them Escobars is minin what rightly belongs to us."

The Mexicans washed sand in the Long Tom, unmindful of the words which they could not understand; but aware of the current of electric hate that surged down the river.

# 20

By the fall of 1848, the once snoring village of San Francisco already felt a growing insomnia. Although the world had not yet rushed in the way it would in the months to come, even now the trickle had begun.

From cockcrow to past can't see, the clatter of hammers, saws, picks and shovels and bawling men gave new zest to once barren, sandy hills. Packed among the few hovels of less than a year ago were new and bigger hovels. Canvas quilted huts, clapboard shacks, a log house here, a brick one there, covered the area back from the old wharf. The best hotel was built of rough boards on top of the hull of an abandoned ship, now high and dry on manmade dirt fill where it had floated only weeks before.

Back of the ship-hotel, Portsmouth Square was already a reality. A large rectangle of tinderbox buildings, Portsmouth Square, named for the United States' sloop of war, was the quarterdeck of a moving, heaving city. A city moving out into the bay as men poured their excavation dirt to fill the tidal flats to make new real estate; a city heaving up the steep, round hills behind. A city ever moving and swaying to the song of gold.

Frank Potts climbed down the ships' ladder from the hull-mounted hotel Niatic to the mud street below. He was clean shaven and clothed in a black broadcloth suit. Still, under the new suit, his last bath had been a swim in the Bear River.

Potts looked out over the bay toward the Golden Gate and the blue Pacific beyond. A hundred ships lay anchored in the bay, sails furled on wide arms, some hulls empty, most still filled with goods of all descriptions, all quiet, deserted, except for a captain's forlorn face at a rail here and there.

Crews have all jumped ship, thought Potts. Jumped ship and headed for the mines just like I done; or to build this instant city for three or four times a seaman's wage. He watched the gulls circle dead hulls.

Ships still loaded with all manner of goods, I reckon. Full-loaded and unguarded. Goods worth more than gold at the placers. Potts pushed the new beaver hat back on his head and picked at greasy-thick, black hair; pinched the life from a lice or two between grimy fingers.

"I wonder," he said to himself and thought about ships full of unguarded cargos.

He walked into the square to the beat of the endless construction music which was the city's anthem. Mixed in with the ballad of hammer-and-saw, he heard the out of place tinkle of a fiddle and guitar coming from the open side of a two story building across the square.

"Pinch 'a Dust" said the hand lettered sign above the wide opening. There was no door because the place never closed. When it rained, the men just packed in tighter.

Potts could smell the liquor from across the square; and he hefted the five pound weight of gold sacked between his skinny ribs and his new shirt and made for the saloon.

Potts had ridden away from the camp on the banks of the Sacramento well before dawn. He was satisfied that the steak and biscuits fed to him the night before by Louy Simonds would last him long enough. He was afraid that the looks and questions of Pete Cortez and Long John Hatcher might last too long. He had found the boat about noon with room enough to take himself and his scraggly mule down river to San Francisco.

He had put up at the Niatic because it hadn't been there when he and Buff had come through the town only a few months before and because it was the best to be had for a gold-rich man.

Now he was ready to bust loose in his own quiet way.

Potts followed the raw liquor smell into the Pinch 'a Dust. The whole left wall was a plank bar mounted on barrels. Even though the afternoon sun was still two hours above the Golden Gate, the bar was stacked like post piles with drinking and talking men. No matter where the sun, day or night, the scene at the bar never changed, only the men rotated in and away and back again.

Tables centered the room where men sat at cards and whiskey. To the right, a few tables were reserved for eating. In the far right corner a Mexican played the guitar; another sawed the violin. Although Potts looked hard, there was not a woman to be seen. Damn, he thought, I need a woman.

Potts shouldered his way to the bar. "Whiskey," he shouted to the bartender.

The man came up to him, a towel in one hand, the other pulling on one handle bar of a two bar mustache.

"See your dust," the bartender said.

Potts reached inside his shirt and pulled out the five pound sack of gold. The bartender nodded, poured two fingers of whiskey and didn't look in Potts' sack.

"When you're through drinkin, I'll take what you owe from your sack," the man said.

Three shouts of "whiskey" pulled the man down the bar. Potts put the glass to his lips and sipped. He felt the harsh liquor burn his innards all the way down. Jalapeño peppers and, maybe tobacco, he thought. Not bad. He emptied the glass. It took three swipes from his sleeve to clear the water running from his eyes.

He turned to look across the wide room. Men were bunched around several tables playing cards for sacks of dust. One man caught Potts' eye.

"Five card schtud, we play," he heard the man say. He thought the accent was German.

The man dealt. Potts watched the gloved right hand wheel the cards and knew immediately that the man was missing some fingers. The man's face was mottled gray and black. A half-moon scar curved from the man's left eye to his jowl.

Potts called for another whiskey. When it came, he opened his sack and watched as the bartender carelessly took two pinches of gold from the sack. He brushed his fingers over an open snuff box on the bar. The cash register. He wiped his hands on the seat of his pants and half a drink's gold sprinkled into the trampled dirt.

Potts picked up his drink and his sack of gold and went to the table where the big man with the mottled face was just finishing the game.

"Again, I lose," the man said, looking around the table at the other three players. He eyed the sacks of dust stacked by each man's hand. Nervously, he rubbed the half-moon scar.

"Mind another hand," said Potts not waiting to be invited before sitting down at the table. He plopped the sack of gold on the table.

"Mind, I do not," said the dealer. "Maybe with you, I be more lucky."

"Maybe," said Potts. "Maybe not."

"With this game, I have today not won a hand."

Potts looked around the table at the other three players. All smiled.

"Deal," one man said.

"Looks like you've done well at the mines," said another, looking up from shaded eyes at Potts.

"Can't complain," said Potts. "You boys seem to be havin the same kinda luck here at this table."

In two hours, Potts had three more sacks of dust to side his own. The shady eyes were open wide as the players whose sacks they had been stumbled away from the table to the bar.

Now Potts played with the mottle faced man. No one joined the game. It was rare for a stranger to clean a table. Rarer still, when the cards and the deal belonged to another. Usually, it was the other way around. Several men watched.

"Way I count, you've got one, maybe two hands left in your poke, friend," said Potts smiling. "Got any more?"

"We play till this is gone; or your sacks I have."

Potts shot a look at the man; saw blue-ice eyes in the gunpowder face.

"About what I said. One or two more hands."

Potts watched the gloved hand deal the cards. Now, he was sure. The last two fingers of the glove were stiff and never moved. Stuffed with paper or cotton, he thought. Two fingered card dealer does all right though.

It took Potts three hands to tap the man out. Slowly, the big man stood. For the first time, Potts saw that the man wore a saber scabbard by his side.

"Soldier?" he asked the man.

"Once a soldier I was."

"Come. I'll buy you a drink."

"Nine."

"Nine? Nine what?"

The man brushed by Potts and walked out of the Pinch 'a Dust into the San Francisco night.

Potts bought more whiskey with the dust he'd won and a steak to go with it. In spite of the meal, he was a little drunk. "Nine what?" he mumbled to himself and counted ten fingers. "Can't be that."

By midnight he was more than a little drunk.

Potts walked straight, or thought he did, seeing an imaginary line bending this way and that in front of him as he melted from the Pinch 'a Dust into the San Francisco night. He steered a course for the Niatic and sleep. The only light came from the bed of stars above and a large fire up the street, beyond the square. The music of construction was still playing around the fire.

Potts saw the narrow passage between the hotel and the store next door; but was too busy following the weaving line to be watchful.

Just as he passed the ally, he felt a thump on his back, to the side and low down. He did not feel the knife slice against his rib. As he was about to laugh at the strange sensation, a gloved hand covered his mouth.

Next thing he knew he was on his back in the pitch black of the ally. Instinctively, he reached a hand to the sacks of gold in his shirt. Too late. The gloved hand was there first. The two hands struggled, four fingers against two. The gloved hand yielded for a moment, was gone.

Suddenly, a heavy weight landed on Potts chest. He felt a razor thin pressure at his throat. His fuzzy brain, which was beginning to register pain and blood at his back, registered knife!

Just then, a voice whispered, "Deliver and stand. Your gold I want."

"'De-de-deliver and stand?'" he coughed. "Hell I'm flat of my back."

He felt the knife blade press on his wind pipe.

"Sore loser," he whispered. "Take the gold."

He felt two fast fingers rip inside his shirt; felt weight leave his rib; heard the plop of a sack of gold hitting the ally mud; then another. Plop! Plop!

"Damn, the gold have I dropped."

Potts felt the man's hot breath leave his cheek; felt the weight of the knife blade hesitate; heard the man scrambling in the mud.

"Hold on there, friend," said Potts. The pressure of the knife blade increased.

"The gold I must have," the knife-man said. "Help me find the sacks I have dropped. Or you I kill."

"Hell, man," said Potts. "You can have the gold and welcome; but I have a better idea."

He felt the knife blade slide across his ribs. In a flash Potts was on hands and knees along side his attacker in the black of night patting the wet mud for the lost sacks of gold.

"Want to hear my idea?" said Potts, who had found one of the sacks and stuffed it into his boot.

"You take my gold and you'll piss it away at cards like you done tonight, or liquor. In a week it'll be gone."

"The sacks," said the man. "Look and shut up."

Potts felt the point of the knife at his side again.

"All right. Be stupid," he said. "But, fool that you are, if you take my idea, you'll get rich in not much longer than a week, and me too."

Potts sat now with his back up against the hull of his boat-hotel. He held a pistol in front of him in the direction of the mud-patting man.

"And keep my gold to pay your way!"

Suddenly, the man stopped his search. All was quiet in the black alley except for the man's rapid breathing and the click! click! as Potts eared back the hammer of the pistol.

"What idea?" Potts heard the man say quietly. "Rich? Black Hess rich? How?"

"Well, Mister, Hess is it? Here's how."

# 21

There was no moon in the cloudless night sky which canopied San Francisco bay; but bright stars creamed the milky way. There was light enough to row by.

Black Hess sat in the stern of the lugger as it slid across the bay toward the brigantine, the Nancy Ann. Two Indios rowed the freight boat with muffled oars. Her sails were furled around her stubby mast. The gaff boom hung loose in the night. Two more men squatted in the bow of the boat ready to board the Nancy Ann. Starlight gleamed dully from their bare-bladed knives.

"Stop!" whispered Hess. "Into the ship's side we will drift. Quiet!"

Hess looked up at the high railing of the cargo vessel. A light reflected across the bay from the stern window. All else aboard the Nancy Ann was still and dark.

Suddenly, with a thump, the lugger hit the side of the ship. One of the men forward secured the lugger to the ship's ladder. The other climbed swiftly to the high deck. The oarsmen drew knives and followed, then Hess, his saber drawn, scrambled up the side.

On the deck, Hess motioned the Indios to the fo'c's'le to check for any crew. Hess climbed the deck to the stern and quietly opened the door to the cabins which lay under the quarterdeck. He stood motionless in the doorway and listened. He heard nothing; saw a sliver of light under the far door.

Like Potts said, he thought. On board is only the captain. All the rest have deserted for gold. Not for long the captain will be on board. Hess curled a lip and thought he smiled.

The door was not locked and moved into the captain's cabin on oiled hinges. Hess saw the man sitting at his desk, a night cap on his head and nightshirt draped about him. His bare feet stuck out from under the desk. He was reading and did not look up. The book he was reading was the Bible. His lips moved silently as a stubby finger slid along the lines of the page.

"It is your cargo we have come for," said Hess. He followed the slicing blade of his saber into the small cabin.

Startled, the captain looked up. "Cargo? You've come for . . . ."

His eyes widened and crossed as they saw the slicing blade rise in front of his face. The captain's eyes exploded as the slicing blade sliced deep into his neck; then the eyes glassed over and the captain was dead before the spurt of blood twice spurted. His head flopped on the deck followed by the rest of him. His night shirt soaked blood. Some colored his gray hair.

Hess opened the cabin window. He dragged the late captain of the Nancy Ann to the sill and dumped him into the bay. He did not bother to wipe the blood from the saber blade as he shoved it home in the scabbard.

On deck he set the Indios to unloading the cargo of men's boots, shirts, hats; bolts of canvas, kegs of nails; one hundred baskets of champagne and four hundred cases of French brandy. It took four hard trips from the Nancy Ann to the beach to fully empty the ship.

As the first rays of the sun crept out to sea through the Golden Gate, Black Hess stood on the beach on top of stacks of boxes and bales watching the Nancy Ann. He passed a bottle of French brandy to Potts. Potts stood in the sand, reached 'for the bottle and looked up at Hess.

"What do you think of my idea now, Black Hess?" Potts took a long pull at the brandy, let the leavings slide down a thin crease in his thin face.

"It is glad I am that stupid I am not," said Hess, curling his lip. "If sell we can these goods to the men in the mines and to the many more coming to the city, it is rich we will surely be. Rich!"

Hess pointed with his two finger hand toward the skyline of San Francisco just emerging from the dawn a couple of miles around the bend in the bay.

Potts laughed. "With the goods we've taken from these three ships, we'll open a store."

Potts waved vaguely at the bay where two other cargo ships had been anchored and abandoned, emptied and sunk along side the Nancy Ann.

"We'll open a store on Portsmouth Square. You'll store-keep. I'll freight the goods to the men at the mines. This winter, the rains will close the roads. The men will pay any price for a boot without holes or a dry shirt. The rains will make us rich."

"Rains will keep the miners at the mines; and, in the city, the new men must stay until spring." Hess rubbed the crescent scar on his cheek with the two fingered hand.

"In the spring," said Potts. "Cortez and Hatcher and the little Frenchman will bring my gold from Buff's Bar unless I get over that way on my next trip to the mines. They work in the cold, wet river . . . ."

"Cortez!" shouted Hess.

He jumped down from the pile of goods. He ripped the bottle from Potts' lips and took Potts by the throat of his shirt.

"Pedro Cortez? From Taos!?"

Spit hit Potts in the face. He pulled back. Hess hung onto the shirt and stepped into the retreating Potts.

"Tell Me!" Hess screamed.

"Pete. Name of Pete Cortez."

"And a man called Hatcher? A mountain man?" Hess hissed. He took his hand from Potts' throat. "The little Frenchman. Simonds?"

"Sounds like them," said Potts. Feigning surprise, he said, "you know those boys, Hess?"

"Them I know," spit Hess. He held up the two fingered hand, now gloved in black. "This they done to Black Hess." He put the hand to the crescent scar. "And this. Them I know!"

"Well," said Potts, "while I'm gone a-packin goods to the mines, you keep a sharp look out for them boys. They owe me my share of their mine. Might forget after a long winter."

"If they come to the city, them I will see!"

Hess lifted the saber; slammed it home with a crash.

"When them I see, them will I kill!"

"Not before I get the gold's comin to me," said Potts.

He picked up the brandy from the sand. He took a long pull; started to hand the bottle to Hess; took another drink and tossed the empty bottle into the bay.

As the sun climbed over the eastern hills, Potts and Hess watched the Nancy Ann, down by the bow and settling, slowly sink to moor her keel to the bottom.

The two men watched air escaping from the sunken ship and saw golden bubbles.

# 22

It was the last week in January when the pack train came to Buff's Bar with supplies for the miners, many of whom had been on a steady diet of biscuits and salt pork or jerked beef for weeks.

Pete watched as miner after miner tossed down his tools and headed up the steep slope to town as news of fresh supplies hit the bar.

Hatcher was quick to cross the river to the meadow and saddle a horse and put frame and canvas sacks on a mule.

"Need coffee and tobacco," he called out to Pete and Louy as he rode back over the bar and into the fork of the river below the town.

"Flour and beans and sugar," yelled Louy. "And stay away from the sacre damn liquor and the monte dealers."

Three Mexicans and two Indios with only three pack mules meant short rations. But, of all of the groups mining on the bar, only the Mexicans did not go up the hill for supplies.

Pete and Louy worked their rocker through the day.

"No Hatcher. No more coffee," said Pete that evening. He pulled hot biscuits from the frying pan and tossed a couple to Louy.

"It's cold and dark and that damned Hatcher, she is not back from the town. By now she is drunk and been fleeced by the card cheats."

They ate biscuits and beans in silence.

It was after nine o'clock when Hatcher rode in.

"Help this old coon with these here supplies," he called into the cabin.

"Where the hell have you been," said Louy. "We got no coffee. You drunk and broke, Mister Mountain Man?"

Louy ducked out of the cabin door to help unload the mule.

"Had me a drink of aguardiente. Mostly listened to the talk. Got ten pound of beans and fifty of flour and five of tobacco. Was a couple-a weeks too late for coffee, though."

Hatcher threw the fifty pound sack of flour at Louy. "Don't drop that 'less you want mud and dung in your biscuits."

Inside, Hatcher produced tobacco and a small jug of home brew aguardiente. He ate cold biscuits and beans. Louy took a pull on the jug.

"Aye, god, she is awful. Poison." He shuddered and passed the jug to Pete. One long swallow was enough for Pete who coughed and wheezed as fire smoked his insides.

"Aint real refined," said Hatcher. "But it'll warm your toes some." He took the jug and tilted it under his sloping nose and swallowed once, twice, before he choked.

After an interval of hard breathing, Hatcher lit his pipe. Pete rolled a cigarillo in some corn husk. He could still feel the liquor burn as he exhaled smoke. Louy stared wide eyed at the fire and did not reach for his pipe.

"This coon has drunk good liquor and bad liquor; and that is the baddest of the bad." Hatcher exhaled smoke and coughed again.

"That Millie girl has moved in with them two miners as was tryin to shoot one another the day we come here. She's the talk of the town. They say them two are well; but won't speak to each other except she repeats what each one says. Say she keeps them two from killin each other. Some say they reckon, eventually, she'll let 'um at each other and ride out of here a rich woman with all their gold."

"This land," said Louy. "She is hard on a man. I say, let a woman make her way as best she can."

Recovered now, Louy lit his pipe and the small cabin was filled with the raw smoke of coarse tobacco.

"Guess you boys'll recollect the man as freighted in the supplies."

Hatcher looked to each of them as if the news was important.

"Potts. Frank Potts."

"The fugitive miner who directed us here?" said Pete. "The one's maybe mentioned in Buff's diary?"

"Yep. Him that was all ragged and torn, except for that shinny, new Sharps rifle. I says howdy and to come over and collect his share of the gold. He says he will. I asks him how come him to come back, if, as he told us, he'd seen the elephant.

"Says he put what little gold he had into supplies. Knew how bad they was needed at the mines this winter. Has mined more dust with bacon and flour and coffee than ever with a pan. I looked over his outfit. His little bit of gold was a damn site more than a little. Twenty mules all packed solid with goods of every description."

"Then, why no coffee? I can not live in this cold place without coffee." Louy blew the words out with the harsh smoke. Even with the fire and the snugness of the cabin, they were always wet, always cold.

"Funny thing about that. Says he was robbed more'n two weeks ago; while he was camped outside of the Mormon Diggins over the mountain on the American Fork. Took all the coffee he had left to sell. Coffee and sugar. Some odds and ends of tools. Didn't see who took 'um, but from the look of the tracks, he thinks, Mexicans. Several Mexicans. Big roweled spurs drug in the mud behind the bootheels."

"Seems Mister Potts just naturally don't like Mexicans," said Pete. "Claims three of them shot Buff and almost got him. Right here on this bar. Now, it's Mexicans who stole his goods." Partly, Pete felt defensive, partly puzzled.

"Higgins says they found Buff and three Mexican rancheros shot dead at the top of the bar," said Hatcher, his eyelids at half mast against the smoke and his thoughts. "And, some markin in Buff's diary. P-a-t-t-t, somethin like ...."

"Or, P-o-t-t-t. Potts, maybe," said Pete. "Well, Buff and Potts was friends, partners. Likely Buff was leavin his pard a word."

"A last word," said Louy.

"But if the rancheros killed Buff and tried to kill Potts, who shot up them rancheros convenient-like so Buff could write about them gettin shot in his book before he died?"

Hatcher put his pipe down, lay back on his buffalo robe and shut his eyes. "Damn!"

"Potts told us nothin about three Mexicans bein shot," said Pete. "Maybe, like Potts said, the three Mexicans shot Buff; and someone else got them Mexicans."

"Somethin, she don't smell right," said Louy, relighting his pipe with a stick from the fire and puffing hard to get it going again.

"It's this sacre damn cabin," said Pete coughing. "Open the door and let the smoke out."

As the smoke was sucked out of the opening, a new smell slowly filled the small cabin.

"Coffee," said Pete. "I smell coffee on the boil."

He stuck his head out the door; saw the Mexican camp across the meadow; saw a man standing by the fire raise a tin cup to his lips.

"Them Mexicans have coffee," he said.

"I told you boys a door'd come in handy," mumbled Hatcher.

The next evening at bat time, Pete called into the Mexicans' camp.

"Hola, la rancheria," he said. "Vengo hablar con ustedes."

He stepped into the ring of fire light. His arms were outstretched. In one hand he held a partly filled sack of flour. Pete could see they were three Mexicans and a pair of Indios.

The two Indios were asleep with heads on saddles. Two men sat by the fire drinking coffee. One, a tall man, stood with a tin cup in hand.

As Pete approached, the tall man dropped the cup and scooped up a rifle.

"Con cuidado," said the tall man. He took a step toward Pete. He wore a heavy wool serape, a long handle bar of mustache drooped from each nostril of a flaring nose. His eyes were muddy pools against the backdrop of the fire's flicker. He wore no hat; but carried the cocked rifle at the port. Thick lips smiled under the mustache.

"Bien venido, Señor. Me llamo, Juan Escobar, de Sonora. Quien es?"

"Señor Escobar. I am called Pedro Cortez from Taos," Pete said in his cultured Spanish. I have flour to trade for coffee beans. Five pounds for one." Pete held out the white sack. "We have run out of coffee, my friends and I."

"Come. Sit by the fire. Have some coffee," said Juan. "We have seen you and your gringo friends on the bar. You do well."

It was not a question, Pete thought. They've been watchful. Maybe too watchful. He smiled and sat down. At a gesture from Juan, one of the men poured Pete a cup of hot coffee.

"That one is Luis," said Juan pointing to the man who had just poured the coffee. Luis smiled from a full, round face and nodded.

"This other one is Sylvio. We are brothers."

Sylvio glanced up at the sound of his name; then resumed staring at the fire.

"Don't mind him. He does not talk much since a mule kicked him in the head more than a year ago; but he works hard, harder than any of us. Why? I do not know."

Pete sipped coffee just off the boil and glanced at the other two men asleep on their saddles.

"Until news of the California gold reached us in May," said Juan, "we worked for the patron in the mines of Sonora. We are miners by trade. In the Sonora mines we work for a few pesos a day in wages. In June we come to Sutter's Fort and work on the American Fork. Too many miners; not so much gold. So we come to Buff's Bar."

"In the time you have been here," Pete said, "I have watched you work. Hard and long and fast."

Juan beamed at him. "Here we mine the gold for ourselves, for our families; not for some fat, rich Spaniard who never soils his hands."

Pete knew that Escobar had seen the Spaniard in himself; but did not apologize.

"It is a new thing for us. Even those two who are Indios," indicating the sleeping men, "have a share."

Juan still beamed as he spread his hands to embrace the entire group. Luis smiled. Sylvio stared at the fire and did not move.

Suddenly, Juan's face sobered. "The Americanos do not like us to take the gold. They say it is American gold, only for Americans. I say it is God's gold to be taken by any man willing to dig it out of the ground and wash it in his rocker."

"Well, it is true. Some of the men complain about you working that Long Tom. They're sayin that, with it, you take more than your share of the gold on the bar."

"Only within the bounds of our claim. We wash the gold in our claim faster. That is all. We work faster so that we can return to our families before, before it is, for them, too late."

Luis spoke for the first time. "Our families have little enough since we left Mexico to come here. But, soon."

He smiled again, rounding his round face with happy anticipation.

"Very soon, they will be comfortable." He winked a round eye in the firelight.

"My Maria and the little ones," said Juan, "will soon live like the patron." Juan laughed at Luis. "Come, Señor Cortez. Your flour is dry and free of weevils?"

"Have a look." Pete proffered the sack of flour. "If you have some coffee beans to spare, we would be much in your debt."

Juan opened the sack and ran his fingers through the flour.

"Muy bueno," said Juan. He nodded at Luis who started to get up from his comfortable place in the fire's warmth.

Abruptly, Sylvio jumped up and went into the tent. Luis settled back on an elbow. In a minute Sylvio returned with a sack of coffee beans. He handed them to Juan without saying a word.

Juan hefted the bag. "One pound of coffee for five of flour."

He handed the coffee to Pete, and a small paper package wrapped with string.

"Some sugar. Sylvio's idea. To sweeten the coffee. We are in need of your dry flour as you are in need of our coffee. Muchas gracias."

Pete gave the flour to Juan who passed it to Sylvio. Pete tried to thank Sylvio for thinking of the sugar; but Sylvio walked quickly to the tent without looking up.

The fire danced on the gray-white canvass. Pete could hear mules in the darkness cropping shoots of meadow grass. Near the tent at the edge of the light he saw a hitching rail set on top of two posts. A saddle straddled the rail. Pete could just see the ornate tooling of the rich leather and a brand burnt into the skirt.

He looked closer and saw: BUFF.

Glassing over the surprise that he was sure had flashed into his eyes, Pete held out his hand to Juan. "Well I must return to my friends. Very much, thank you; and they will thank you when they see you in the morning. This California winter is wet and cold; but with hot coffee, it is bearable. Without coffee?" Pete shrugged.

"Buenas noches," said Juan as Pete turned to go across the meadow to his own cabin. He waved as he entered the dark.

What are they doing with a saddle marked BUFF? thought Pete. The saddle of a man murdered out on the bar for his gold? Murdered by Mexicans? Three Mexicans? So says Potts. Damn!

# 23

It was the end of the week when Frank Potts rode his mule down the hill and onto the bar. He wore new boots, heavy wool pants and shirt and a beaver hat which brim-shaded his eyes. He sat his mule looking down at Hatcher.

"Come for my gold," he said without ceremony. "Hear you boys've done well."

"Mister Potts. You put us onto gold, sure enough; and we're obliged."

Hatcher got out of the five foot deep hole he was working.

"We've kept yours separate. About five hundred dollars, I reckon, at ten percent until the end of December. It's at the cabin."

He pointed toward the cabin on the other side of the river.

"Five hundred?" said Potts, sounding doubtful.

"Give or take," said Hatcher. "Almost half come from a pocket Pete here found the second day."

Still sounding doubtful, Potts said, "Talk in town is you boys done better than that."

His hand was at his belt just above the butt of a new Walker's Colt.

Hatcher looked at Potts for a long moment.

Suddenly, he took a step and with a paw of a hand swept Potts off the mule and into the wet sand. Just as suddenly, he jerked Potts to his feet.

"Five hundred." Hatcher breathed an inch from Potts face. "Honest count."

Potts shoved Hatcher back and dropped his hand. Hatcher still held a chestful of wool shirt.

"This shovel," said Louy Simonds. "She is sharp from the sand."

Louy stood next to Potts with his shovel in the air. Potts' hand moved away from the gun. He brushed the sand from the butt of his new wool pants.

"Just jokin. What the hell's the matter. I accept your count."

Potts laughed and stepped back. Hatcher released his grip on the man's shirt front and laughed too.

"Be it beaver plews, tobacco, powder or gold, this hellion aint seen the man, white or Indian, he'd hold back on."

Hatcher laughed again, but his eyes did not laugh.

"Potts here, maybe she be the first man we cheat, eh, Hatch?"

"Don't tempt me." Hatcher turned and went back to his hole in the sand.

"I'll take you over to the cabin," said Pete. He led the way across the river. Potts followed on the mule.

As they stepped out of the water, Sylvio was approaching from the Mexican camp. He carried a shovel and was stuffing a biscuit into his mouth. He did not look up as he went into the river.

"Damned greasers. Robbed me a while back. That their camp?"

"It is the camp of men who have claims just above ours on the bar," said Pete.

At the cabin Pete left Potts sitting his animal and ducked inside. In a minute he was back with a heavy can which he handed to Potts. Without opening the can, Potts nodded and, reaching around, put the can in a saddle bag. Then he rode straight across the meadow to the Escobars' camp.

Pete watched Potts get down from the mule and walk into the tent. In a matter of minutes, Potts was back outside. He held up several bundles.

"Mine!" he shouted across the meadow. "Stolen from my camp over on the American Fork. It's all here."

Pete walked across the meadow. At Potts' feet was a pile of coffee bags. Potts ducked back into the tent.

"And, here's the sugar."

He came out with an arm full of smaller sacks. He piled them with the coffee and began to walk around the camp. He passed the hitching rail and the saddles, and went out into the meadow where the Mexicans' animals were grazing.

"See! My mule," he yelled back at Pete. "My mark in his ear."

Suddenly, he pulled the Walker's Colt from his belt and fired three shots in the air.

"C'mon, boys. Here are the thieves. It's them Mexs."

Pete looked across the river at the men on the bar. They had heard the gun shots; but not the words. The three gun shots were enough. As one, they dropped their tools, crawled out of holes and began to cross the river. The Escobars, seeing Potts and Pete at their camp, were the first across. Their two Indios, not understanding; but curious, started too. Juan waved them back to their holes.

Higgins and Bailey and Henry brought up the rear as about fifty men gathered around the Escobars' camp.

Juan strode forward. "What passes in our camp."

His English was gritty with accent like sand in the beans. He came to a stop in front of Potts and looked down at the pile of bags.

"Here's my coffee and sugar," said Potts loud enough for all to hear. "Stolen by these Mexicans over on the American, and my mule." Potts pointed to the mule cropping grass in the meadow. "Them greasers loaded my goods on my mule and walked off into the night slick as you please."

Potts had a chin raised up in Juan's face and a finger in his chest.

"Grab 'um boys!"

"Señor, a moment . . . ." Juan tried to talk; but the men were shouting now.

"Hang 'um!"

"Flog 'um!"

The miners took hold of Juan, Luis and Sylvio.

Now, their two Indios understood. They quietly managed to slip across the bar, into the river and up the hill to town. No one paid them any attention.

Juan spoke to his brothers in Spanish. "Do not resist or they will kill us as we stand."

In an instant, their hands were bound. The men formed a circle around the Escobar brothers in front of their tent.

"We'll hold a miners' court on them," said Higgins.

"Then hang 'um," yelled a man from the rear of the crowd. Many of the men laughed.

"Trial's a waste of time," said Potts. "There's the goods. Taken from their tent. Over there stands my mule. Stolen with the goods. I say . . . ."

"Hold up a minute," said Pete. "They may be guilty. But we got to give them their say."

"Then hang 'um," the man in the back yelled again. This time a few laughed.

Pete held up a hand for quiet and turned to Juan.

"How did you come by so many bags of coffee and sugar? And, the mule?" He asked Juan in English. Then, in Spanish: "Tell the truth. Tell it fast. You're next to death as it is. I'll help if I hear truth!"

Juan started to speak in English. His face was bathed with sweat in the cold. He stuttered and mixed Spanish in with the English words.

"Can't understand a word he says," said Hatcher. "Pete, tell him to talk Mex and you tell us what he's sayin."

Even in Spanish, Juan stuttered and shook. Pete translated.

"Since three weeks, maybe more," explained Juan, "we are on the American Fork. Forty, fifty miles above Sutter's Mill."

"That's where . . . ."

"Hold on Potts. You'll have your turn." Hatcher held a hand up to Potts face. "Go on, Pete."

"He says, him and his brothers was workin up a creek bed off the American when they come on that there mule. Loaded with coffee and sugar. They hadn't seen another soul in days so they took the mule in hand. Figured the man who'd lost him would come along and claim him and the goods. No one came in more'n a week. So they brought him and the goods over here to Buff's Bar. He swears it on his mother's grave. So does his brother, Luis."

"Damn lies . . . ."

"Potts!" Hatcher's one word voice was like the snap of a dry branch.

Juan said something more. Pete walked over to the hitching rail.

"One more thing. Juan says this saddle was on the mule when they found him."

Pete picked up the saddle with BUFF branded in the skirt and held it up so all could see the name.

"Underneath the pack tree."

Luis said something to Pete. "As if the mule had been rode by this Buff; but used as a pack mule by someone else."

"These Mexicans have taken our gold with the Long Tom," said Higgins moving to the front of the crowd. His speech was Boston. His tone was imperious. "They have taken Mister Potts' goods and a mule wearing Buff's saddle. We found Buff shot dead not more than a month ago. Gentlemen. I think we have found Buff's killers!"

"Murderin Mexs," said the man in the back. "Hang 'um, by god!"

"Hang 'um. Hang 'um," cried the chorus of miners.

Now no one laughed. A man ran into the tent and came out with a long riata. Pete pulled his pistol from his belt and fired a shot in the air.

"Quiet," he shouted. "It's just as likely that they found the mule like they say. If they shot Buff, almost a month ago, how come Potts has Buff's mule for them to steal?"

"Aint Buff's mule," shouted Potts. This time Hatcher let him talk.

"It's my damn mule."

"What about Buff's saddle?" said Higgins.

"Last time I seen it, it was layin next to where Buff was shot; and me fleein for my life down the river with rifle balls buzzin my head like hornets," said Potts crossing his arms over his thin chest. The bullet-hole eyes were ablaze in his tear drop face as he shot light beams into the crowd of miners.

The crowd stood quietly, waiting. After a minute, Potts continued.

"They stole my mule from me in the night," he said, suddenly pointing to the three Mexicans standing in the center of the circle of men. "And, they stole Buff's saddle from him after they shot him and three rancheros and damned near killed me."

Potts' pointing finger was like a shaft of death.

"Seems like you told us Buff was done in by three Mexican rancheros, not that Mexicans was killed with him," said Pete.

"Mexicans killed Buff. I seen it. How them three rancheros got killed don't matter. What does matter is they done it!"

Potts was pointing at the Escobars and shouting at the crowd of miners. The miner with the Escobars' riata shook it high in the air.

"Matters a whole lot," said Pete, "when it's your story that don't match itself; or what the boys found when they come on the bar."

"Hang the Mex bastards," sang the man in the back. All of the men joined in the chorus this time. "Hang the Mex bastards!"

"It's u-u-nanimous," said Bailey, shivering.

"If'n you men hang them on such a story as this, you condemn yourselves to the same," Pete shouted over the crowd. "Higgins! What about the entry in Buff's diary? 'Pats' or 'Potts.'"

"Don't mean nothin now," yelled Higgins. "This here is miners' law."

"This aint law, it's a lynchin," said Pete. "Lynchin Mexicans!"

"Hang you too, you Spanish speakin son of a bitch, you keep up this talk."

Potts took a step toward Pete, saw the Colt still in Pete's hand.

"Take care of you later you cheatin, lyin greaser lover," he said quietly with the hiss of a snake. Then he turned to the crowd.

"Let's hang 'um afore it rains and we lose the whole damned day."

"No! Listen!"

The crowd surged past Pete. Two men grabbed each of the Escobars and marched them to the nearest stand of pines. Pete raised the muzzle of his pistol at their backs. Five shots against fifty men with blood in their eyes. He felt pressure on the Colt's barrel pushing it down.

"You done all that could be done," said Hatcher quietly.

Hatcher pulled the Colt from Pete's yielding hand and shoved it into the red sash at his waist. "Some things is just bound to happen."

"We can't let them."

"Can't stop them either, Pete."

In the shadow of the tall pines, one of the men cut the Escobars loose and handed each a shovel.

"Dig your own hole. Right under that branch."

"Th-th-that's it, Eli. Make 'um di-di-dig their own graves." Bailey laughed and gave Juan a push.

Juan and Luis stared wide eyes at the flesh menace pressing in all around them; then plunged their shovels into the soft, wet ground.

Sylvio held his shovel in both hands. He did not make a move to dig. Eli bent at Sylvio and pointed to the ground.

"Dig!"

Slowly, Sylvio nodded his head at the ground to which Eli pointed. Slowly, he looked at the spot and wagged his head back and forth.

"Dig, god damn it!"

Suddenly, Sylvio swung his shovel at the man who had given it to him and who was pointing at the ground. The shovel sliced Eli's throat from ear to ear. Only the man's bony spinal cord held the head a-dangle from the severed neck. Eli slumped to the ground at the end of his pointing finger. He fell front down; but his head twisted on its stem, like a puppet's head twists on the marionette's string. Eli grinned at the miners, his face perched atop his back.

Three of the miners grabbed Sylvio, seized the murder shovel and pinned his arms.

"Eli's dead. The greaser killed him."

A man looked up from the body of the fallen miner, a tear in his eye.

"Eli kept more'n his share of our gold," the man said. "Ate more'n the grub, didn't talk much, 'cept to cuss a feller. Still, I didn't want him dead. He were my partner."

The man picked up the shovel and began to dig.

"I'll make it big enough for two," he said looking over at Sylvio.

Sylvio stood quietly, his face to the ground. They tied his hands behind his back. One of the men looped a riata over his head and threw the handful of coiled leather rope over the tree branch.

Juan tried to tell them that Sylvio was not right in the head; he did not understand the men. But the men did not care.

"Sylvio!" Juan cried.

Sylvio did not look up.

"Shut up, greaser, and dig," said Higgins. "Put Buff's saddle on the mule," he said to Bailey. "A nice sense of justice."

Bailey led the saddled mule under the tall pine. They sat Sylvio on the mule. Without any ceremony, Potts slapped the mule's behind.

Pete heard Juan whisper to Luis in Spanish. "Now, Sylvio knows: a California tree is a gallows tree."

Like the sound of an ax on bone, Sylvio's neck cracked from the force of the drop; and Sylvio heard nothing.

Pete stood paralyzed as the mule lurched away. There was no spasm, no struggle. Sylvio just sagged to the end of the rope and swung peacefully from the limb of the huge pine in the afternoon breeze blowing in from the river.

Luis was next on the mule. He sat Buff's saddle with head held high.

"Your turn, Bailey," shouted Potts. "Whip you up a dead Mexican."

"No th-th-thanks, Potts." Bailey was looking up at Sylvio.

"For Eli!" yelled Potts.

With a quirt, he hit the mule's rump. The mule jumped and, with a neckbone snap, Luis too, hung in the gentle breeze, dangling, dead.

They hung Juan the same way; but Juan was strong in the neck—or unlucky. He cried, "Maria! Maria!" and kicked at the end of the riata until the vomit trapped in his throat choked him to death. It took Juan five minutes of violent struggle, to the delight of the miners assembled, to garrote.

And his body, too, in unison with his brotherhood, swung peacefully from the huge limb of the California tree in the afternoon breeze blowing in from the river.

The crowd of miners quietly savored their justice. Soon, the men moved back toward the river.

"Cut 'um down and bury 'um tonight," Eli's partner said. "I was workin some promisin dirt when this ruckus started."

The man took a last look at the bodies, spit and, abruptly, turned and splashed quickly through the river to the sand and gold of the bar.

Pete watched the three brothers swing side by side. A tightness in his throat was all he felt. Maybe they done it, he thought, studying their faces, peaceful in death. Maybe not. In case of doubt, hang the Mexicans. Pete wiped a hand across his face as if to wipe away his own heritage. They don't have to fret about makin a mistake—if the mistake is Mexican. Hangin is fast and final and soon forgotten. He looked across the river to the bar and saw the men hard at work, digging, washing, rocking rockers.

Louy waved and pointed. Higgins, Bailey and Henry were already shoveling dirt into the Escobars' Long Tom.

Pete saw that Potts was already half way up the hill to town; saw him occasionally look back down on the bar as the mule struggled up the slippery trail.

I'll be seein you, I guess, thought Pete. Absently, he fingered the walnut grip of the Walker's Colt tucked again in his sash.

After a moment, Pete walked to the Mexican's camp and went into the tent. A few minutes later, he came out of the tent carrying three large, heavy sacks. He walked toward the cabin. Before entering, he looked again across the river. He saw the men working their rockers—and the Escobars' Long Tom—on the bar.

He saw Potts sitting his mule at the top of the steep hill, the shinny Sharps rifle in his hand. He saw that Potts was looking down at him—and the heavy bags he carried from the Mexicans' camp. Pete hugged the bags and ducked into the cabin.

Soon after Pete had walked away from the lynching pines, one of the men on the bar wadded the river. He stopped at the row of open, empty graves. He did not look up. He seemed not to see Eli's leering corpse slumped at the foot of the hanging tree, head on front-to-back.

He studied the mounds of new dug dirt as if he were questioning justice. After a few moments, the lone miner walked back to the river and dipped a bucket into the cold water. He dragged the full bucket back to the mounds of dirt piled at grave side. Beneath the swinging boot heels of the dead Mexicans, the man began to wash the dirt in his pan. He looked at the bottom of the pan, then glanced slyly off toward the river.

"Color, by god," he whispered under his breath. He scooped up another pan of dirt. "Chunks of it."

In the dark, lit only by a small fire, Hatcher cut each death riata with the Green River. Pete and Louy gently lowered each body into its shallow grave. They lay crazy Sylvio in the hole with headless Eli. Juan and Luis had dug separate beds for the long, static trip to judgment day. They covered each purple face with gold-laden dirt.

No miners came over from the bar to help bury the cadavers they had made that day.

"I took the Mexicans' gold and put it in our cabin," said Pete. "I'll find a way to send it to the Escobar families in Sonora."

Rain started to fall and the small fire sputtered and went dark.

"One hell of a day," Pete said. He kicked at the last of the dirt mounded over the spot where Sylvio was buried with Eli, the man he had killed.

"Still and all," said Hatcher, "this child could stand to eat."

"Get out of this rain, too," said Louy.

"Done all we can for these poor bastards," said Hatcher. He and Louy walked back to the cabin and supper.

Pete stood in the rain alone over the graves. So much for foreign men different from the common crowd, he thought. Face burned a little tanner, the crowd hangs you. Don't speak the lingo, they hang you. It aint so much that you boys was Mexican; it's that you was some different. As inside, I, too, am different. A Mexican? A Spaniard? Yes! Had they really seen, they'd-a hung me with you. Almost did.

Pete took off his hat. He saw the California tree framed against the shrouded sky. Wet beads of gently falling rain and tears purified his prayer.

Please, forgive me.

# 24

After supper, Hatcher poured a liberal shot of aguardiente into each cup, filled the cups with coffee and lit his pipe.

"Way you boys drink coffee, should have bought another bag or two and sugar off Potts while he was here today."

"I'll go in the mornin," said Pete. "Aint been to town since we come here. I reckon I got enough gold put by to afford a second set of underwear. That way, maybe I'll be able to sleep dry sometimes."

Pete pulled on his cigarillo and exhaled. He looked over at Hatcher who was slouched against a log wall.

"If you learn how to sleep dry in this rain-wet river bottom, you'll be the only one. This coon don't know the feel of dry."

"Besides," said Pete. "I think Potts wants my ass. I'd just as soon call him out and face him than get shot while I'm squatin behind a bush with my pants down."

"The Sharps, she shoots far and straight." Louy's eyes were lidded against the smoke which lay heavy in the small cabin room. "In the morning, I think I also will go to the town." Louy poured the last of the aguardiente into the last of his coffee. "Comes to the shootin, you will need me and my fusil." He emptied the cup.

The early morning air was damp, even inside the cabin. Pete pulled on his wet boots over wet-legged pants and long johns. He listened to the splatter-splatter-splatter of rain beating on the brush and mud roof of the cabin; heard the water-torture plink-plink-plink of droplets falling from the leaky roof into the cooking pot. Pete looked over at Hatcher's buffalo robe and met eyes open and alert.

Louy snored.

Picking up the Walker's Colt revolver from his blanket, Pete removed the paper-wrapped powder and ball cartridge from each cylinder and inserted a fresh, dry load. He did the same with each percussion cap. Then he wrapped the action of the pistol in a piece of dry deer skin to keep the rain out.

He put the gun in his sash and took a stick to poke the ashes of last night's fire, looking for a live coal. Finding one, he lay kindling next to it and blew on it until the dry sticks were ablaze. He reached out for a larger log.

Abruptly, a strong hand grasped his shoulder. Quickly, Pete looked up. Hatcher stood above him with a finger over his lips. Carefully, he gestured toward the door with his thumb and mouthed the word "company" without making a sound.

Silently, Pete moved to the door. In a minute Hatcher was beside him with his rifle in one hand and powder horn and bullet pouch in the other. He held up three fingers and mouthed "on three," again without making a sound. Pete nodded and pulled the pistol from his belt with one hand and ripped off the covering with the other ready to spring out the door.

Louy snored.

As the third finger snapped into the palm of Hatcher's hand, Pete pulled the deerskin door aside and lunged into the meadow. He hit on his right shoulder and rolled in wet grass to his belly, the pistol up and pointed. He heard Hatcher step out behind him.

Pete looked over the barrel of his pistol at the legs of a horse or mule. Just as the thought "too low" flashed in his brain, he heard the click of a pistol hammer falling; heard the sharp pop of a percussion cap. Tensely, Pete waited for the explosion; could almost feel the impact of the ball.

Instead, he heard another click, another pop.

Behind him a rifle exploded. His eyes rose to meet the thickness of a man's body falling to the ground.

His revolver was up now, the hammer eared back. He saw two men who sat mules on either side of a third mule with an empty saddle. He aimed at first one man and then the other.

Each man had a pistol pointed at Pete.

"That one's dead," said Hatcher from behind Pete. "I drilled him plumb center. The boy here'll get at least one of you. Probably both. I seen him shoot."

While he was talking, Hatcher was ramming a patch and a fresh bullet down the barrel of his rifle.

Pete saw the man on the left swing his pistol barrel to cover Hatcher. The man said nothing. The muzzle of the pistol said it all.

"Hammer's eared back and trigger's pulled," said Pete, holding steady on the man to his right. "No matter what happens to me, mister, you're goin to die." Pete heard himself saying the words, while inside, his belly wrenched itself into a knot. "My loads are fresh and dry."

"His weren't and he's dead," said Hatcher nodding toward the body which lay sprawled at the feet of the middle mule. "Two misfired. He didn't get a chance to squeeze off a third. Your loads wet too?" Hatcher raised the reloaded rifle at the man on the left.

"Mine aint."

The two riders glanced at each other across the short, killing space. Suddenly, the man on the ground groaned. The man under the barrel of Pete's gun jumped in the saddle. At the jump, Pete fired, missed. The man's mule bucked a little; then steadied.

The man raised his pistol. Then both hands and the pistol shot up in the air.

"I quit," the man yelled at Pete. Slowly, Pete stood up.

"See, I done quit," the man said again. Pete saw the fear in the man's eyes.

"Drop the gun," Pete said.

The pistol fell to the sand.

"Now, you've quit," said Pete.

Hatcher's man slowly lowered the muzzle of his gun and let it rest across the pommel of his saddle.

Hatcher sighted his man down the long barrel of the reloaded Hawkin.

"If'n you quit, drop it. If'n not . . . ."

The pistol fell to the wet sand. Pete saw no fear in the man's eyes, only good sense.

The man on the ground groaned again.

Hatcher took a careful step forward and turned the man over with his foot.

"Potts!" said Pete.

"Aint surprised," said Hatcher. "Him and them come after the Mexicans' gold, I expect. Must have seen you haul it into our cabin. Probably our gold too. Potts is still alive. Smells alive. In my haste to save your ass, Pete, I shot a might high."

"My ass? I was just gettin set to take all three when you butted in."

Pete laughed and the belly-knot came undone.

"Mex gold aint worth dyin for," he said to the two men. "Nor ours. Leave your weapons and ride on out of Buff's Bar—and live awhile."

Two mules turned as one and headed for the river. Two riders never looked back. The third mule with the empty saddle ambled along behind. The empty saddle had BUFF burned in the leather skirt.

Pete knelt down over Potts. Blood and pink bubbles spilled from his thin lips. Potts' breathing was a wheeze and a wheeze again and each surge of his chest was followed by a deep slump as if it were his last.

"What the hell!" Higgins had heard the shots and had just come around the far end of the cabin. He stopped and Bailey and Henry piled into the back of him.

"Sh-sh-shit," mumbled Bailey as he mashed his nose into the back of Higgins' head. "Shit."

"Damn it, Bailey," said Higgins, pushing him off. "Have you got the peedoodles?"

"No. Ne-ne-never. I aint go-go-got them peedoodles."

Bailey stuck his nose around Higgins' shoulder and looked down.

"It's Po-po-pot-te-tes." He gave Higgins a friendly shove. "Three te-te-tees."

Pete leaned close to Potts. "You killed Buff and his friends for their gold and lied about the Mexicans." It was not a question.

The bullet-hole eyes looked up at Pete and held. The lips spit pink bubbles.

"No!" Potts breathed.

"Don't lie! You son of a bitch."

"His own friends," said Potts loud enough for all to hear him through the pink bubbles and the faint smell of death, coming.

"Them, them rancheros. They wanted more than their share of the gold. Buff protested. Them Mex rancheros said, `we split even with you; not him. Meanin me. Buff joined 'um. Said I worked too slow; said they'd take three quarters of what I dug and share none of theirs with me. Me? I said okay."

In spite of the shortness of his breathing, Potts' words oozed, like sudden truth sometimes flows, evenly.

"They was four to my one and no share in them. I dug and panned and bided my time."

Potts coughed and the pink bubbles spilled from his lips and smelled like present death. He sucked air.

"Then, one mornin, from the top of the bluff, where the town is now, I laid for them with the Sharps. In a wink, they was shot. When the shootin was done, the Mexicans was dead and Buff was nearly so. I took all the gold and rode out of there."

Potts coughed up more pink bubbles. His chest stopped heaving for a long moment; then raised up again for another breath.

"Gold was easier to take than to dig—that day."

"When you run off," said Pete, "was Buff still alive?"

"I knew it! I know it, now!" Each whispered phrase a labored breath.

"He was your friend."

"My friend? He sided with them—agin me."

"You took his gold and left him to die like a gut-shot deer you was too lazy to carry out."

"That I done."

Pete looked into Potts' eyes. In spite of the wheezing and the bubbles and the darker blood beginning to seep at the corner of Potts' mouth, the eyes were clear and sharp like bullet holes through target paper.

"Why the Mexicans? You lied about them stealin your mule and supplies. Murdered them with your lies. Why?"

Potts spit and Pete smelled the death spital as it dribbled down his chin.

"To cover what I done to Buff. It was eatin at me. I could see it. Others suspected. You suspected. In their eyes, your eyes. I seen it. I had to." He coughed. "Stop the starin eyes."

"And your own hangin."

"That too."

"And the mule, all loaded with coffee and packin Buff's saddle?"

"Over, over on the American. Wandered off in the night. Like they said, them Mexicans found him." Potts' breathing grew slow and shallow now. "They was three to my one. They had Buff's saddle." He tried to spit, couldn't.

"It, it almost worked!"

He did not have to spit now. The blood seeped from his mouth like water from a long-dry desert spring recharged with new rain. Slowly at first. Then faster until the rushing dark blood cleansed the pink bubbles of his last breath from his lips. The bullet-hole eyes were paper target eyes now, tiny dead eyes ringed with white; and, Pete thought, smells somehow clean in death.

"I'll be damned," said Higgins. "I would never have believed it if I had not witnessed it. Just like in Buff's diary: 'P-o-t-t-s.'"

"He got them Mexs ha-ha-hanged. He done it," wailed Bailey. "It wasn't us. Ho-ho-how'd we know?"

"He lost them goods," said Higgins. "Like them Mexs testified, and Buff's saddle."

"And the three Mexicans you all hanged by miners' law were innocent." Pete spit into the sand.

"Ho-ho-how'd we know that there?"

Bailey put hands on hips and stepped over Potts' body to stick his nose in Pete's face.

"We couldn't know."

"Mistake! That is what it was," said Higgins pushing Bailey aside to look Pete in the eye. "Miners' law serves where there is no other; but it is not perfect."

The Boston accent, more pronounced than ever, was like a nose in the air.

"Mistake. Plain and simple."

"This child has seen a heap-a men's doins. He's seen justice where there aint none. Mountain man's justice. Indians' justice. And now, miners' justice." Hatcher looked down at Potts.

"To this child, they're all the same. Justice-afyin. Killin the most likely coon. Sometimes it's by fire or bein drug behind a horse or a bullet hole or the chokin rope. Maybe the coon that's dead done wrong. Maybe not. Right or wrong of the killin don't seem to matter much s'long as some poor coon pays up for what he—or someone—done."

Hatcher leaned on his rifle and looked around at the men. Absently, he toed up some wet sand over Potts' death mask.

"S'long as we feel justice-afied!"

"They were foreigners," said Higgins, shrugging. His Boston nose poked as far as it would reach up into Hatcher's face.

"Aint we all," said Hatcher and he turned away like a man does who can't abide fools.

From inside the cabin, Pete heard a cough, a sputter, lips smacking, Louy's contented snoring.

"Just Mexicans," he said to himself.

# 25

Six days after Potts was buried, Buff's bar was awash. The Bear River had risen more than four feet. Mining came to a stop. What was left of Potts' supplies and the Mexicans' was divided among the miners by lottery. Secretly, some of the men wondered if hanging the Escobars brought the month long avalanche of rain that began with their deaths at the beginning of February 1849.

Now the men stayed under cover in the town on the hill, played three card monte until much of their hard-dug gold was in the hands of a few monte men who banked the games. Rain-fat rivers and bottomless mud prevented all travel. Within days the last drop of liquor had been consumed. Other supplies ran out.

For most of the winter, the men had relied on a diet of salt pork, jerked beef, biscuits and weevil-bread. There had been no vegetables in camp for weeks.

It began with the taste of blood in the mouth from bleeding gums. Bailey was first. He watched his legs turn blue and mushy and swollen. He poked a dent in the blue flesh with a finger and the dent stayed.

Rheumatism?

Soon the blue legs would not support even a walk to the latrine. He pissed his piss-stained blanket. He cried out with intense pain. Blue legs turned black.

"Land scurvy!" the miners of Buff's Bar cried.

---

It was the third week of rain when Hatcher, Louy and Pete could stand the small cabin no longer.

"This coon'll swim his mule across the river or die a-tryin. We need supplies of every kind; and, I need a different face to look at from yours, damned Frenchy face, all sacre damn black with soot and full of nothin."

Hatcher pointed a finger at Louy. "Sleep through a gun fight and, then, come out yellin 'where is the sacre damn breakfast.'"

"It were your turn to put on the coffee and broil the bacon," Louy said and wagged a hand at Hatcher. "Can I help it if you don't shoot so loud."

Beneath the attempts at humor, they all felt the scratch of building irritation. Pete rubbed his shoulder where Black Hess had slashed it to the bone. When his shoulder ached in the cold and wet of California, he remembered the ugly, red crescent on his mother's cheek where Black Hess had carved a new-moon imprint like a dreadful eclipse across his mother's beauty.

He remembered the fight at Estis' Tavern in Taos only in confused patches; his own vengeance-driven challenge, the weight of the man; his killing eyes blue as ice; and the arching, cleaver-edged blade hanging over his head; and panic as it slashed down, down, down. For an instant, in the ache of his shoulder, he felt the panic again.

Louy looked at Pete. "You are too young to have the rheumateeze."

"Aint age or youth," said Pete, exhaling. "It's that damn Black Hess; his sword. Aches hot in this wet weather, like the blade was still cuttin me." Pete smiled to hide his pain and the moment of panic that had just passed.

"Don't surprise me a-tall," said Hatcher. "The way you let him . . . ."

"Let him?" Pete was angry. "He was strong and mean; and he knew how to use that sword. Like the way he done Ma."

"Still, you was a mite slow. If it weren't for this," Hatcher patted the thick handle of the Green River at his belt.

"Damn it. I got out of his way as fast as I could scramble. He cut me anyway." Pete rubbed the shoulder, embarrassed.

"That fight, she was some conboberation," said Louy. "Saber against the Green River." Louy looked over at Hatcher. "Till Hatcher, he stop you from killin the bastard."

"Man was spurtin blood where his fingers had just been and his sword was broke by then," said Hatcher. "Weren't fair to kill him. Let him live his life shy two fingers; and his face cut to ribbons to boot."

"I bet Hess's fingers don't hurt like this here," said Pete, still rubbing the soreness in his shoulder.

" 'Course not." Hatcher held up his right hand with the last two fingers bent down into the huge palm of his hand. "You cut them fingers clean off." Hatcher opened his fingers and rubbed his chin. "Mean as that bastard was, nothin hurts him now, I expect. Probably dead."

"Did you mean what you say, Pete? If you see him again, you will kill him?" Louy looked doubtful.

Pete laughed. " 'Less'n he sees me first!"

They all laughed; but, now, Hatcher looked doubtful.

"If he aint dead, you'll run across his trail one of these days. You'll have it to do. I was wrong there at Estis.' I should have let you kill him then."

"It was your talk; my decision. Maybe we were both wrong."

"It aint sacre natural; but now, Hatcher, she is right for once. Black Hess is likely dead by now. Too mean to live long among men."

Hatcher nodded, still looking doubtful. "Need tobacco," he said. "Louy fetch me some of yours." He picked up his pipe and waved it at Louy.

Louy reached for his tobacco pouch, squeezed skin against skin and tossed it at Hatcher. "Empty. Like your head. Empty." Louy's quick smile was crooked.

"Let's go over to the town," said Pete. "See what's goin on. Get some coffee and Louy some tobacco, at least." Pete threw Hatcher his own tobacco pouch which was not far from empty. "Help yourself."

"Little Frenchman smokes too damn fast. That's his problem."

"You're just throwin good tobacco after bad," said Louy.

"It's my generous nature to share what I have," said Pete to Louy. Then to Hatcher, "you've smoked most of my tobacco anyhow, Long John Hatcher."

"Done you good, Pete. If'n I'd let you smoke all that rough weed, you'd have choked to death, and us too. Aint that right, Louy?"

Louy made no answer. Hatcher filled his pipe and passed Pete's pouch back to him. Before lighting his pipe, Hatcher threw Louy's empty pouch into his face.

"Frenchman without tobacco aint no use a-tall."

He reached toward the fire for a light. In a wink, Louy was on top of Hatcher. "Sacre damn lie. See who chokes."

Hatcher rolled Louy off of him; but not before Louy had pulled Hatcher's own tobacco pouch from his belt. Louy settled back against the log wall of the cabin and reached for his pipe.

"Sacre damn Hatcher, he hold out on us. There's still a smoke or two in this here skin."

Hatcher crouched on the other side of the small room, ready to spring. Louy waved a soot-blackened hand.

"Sit down, Long John. Let a mountain man smoke in peace."

"Damn little Frenchy. Always stealin another coon's possibles."

Louy tamped tobacco into his pipe and flipped the pouch back to Hatcher. He pulled a flaming twig from the fire and lit the pipe, showering the room with rich smoke. "When I finish this pipe we will go." He lay his head back against the logs, closed his eyes and inhaled deeply.

Hatcher settled back on his own side of the cabin, picked up the discarded, empty pouch and stuffed it in his belt.

"Louy, hand me a light."

Pete laughed when Louy did not move and pulled a burning end from the fire. Hatcher nodded and smiled.

"Little Frenchman gets nasty of a time. Seen it a-fore. Reminds me of that winter up on the Musselshell. Froze in solid for more than a month. No wherewithal for to eat or smoke. No squaw."

With eyes still closed and puffs of smoke coming regularly from the side of his thin-lipped mouth, Louy smiled, said nothing.

" 'Cept Louy."

They smoked in silence until wet dottle drowned the last ash.

Pete pulled out a deerskin, well worked with grease. He laid the Walker's Colt in it along with some spare caps and cartridges. Adding cotton tinder, a flint and the empty tobacco pouch, he closed the package tight and stuck it inside his shirt.

Louy pulled a large sack from among their meager supplies at the end of the cabin. He began taking items from the sack and putting them in a smaller bag.

"What for you takin them weeds and such?" Hatcher asked, looking puzzled.

"I have seen her before in camps like this. Without the acids, men die. These give the acids. The bark of the spruce tree. I have put it in our coffee. We stay well. Wild mint, watercress and onions, I find along the river. And peas, beans. All these give the acid. I will trade these for coffee and flour. You will see."

They crossed the river above the bar. Although, wider, the river there flowed more slowly; and they could more easily dodge the tree trunks and branches that came rushing at them as their swimming animals fought the current.

Pete was pleased that the smoky horse turned out to be a good swimmer. He and Smokey were first up the bank on the other side of the river and first up the slippery trail to the town at the top of the hill. Pete let Smokey catch her breath.

He saw many more tents and shacks stretched on either side of the mud track. What's it been? he thought. Three, four months? Look how she's growed. But, the track between the tent shacks and cabins is still running with mud just the way it done when we first saw it. Does this California ever dry out? He was so used to being constantly wet, that he hardly noticed the rain slanting into his face.

Hatcher and Louy huffed and puffed to the top of the hill and pulled up along side of him.

"Look how she's growed," Pete said.

"All the same to this coon," said Hatcher.

They moved slowly down through the fetlock-deep mud and stopped at the first saloon tent. Pete slid from the wet saddle and pushed aside the tent flap. He started to go in, suddenly fell back.

"What the hell," said Hatcher as he arrested Pete's backpedaling.

"My god! The smell."

Hatcher pushed past Pete and into the dimly lit room.

"Scu-scu-scurvy! There's ten of us. Two died. They smell."

"That you Bailey?" said Hatcher, his eyes beginning to adjust to the rain-filtered light.

"It's me. Or what's le-le-left."

Hatcher stuck his head out of the tent. "Louy, you was right. Bring your acids."

Pete built a fire in the cold, iron stove. Louy filled a pot with his herbs and vegetables and water and put the mixture on to boil.

Around the tent-room, laid out on the few pine-log tables, were eight men, barely alive and shivering under thin blankets. A look under the blankets disclosed advance stages of black-leg scurvy. Two men had been dead for more than a day. Hatcher and Pete piled their stiff bodies in the mud outside the tent saloon.

While they waited for the soup to boil, Hatcher rummaged around for a bottle of aguardiente or rum or brandy.

"Aint had no liquor for weeks," said one of the men from his bed on a table near the fire. "Saloon keeper's gone to Sutter's Fort for more."

"And some potatoes and beans," said another. "For this scurvy."

"Wo-wo-won't do me no good," said Bailey. "I'm a goner." He sighed into the room and it sounded like the last breath of a dying man.

Pete went over to Bailey. "Louy's fixin some soup. It'll cure you. Hang on."

"Been hangin on. 'Bout to le-le-let go."

"You'll make it."

"Pete?" said Bailey. "What we done to them Mexicans? Brought us down hard on our luck."

"Maybe," said Pete. "More like a mean winter, lack of supplies or any ways to get 'um in here. Luck a feller has from time to time, no matter what he done."

"We-we-well, she sure done me in, did Lady Luck. I'm-a dyin."

During the next two days, Louy boiled spruce bark and wild peas and onions until he ran out. Pete and Hatcher fed the soup to the scurvy men. They sent Higgins and Henry and some of the others out in the rain to comb the river bank and the hillsides for more of the curative herbs and vegetables. Louy showed them what to look for.

In midweek one of the scurvy men died. But, during the same time, Bailey's pain eased. By the end of the week, his black legs turned blue again and the blue began to fade. In another week Bailey could walk to the latrine and he welcomed the pain of it. When he poked a finger into the flesh of his leg, the flesh popped out again.

Seven of the scurvy men survived to shove sacks of gold and hallelujahs at Louy Simonds.

"I owe yo-yo-you my life," said Bailey over and over. "My life!"

"It is not much, the life of this miner," said Higgins. "But Bailey does move a good amount of dirt. That is worth something."

The Boston voice still sounded to Pete like a snub.

Louy took the thanks; handed back the gold.

"She is easier for Louy to dig than to take," he said.

"Damn fool Frenchy," said Hatcher.

They had beaten the scurvy with wild things from the land: spruce bark, onions, pine pitch tea, more precious by far than gold—and harder to dig, by god, Pete thought.

# 26

A flight of three butterflies hovered for a moment on gentle air shafts, then darted away into the coming California spring. Sparrows, robins and woodpeckers fought with the blue jays for the best nesting spots. The noisy aerial show was warmed by the low-flying sun. The new-built porch on the front of the cabin Millie shared with Sam and Jed cast the scent of wet pine pitch into the evening air.

"Tell him cornbread or sourdough," said Jed. "Don't make no nevermind to me. Biscuits is biscuits."

Jed looked straight ahead as he spoke. He sat on a rawhide stool on the left side of Millie. Sam sat a-straddle a log saw horse on her right. Millie rocked between them.

"Jed says," said Millie. "He don't care . . . ."

"I heard him," said Sam. "I can definitely hear him. Wish to hell I couldn't; but I can."

"Well then?" she said. "It's near supper time."

"Cornbread," said Sam. "My choice? Like always, cornbread muffins."

Sam gave Millie a big smile. Millie started to get out of her rocker.

"Sourdough," said Jed. "Tell that son of a bitch, sourdough."

"But you said . . . ." Millie stood up and stamped her foot.

"Changed my mind, Millie. Sourdough." Jed frowned his choice at her. "You asked me. It were my choice. I was just bein generous. But, now, I changed my mind. Sourdough."

"Aint got no mind to change," growled Sam. "Tell him so. And, if'n he did, changin it would twist his ass betwixed his knees."

Sam spit a stream of tobacco juice out into the dry street which had recently recovered from a long winter's mud bath.

"Cornbread," he said. "By god, I mean to have cornbread."

"Oh, damn you both." Millie stomped into the cabin.

"Been livin with you two for all of the winter; and I'm gettin good and sick . . . ." Her words faded into the knock of pots and pans.

Sam and Jed did not move, except to work tobacco in tight jaws. Each stared straight ahead as the bats flew mission on mission, bringing in the night.

In the cabin, Millie's noise, banging pans, a note of song, a cussing phrase, a laugh out loud; the way she did every evening, filtered out to the silent men.

Each man heard Millie's noise as just for him or just for the other, depending upon the sounds he heard. Sweet sounds for him; harsh sounds for the other.

Tonight, all of Millie's noise was harsh. Jed thought Sam was getting cussed; Sam thought Jed's head was under Millie's crashing pans.

Each man believed Millie loved him true!

After a good number of choruses from the kitchen, Sam got up and went into the cabin. Jed stayed on the porch until he heard Millie sing out the "come and get it." Then he, too, went in and sat at the end of the table opposite Sam.

"I recollect the night," said Millie. "You stood shoulder to shoulder in that doorway; neither one wantin to let the other in first. Found you in the mornin. Sam laid out on the porch. Jed on top. Both asleep in the jamb. Not even a nose whisker inside. Damn fools. At least you got the sense to come in the door in your own time since."

She smiled at them.

"I don't know," said Sam. "How you put up with that bastard. He's mean. He's stubborn . . . ."

"What the hell is this here?" said Jed waiving a biscuit into Millie's face, crumbs popping from his mouth into his beard as he shouted.

Sam looked over at Jed. "Well, I'll be damned," he said, a look of pure surprise creeping over his whiskered face. "That aint no kinda biscuit."

"Sure aint," said Jed. He tossed the biscuit onto the table.

"I mixed 'um," said Millie. "Cornbread and sourdough. You can each eat the part you want. Feed the rest to the birds, all I care."

Millie looked first at Jed, then at Sam. She smiled at each.

Sam smiled and popped a biscuit into his mouth, chewed.

"Tastes like cornbread to me," he said. "Mighty good."

Jed picked up the discarded biscuit. "Sourdough, you damn fool. Tastes like sourdough," said Jed, filling his own mouth.

Sam scowled, crumbled another biscuit into his plate of beans and beef. He scooped up a spoonful and fed his mouth.

"Bastard don't know sour from corn."

A solitary bean rolled back past the gate of his lips as he mumbled.

"Suit yourselves."

Millie put a hand over her mouth to hide the smile. She thought of the sacks of their gold piled in the corner of the cabin, maybe five hundred pounds. Take seven, eight mules to haul it, she thought. More than one hundred thousand dollars for my winter. And, neither one'll let go of the other long enough to touch me. This time the hand across her mouth could not stop the laugh.

Some special whorin I've done. She giggled.

Each of the men smiled at her.

"Record-settin stubborn," she laughed at them, surprised at the deep feeling that welled up in her breast.

Jed shoved the empty plate back and wiped a sleeve across his mouth. He pointed at the dark corner piled with gold-filled sacks.

"Surprised you've stayed on. Now that it's turned warm and the ground has dried. You could have taken it all while we was down at the diggins."

Jed got off the rawhide stool and went to the cupboard for his pipe. He forgot to use a rag when he pulled the burner plate off the stove to get a light and burned his fingers.

"Damn," he yelled.

Millie jumped up and ran to him. She looked at the burn and put butter on the red spots.

Jed put his arm around Millie then. Sam saw but pretended not to notice.

"Tell Sam, I think you've stayed because, well, shucks, you care a heap about me!"

"Afraid if she left," said Sam, "I'd blow your damned head off."

"You would, too. Damn your eyes."

"See Millie!" said Sam. "He knows I'd do it." Sam picked up another mixed biscuit and waved it at Jed. "Tell him that's the first truth I've ever heard him utter. God knows, he aint used to truth. I hope it poisons him."

"Jed. Sam says . . . ."

"I heard what he said."

Millie pulled away from Jed's arms; but gently. She walked up to the table behind Sam and planted a quick kiss on his forehead.

"Aint enough gold to make me leave just yet! But mind! Keep on diggin. Keep on, boys."

She picked up the empty plates and walked them to the side board. She looked out the window at the few winking lights from shacks behind and smiled, remembering.

All she'd said, Millie's noise, was how nice it'd be to look out; and next day there was a window cut out of the solid log wall and filled in with real glass. When it snowed so a girl froze goin to the privy at night, Jed and Sam had covered the pathway. And, in truth, if I don't stand between them, they surely will kill each other.

"Someday," she said quietly, "I'll go, when there's enough gold," feeling that in her lifetime there'd never be enough.

# 27

Like fingers in water slowly warming on the stove seldom feel the heat until: "ouch!" the men of Buff's Bar scarcely noticed the world rush in until it was already there.

In the spring of 1849 came Kanakas from the Sandwich Islands, farmers from Oregon, more Mexicans from Sonora, Spanish from Chile and Peru. These were the early lukewarm trickle; but the boil was on, as men in droves left the States seeking the shiver of golden adventure.

Thirty mules came up the dry mud track from Sacramento to Buff's Bar. They brought the first fresh supplies in months. Flour, coffee, preserves and vegetables. They carried brandy, too; and the saloon keeper was back in business.

The freighter was followed by small groups of men, some few on the backs of animals, many pushing hand carts, most on foot with huge packs of goods, tools and food stacked on bent and weary backs. In all, that early spring, nearly half a thousand would-be miners came to Buff's Bar.

And a monte dealer. And half-a dozen honest-to-god whores.

The new miners found the sandbar in the middle of the Bear River fully claimed.

The meadow was partly taken by Higgins, Bailey and Henry who washed the sands of the Escobar camp. Pete, Hatcher and Louy worked the rich dirt around their cabin and up the ravine. They made it clear that new comers to the meadow would be shot. The new comers went back to the sandbar and bought near played out claims or scurried upstream or down or into other small riverbank meadows.

Still, they came. It took at least two men, day and night, to guard the claims. Even then there were fights.

Pete dug and hauled dirt from the steep banks of the ravine at the rear of the meadow to the river where Louy had set up the rocker. Hatcher shoveled dirt while Louy rocked the baby.

Then one day, word spread down the mountain like lava. The saloon was open. Brandy, well aged on the three week trip up the Sacramento, flowed from barrels scarcely another week older.

The morning after the glorious news, Hatcher took a large sack of gold and went to town. For the next three days, Pete and Louy worked the claim alone.

On the fourth day Hatcher came back to the cabin. He looked no different except when he walked. Then he weaved and stumbled, putting first one hand and then the other out in the air to balance the load of brandy that gurgled inside.

In answer to an inquiring eye, Hatcher put his face in Louy's and laughed and spit fumes wide and far.

"This child aint felt better since before he were born to that good woman, his ma. They's gold for the takin up yonder from the damn fool mountebank. And women. By god, women."

He took the rest of his gold and started back to town. When Louy said something to him about shoveling, he said, "this coon got more and better things to do than throw dirt, dirt and dirt."

Pete tried to stop him; but got pushed into the river for his trouble; and Hatcher trudged and stumbled off to climb the brandy trail.

"Muy borracho," said Pete.

"Been drunk these three days, I think," said Louy, licking his lips. "She was the same at rendezvous. He'll drink until all of his gold, like the beaver, is played out on the monte cards or stolen by the whores or lost in the sawdust."

"Maybe we should go on up there. Make sure Hatch don't get his toe caught in a mousetrap, so to speak," said Pete.

"No way now. He'll stick his toe, and anything else, where he wants. When that child, she is taken by the rendezvous fever, there's no holdin Long John Hatcher."

Louy looked up the hill across the river. Hatcher was almost to the top. He stopped to puff and to wave at them. Pete waved back. Louy turned back to the rocker.

"Soon, all his gold, she will be gone," said Louy.

"Well, judgin by what we've found in this here ravine, there'll be more he can dig when he gets back."

Pete headed up the meadow for another load of the rich sand. He heard Louy mumble, "if'n he get back!"

The next morning, Pete was dumping a load of dirt from the pack on his back near the rocker in which Louy was washing sand as fast as he could shovel and shake. Pete heard a shout and looked over to the bar.

"Louy!" Pete said quietly. "Quick. Get the guns."

Pete watched six men drag the limp form of Long John Hatcher across the lower end of the bar and into the river between the bar and the meadow. As the men crawled out of the river and dumped Hatcher on the bank, Louy scampered back from the cabin with Pete's Colt and cartridge bag and his own fusil, powder horn and bullet pouch. Seeing Hatcher lying beside the river, Louy ran up to the men.

"What has happen to him," he said. His eyes were on the men. He held the flintlock musket in both hands. The hammer was all the way back.

"Drunk," said one of the men. The man who spoke was no taller than Louy. Except for black whiskers, his face was a ghostly white. The black eyes flicked from Louy to Pete like snake eyes. He ran delicate, pink fingers through thick, black hair. The delicate pink fingers reached out and pointed.

"This here man," he said, "bet his claim to this meadow on the turn of the cards. Lost."

The other five men began slowly to fan out along the river bank. Each man carried at least one pistol in his belt. Some wore two.

"He threw in your claims with his," the pink-fingered man said.

"Like the hell he did," said Louy backing up some so as to be able to swing his musket better.

"No need for trouble," said the pink-fingered man. "You and your friends can take your possibles from the cabin and go. Of course, leave any gold. That was part of the bet. Take your possibles and go. Now!"

The man's hand rested on the butt of his pistol.

"Louy, I think these boys intend jumpin our claim." Pete said it softly like he was whispering in church.

"You kill this dandy with the lady's fingers," he whispered. "I'll take the rest."

Pete stood by the rocker. His Walker's Colt was leveled in the direction of the men spread out along the river bank behind their leader. No one moved for a long minute.

Suddenly, Louy thrust the muzzle of his musket into Pinky's belly.

"This one, the big mouth, she is dead."

Just as quickly, the man backpedaled into the river. The fast water tackled his ankles and he went for a swim. The other men stood with hands on or near their guns; but did not move.

"Who wants to be first can pull his pistol and die," said Pete.

Still no one of the men moved. Grasshoppers hopped around their ankles. Bees buzzed them to see if they were flowers. No one moved to dodge the bees. The sun was hot. The five men sweated. They sweated and watched the slow swing of the muzzle of Pete's Colt, waver and hold, waver and hold, from belly to belly.

"Guess these boys don't feel like winners today," Pete moved slowly toward the five men, motioning them to close up. "Get their guns, Louy."

Louy went from man to man removing pistols from waist bands and coat pockets.

"Five men. Eight pistols. Two Colts. A sacre damn army."

Pinky crawled out of the river and came back to the spot where he went in.

"Damn you. We won this claim fair and . . . ." He spit river water. "Square." More water seeped from his gray coat and pants to fill his boots.

"Don't the man get a chance to win it back?" said Pete.

Pinky started to finish his pitch, stopped, smiled in spite of his shivering. He shook water from his black hair and eyes. Wet whiskers gleamed in the sun.

"Sure. Why, sure. Cards?"

He looked at his companions. One of them pulled a deck of greasy cards from his coat pocket.

"Not cards," said Pete. "We choose the game."

"You throw in your share of this here meadow. Both of you!" It wasn't a question.

Louy looked over at Pete. "Sacre damn no . . . ."

"It's a bet," said Pete. "All he lost agin all we have."

"Pete?" Louy almost shouted.

"Well, sure. What game?" Pinky looked around at the other men and smiled.

"You goin to play for yourself and these other boys, are you?" Pete asked the man quietly.

"Yes." He looked around again. The men smiled and nodded. "What game? Poker? Twenty-one? Name it."

Pete walked over to Hatcher and rolled him over on his back. He splashed cold water in his face; and Hatcher began to stir. Quickly, Pete snatched the Green River from Hatcher's belt and tossed it to the pink-fingered man. The man dodged the heavy knife which buried itself in the sand at his feet.

"Pick it up," said Pete. "You'll need it."

The man bent down and pulled the huge knife from the sand.

Pete slowly pulled his own knife from his belt. It was the knife he had taken from Montoya. Montoya had killed Papa Cortez and taken this knife. In life's turn, Pete had met Montoya on the banks of the Purgatoire and had killed him in a duel of rawhide and knives. His father's knife was now his own.

A pistol in one hand and the knife in the other, without taking his eyes off the monte men, Pete walked into the meadow and drew a wide circle in the sand with the heel of his boot.

"Louy, get the rawhide."

Louy ran to the cabin and returned with a thong of braided deerhide about ten feet in length.

"What the hell kind of game is this."

"It is an Indian game."

Pete saw that many of the miners from the bar had come over to the meadow. For the moment, curiosity—and deadly diversion—overcame gold-lust.

"Come," said Pete. He handed the Colt to Louy and walked to the circle. Pinky followed. Louy covered the other monte men with his musket in one hand and the Colt in the other.

"We are mated by the rawhide."

Pete pointed to Pinky and to the coil of deerhide thong.

"Left leg tied to right leg. In our right hand, the knife."

He raised the blade to the sun. The knife was not thick with a curved blade like the Green River. The stiletto-like blade had been forged in Toledo by the Cortez men of Malaga almost a century before. Razor sharp edges swooped to the killing tip.

"We play the game in this circle."

"Play? Game?" The man looked at the sun dancing on the foot long blade of Pete's knife. "Fight, you mean. Like savages."

"The man who lives, wins," said Pete quietly.

The pink-fingered man looked shocked and dropped Hatcher's Green River. "That aint no gamblin man's game," he said.

"Hell it aint," yelled one of the miners in the crowd.

"Carve his guts out, Cortez," shouted another.

"Serve him better than he served me," said a new miner. "He shilled me into the game with these other fellers; then cleaned me out, mule-dumb that I am."

Other miners joined in, hot for blood on the sand, when it was not their own.

Pete ignored the crowd. He walked over to Pinky and lightly thumped his wet chest with the point of his knife.

"Aint no game, I say," said Pinky.

"It is the game you must play if you wish to have this claim. The man who refuses to play the game loses the bet—but he, too, wins."

"Wins? Loses but wins? How?"

"He lives!"

Suddenly, a growl erupted from behind the group of men as if it had come from the river's angry spirit.

"This child has been drunk a-fore. Drunk as the Lord God almighty."

The crowd parted as Hatcher stumbled in among them. His eyes were wild and his breath killed flies that flew to close.

"This child has been shilled a-fore. Shilled by the Nez Perce, the Crows, a Saint Louie mountebank and a Saint Jo whore."

He stepped up to the gambler and withered him with the fly-killing breath. He felt in the ground with the toe of his moccasin, bent over, wavered and picked up his Green River.

"This child aint never been drunk and shilled like these men done it."

He turned and weaved his head full of bloodshot eyes at the crowd.

"Experts. By the blood stainin the blade of this here knife." He wagged the long, sharp blade under the gambler's nose. "Experts!"

Higgins stepped forward. "I saw the game," he said. "Lost some gold myself. These boys have been bragging around town and on the river about how easy it was to beat the monte man." Higgins indicated Pinky's friends and then Pinky, the gambler, himself.

"This here's the monte man," said Hatcher wagging the knife blade much closer to Pinky's nose this time. The gambler took a step back.

Another man spoke up from the back of the crowd. "That one there," he pointed to one of Pinky's friends. "That one showed me a sack full of gold and said, 'why spend the days belly deep in cold river water when you can win all the gold you want right here in town. Do like me,' he said. 'Bet it all, like I done; and clean up on the dumb monte man.'"

"All of these men have posed as players against the monte man," continued Higgins. "Winners. Made it look easy. Just cappers.

"When some of the miners started to play, the cappers pulled back. At first the miners bet a little and won. Hatcher and I started to play. In the beginning we won too. Then Hatcher put a large sack of gold on the table and told this pink-fingered man to turn the cards. Hatcher lost. Hatcher was pretty drunk and I took him over to Millie's to sleep it off."

Pinky looked at Higgins and then at Hatcher. "Later he bet his claim, and yours, and lost," said the gambler to Pete. "Weren't no shill to it. Fair and square, my game is."

"So is mine," said Pete like ice. "Take the knife or take out of Buff's Bar. Your choice."

The crowd cheered. Most of the men had lost dust and pride to the monte man.

First one and then all of the cappers headed back across the river. The gambler followed, his face a match for his delicate, pink fingers. The crowd of miners frolicked, laughing and shouting, at his heels. Some splashed the monte men with cold water.

The exodus was fast, too fast for Hatcher. "Where'd them card-cheatin skunks go?"

He waved the Green River in the air. The weight of the blade caused it to propeller until it took Hatcher around in circles with it. After three or four turns, Hatcher melted onto his knees, then floated down to plow his face in the meadow sand. He snored before the dust settled. With each expulsion, more flies died.

That night six men on mules—and four mules packed with gold—headed out of Buff's Bar and into the golden moonlight.

"There's still many a man in these mountains aint seen the elephant," Pinky sang into the night.

"They will," he sang. "They surely will!"

# 28

The man who brought the mail for a pinch of gold per letter started it. It swept through Buff's Bar like dysentery.

"Middle Fork of the Yuba! More gold than sand. Avalanches of it! Miles of it! Up and down the river. Gold! Gold! Gold!"

Within hours the stampede was on. Within a week, Buff's Bar was almost empty, deserted. Higgins, Bailey and Henry were among those leaving for the new strike. As they sat their mules, saying their goodbyes, Hatcher erupted.

"When we come on this bar," he said, "a feller was leavin for the Trinity on news of a strike there. He told of the time this here prospector got to heaven."

"No-no-no one from around Buff's, I expect," said Bailey.

"Well," said Hatcher. "Accordin to this here feller, one prospector made it. Seems Saint Peter wouldn't let the man in."

"Nor would I," said Higgins.

"'Too many miners in heaven just now,' says the Saint. 'I'll clear 'um out in a minute,' says this here miner. 'If'n you let me in.'

" 'Course Saint Pete has to give him his try. Soon as the miner gets into heaven, he passes the word, 'they done struck it big, mighty big—in Hell!'

"Soon the story is all around heaven. Them heavenly prospectors stampede out-a the pearly gates 'till that miner is the only one left."

Hatcher looked up at the mounted men and smiled.

"Wasn't long afore this here prospector, he goes up to Saint Pete and says, 'I got to get shut of this place; and I'm in a awful hurry.' Surprised as a possum tryin to bed a skunk, Saint Peter asks him why.

" ' 'Cause there might just be somethin to that story of a big gold strike in Hell.'"

Higgins waved as they started for the Yuba. "We'll all meet in Hell," he said.

Liking the cabin and the river and the meadow almost as much as the gold, Hatcher said, "let them run off to the next mine. Leaves plenty for us. Right here." And the steep sides of the ravine leading into the meadow were rich with gold.

The March days, empty at first of miners' voices on the bar, soon filled again with the sing-singing of fresh hope as newcomers settled in the abandoned shacks and began to pan the leavings of those who had departed for new hope on the Yuba.

In days, Buff's Bar recycled. Although the river was still high in March, work on the bar was soon as furious as ever. The difference was that now, the men mined a week's wages in a day; no longer could they dig a year's wages in a week.

Still, those who rushed in knew no better. Back home, a man traded his twelve hour day for fifty cents or, at most, a dollar; and he owned nothing but his sores at the end of the day. Here on Buff's Bar, he made an ounce or two a day, worth eight to ten dollars per ounce in trade goods. And, as much of the river banks, meadows and mountains as he could dig were his.

Blue lupine, periwinkles and orange poppies gilded the April meadow. The ravine was still rich; but now, others, strangers, were working the Escobar camp.

"Our meadow's gettin crowded," said Hatcher. He shoveled the day's last pile of dirt into the rocker. Louy pumped the handle as Pete poured bucket after bucket of river over the screen.

Several men walked past them and into the river heading back to the town. The sun had set behind the high ridge of the mountain. The early bats darted here and there leaving dark night trails.

Louy scraped the rifflers and put the deposits in a can.

"Can't see."

He took the can and started toward the cabin. As he walked, he hefted the can.

"She is somethin over two pound, if she is not all black sand."

"A-fore this here meadow gives out, we'll have more gold than we can carry," said Hatcher, wiping muddy hands on the tops of his long johns as he willingly followed Louy and Pete to the cabin.

After a supper of bacon fried with wild onions and biscuits with honey, Hatcher picked up the last remains of *Paradise Lost* which he had found abandoned and lost beside one of the empty shacks in town. He thumbed the few pages and went out the door.

Pete lit his pipe and settled back against the log side of the cabin. Louy reached for a twig from the fire with which to light his own pipe.

"I got a letter from Anna," said Pete. "First since we've been in California. Mail rider saw it was written in a girl's hand. Wanted two pinches of gold. I told him it was just my sister. He looked at me kinda funny-like; then handed me the letter. 'Sorry,' he said, 'on the house.' He shook his head and rode on his way."

For a moment, the flash of his sister's Spanish cat eyes flecked with green and Missouri red hair caught at the back of Pete's memory.

"What does the beautiful Anna have to tell of our friend Garrard?" said Louy. "Is he still with your mother and sister at the rancho in Taos?"

"Garrard is still there. Seems he's made a good ranch hand and Missouri farmer. She thinks he'll make her a better husband—soon as he gets up the nerve to ask her."

"She will have to ask him, I think." Louy smiled through a wreath of smoke.

Hatcher came in from the out-back. "Last of the Paradise book," he said, tossing the hard covers into the fire. "Read a page or two till I found a better use for it." He thumb-gestured out the door.

"Anna Cortez' letter, she say Anna and Garrard will marry." Louy pointed to the sheet of paper Pete held in his hand.

"Garrard's the marryin kind," said Hatcher. "Could see it right off. Don't know why I took the time to teach him about the mountains."

"Because Captain Saint Vrain asked it of you. And the boy was willin and handy at times."

"Like when he shot me for an Indian," said Pete rubbing the deep scar along the right side of his head. They laughed, remembering.

Hatcher threw a log on the fire, stuck a twig in the flame and lit his pipe.

"Miss your family?" he asked looking under draped lids at Pete.

Pete veiled his eyes and nodded.

Hatcher sat up. "Can't say as I do mine. Each year since I was born seemed like, I'd get a new brother or sister. Wasn't long, Ma forgot me for the young 'uns. When I was about fourteen, Pa took a hickory branch to my back once too often. I traded him blow for blow, only I had picked up a stout log, by mistake. Last I saw, Pa was laid out in the barn, some bloody. I lit out up the wide Missouri. Aint seen nor heard of them from that day till this."

Pete looked over at Louy. He shrugged. "My mother, she feed me in summer and I take care of her animals in winter. My mother, she is the Hudson Bay Company. My father is a French trapper from Quebec City. In summer he is gone to the mountains; in winter under the buffalo robe with a squaw. Still, he teach me to trap the beaver and to smell the Indian. And, when he die one winter under the robe; just die; I pick up his fusil and his plews. I trap ever since."

Pete looked his surprise. It was more history than he had heard from them in all of the last two years and more.

"I reckon me and Louy have thirty, forty thousand dollars in gold put by," said Pete.

"Monte man got mine," said Hatcher. "I'm poor as when I came to this here gold mine."

"Louy and me won't let you starve," said Pete.

"Sacre damn hell we won't. He lost his gold. Let him find more." Louy kicked a moccasined foot at Hatcher and laughed.

"I aim to do just that; and this hellion would take no gold from a Frenchy. It'd be full of his fleas just like his beaver plews was. And there aint nothin like a flea as has fed on a Frenchy. Swoop down like a vulture. Bite like a grizz. Hold more blood'n a swamp full of skeeters. No Frenchy gold for Long John Hatcher."

He lunged a foot back at Louy; and they toe wrestled for a moment. Pete watched and laughed.

After a long silence, spliced with smiles and flashing eyes, Pete said quietly, "I can make a fine horse herd easy from the wild stuff here in California. Hire a Californio or two to help with the drive. When I find that valley, I'll have gold enough to last a lifetime of ranch-buildin."

"You do not think your valley, she is here in California?" Louy looked at Pete, a thin smile on his lips.

"No; but even if it could be, the call of gold will fill it with strangers, just as Buff's Bar is again overcome with new men. No. I think my valley is in the mountains of my boyhood. In the Sangre De Cristos of New Mexico." Pete looked first at Louy; then at Hatcher. "And some nearer to my family." Embarrassed, he cast down his eyes for a moment. Still, he went on.

"I have a horse herd to gather while the spring weather lasts and a hell of a long trip home."

He pulled at the pipe; but it had played out. He did not relight it.

"I'll leave tomorrow," he said simply. "I'll go to San Francisco. To ship the Escobars' gold to their family in Sonora, if'n I can. Save me a long trip into the Sonora desert. Then I'll collect vaqueros and my herd of Spanish horses. By late summer, I should be home. Taos! Mama! Anna!" Pete sighed, but his face was lit with longing.

Hatcher and Louy smoked in silence. Pete stared into the faces of his mother and sister in the leaping flames of the fire.

After a while, Hatcher said, "I seen the Sangre De Cristos. Hot, mostly dry. Damn few beaver."

"There'll be a long, green valley with water . . . ."

"Pete. Louy and me'll stay awhile. Louy is rich. He can help me with my own fortune. Maybe when we're both rich, we'll come on over to see how you're gettin along."

"Then it's . . . ."

"Hasta la vista," said Hatcher.

"Yes," Pete said quietly. "Hasta la vista."

Pete tried to swallow, but couldn't get the spit past the lump in his throat.

"Until we meet again."

# 29

In the Spring of 1849, Black Hess was already nearing rich. What he and Potts had begun with Buff's gold and the goods stolen from abandoned ships had grown with the needs of the world of new arrivals who rushed into San Francisco.

With word of Potts' death, Hess was now sole owner of Potts and Hess Mercantile. The store occupied a two story brick building across from the Pinch 'a Dust in Portsmouth Square.

During the wet winter, the city had filled with men anxious to get at the gold of spring. They spent eastern cash for all manner of goods; and Hess had all manner to sell. As the rains faded and wild flowers pimpled the hills, more of the free spending world rushed in at the moving, heaving city. Hess was nearly sold out by May.

To steal from the ships is now harder, Hess thought, remembering. He sat behind the counter of his store and looked at the gaps in the shelves and empty pegs on the wall. He remembered the Nancy Ann and other ships he and Potts had plundered. Then, it was so easy. Now, to get more goods, them I must buy. Hess scowled and the crescent scar wrinkled along his powder darkened cheek. I buy, maybe.

Potts' trip to the mines had been a bust. That's for sure, thought Hess, as he counted the day's take in paper and dust. Still, it I hardly miss. Potts I miss not at all. Hess scraped the paper money and gold dust into a large sack and tied the string. Maybe, if he does well, I let Mister Wells keep my gold and money. In the city, honest gold is not safe from thieves. Hess scowled again and rubbed the scar with the two fingers of his gloved hand.

Long John Hatcher and Cortez done for Potts! Hess curled a lip and thought he smiled. Know it they do not; but for Black Hess they done a favor, killin Potts. The curled lip twitched. Here they will come. Later or sooner, they will come. Everybody does.

He looked down at his two fingered hand. Come they will. To Black Hess!

Stuffing the money bag in a tin box, Hess went to the back of the store. After looking all around, he lifted a floor board and put the box into the ground. He replaced the board and carefully tamped it down with a polished boot. Then one by one he blew out the four lamps that hung in a row across the store and left the large room to the night, careful to lock the door behind him.

To the Pinch 'a Dust, I go. For a drink and cards with my friends. As he crossed the square, Black Hess returned the amiable nods and greetings of several other merchants, a sea captain and Doctor Samuels from Boston.

In the Pinch 'a Dust, miners and workmen made way for Black Hess at the bar. No longer did he wear the long saber at his side. He wore a plush, gray, frock coat and striped pants. A red cravat puffed out from his thick neck. To each man he curled his lip and thought he smiled. He thought each smiled at him in return. Some few did.

Like a Spanish stallion to a mare in heat, Pete Cortez was drawn to the names on the sign over the two story brick store front opposite the Pinch 'a Dust saloon in Portsmouth Square.

"Potts and Hess Mercantile," the sign said.

"Potts and Hess," Pete said aloud. "My god Smokey. I'm just rid of one and now here's the other. Black Hess!"

Quickly, Pete looked all around the square. I better see Hess first. He let the thought drift into remembering.

He remembered the deep, slanting scar across his mother's face etched in blood by the long, curved saber blade, carved by Black Hess in his mother's cheek. He scowled at the sign, "Potts and Hess."

Hess!

Past remembering, he saw again the long, curved saber blade shinning above his head in the morning light slanting through the window slits of Estis' tavern in Taos; felt the deep bight of cutting steel sear his shoulder; heard the crunch of steel on bone, his bone; smelled the unwashed sweat of the killing man with the powder burnt face. He saw the same two-fingered man pick up his severed digits from the tavern floor; saw the spit of death from blue-ice eyes, shot with killing anguish from deep in the man's black soul.

He heard again his own hot words washed in blood. 'If I see you again, I'll kill you, Hess.'

Hess' savage reply now echoed in the cavern of sudden remembering. 'You will not see me again—first.' His words remained hot. So did the echo. Pete remembered the Prussians' words as Black Hess had retreated from the tavern. Called me a fool for not killin him.

"Long John Hatcher," Pete said to himself as he stared at the sign and tried to see in the window of the store. "Sometimes you talk too much. But for you and your talk, I'd a killed the bastard. I'd be done with him. 'Fool' aint far wrong."

Pete could see nothing inside the dark store. He heard guitar tinkle and fiddle scrape coming from the Pinch 'a Dust. All around the square and beyond, he heard the gentle roar of grumbling, laughing, crying, dying, living men. A wagon loaded with cut boards lumbered in front of Pete and cut off his vision of the dark store. Still, Pete saw the store just as it was the moment before the wagon crossed his eyes.

"Now I got it to do all over again," Pete said to the store front. "And, I better, before Hess sees me first."

Pete Cortez had taken most of the month of May to trail three, gold-laden mules and follow the Sacramento to its gaping, tule-marsh mouth at the northern end of Suisun Bay. There he met Captain Hughes of the lugger, Ann, camped alone on shore in an open flat among the tules. The lugger was full of empty barrels and boxes, some packs, a few tools and seven pinewood coffins.

This time of the season, men were going to the mines in the opposite direction. Captain Hughs brought out the dregs of the long winter.

"Sure I can take your mules and you to San Francisco," bellowed Hughes. "I pleasure for the company, son. All I've had since leavin the American is wind through the empty barrels and them coffins. Get down wind of them fellers and you know what smellin the elephant is."

So, Pete, Smokey and the mules rode the lugger, Ann, against a contrary wind across Suisun Bay, past the city of Benicia, through the Straits of Carquinez, down San Pablo Bay and into San Francisco.

"Look sharp, son," said Captain Hughes as Pete led the animals onto the wharf. "City's growed by about thirty thousand since the fall of last year. Yep, as many as that. Most is okay folk, headed for the mines. But they's some as evil as the Devil hisself. A few of 'um more so, I'm thinkin."

"Thanks," said Pete. "Any place a man's gold will be safe?" he asked.

"No place and anywhere. In San Francisco, only thing cheaper'n gold is life. Few men steal. It's easier to take a man's gold peaceable-like. Cards, high priced supplies, whores and liquor." Hughes waved a rope-hardened hand across the sky-line of the city. "Still, if your gold's just layin around, someone too lazy to cheat you might just up and walk off with it." The Captain laughed. "Providin it weren't too heavy."

"Pretty much the same way at the mines," said Pete smiling. "Still, there are exceptions." Pete remembered Potts had been one of those. "I'd feel less a fool if some one watched my gold, at least while I take a bath and get a restaurant meal."

"Safe? Try Henry Wells. He's been a freighter back East. Boys seem to trust him. Some have used him to ship their gold home. None lost any that I know of."

Pete found a stable for the stock at twenty dollars a day and found per animal. He deposited his gold and that of the Escobars with Henry Wells. Wells agreed to hold his gold for safe keeping until he left for the south to collect his horses; and to ship the Escobars' gold home to their families in Sonora.

Pete tried the hotels; but found them packed with traders, mechanics, carpenters and gamblers. Most hotels wanted long term guests and refused to rent for the night. Pete intended to stay only so long as it took to see the city and send off the Escobars' gold. He'd arranged for the latter. From what I've already seen and heard, he thought, I can see the city on the way out.

He was headed down the coast to Los Angeles where he planned to round up a hundred or so of the free-running Spanish horses in the San Bernardino Valley to herd on home to Taos.

Pete found a hip-wide bunk in a clapboard warehouse where he could sleep for two dollars a night. The large building held about five hundred rough cut, hardboard shelves, five and a half feet to a man. Each lodger had to provide anything else he needed for himself, straw or a mat, blankets; or he could buy them from the seaman who ran the place, at thirty to fifty times their cost anywhere on earth but San Francisco. No extra charge for the ticks and fleas.

The seaman who ran the place called the shelves "beds."

"My horse and mules have got better than this," said Pete.

"Sleep with them, then and be damned," said the seaman.

Knowing he had a sale, the seaman smiled slyly.

" 'Course, stableman'll charge you five dollars, in case you might try sleepin in the hay. Three dollars for a horse apple bed, 'less its still warm. Warm apple bed's five, 'less there's other fellers biddin for it, and so on."

Pete paid his two dollars and another twenty for a place to store his possibles.

"For ten dollars, I stores 'um. For twenty, I makes sure they're all here when you come for 'um, provided you gets here by noon tomorrow."

"I aint storin this here Walker's Colt nor my pa's Indian sticker," Pete patted the foot long knife in his belt.

"Like I said, safe till noon. Another twenty, in advance, if'n you're plannin to be late."

Suddenly, Pete's hand flashed and the stiletto was at the seaman's throat.

"Keep my possibles safe till I come for 'um." The seaman's eyes bugged at Pete. "And, you'll have to trust me for the other twenty, if'n I'm late."

The seaman nodded urgent assent.

"You're an understandin man," said Pete.

As fast as the knife had appeared at the seaman's throat, it disappeared in Pete's belt sheath.

"Goin to get my horse and see some of this here town a-fore it blows away or burns down."

And so, Pete Cortez rode into Portsmouth Square; and, drawn like the stallion, by fate, he'd seen the crooked facade of Potts and Hess Mercantile and memories past remembering.

It was dark when Black Hess left the Pinch 'a Dust, his belly full of fresh meat and his pockets jingling to the clink of fresh coins. Whiskey, meat and poker. Black Hess felt like a happy man as he walked across the square toward his store. He did not look toward the rider mounted quietly on the smoke-gray horse in the shadow of the square. With a brass key, Hess opened the door and went inside. In a moment, he lit a lantern and felt the warm comfort of the dim glow.

Pete nudged Smokey with a knee and the horse began a slow walk from out of the shadows and across Portsmouth Square. Pete could not see the sign in the dark; but he knew it was still hanging there above the door.

"Potts and Hess Mercantile."

Pete fingered the smooth, walnut grip of the Walker's Colt.

A cold wind, smelling of salt-decayed wood and dead fish, blew into the square from off the bay. The chill made the place seem darker, the light-shafts from the taverns, hotels and stores bleak as light in the hangman's eye. In front of the door of the Potts and Hess Mercantile, it was pitch dark.

To the seeming shriek of saddle leather, Pete dismounted. He had to feel for the door. The knob turned quietly. Unlocked. Pete stepped into the room.

"Black Hess! I'm seein you first!"

"Was ist los?" Hess stood frozen behind the counter. "Cortez?"

Eyes locked. Prussian blue-ice spilled into Spanish liqueur. Blue froze; Spanish burned. Each man saw his own death in the eyes of the other.

Suddenly, Hess held up his gloved hand; and the grip of eyes was broken. Slowly, finger by finger, thumb, index, middle, he slipped the glove off. Thumb and two good fingers, the last two, ragged stumps.

Pete stood with his hand on the butt of the Colt.

"In Taos," said Hess in a quiet voice, "you, Cortez, took my fingers with the long knife."

Hess' lip twitched and he thought he smiled. He shook the black glove until two small objects spilled from the empty finger holes.

"These have I kept. At first to remind me of you."

Two shriveled, mummified fingers spilled, clickity, click on the counter.

Pete stared at the clickity-clicking; jumped his eyes back up to Hess.

"After what you done to my mother, you got off lucky in Taos."

"After skin grew over these stumps and I learned to use a two-fingered hand. You I looked for. To kill."

"Here I am!"

Hess waved his five-fingered hand as if to clean the air into which Pete had spit his challenge.

"You were from Taos gone."

Pete gripped the butt of the Colt.

"I'm here now and waitin, Hess."

Hess thrust out his good hand, palm forward like Christ calming the multitude.

"But, please. Understand, you do not."

"I understood then and do now."

"No! No! Please! Let me explain."

"As long as I can see your hands and nothin in this room moves, you can talk all night."

"Good, good. Thank you. Soon it will all be clear."

Hess put both hands flat on the counter. His powder blackened face softened. In the dim lamp light, even the ridge of scar paled.

"My unit was ordered to join Colonel Doniphan in Mexico. To Chihuahua to fight. Fighting Mexicans for no profit was, for me, not possible. I am crippled in the hand. So was I mustered out, so to speak, from the army. New Mexico I left and here by ship I came. Here have I prospered. See!"

Hess swept the store with his two-fingered hand. Open barrels held shovels and picks; sacks of dried beans and peas lined the wall; all manner of pants, coats and shirts hung from wooden pegs above the sacks; pots, pans and pistols filled the counters.

"I see," said Pete not taking his eyes off Hess.

"Potts and me, we have mined more gold with these than you have from the mines."

"Potts aint minin it, Hess. He's fertilizin the gold in a ravine up on the Bear River. He come gunnin for our gold and got his pay in lead."

"This have I heard. You or Hatcher?"

"Hatcher shot him from his mule. He was shootin at me at the time. Leastways, tryin to. His powder was wet."

"Or you, he would have killed." A warm chinook flashed across the blue-ice eyes.

"Had me on my belly in the rain. Dead to rights. That winter of rain was bad; but not all bad. His powder was wet and he died for it. I've kept my powder dry. Now I'm here, Hess."

He heard himself. It suddenly sounded to Pete more like a question than a threat.

"Cortez. Between you and Black Hess, it is finished."

"Finished?"

"You I forgive!"

The moon scar on Hess' cheek gleamed oily in the pale lamp light. He held out his bare, two-fingered hand in forgiveness. His eyes chilled the room; but Pete saw the hand. Pete stared at the finger stumps.

"It is true, Cortez. Here have I prospered." The hand across the counter did not waver. "Now, an honest merchant I am; who does not fight. Peace I offer. Between us, peace."

Pete stared; said nothing. Maybe Hatcher was right, he thought. Killin is too good for this man. His fingers eased their grip on the Colt. Maybe?

"Peace till I turn my back. Is that it?"

"Peace. Always."

Still, the crippled hand tried to bridge the gap between them.

Maybe. Maybe not, thought Pete. Fool that I am, I can't just gun him down while he waves the hand of peace at me. That makes me twice a fool, I think.

"So be it," said Pete. He did not take the offered hand. "You cut my mother cruelly. I gave you the same brand to wear."

"And more you give to Hess."

Hess held the finger stumps up to the light. Dropping the other hand he picked up the black glove. One by one he held up his mummy fingers and stuffed them into the empty sockets of the glove.

"Now, it is just space in the empty glove they take up." Hess curled his lip as if he were trying to smile.

"We're even is all," said Pete.

He took a step back; saw the hate in Hess's eyes; hesitated. Then, he turned and felt the short hairs fire up along the back of his neck. He walked through the open door and into the night.

He heard Hess call out.

"Cortez. Goodbye. As rain we are now right."

Pete mounted the smoky horse and headed for his two dollar bunk.

"Smokey, I'll surely be glad to quit this place if'n Hatcher's words and my own chicken hearted foolishness don't kill me yet. A twice-a-fool don't deserve to live, 'less'n God's workin overtime."

Although Pete was well out of Portsmouth Square, the fired short hairs still tickled hot at the base of his skull.

———

Pete followed the wagon rut road under a canopy of dense fog. South of San Francisco, the road cut between furry hills of wild grains, turning gold, and speckled poppy blossoms, still bright orange in the lateness of the spring and made more beautiful by the drape of whispering fog.

The mules, repacked with Pete's gold and new supplies, pulled and jumped at their leads, eager in the early morning. The animals fed at the wild wheat and oats as they walked at the end of the lead rope. Smokey pranced among petticoats of dancing mist that wet her pearly-gray socks to her knees.

El Camino Real, the road of the mission fathers, would take Pete to San Juan Bautista, west of the Diablo Mountains; to Monterey on the Pacific; then, across the coastal mountains, down the long valleys past Soledad, San Miguel, San Luis Obispo, Santa Barbara, San Buenaventura to Los Angeles. There he intended to hire his vaqueros. Together, they would gather Spanish horses from the wild herds of the valley of San Bernardino. The new Cortez horses.

By late summer or early fall, I'll be home to Taos and Mama and Anna. I'm rich with the gold I carry and the herd I will gather. I'll find the valley of my dream. My rancho. My Cortez!

"C'mon mules! Smokey! C'mon." Pete tickled the horse's ribs with his heels.

Suddenly, Smokey jumped, crow hopped, cried out in pain and sagged to her knees under the fog-wet shroud.

Only then, did Pete hear the rifle shot peel back the misty pall. He felt Smokey quiver between his knees.

Suddenly, he was rolling, all arms and hips and bootheels. He noticed the smell of poppies as the gunshot echo rustled the heavy headed grain.

He heard the mules trot away to feed and the squeal of pain as the mare tried to get to her feet. He saw her rise a few yards away; saw the blood spill across the light gray of her neck where the bullet had exited; saw the electric pulse of fear and shock ripple under her skin.

"Smokey!" he cried out. "Smokey!"

"Dead the horse is not, Cortez. Soon will you be—dead."

"Black Hess!" Pete rolled on his back to face the voice. "Hess! You lyin bastard."

In a step, Black Hess was on him, standing over him with legs spread and the curved blade of the saber arched high. Pete saw the blade cut down through the fog.

His hand went to the Colt at his waist. He rolled in the wild grasses, rolled again. The Colt was free and firing as he rolled—and the blade following.

Suddenly, the blade swung sideways. Pete felt the whirlwind of its passing as it cut a swath like a farmer's scythe. Black Hess followed the blade into the cut it made. He sowed splotches of gunshot blood in the furrow he plowed across the fresh-cut, spring wheat.

Instantly, Pete was up. He pointed the Colt down at the still body of the forgiving man. Pete stood poised to shoot and time packed in around him so he could hardly breath. Breathless eternity was but a minute or two of man's time in the killing day.

Suddenly, Pete exhaled poison from his lungs. He coughed. The pistol wavered over the unmoving body. The grip felt greased in Pete's sweaty hand. Though he willed another shot, a killing he could remember, Hess did not move.

Finally, Pete gave up his dead. Slowly, he loaded and returned the Colt to the red sash. He took a last look at Hess.

"He gathered what he sowed," said Pete.

He looked over at Smokey and saw flies swarming at the blood on her neck. Smokey stood and shook her head and cried out in pain. He felt the ache in his neck, as if it, too, had been drilled.

It seemed to Pete to take forever to stop the bleeding. The wound in the horse's neck went clear through; but looked clean like it had cut only the muscle between bone and sky.

"You'll be sore as hell for a while, Smokey horse; but by San Bernardino, you'll be ready to chase the wild bunch, frisky as ever."

The mules were easy to catch as they fed on the lush, mountain table. They fought to stay at it; but Pete finally got their hides behind and ready to trail. He hung Hess's saber on the saddle horn and mounted Hess' horse. He trailed Smokey. She snorted at the pain of walking. Gently, he nudged her forward. She stepped out, at first one halting foot at a time. Soon, she adjusted to the new pain in her neck. Pete spurred Hess' horse as if it were Hess, pulled the lead rope with a jerk and the animals followed.

He did not look back at the field he had plowed that foggy morning. In less than an hour, Pete Cortez had lost himself beyond the horizon of fuzzy, slowly waving grain.

Soon, the gentle breeze swept under the skirt of fog and, almost gaily, lifted it above the field. Black Hess lay at the end of his furrow. Flies fought to drink his blood before it dried in the coming sun. The gentle breeze licked Hess' scared cheek with a salty tongue.

Suddenly, Hess groaned and the flies jumped.

III
1853
THE DEADLINERS

# 30

Beckey Goddard was stuck and scared. She sat the heaving seat of her four-wheeled buggy. Her matched pair of grays plunged and reared as the roilly, rain-swollen current of the Cimarron River hit them full force.

"Help me!" She screamed. "Captain Gray. Help!"

She saw Captain Gray sitting his roan horse on the opposite bank of the river. His feet hung loosely out of the stirrups. He waved a beckoning hand; but made no move to come to her aid.

Suddenly, Beckey felt the buggy sag by the downstream front wheel; felt the back end begin to swing around with the river's surge.

She grabbed the whip and snapped it at the horses. The horses jumped and plunged even more. The buggy moved forward a foot or two, straightened out some and stuck again.

Still, Captain Gray sat his horse, motionless, watching her.

"Lead them horses," she heard Gray yell.

"I can't. The river," screamed Beckey as the rush of muddy water came up almost over her boots.

"Jump in and grab the reins," she heard. "Jump in and take them by the head and lead them out."

Still, Gray sat his horse. She saw a smile play over his face.

With sudden resolve, Beckey stepped from the buggy into the river. Slowly, she worked her way to the horses' heads as they swayed back and forth in the swirling water. First she took hold of the halter of one horse, then the other. River hands yanked at her dress, wrapping it around her legs. For an instant, she stood waist deep, facing the horses, her back to the shore and the watching Captain Gray.

A tossing head pulled her almost out of the water. She let go of the halter of the off horse. The near horse reared and plunged in the traces. She lost her last leather grip. Then she was under the water shooting down the river.

Gasping for breath, she got her head up. She stabbed the sandy bottom with her legs. After several tries, her boots gripped sand; and she stood, her bent back and flexed buttocks an island in the surrounding current. Slowly, bracing each step with bent knees, she turned to face upstream. With bent knees quivering, she saw that she was only down from the buggy by maybe thirty yards. She searched right and left for a way out of a watery grave. Thirty yards to the buggy. About the same to the far shore. She saw the horses lunge and duck as the mad river swirled around their bellies.

If I unbend a knee to take a step, the river will surely get me, she thought. But, if I don't? She felt the growing weakness in her legs. And then she saw it.

A giant tree, skimming and bobbing down the river and past the buggy. Spiky roots danced across the blue of the low sky. Root spikes plowed aside the angry water as the tree drove right at her belly-band.

Beckey Goddard was a Missouri girl from Illinois. When she was eleven years old, her family had moved from Franklin, Missouri to Carthage, Illinois just in time for her to witness the storming of the Carthage jail and the gunshot death of the Mormon prophet, Joseph Smith, and his brother Hyrum in 1844.

There, near Carthage, her father grew corn and pigs on a section of forgiving bottom land. Her father was not so forgiving as the land.

Presbyterian from birth, narrow by nature, her father filled her growing up with rigid God rule. Still, the Goddards prospered on the land. From her mother, Beckey learned that God in the body of her father came first, then the pigs. Mother taught her to read from the Good Book and from the local papers. From the Book, Beckey learned of the trials and wanderings of ancient peoples, of Moses and Jesus. From the local papers, she saw that the struggles of her own people were far from over.

Mostly, she studied the stories of a wagon wheel people moving West to Oregon, California, Santa Fe. Secretly, she yearned to see the distant lands; feared the excitement growing in her breast. Occasionally, her excitement would pop out at supper and she would start to read a story from the paper of families pulling up stakes and heading for new lands.

"Mostly poor folks," her father said. "Some shiftless no accounts. Others who have settled on land that won't yield them a living. Here the Lord has provided all we need. Here we stay. And, girl, that's an end to it."

Yet, Beckey read and dreamed as she saw neighbors and friends mount wheels with billow capped wagons to follow plodding oxen into a hundred sunsets.

From the leaded window of her room at Missus Pritchard's Presbyterian Seminary for Young Women, where she lived and studied spring, summer and fall, she watched the steady whirl of wheels heading into her westering dream and beyond; and each time, a part of her rolled with them.

Trained in the seminary to teach, she took up her first assignment at the local school. Here, children of all ages from tykes to grown men and an occasional woman came to learn to read, to cipher, to see something of the world beyond the nearby fields of corn and wheat. She loved the teaching because the books and the draw-ings flew her, too, over Presbyterian walls.

In winter, when school was out, Beckey returned inside the walls of her father's farm. There, she helped with winter work. The work brightened her round cheeks. Even in the low sun, her auburn hair flashed a reddish light back at the dull sky. When her students came to visit her or to borrow a book, bright eyes flashed their greeting, and she puffed out her womanhood with pride in their need of her.

Young men came too; but not for books or teaching. Oh, they pretended to a need for learning. At first, Beckey took the men at their word, until yearning eyes gave her the clue. Then she looked them over, always found them a part of Presbyte-rian narrowness—and no part of her westering dream.

Beckey's eyes filled with the spiky roots of the oncoming tree. She took a stumbling step backward and the swift current grabbed at her skirts and tripped her. Under the water again, sand and mud stung her eyes until she shut them. She prayed.

Oh! Papa. Help me!

She clawed for breath and to see the gray sky again. Death hands squeezed the last air from her lungs. Boots dragged sandy bottom and she pushed with the last of her failing strength. Her head popped like a cork above writhing white caps. She sucked wind. Coughed and spit. Boots gripped the sandy bottom. Froth rinsed mud and sand from her eyes. She was standing. The river's current broke in eddies around her bent waist.

The gray world filled her eyes; and, then the spiky-rooted tree—still on-com-ing right at her.

It had happened late that winter; and, they all knew. On that cold morning, without a word or a tear from anyone, she found her things in a bundle on the porch, a white piece of paper stuffed in the leather strap. Folded in the paper was two hundred and fifty dollars. The paper had writing on it in her father's stiff hand:

"You have shamed us and we are quits. Take this money and go with Mister Schyler. He takes a load of goods today to Santa Fe."

Without a word, for she knew her shame, Beckey hitched her own matched grays to the buggy and urged them out of the yard of the farm that had been home for most of her twenty years. She saw her mother, framed by the farmhouse window, half wave a last goodbye. Her face was twisted and her eyes shone.

Beckey met Mister Schyler in Carthage for the trip to Saint Joseph and through the lonely desert beyond. Missus Schyler stood behind him, a black pill box set squarely on her gray head.

"Aint fittin we take a single woman," she said so Beckey could hear. "And, one such as—such as her."

Schyler turned to his wife. He rubbed the wart on the side of his nose with a dirty finger and the nosy wart shown red in the sun.

"Now, Missus Schyler. What she done mustn't follow her where we go. I promised her pa. She's to have a chance to mend her ways afore God; or to keep on with the way she took up with here. It is to be her choice. We will not interfere."

"The folks we travel with are God fearin. They have a right to know," said the pill box hatted woman through thin, dry lips.

"No, woman! Her secret shall be safe with us."

There on the banks of the Missouri River, Beckey paid Mister Schyler one hundred and twenty dollars to cover supplies for the trip and, he said, "my protectin of you along the way."

At Saint Joseph she met the small party of traders, headed by Captain Gray.

"Roll 'um. Roll 'um out," sang Captain Gray one morning before dawn.

Whips cracked over the heads of oxen yoked six to a loaded wagon. The party numbered sixteen men driving or herding more than sixty oxen for the seven freight wagons and three conestogas. Six women, wives to that many of the bullwhackers, and ten children, rode the three family wagons with high, white covers. Beckey drove her buggy behind the last of the schooners.

Together at first, they started the wheels rolling toward the southwest—and Beckey's dream.

During the first few days, the women were friendly enough to Beckey. She ate from Mister Schyler's supplies at the common fire, sang along as she helped wash the dishes and tend the children. At the urging of the women, she held school in the back of a bumping, rocking prairie schooner while one of the drovers handled her buggy and the matched grays.

Then one night on the far side of the Kansas River, Mister Schyler dumped a sack of flour, some salted bacon, dried fruit, coffee, a pot and a frying pan in the back of the buggy.

"They know," he said. "You'll be tendin your ownself from now on."

"Know?" Beckey put a shaking hand to her mouth. "How?" she cried at his back as he walked away. "You told?"

He stopped then and faced her over his shoulder.

"You can follow; but don't try to mix in. Women won't have you. Men neither. You try. They'll cast you out."

"But, I paid you to take me. Protect me."

"That's the only reason."

"Reason? For what?"

"You can follow, even. I told 'um I had a duty. They said, 'give the money back.' I told 'um it was spent. That's the only reason. If I hadn't-a spoke up, they'da throwed you out. Still will if'n you butt in." He turned. "Your on your own from here out."

She watched him walk back to the camp.

"How?" stuck in her throat until she knew how.

Since the Kansas River she had been alone, riding drag in the April wind which brought dust and the faint sounds of children singing. She made do with slim supplies over a small fire, trembled at the night sounds, crossed swollen streams and rivers, fat with spring rain, by guts and luck.

And, now, here she was barely standing against the angry current surging down on her in the cut-bank throat of the Cimarron River. She was terrified; but guts kept her from just sinking and floating away.

The root of the great tree trunk hit her ribs and knocked her sideways off her feet.

As the tree hit her she grabbed. She grabbed and held and felt the pain in her side and belly. She lost her breath and a scream froze in her throat. Still, she did not let go; but scrambled with her hands up the root spikes as the tree slowly began to roll with her weight.

The impact swung the tree cross-river. The tree listed. Hand over hand Beckey climbed the spikes. Still, she felt the river rise around her shoulders. She took a swallow of river and mud through lips sucking wind. Choking and coughing, she felt her hands slip, once, twice.

Grab! Grab another spike. Hang on! The root spikes pushed grasping hands away as the tree twisted her down.

The current ran up against the ten foot tree and sent it diagonally toward the far bank. The spin of the huge log slowed. Beckey felt a sandy bottom scrape across her butt. The brute tree lunged against her breast; then, sliding slowly by her, it let her go. Sitting breast high in the sluggish back eddy of the cut-bank shore, she watched the tree glide back into the river and resume its thousand mile ride.

Alternately, she sat and panted and slowly inched her way out of the river. Her breathing slowed. She turned over to hands and knees on the muddy shore. When finally she stood, the bank was as high as her head. She looked around. The bank blocked her view of the shore at the crossing where Captain Gray had sat his horse to watch the spectacle. She looked upstream, but the buggy was gone.

Walking at the edge of the river, she went toward the crossing. After a quarter of a mile, the bank sloped away and she could see her matched gray horses pulling at the short grass. Reins were dropped to the ground in front of them. Black and dripping mud, the buggy stood, still hitched behind the horses, in the middle of the wagon road. Somehow, while she was fighting the river, they had crossed.

In the distance, Beckey saw the dust puffs as Captain Gray galloped his roan back up the trail toward the wagons now receding from her sight.

She walked to the buggy. No harm done, she thought, as she checked the rig and the horses. Quickly, she pulled off her soggy dress and long johns and stood naked in the desert wind to dry. As the cool spring winds danced over her supple body, goose bumps jumped out on her skin and her nipples wrinkled up. She examined her belly and thighs and watched the red welts sprout where the tree had grabbed her gut. Be black and blue come morning, she thought, and sore.

Here I am standing in a sea of sand and brush, naked as the day I was born. This can't shame me more than I already am. She cupped shivering hands over wind-chilled breasts and didn't even look around.

When she was dry, she put on her other dress over shirtwaist and bloomers. The long johns were still wet and would be till past evening. She knotted the arms of her union suit to the buggy stays so the wind could work its drying way.

Then she crawled up on the buggy seat. Damn. Can't drive without the reins. Slowly, she climbed down and trudged to the horses and gathered up the reins. Just as slowly, she mounted the seat again.

Take me most of the afternoon to catch up, she thought. Better get a move on.

"Hi yee, you gray horses. Git along!" She shouted and slapped the reins.

The horses pulled one last wisp of grass and moved out along the wagon road. Ahead, it sloped up to the horizon. On all sides, the desert began flat, scrubby and empty. Beyond, buttes stuck twisty fingers into the pastel sky of fading day. Way off, a vulture rode a heat spawned dust devil.

Missus Schyler's told them for sure, she thought. He promised; but she never did. My secret's among 'um; and they hate me for it and shun me.

"But, why?" she cried out loud. "Why can't they understand?"

Hearing her voice, the horses picked up the pace; but now Beckey Goddard was all alone on the Santa Fe Trail.

# 31

Pete Cortez sat the smoky horse and looked out over his valley. Below, pines gave way to aspen and juniper and grama grass belly high on the gentle downward tilt. A spring creek bounced off the high mountain and hissed and snaked across the valley floor to hide in the grama.

The flat of the valley hung high for more than three miles before it fell off the end of the mountain and into the forever desert. Pete's valley, now called The Cortez after his name, lay between rocky buttresses, at least two miles apart, which seemed to brace the Sangre De Cristo mountains from falling into the eastern sky.

Beyond the valley, Pete could just make out green cottonwood tops that marked the slow, twisty flow of the Canadian River. He winced as his coal black eyes picked out the spot of green on the Canadian which always reminded him of a like place on the Purgatoire where it'd happened.

Behind the black eyes, knives flashed again in the sun and the blood. Strapped ankle to ankle by a rawhide leash, he and Montoya had fought to the death. He'd killed his trusted boyhood friend because Montoya had suddenly defected to the insanity of the times and butchered Papa Cortez in the Pueblo uprising at Taos in '47.

"Does every man remember the first time?" Pete wondered aloud. He smiled at himself. The bullet shaped scar on the right side of his head just below his hat band reddened. Wrinkles smiled at the corners of his Spanish eyes. Firm lips bent a little below the trim, black mustache which centered the square-jawed face.

I'll betcha Hatcher nor Louy don't remember the first, or even the tenth man they killed, he thought.

He had not seen these two friends for almost three years. Pete left the California gold mines in spring of 1849. Before he left, he'd gathered a herd of nearly a hundred of the wild Spanish horses that roamed the California valleys and coastal plains. Driving his herd with the help of two Californios, he'd come home to New Mexico and the Taos Valley, leaving his mountain man friends, Long John Hatcher and Louy Simonds, to pad their own riches in placer gold.

Hatcher and Louy had stayed behind to work the gold claim they shared to make up for gold lost to the monte dealers. Seems Hatcher could always find his card until the stakes got high and the bottle low. Louy thought he was smart and played table stakes poker. Louy had been scalped a few years before; and Hatcher always allowed them Indians took some brains along with skin and hair.

Pete brought the horse herd into his mother's rancho at Taos. Along with the horses, Pete carried twenty thousand in gold he had dug from the Bear River placer with his own hands.

At the rancho, Pete found his mother and sister, Anna, busily planning for Anna's marriage to Louis Garrard. Garrard. The young man who bullet-marked Pete's head with a shot in the dark of a rebel night. Garrard. The young man who'd kept Hatcher's Green River from Pete's scalp as Pete lay bleeding from the bullet wound. Garrard. The young man who paced him brandy-for-brandy on the night before they helped the army of the United States hang the rebel Pueblos from make-shift gallows on the field at Taos.

Companion for a time, Garrard had chosen Anna instead of California gold. Now Garrard would be brother to Pete.

"He aint the loser by not goin with us to the mines," Pete had said to his mother. "Look how Anna shines in the light of him; and him in hers."

Pete turned the California horses in with his mother's few head of Spanish breeds and let them run together.

"When I find my valley, Mama, I'll be back for the horses and their yield. This gold is yours."

"Ten thousand, Pedro? Half of all the gold you took from the freezing river of the bear? I do not need it, and so much."

His mother pushed the sacks of dust and nuggets away.

"For your safety and the safety of the rancho, and Anna. You must take it."

Pete grinned and, he knew, his own lights filled his mother's heart.

"Besides," he said. "Where I go, it is too heavy to carry; may mark me as a good man to kill and rob."

He pushed the sacks back across the table and got up.

Pete buried the rest of his gold under his father's head stone in the family cemetery behind the adobe ranch house.

After the wedding, Pete mounted his smoky horse; and trailing two pack horses and an extra mount, he headed out of Taos to look for the valley of his dream.

The looking took most of a year. A year of high mountains and lonely night fires. Then one evening as he slid the smoky horse down a pebbly incline, he saw the miles of belly high grass and laughing waters suspended from the side of the mountain below. The smoky horse had slid to a stop on the spot where he now stood. For an hour or more, Pete had sat the saddle and just looked.

"At last," he said to himself. "I've caught up with my dream. Here is my valley."

He found an animal trail down to the grass. That night he camped by the chuckling stream where the flat began.

It took him a month to make a full circuit of the place. He saw signs everywhere of deer, elk, wolf and bear; but from all he could see, he was the first man to bend the grass.

As he rode the circuit, he piled stones at the corners and at points along the way where the flat met the upthrust of buttress slopes. In the same way, he stacked rocks across each animal trail into and out of the valley. He mapped his valley, marking the location of each pile of stones and the other prominent features. He drew in the course of the spring fed stream as it marched back and forth down the valley and off the edge into the desert. He marked clumps of aspen and juniper; rock outcrops, rounded mounds, dips and hollows in the valley floor. He drew them in as best he could until he had a detailed chart of his land.

He spotted the valley in relation to the points of the compass, sunrise and sunset, the thirteen thousand foot high Wheeler Peak to the south and the ribbon of the Canadian River far into the desert to the east.

When he was finished, he was also out of grub; so he went down to Taos. There he found the land of his valley was unknown and unclaimed. So he claimed it.

Back in the valley, Pete cleared and leveled a flat projection of the north buttress. There he built a make-do cabin from milled lumber hauled over the mountain from Taos; but primitive, nevertheless, although it had glass in the windows. Inside, he laid a fireplace and chimney made of the local rock. The fireplace split the cabin between eating and sleeping. At one end was a side board and shelves for food and utensils; at the other four bunks lined the rough plank walls.

Outside the cabin, Pete installed a large log-post and rail corral, a clap-board shack for equipment storage and an elegant one-holer privy of milled wood to match the cabin.

Water from a small spring creek giggled past the cabin and chuckled its way to the larger stream below. Using what he had learned in the California placers, he routed the creek along a wooden flume to spill into and out of a barrel by the side of the cabin and to flow back to the creek.

It was not much of a place compared to his mother's rancho where he had grown up; but it was a start. His start. Not fit for a woman, he thought. *I aint got a woman to fit it for, except, maybe, one from across the desert, from the other part of my dream. Don't know who she is; or if she is, even.* He laughed at the cabin and the corral, the elegant privy and running water, and at the dream woman of his loneliness.

In the months that followed, he brought the California horses from his mother's rancho near Taos to the valley. Pete saw the future of men from Missouri who yoked ox power to haul endless wagon-lines of wheeled freight to Santa Fe. So, Pete dug up his gold and bought three hundred head of oxen to strengthen on the high valley's blue grama, and to breed.

He hired hands as he needed them to move the stock into the valley or down to Santa Fe for sale. While in the valley, the cattle needed no tending.

The herd of a hundred Spanish blooded horses was another matter. Born to the freedom and wild grains of California, the horses needed breaking to the saddle and harness. Pete put the word out in Taos and Santa Fe for a bronco buster. He interviewed several; but, so far, none had been willing to spend his nights for long a many-day's ride from liquor and women.

Pete took up the breaking chore alone. His way was special. A good gentling took him six, maybe eight days. Instead of just mounting and spurring the horse into submission in the normal fashion of the contract busters, Pete took the first couple of days to get acquainted and to let the horse learn about the rope, the snubbing post and the man. He talked softly, even fed the horse from his hand as he worked.

By the end of the third or fourth day, the animal had worn bridle, saddle and blanket, had done his biting and kicking, head throwing and crow hopping. The fifth or sixth day he felt the weight of the man, did his protesting, learned the man would stay in the middle of his back. The rest of the time Pete taught the animal to turn on a spot, respond to the man's knees for guidance, not shy at surprise, stand against the rope and other tricks which distinguished a Cortez horse from all others.

Most of the broncs traded freedom and defiance for a kind word and a handful of rich grass sprinkled with a few kernels of corn. A Cortez broke horse stayed gentle and mindful of his master's needs.

Still, with a hundred horses, the work was slow; and he needed help.

Now, Pete gazed down on The Cortez at the mixed dots of Spanish horses and young oxen grazing along with deer and elk far below. He had come up here, as he frequently did, when he had a problem beyond the usual ache of saddle hours and loneliness. Here, at the point of his discovery of the valley, his Discovery Point, he could consider the valley and his problem as a whole.

This morning, not far from his corrals and cabin, two days ago down the stream a-ways and last week at the edge of the juniper grove, each time, he'd found an ox, dead in the grass. He found bear sign, too. Each time the droppings or a paw print were written on the ground near the slaughtered animal as if a maverick grizzly were systematically killing his beeves.

The soft under belly of each dead animal had been slashed and a good part eaten. The rest lay fly-blown and bloated. Bear for sure, except for that chunk of rump meat. And, the throats.

Funny. Each animal the same. Throats razor cut and that rump meat sliced neat as you please.

"Aint no bear can cut that clean. No, Smokey. There's a man on The Cortez. A man is killin my animals."

As Pete spoke, the smoky horse flicked her ears back, shifted her feet and snorted. Pete gave the horse a nudge with his knees and started her for home.

"Bright and early, we'll track us this ox killin man."

# 32

Although the Missouri day had started out cool and cloudy, Blair Halluck was sweating. Rivulets of moisture rolled down his well tanned brow from thick, black hair that bunched in curls across the top of his forehead. He wiped a deerhide sleeve over drooping lids which veiled black, Irish eyes which seemed always to be looking at the sunset after a grueling day on the trail.

Blair Halluck was a freighter. Since 1848, he'd carried on the trade between Independence, Missouri and Santa Fe, at first with six heavily laden wagons; then, as the years passed and his trips grew more profitable, ten wagons, until year before last, a full train of twenty five.

Last year, he'd sold his wagons and stock to concentrate on farming his section of Missouri river bottom land; but, the sunsets had never left his eyes. Now, he was back in the freighting business; or, he would be, if Colonel Joseph Alexander would give him the loan. He would need six large wagons for freight, half a hundred mules and horses and at least fifteen good men to succeed in this new venture: hauling the United States mail between Missouri and Santa Fe.

Just that month, May 1853, Blair had been awarded the contract from the government to carry the mail, monthly, from Independence to Santa Fe and back again. Now, he would have to borrow to buy the wagons and animals and to pay the men until payment from the government, always slow and iffy, could be collected.

Colonel Alexander had agreed to the loan. Blair stepped into the colonel's plush office to sign the papers and draw down the cash.

"Mister Halluck, good morning," smiled the colonel from puffy cheeks. The colonel heaved up soft bulk from behind his ornate Louis XIV desk and extended a manicured hand. "Sit you down, Sir."

"Thankee kindly, Colonel."

Halluck perched on the edge of a needle point chair which felt like it could not hold air much less Blair's two hundred pounds.

"I aint used to borrowin; and these papers seem mighty weighty." Halluck pointed to the stack of loan papers on the portly man's desk.

"Unfortunate necessity of business; but, the short of it is that I will give you the money you need and you will secure your promise to repay within the time set, with interest. That's the nut shell of it. Simple, really."

"Securin is one thing; but, my farm, the wagons, animals, the whole kit and caboodle. Seems if I have trouble on the trail and need more time, you can wipe me out. And all that I'm puttin up is worth a good deal more than ten thousand dollars."

"The excess value covers my risk."

Alexander shot a scared look at Halluck the way a melodrama actor looks out at an audience. He puckered his plump lips.

"I take due dates seriously. I must. But, of course, in unusual circumstances, I might . . . ."

"Always unusual circumstances on the trail. The time set aint much, considerin the obstacles of every trip and the government's stipulation that I make the mail run to Santa Fe in thirty days or lose the mail contract."

Halluck ran the sleeve of his deer skin jacket across his forehead again; and, again, it came away wet.

"Well, Sir, if you have doubts?" The colonel picked up the papers as if to return them to his desk drawer.

"Doubts? No, I aint got doubts it can be done. It's the shortness of time that gives me some pause."

Blair's eyes saw the trail, storms, swollen rivers, burning prairie grass smoking the horizon, dry desert crossings, the skeletons of wagons raided and burned by Indians, and the distant sunsets.

The papers in the colonel's white hand fluttered in midair, then came to rest again on the desk.

"Let's git her done," said Halluck. "A-fore my nerve turns to jelly."

His nerveless eyes tried to hold Colonel Alexander's blue; but the latter danced away above a flash of cunning smile.

"Just as you like," said the colonel.

They signed the papers, a note for ten thousand dollars at twenty percent interest, a mortgage on Halluck's section of farmland and on the wagons and animals. The colonel reached into his desk drawer and shoved a stack of bills across the desk.

"Ten thousand. Count it to be sure it's right."

"No need," said Halluck, holding the money in his hand, as if weighing it. "Thankee, Sir." Blair Halluck stood and extended a rough and scarred hand.

"It is a risky venture you embark on," said the colonel, not standing. The cunning smile snuck by the puffy cheeks, then, like the actor's, turned sincere. "I wish you luck."

"Aint the risk, I mind. That's part of the game. I've pledged my word to pay you. To me, that's worth more'n all them papers."

"I am sure of it," said the colonel now rising. "I need not remind you that payment is due, promptly due, sixty days from this date. I know you'll . . . ."

"Kin I help it, you'll get every cent, Sir, when due, if not before."

"Sixty days, then, Mister Halluck. I will see you in sixty days, or sooner."

Blair Halluck nodded and left the office. Clouds drifted with the winds aloft across the Missouri sky, pushed by a late morning sun just there on the horizon.

Government deadline, thirty days for the mail, each way, Blair thought. Alexander's deadline, sixty days—and I've given my word on it.

He walked swiftly toward the river and the wagon maker's huge barn. Well, Blair Halluck, you've got some butt-hustlin to do. That's the size of it. Deadline—or dead.

# 33

As sundown pinks and blues faded into violet, Beckey Goddard urged the team up the trail at a wearing pace. Deep purple pushed violet over the horizon; but, still, she saw no wagons, no telltale dust to mark them. The ribbon of trail disappeared into the black of night.

From time to time, the team missed the trail, sending buggy wheels into the soft sand or up and over boulders at the side of the wagon road.

The wind had died at sunset; but the cold it brought stayed into the night. Beckey pulled a shawl around her shoulders. Each jolt of the buggy pulled at her bruised body. She winced and bounced and winced to the footfalls of the gray horses.

Distant flashes of lightning lit her imagination and showed her the way. At last, she saw the far off spark of a camp fire; but it took another two hours before she reached the wagon train.

"Hold, there!" a voice whispered.

Beckey could not see Johnny Benson, one of the bullwhackers; but, she knew his voice.

"It's me. Beckey Goddard."

"Pull off by that big rock. Aint welcome in camp, I was told to say. If'n you showed. Fix your own fire."

"Oh, Johnny. I'm too tired to do anything but sleep."

She pulled the buggy off the trail, got down and unharnessed the team. Then she led the horses out into the black desert, feeling with her boots for grass. As the horses began to feed, she crawled on hands and knees to hobble their forelegs so they couldn't wander far in the night.

Then with a last ounce of strength, Beckey found her blankets in the rear of the buggy. She dove in, fully clothed. Despite the pain in her ribs and gut, she slept.

Moments later, it seemed to her, through a fog of sleep and pain, she heard Captain Gray.

"Rise and shine. Breakfast at nine!"

Beckey awoke and knew it was just past four in the morning. She'd slept about three hours. Others in the camp picked up the song.

"Rise and shine. Breakfast at nine."

She would not eat for another five hours or more.

Somehow, she managed to find and hitch the horses in time to leave with the others. In the cold predawn, she took up her position in the drag of the column. In spite of the bounce of the buggy against aching belly band and the pull of the reins, she dozed on the buggy seat through sunrise.

The new sun was shoulder high when they stopped at a thin trickle of water which twisted across the trail and curled up in a depression a hundred yards to the southeast. Beckey did not stop to unhitch; but gave the horses their heads. She was the first at the pond. The gray horses buried their dry muzzles in the shallows. Slowly, with one hand across her belly to squeeze at the pain, Beckey got down and knelt at the water to fill a water skin.

Alone and away from the others, she turned the horses loose to graze and drink, hoping they would not roam too far from her camp. She was about to leave the buggy in search of fuel for her fire, when a small boy called her name.

"Miss Beckey. I brung you some chips for a fire."

In spite of his size, his voice cracked when he spoke. He dumped a shirt full of buffalo dung at her feet and backed off.

"Thank you, Mister Brant," she said, smiling at the boy.

"Josh. Just Josh, ma'am. My pa is the only Mister Brant in our family."

"Josh, then. Care to stay and eat?"

"No ma'am. I can't." He turned to go back to the wagon train camp. "You know, I can't."

"Well, a-fore you go, tell me. How's your mama?"

"Poorly. Lays on the flour sacks in the back of the wagon and moans. Pa says she complains when the wagon rolls and when it don't, no matter which."

"She's about due, isn't she?"

"Don't know about that. Some of the other women seem to think it, though."

"Tell her I'd be glad to help if she needs . . . ."

"She won't, well, take help from you. You know . . . ."

"Tell her, just the same, please."

"I better not. Else I can't come again. To help you, and talk a minute."

"I see. Well, you call me, then, if you see she needs me."

"Maybe."

"All right. Thanks again, Josh, for the chips."

With one eye on the horses grazing contentedly nearby, Beckey rolled and dropped biscuits in hot bacon grease. While the biscuits rose, she wolfed down the salty meat between sips of scalding coffee.

Several hundred yards away, the others were busy cooking, eating, checking equipment and stock. She could hear their voices on the wind; but not what they said. The sound of forbidden voices deepened her sadness as she ate alone.

After breakfast, the train headed down the trail again with Beckey still eating their dust in the rear. They stopped at ten o'clock that night, having come almost fifty dry, sandy miles to cross the Cimarron for the second time on the way to the

Canadian. At this crossing, the river was a dry bed with a few stagnant pools growing mosquitoes.

Coyotes and, she imagined, wolves sang her to sleep under a dark canopy lit only by flickering and falling stars. Sometime late in the night, a cry woke her.

Instantly, she was wide awake. Pain cramped her belly. She pulled a box of dried fruit from under her stomach. The pain eased across her bruised middle; and she realized that the cry that had startled her from sleep was her own. Her belly-band relaxed and she rolled onto her back under the blankets.

Suddenly, another cry, a scream, sent her upright and out of the covers. She shivered as another sharp cry warmed the cold of deep night.

Beckey crawled out of the buggy and pulled a blanket over her shoulders. The noise was now commotion, cries mingled with voices, coming from the wagons. Beckey hurried over to find men running this way and that, one collecting buffalo chips in the dark to charge the fire. Another called for water. A third said, "I'll check the stock."

The cries came from Josh's wagon. Beckey stopped outside. Josh was standing alone by the rear of the wagon. As Beckey approached, she sensed that the boy was shaking, but not from the cold.

"Josh? That you? What's . . . ."

Another scream, close at hand, sent a shiver along Beckey's spine.

"Your mama's time is here!"

"Ye-ye-yes, ma'am. The others, the women, are afraid."

Beckey looked around in the dark. She saw no one coming to help the crying, birthing woman.

"Why?"

"Say somethin's wrong with Mama. One said, 'aint natural. She'll die—and the baby.'"

Beckey caught the wet in the boy's eyes from the light of the newly kindled fire.

"I'll help her all I can, Josh. Tell them to bring hot water and clean bunting. Don't you worry."

Beckey patted the boy on the shoulder and climbed into the wagon. She found the woman by following a long-noted scream. Missus Brant lay on her back pushing at the canvas top with wheeling legs. Beckey felt the bedding and it was wet.

"Your water's broken. It'll be soon now. Keep pushin. Don't be afraid to yell out."

Beckey took the writhing woman's hand and squeezed. The woman squeezed back and breathed, "thanks."

But this baby was not a "soon" baby. It hung fire past daylight, past breakfast, past all endurance. The other women watched from the back of the wagon. Finally, when the woman's strength seemed all but gone, Beckey reached in, found a foot, a leg, another leg, and pulled.

"He's backwards," she said to no one in particular. "I'm taking him feet first."

Missus Brant lay in sweat, panting out her exhaustion. The baby was a boy; but it gave no lusty cry. Beckey slapped its rump; but she knew it would never cry. A necklace of cord wrung its throat.

She finally quit slapping and wrapped the dead child in a blanket. Then she crawled out of the wagon to the bright of new day and the hostile stares of the people gathered around.

A thick man shouldered past the women. "My wife?" is all he said.

"Exhausted. Resting. I don't know. She's had a hard time, Mister Brant."

Josh came over to stand by his father. He looked up to see the sleepless fear in the man's face.

"The child, a boy, is still-born. I'm sorry. I wrapped him in a . . . ."

"You!" A large busted woman pointed a shaking finger at Beckey. "You done it!" she screamed. "Killed that child and, more'n likely, the mother, too."

Beckey took a step back from the seething bosom of the accuser. She put a hand to her mouth, saw it was covered with mother's blood.

"How can you say such a thing. The baby came out backwards, feet first, with the cord wrapped around his neck. See for yourself."

Beckey pointed to the opening of death in the canvas and the small bundle entombed in the wet blanket.

The buxom woman did not move. She still shook her finger at Beckey.

Mister Brant slowly moved to the opening and reached into the wagon. They saw his back and shoulders freeze for an instant in the sunlight and then begin to shake.

"Martha. Martha." He sobbed the name. "Martha!"

Josh walked to his father and took his hand. Mister Brant looked left, then right, then down at his son.

"She's gone, boy. Your ma, the baby. Both gone to the Lord."

<hr>

"Move 'um out. We've time to make up."

Beckey heard the distant call of Captain Gray's command. She was ready. She hadn't attended to the trail side burial. The buxom woman had seen to that, and Missus Schyler. Exhausted, she had trudged back to her buggy camp, eaten a breakfast of cold, hard biscuit and dried fruit and curled up on her blanket bed to await the call to leave.

Now the grays were hitched and eager after almost a whole day's rest. Black clouds had piled up in the western sky; and she could see threads of rain sowing new life in the land ahead. She watched the wagons slowly snake out of the death camp and into the deep ruts, cut in the earth by years of wheels-west, which marked the way to the Canadian River and Fort Union beyond.

Beckey said her own silent Presbyterian goodbye as the buggy passed the two small mounds of sand on the edge of the dry Cimarron. From the last wagon, now far ahead, she saw Josh looking long at her. Then, slowly at first, his hand went up; and he waved.

"Takes a child to understand," Beckey said to herself as she waved back.

Suddenly, wind whipped rain-threads soaked her and blinded her eyes. Thunder pounded the ground. Lightning forked the trail. In a matter of minutes the drenching squall passed over the trail, pushed east by a lowering sun. Long after the sun-dried wind had sucked all moisture from Beckey's clothes and hair and face, wet pools stained her eyes and dusty cheeks.

It took nearly five days to reach the Canadian River. Along the way, Beckey wondered at the vast networks made by the prairie dogs. For hours she watched the animal antics.

Each time she approached a village, rodent heads popped from the earth. A hundred eyes watched her for a moment; and then, instead of disappearing into the safety of their holes, the creatures jumped up and ran to their neighbors, chattering all the way. More dogs appeared until the entire village was out on sand hills to watch her approach.

Many formed into committees. They seemed to confer. As fast as one committee formed and its members deliberated, its members scampered away to join new groups. Always the dog chatter continued.

Finally, at the moment agreed on by committee, each dog dove for the nearest hole; and, in an instant, all were gone as Beckey passed too close for comfort.

At Rock Creek, the wagons stopped early to fix supper before the night time drive. Just as Beckey was unhitching the grays, a great commotion of dust and shouts and tramping hooves surged from the sunset.

Out of the dust cloud rode a band of Mexicans, sombreros flying in the wind, rifles waving in their hands. This band camped about a mile west of the wagons. They proved to be an advance party of buffalo hunters, about one hundred and fifty men and five hundred animals in all.

Beckey learned from Josh that the Mexicans came from a small town called Taos in the New Mexico mountains. They hunted buffalo each spring and fall. The butchered meat was dried in camp and sold as far south as El Paso in Texas and Jaurez in Chihuahua, Old Mexico.

Josh brought her a loaf of Taos bread, coarse, dark and sweet, which one of the hunters had given to him.

"Them Mexicans have liquor they call 'aguardiente.' I tasted it when Pa wasn't lookin. Didn't like it; but Pa and the freighters took to it some, Captain Gray included."

Beckey could hear the loud talking from the wagon camp.

"I can hear them takin to it," she said with a laugh.

The next morning broke cold and clear. Far to the west, Beckey saw a sweep of tall mountains, still snow-crowned.

"The Sangre de Cristos," she heard Captain Gray say.

"The Sangre de Cristos," she whispered to herself, wondering at the strange sound of the words and their meaning for her.

They breakfasted that day at the Point of Rocks and reached the Canadian River in the evening. The wagons crossed the river before stopping; but Beckey was afraid to risk it alone in the dark. So, she camped on the east bank to await the dawn.

The next morning, a shout from Captain Gray aroused her from a sound sleep. Quickly, she chased down the horses and, fumbling in the dark and cold, she managed to back them into the traces. Then she climbed up on the buggy seat to shiver under her shawl and await first light.

Slowly, the new dawn began to creep under night's veil, so slowly that she was surprised to see the river banks and ribbon of water emerge before her eyes as if just created that instant.

First she heard the splashes, then saw someone wadding the river toward her.

"It aint deep and the bottom's sandy and smooth," Josh said. "You can make her easy this mornin." Josh stopped at the heads of the horses and checked the rig. "You're all hitched up. If you want, I'll walk by the horses while you cross. See they don't act up on you."

"Thank you, Josh. I guess it's light enough."

Beckey shuddered as she remembered the Cimarron and the tree-trunk ride in its cold waters. She nudged the horses with the reins and spoke quietly,

"Gee up, now."

The buggy began to roll toward the river. Josh held the near horse's halter as the matched pair stepped into the shallow water.

"This aint nothin," he called back to her.

In the soft blue light, she could see the wagons several hundred yards ahead of her, already on the move.

"I'm all right, Josh. You'll have to run to catch up, unless you want to ride with me."

Before the boy could answer, she saw a horse and rider emerge from the rear most wagon and race toward them.

"Looks like Pa's seen me," said Josh with a tremor in his breaking voice. "I better hoof it."

Quickly, the boy waded across the river and began dog trotting up the trail. The rider flew on past him and into the river. He almost did a header with the grays; but his madly running horse reared at the last minute and turned aside.

In their turn, the grays reared and plunged. Beckey lost the reins. The grays were running now, out of the river and across the boulder and sand desert. The reins blew by her face like lacy ribbons. She reached for the lace; it fluttered away.

Beckey screamed and held on as the buggy bounced and lurched. The wind of speed pounded the breath from her lungs.

And then the wild ride was over. The grays had pulled up sharp at the edge of a deep, wide gully. The buggy slued around them and stopped with a sudden, sharp snap at the brink. It was down by the right front wheel which lay spoke-shattered in the sand.

Beckey was almost pitched out of the buggy by the wheel's impact cross-ways of a large boulder. She could scarcely breathe as she scrambled to stay on the leaning buggy seat. She looked into the deep of the gully, peopled by jagged rocks whose knife points were just then tipped by the first shafts of the morning sun.

Brant rode up to her. He sat his lathered horse, careful to avoid the plunging of its head, and stared.

"Help me, please," panted Beckey.

The man laughed then.

"Help you? The way you helped my Martha to the grave? Gladly!"

Becky Goddard felt the shame heat her cheeks as she listened to him curse her.

"Whore! Godless whore!" Brant shouted at her and wagged his fist in the air. Then he raced his horse around and around her broken down buggy.

Suddenly, he pulled his horse to a sharp stop. Dust flew over her and into her eyes where she sat sideways on the leaning seat.

"Now you've come to your just deserts," he panted. " 'Less'n a Indian finds you before your time, you'll whore no more, I'm a-thinkin."

"Nooo!" The protest crawled from deep in her soul. "You're wrong! Wrong about me! Wrong!" Beckey's soul cried out. "Oh, Mister Brant, I did the best I could for your wife and baby."

"Had no business doin anythin."

"None of the others, the women, were helping. Can't you see. She was alone and scared. I think she knew the baby was backwards. I held her hand is all, to give her what little comfort I could."

Brant sat his horse and looked down at Beckey.

"All I know is she's dead. And the baby. And what Missus Schyler says."

He pulled up on the reins of the dancing horse; then let them out as the horse's head shot down between its forelegs.

"The Schyler woman lies. Not about what happened to me, but why. I would never . . . ."

But Brant was suddenly gone. He galloped his horse back to the last wagon of the train now some ways on down the trail. He left Beckey and her broken buggy, alone, in the middle of the road to Santa Fe.

"Why can't they understand?" Beckey cried out to the empty sky.

"They'll be back. They won't leave me here to die."

For a long time Becky watched through tears perched on the lips of her eyes as the wagons receded until their dust almost disappeared. Then the tears fell off their perch and washed dust-trails down her sun-red cheeks.

Past the wind of afternoon, she still sat on the crooked seat until there was nothing more to see except the vast emptiness of the desert. The buggy was down to the right. The front axle was broken. The shattered wheel lay in the sand.

The setting sun cast its pastel magic over the desert; but, Beckey didn't see the magic or feel its spell. The last rays mixed gold with purple; and the wind stopped.

The rear of the buggy was open to the east where the shadows rushed in and where the sun would rise.

Her horses stood quietly now on the edge of the ravine, still in the traces. Now and then, one would switch a fly with its tail or nuzzle the dirt with his nose.

It was after dark when she finally got down from the buggy. She unhitched the horses and hobbled them to do the best they could on the short grass and grease-wood brush by the side of the gully.

Then she searched the back of the buggy for something to eat. In the last of the twilight, she ate jerked buffalo and dried fruit—and remembered.

The members of the wagon train had turned nasty after Missus Schyler gos-siped Beckey's disgrace to the party.

"Claimed rape; but went willin enough," Missus Schyler said as if she had been there to see.

"Missus James found them together. Right there in the middle of the school house. Mister James, her own husband, and her with three babes and one on the way—and this here Goddard woman.

"I don't need to tell you what Missus James found them a-doin. Couldn't tell it if I had to."

Missus Schyler looked all around the camp. She pointed a sharp finger.

"Well, Missus James went straight to the preacher. A meeting was convened and they was brought into the church, chalk on their faces, and guilt. 'Confess your sins,' says the preacher.

"'I aint done nothin,' says Mister James, sheepish like.

Missus Schyler stood in the firelight, bony finger still pointing.

"Cryin and shakin, this here Goddard woman says, 'I was clearing the books and things like I always do after school. Suddenly, there's Mister James. Just stand-ing at the door and looking at me. I ask him, "what can I do for you?" All he does is shut the door and grab me. He's too strong for me and he hurts me. And that's all.'

"No one believed her. Right there in church, the congregation cried her down. Her own pa put her out. We brung her with us out-a kindness."

"That was not the way of it," Beckey yelled at the empty desert. "But that's the way they believe it was."

Beckey found an apple and three biscuits left over from morning as a finish to her dark supper, and her remembering. Then she crawled into the back of the buggy, pulled her blankets around her chin and slept the stars toward sunlight.

A half-mile away the red crescent of the new sun nosed the morning over the mound of a sandy hill. Black against the arc of flame, three horsemen sat there, motionless, watching the matched grays crop the dew crested grass. Beads of Comanche-eyes coveted the horses and the white woman so peacefully asleep in the bent-down buggy, her pale face aglow in the sun-filled bow of the buggy top.

# 34

The morning sun's arc of flames cooked the dew from the grass and misted the surface of the mountain stream.

Pete Cortez stood at the doorway of the cabin high on the north buttress of the valley. He sniffed the cool morning, a cold biscuit jammed between even, white teeth. He looked east and saw the sun gently cupping the tops of the cottonwoods along the Canadian River just about as far as the squinted eye could see.

"Time to see about that ox killin man," he said to the new morn.

He pulled the Colt Dragoon pistol from its holster and tapped each of the balls back into its nesting place in the cylinder to make sure the powder end of each paper cartridge was tight against its touch hole. He pressed each cap hard upon the nipple and eased the hammer down. Then he picked up the Sharps rifle, lowered the lever and inserted a paper cartridge in the breech. He pulled the lever up to cut the paper and expose the powder to the vent at the rear of the breech. He pressed a percussion cap on the nipple and dropped the hammer to half-cock. Armed for bear or man, he thought.

He walked to the corral and caught up the smoky horse. Within minutes, he was down the trail headed toward the last ox kill.

The dead animal lay stinking and bloated in a pile of gorging flies. Pete searched the area along the stream for tracks; saw none. The first kill had been close to the desert lip of the valley; the next higher up; this one higher still. The man is climbin my valley, Pete thought. Climbin like a vulture on wings, 'cause I see no boot tracks in the sand. Mighty sly of foot, this climbin man. He turned Smokey upstream. He'll stay near water; lay low in the can-see; kill and eat at night.

Pete trudged the horse along the sandy bank of the stream looking for tracks, sniffing the light morning air for wood smoke. Man can't fly; got to cook that tough ox meat; got to drink.

From time to time, Pete crossed and recrossed the slow moving giggle of water. His black eyes cut the sand for sign. An hour later and a mile upstream, he came to a large stand of junipers, so thick along the bank that he had to ride in the winding creek with Smokey's fetlocks pushing half circles against the current. Under the flow, Smokey's dainty hooves hit rock river bed with a clack and a splash.

"Shuss," whispered Pete. "That ox killin man'll hear us sure." Pete slowed the horse. The clacks and splashes were farther apart; but just as loud. "Damn!"

Wading the smoky horse upstream, Pete circled clumps of overhanging branches until he came to a break in the trees. There, in a back eddy along the bank, he found the first track. A bear track, three hands long and two wide. A trickle from the back eddy's pocket had filled the bear track by half. Not more than an hour old, thought Pete.

Pete shifted in the saddle and looked as far as he could see through the dark overhang of branches. Nothing was visible. Still, Pete felt uneasy. He put his hand on the stock of the Sharps, ready to pull it from the saddle scabbard.

The smoky horse tossed her head and gamboled dainty feet from side to side. Pete laughed at his own jitters.

"Quiet, Smokey. No need to fuss just yet."

With both hands on the reins, Pete steadied the horse and dismounted to study the bear sign.

"Big fella, this bear. Whoa! What's this?"

Next to the bear track, almost hidden by the arm of a juniper which leaned over the water as if to drink, he saw the barefoot print of a man. Pete pulled the branch aside. Water was just beginning to seep into the impression. Fresh as Mama's sopaipillas hot from the grease. He smiled as he got back up on Smokey.

"Let's go find this ox killin man," he whispered.

Pete turned Smokey into the break in the stunted trees. Slowly, he rode into the shade. Here and there, he saw prints in the sand; but he could not tell if they were made by bear or man. Branches whispered off his chaps, caught at his hat, spilled needles down the neck of his buckskin shirt. The plop of the horse's footfalls sounded like thunder, the creak of saddle leather like the hinges of a dozen rusty doors swinging in the wind.

A sudden explosion! Pete arched in the saddle as if struck by a lightning bolt. Smokey crow-hopped and stood quivering. A monstrous whir cut through the overhang of shadow. Branches jumped and dust flew. Pete's hand hit the butt of the pistol before he could laugh at his own fright.

"Quail" he repeated to his subconscious. A huge covey of perhaps thirty birds whirred through low branches and ran in the sand across the narrow path.

The violent wing-thunder ceased almost as quickly as it began. The birds settled in hiding and cautiously clucked reassurance to each other, and to Pete. He pushed Smokey forward against the steady buzz of flies and the hum of bees. He kept his hand on the pistol butt.

The bear tracks or the man tracks, which, he could not tell, walked in front of him along the sandy path as it twisted this way and that through the trees.

Just before he rounded the next bend in the tree shrouded trail, he smelled the scent of fresh death. Smokey smelled it too and stopped. Pete urged the horse forward. As he slowly made the turn, he saw the ox lying across the trail, gutted from crotch to breastbone.

Then, he saw the grizzly down on all fours. His forepaws were on the ox's ribcage. A string of entrails hung with blood and slobber from powerful jaws not ten feet in front of Pete's staring eyes.

At sight of the bear, the smoky horse snorted through wide nostrils, threw her head and pranced backwards in an attempt to turn away. Pete dug in spurs; grabbed for the rifle; missed.

The bear turned its head. Pig eyes glowed red like anger in the dusky glen of death.

With a scream the horse reared and crashed sideways into the clumped junipers and fell. Pete hit the trees with his right shoulder and then his face. Smokey lunged up. Pete reached for the saddle horn; but the trees held him. With a crash, Smokey was jumping over and around and through the trees. In an instant, the horse was gone.

Stunned, Pete tried to wrench himself free of the grasping branches. His shoulder hurt and his face was scratched and bleeding; but, finally, he stood. His breathing came and went in short spurts. He looked down the trail and sucked wind; but it froze in his throat.

The great grizzly was rearing up on hind legs, gore dripping from bared teeth; so close, Pete felt hot bear breath on his cheek; smelled the blood and the anger. With a low growl, the bear raised his right forepaw. His jaws snapped shut just inches from Pete's face.

Pete heard the angry roar and the click of snapping teeth. He took a step back into waiting juniper arms. His hand flashed to the Colt; but his holster was empty. He sensed rather than saw the mighty swing of the clawed paw.

Just then, a shaft of the rising sun flashed like lightning into the dark forest; but for Pete Cortez, caught in the juniper's embrace, there was only the thump and roar of thunder.

The great bear dropped to all fours and sniffed the inert man, pushed the quiet form a time or two with the three-hand paw. Then the bear turned and lumbered up the trail to the ox carcass. Again, as if horse and man had never intruded upon his breakfast, he stuck his snout inside the split belly and began to feed.

He ignored the large, open wound on the ox's rump where five pounds of prime meat had been sliced off razor clean.

# 35

Colonel Alexander steepled pudgy fingers and puffed his weighty cheeks at the man sitting across the desk from him.

"For reasons that suit me," he said. "I want to see a man delayed on his way to Santa Fe."

Red Hickman looked at Colonel Alexander with one eye. The other was purple and puffed shut.

"What man?"

Hickman tried to speak through fist-swollen lips and winced.

"Man named Blair Halluck. Freighter. Has the new mail contract. If he can make the run to Santa Fe in thirty days or less."

"I know him," said Hickman. "I worked bullwacker for him a time or two. He don't like me much. Nor me him."

Hickman started to rub the shut eye, hesitated and looked at the colonel.

"I musta run into a hard man last night. I don't usually look like this after a saloon fight."

"You don't remember?"

"I was some drunk."

"I heard you called a man some names he didn't like. Something about 'flesh peddler, niggah chasing son of a bitch.'"

"I might have."

"Seems the man is an Ozark sheriff from around Lebanon. Potter by name. He and his posse are looking for an escaped slave who murdered his master in cold blood. They think the slave is headed down the Santa Fe Trail."

The colonel slapped a pudgy hand on the desk and laughed.

" 'Flesh peddler.' From the look of you, he took offense."

"Damned if he didn't. Musta been a hell of a fight. And, I can't recollect it."

His open eye blinked and his face screwed up in a show of disappointment.

"That sheriff musta looked a sight, if he lived."

"Sheriff Potter? He and his posse rode out this morning. Not a mark on him." Colonel Alexander smiled. "I surely hope you'll do better with what I have in mind for you."

"That makes two of us, Colonel. Why, there's many the time I marked a man bad or worse'n he marked me last night. Aint nothin . . . . "

"Look here Hickman. To business. I do not want Halluck to, let us say, succeed. A broken wheel here. Lost stock. A bullwacker laid up. A mad Indian who makes a visit with his friends. Cholera. Anything can happen on the trail. I want you to see that it does."

"Anything, Colonel?"

"That's up to you."

Red Hickman smiled. "When did Halluck pull out?"

"Almost a week now. It'll take some hard riding to catch up. Can you . . . ?"

"Easy. Providin the price is right."

Colonel Alexander pushed a stack of silver coins across the desk at Hickman.

"A hundred dollars now. A hundred more if Halluck does not make Santa Fe within the month. Two hundred more if he and the mail don't get there at all!"

Hickman scooped the coins into his hat. Swollen lips parted in what passed as a smile. He stood and stuffed the coins from his hat into the pockets of his cheap wool coat.

"Hundred's better'n I had all winter. Two hundred's better still. And, maybe killin Halluck. That beats all."

"I did not say anything about killing." Colonel Alexander struggled his bulk from the chair.

Hickman turned to leave. Stopped. He looked over his shoulder at the colonel. The closed eye opened a slit as if to wink.

"Killin is what you meant."

The colonel raised a fat hand in protest; but Hickman was gone.

Colonel Alexander slid back into the soft chair and smiled.

# 36

The smoky horse stood fetlock deep in the stream, her muzzle sucking water. Her charcoal flanks shook. Between drinks, she raised her head, pulling the dragging reins from the water, and sniffed the quiet air with nostrils flared.

A man crept ever so slowly from the brush toward the horse. The man stepped bare feet, toes pointed down, into the stream.

With a sudden lunge, he seized one rein, then the other and rolled easily up into the saddle. The smoky horse quivered, arched her back and bucked high in the air. Pounding hooves sent water flying over horse and man. But, the man stuck to the saddle like molasses to a griddle cake.

After a couple of crow-hops, Smokey settled down, aware that the man would stay in the saddle as good as Pete. But, the horse's nose told him the man was not Pete. Legs still a-quiver, the horse looked around at the new rider.

He was a stranger. Stranger than strange, the man's feet were bare, bare legs showed through long, vertical splits in old cotton pants. The legs wore pink scars, some just scabbing over, across ebony skin. The remnants of pants were cinched around a slim waist with a piece of rope. He wore no shirt. More scars welted in pink slashes across his smoky chest and back.

The man leaned over the saddle horn to pat the horse's neck with a hand as big and hard as a skillet. The hand dangled from a long, thin arm. As the hand and arm moved, they seemed to be joined to each other and to the man with puppet strings.

He smiled down at the horse through a picket fence of pointed teeth. His tall, bony face disbursed the sunshine like wax off a glossy, black boot. Kinky hair flecked with white topped the man off.

Without a word, he leaned the reins over Smokey's neck in the direction from which she had just fled. The horse balked. Thick bare heels dug into her ribs and her Cortez training.

Slowly, horse and rider entered the shaded path into the trees.

Pete Cortez watched a dizzy whirl of brush and dust, flies and slits of red sky. He'd seen the inside of dizzy before when Garrard had bounced a musket ball off his head; and he knew to wait until the spinning slowed. He heard a groan; did not recognize it as his own. Then, he heard the slurp and rip of flesh being torn from the ox and remembered the grizzly. Again, he groaned as the whirl inside his head went faster with remembering.

Then silence.

The slurping and rip of flesh stopped.

Silence.

Pete opened his eyes. The spinning inside his head began to turn in slower, wider circles. He heard the flies buzzing and the sharp crack of a branch. A cold nose touched his. He smelled the breath of decayed meat.

The great bear licked his cheek where it ran with blood from deep scratches. Pete saw beady black eyes inches from his own; heard the pulsing sniff-sniff, felt the thick tongue on his face; and smelled the blood smeared muzzle. The mouth opened. Filtered light flamed and flickered on sharp, white teeth caked with ox flesh.

The black man sat the smoky horse watching the bear nuzzle the face of the white man lying in the grasp of juniper branches. The black man smiled. His pink tongue wet protruding lips. He held the smoky horse still with the iron grip of his skinny knees. He saw the huge mouth of the bear ease open, saw the purple skin of the muzzle slide over the glint of saw-teeth in a dance of sunlight.

Suddenly, he saw the white man lash out. A balled fist hit the bear square on the tip of its nose. With mouth wide open, the huge bear squealed like a baby and put a giant paw to its nose. Then with a crack, the jaws slammed shut on air, saw-teeth just a breath away from the fisted hand that swung again and again against the grizzly's pug nose.

The black man watched the bear step back from the flying fist and rise on hind legs. Front paws high, the bear raised up on tip toes to plunge down on the fist waving body. The black man laughed out loud; but his hand went to the stock of the Sharps rifle, still in the saddle scabbard.

Pete saw the great bear rise over him poised to pound him with claws and teeth and tons of death. He squirmed and pushed and pulled to free himself from the juniper's grip. He moved a little; but the bear moved too. Pete's whole world was filled with the bulk of fur-belly, paw-claws and saw-teeth. He tried to hide behind closed eyes; but the bear held him wide eyed.

A rumble hit Pete's ears. The grizzly took a sudden step back. One paw came down to its side. Then the other. The great bulk seemed to sag onto haunches. The head poked out at Pete. The back feet came up. The bear sat on its rump and rolled over on its side. The huge bulk shuddered, froze. Then it collapsed in on itself.

"Madre de Dios." Pete exhaled the last breath he had taken so long ago. He felt the sweat sting his eyes, heard the forest come to life again with the buzz of flies, smelled the animal smells mixed with rising dust from the bear.

He could see that the bear had fallen against the trunk of the juniper that had held him prisoner. Slowly, he rolled away from the branches and into the dust of the trail. He lay in the dust for a long time sucking wind and regaining his belief in the continuation of life.

Pete saw the dainty hooves of the smoky horse before he heard the footfalls stop next to his head.

"Smokey," he said, a catch in his voice. He grabbed a leg to pull himself up; but the horse backed off.

"Where you keep loads for this here 'gator gun," Pete heard a gravely, accented voice say. He looked up and saw the black man sitting high above him in the saddle.

The black man sat slumped in the saddle seat. The Sharps hung from a skillet-hand. The rifle and the hand seemed to dangle from a string-arm. The picket fence smile flashed pure white from the man's bony, bootblack face.

Watchfully, Pete pulled himself to one knee, then got to his feet.

"You're him," said Pete still pulling for breath.

"Who's 'him?'" said the black man, still smiling.

"You're the ox killin man. Four with this one," said Pete, pointing to the carcass lying across the trail.

Slowly, one at a time, the black man held up three fingers of his right hand. "Tha's right enough."

"I said four," said Pete. "I only see three fingers."

"They's four fingers up. You all might miss the little finger 'cause it got cut off an' you all can't see it so good; but, it's up with the rest. Four."

Pete looked for the little finger; could not even see a stump.

"All right."

Pete walked over to look at the bear. He heard the creak of saddle leather and in an instant the black man was beside him. He held a two foot long knife in his hand.

"Gonna skin him some bear meat. Your ox meat am tough."

"Raw? I reckon it is," said Pete, keeping an eye on the knife and missing the Colt right then.

"He don't have no fixins. No flint, no tinder. 'Sides, fire make smoke."

Pete poked the bear a time or two with his boot and then sat down on the haunch. He looked the bear over and then the man.

"Who the hell are you? How come you're way up here?"

"Dibble. He come here to eat ox meat." Dibble stood with legs slightly apart, the knife poised in his skillet hand.

Pete laughed; then put a hand to the hurt in his head which had not fully stopped its spin. He shook his head.

"That bear fetched me a hell of a knock."

"Dibble see. From the blood."

"Dibble? What the hell's a dibble?"

"That's him," said the black man pointing to his chest with the knife. "Dibble."

"Dibble? What kinda name is that for a slave."

"Massa say, 'a boy wicked as y'all must-a come from the Dibble.' So, he am Dibble. Slave? He aint no more. Dibble starve, he die. But he won't be no slave to no man—again."

Dibble knelt beside the bear and slit his belly with the long knife. Pete saw that the knife was razor sharp. He searched for the pistol. The Colt lay in the sand among the roots of a juniper clump. Pete picked it up and wiped and blew sand from the action. Satisfied the Colt would work if need be, Pete filled the holster.

He turned to the black man, saw the pink welts across his bare back and the bony arms slicing away at the bear skin as Dibble rolled it back from the ribs. Dibble whistled a dry whistle as he worked.

My God, thought Pete. This is one skinny black man. Thin as a barefaced lie. If he's filled his meat bag from my oxen, it don't show. Pete saw the man's neck muscles bow and jump like India rubber bands as the narrow head bobbed with the work. He's near gone before my eyes.

"Scrape the hide clean," said Pete. "I'll want it. Pile the choice meat on the hide. And wait." Pete started for the smoky horse.

"You all askin or tellin," said Dibble.

Pete turned to look at the black man. Dibble was on his feet, the knife poised in his three-fingered hand. The veins bulged purple and pulsing along bone arms. He panted slightly.

"Tellin! You owe me four oxen killed and left to rot. Take you the summer'n more to work that off." Pete put his hand on the butt of the Colt.

For a moment, Dibble said nothing. Pete thought he saw a flash of give-up in his eyes. Then Dibble said, "Dibble owe for the oxen, now that you've catched him."

The voice was deep and slow.

"But you owe Dibble."

"Owe?"

"For your life!" Dibble stared Pete in the eye. There was no give-up in that look.

"I took that into account. Out here it's no more than one man does for another."

"Here or back in Missouri, you owe. 'Less'n y'all figure you don't owe nothin to no niggah."

"You got sand, boy; but you don't know nothin." Pete smiled. "Out here you're a man or you're not. If'n you're a man, Gringo, Mexican, Indio, black man. Don't matter, except in talk. If you're not a man, well . . . ." Pete smiled a knowing smile.

"I need a horse buster," he said, "and you're him. Give me a man's work and you'll get a man's pay and found."

"Y'all pay Dibble. Dibble work." The black man's face screwed into a question mark. "What's this 'horse buster?'"

Pete laughed. "You don't know how to gentle a wild horse, you'll learn on the seat of your pants in the saddle."

"Aint a horse born Dibble can't gentle." A broad smile made the sharp cheek bones arch and wide nostrils slant up.

"We'll see," said Pete. "Now skin that bear. I'll be along directly with animals to pack the meat and hide to the cabin."

"Yassa massa." The words cut a challenge in the air. Dibble stared at Pete.

"Name of Pete Cortez. This valley and all that's in it is mine."

"You includin Dibble in that 'mine,' Mister Cortez?"

White teeth gleamed even in the shaded light of the glen; but the show of picket-fence teeth was not a smile.

Pete chuckled and shook his head back and forth. "You're some touchy, aint you?"

"Gettin the lay of the land, Mister Cortez." The white gleam vanished. "If you been where Dibble been, you be touchy, like Dibble."

The man glanced down, then up again. Pete saw the criss-crossed scars on rib bone and legs; and sensed what the man meant.

"Sensible. And you call me Pete. That's American for Pedro, the Spanish name my mama gave me."

"Dibble think on it."

The sharp ridge of high cheek bones had settled back to flat and bony; but the question mark was still in his look.

"Dibble, he aint never called a white man by his given name."

⁂

Pete sat in front of the fire place in a chair made of boards left over from the cabin. Fat bear meat sizzled in the frying pan.

"They after you?" he asked.

Dibble squatted on the dirt floor scraping bits of clinging flesh from the underside of the great bear skin. Now and then he stuck a bare foot out to the fire. Faded long johns hung loose around his ankles under balloon-size cotton jeans from

Pete's possibles bag. A deerskin shirt sagged from his shoulders like unstuck wallpaper. He looked up at Pete; but the knife still angled up and down across the hide.

"Does they follow? Dibble do believe so. Massa were a powerful man. At first Dibble hear they dogs and he run. Run clear across Missouri, 'till he don't hear no more dogs. Hire on at the river. Freight man say forty dollars if Dibble ride drag and not lose none of the animals."

Pete turned the meat, jumped as grease sparked his hand.

"What freighter?"

"A Mister Halluck. Takin the mail and goods to Santa Fe."

"You was drovin Cortez stock. I know Halluck. Good man."

"Right enough. We was six or seven days out when a fella rode in. A Mister Hickman. Red hair, purple eye just healin.

"Durin the talk, he say a posse is in Independence lookin for a runaway slave. Mister Halluck look at Dibble; but he don't say nothin. Hickman say they posse is gonna chase this slave right on to Santa Fe. Say he killed his massa."

"Did you?"

"That night, Dibble take he some bacon and a horse and run some more. Bacon soon gone. Horse give out. Feets bring Dibble here."

"Did you kill your master?"

Dibble kept his eyes on the hide. The only sound was the rip-rap of the knife on the hide and an occasional grease-pop from the frying meat.

Pete pulled the meat from the pan and cut it in two. He scooped some beans from a pot by the side of the fire on to tin plates for each of them. He handed a plate to the silent black man.

"Well, aint likely any posse'll come lookin up here," Pete said through a mouthful of meat and beans.

Dibble nodded thanks to the plate and grabbed the chunk of bear meat in his skillet-sized fist. In an instant, the meat slid past chewing before teeth could catch it. He gulped for air. Then he dug the knife into the beans. He sucked the beans off the knife blade without drawing lip-blood or losing a single bean. When his plate was clean, he looked up at Pete.

"Dibble aint et such goodsome beans in a while." He smacked protruding lips.

"Help yourself. I put in extra. Fry some more bear meat. Get some fat on you; or my horses'll be a-breakin you."

The black man threw a two pound chunk of meat into the frying pan and put it on the fire. Then he filled the plate with beans and sucked them up, again without a cut lip or a bean missed. He scraped at the hide while the meat sizzled.

Pete finished eating and put his plate down on the stone hearth. Walking to the far end of the small room, he picked up some rawhide strips from one of the four bunks and came back to sit by the fire. The loose strips of hide dangled from the end of what would become a lariat already partly completed. The finished end was tied to the bunk. In his hand, Pete twisted and wove three rawhide strands together.

Dibble ate the second chunk of meat more slowly and some of it got chewed on the way down. After he was done, he picked up the plates and the frying pan and walked out of the cabin.

Pete kept at the rawhide rope for longer than it would take any man to rinse a couple of plates. Just as he was about to get up and look out the door, it opened.

"If'n it takes you that long to clean up plates, I'll never get no horses broke." Pete was not smiling.

"Long walk to the creek," said Dibble looking surprised.

"The creek? You mean the stream in the valley?" Pete laughed out loud. "You went clear on down the mountainside to wash in the stream?"

He bent over laughing. Dibble said nothing. Pete got up when he could slow his splitting sides.

"Come here."

He led Dibble out of the cabin and around to the side. Not ten feet from the cabin, a flow of water, silver under the low-rising moon, slid quietly down the slope of the high buttress above the cabin. The water was funneled from the high side of the hill along a wooden flume into a large barrel next to the cabin. The spill-over fell from the barrel into another flume which took the flow back to the spring on the downhill side.

"Barrel's always fresh and full. Runnin water. Neat as you please."

The moonlight pooled in the black man's eyes. "Could-a told Dibble," said the black man, a pout sounding in his voice.

"Man has to learn for himself," said Pete. "But I should-a showed you around some before dark. We'll do it in the mornin. You'll see it all. The Cortez. What's here now. What will be."

Pete stuck his head in the water barrel, shook the water from his long, black hair and rubbed the claw marks on the side of his face and head.

"Still hurts some," he said. "That was one big bear."

"Dibble kill him." Moon-eyes flashed pride.

"My Sharps was what killed him. You was just lucky." Pete chuckled.

"Dibble lucky. Pete lucky."

"I see what you mean. C'mon. I need some sleep a-fore I can stand to watch you eat again. I'm plumb wore out."

Still rubbing his sore head, Pete led the way around the cabin to the door. He went in. Dibble did not.

"C'mon." Pete looked out the door and saw the black man walking toward the corral. "Where you goin, boy."

"To sleep."

"Out there? With the critters and the cold?"

Pete saw the black man's shadowy figure stop and turn.

"Niggahs," said Dibble quietly as a matter of fact without complaint. "Niggahs always sleeps with critters and cold."

The figure turned away.

"Hold up there," said Pete. "On The Cortez, a man can sleep where he wants long as he does his job. Most of the hands sleep in the cabin. That's what the bunks are for. Suit your ownself, though."

The shadowy figure stopped and turned again. "Niggah hands sleep on them bunks?" Pete saw moonlight in the eyes.

"Don't know. Aint had any such hands. Maybe they're some uppity—about sleepin with the regular hands."

Slowly, the shadowy figure moved toward the cabin. In the firelight from the doorway, Pete saw the eyes glisten.

"Aint no promise," said Dibble. "But he give it a lick."

Pete and Dibble stood under high clouds hinting at the pink to come in the dawn sky. They looked over a dozen of Pete's Spanish horses in the pole corral.

"Massa say, 'dig in spurs, club they heads, salt they cuts. Break them horses.'"

"Aint my way," said Pete.

"Aint Dibble's, neither. He tell Massa: 'Spur and club and salt. Horse may mind after a while; but he still wild inside or he dead inside. Either way, can't trust no horse like that.' Massa tell Dibble: 'spur and club and salt; or Massa break Dibble same like he break horse.'"

"Them are spur cuts all over you?"

"Spur cuts. Nails on the end of they rawhide whip. Salt the worst, though."

The black man looked off at the far desert beyond the valley.

"Dibble weren't never no horse. Massa can't ride Dibble nor trust him. Dibble stay wild inside and out. Massa cut Dibble once more too much. Dibble slit Massa from balls to breakfast."

He made a sweeping upward motion with a skillet hand and glanced at Pete.

"Dibble gentle a horse kindly. It take longer; but, when he done, that horse know Dibble. He friend. Dibble trust horse. Horse trust Dibble. That be horse man can depend on."

"That's my way," said Pete. "Seems we'll get along."

"Seems," said Dibble. He picked up a lariat and jumped the pole corral.

"You work your way through that dozen, there's plenty more hidin out in the tall grass." Pete swept the valley with his arm.

After a few days, Pete was satisfied that Dibble knew horses and how to bust them Pete's way.

One morning, Pete saddled Smokey and threw a pack tree on a mule.

"Way you eat," said Pete as Dibble passed him on the way to the corral. "We need grub. Flour, sugar, coffee and such. Halluck should be near the Canadian; or maybe across by now. He'll sell me supplies and save me a week or so it'd take to ride to Fort Union or across the high mountain to Taos."

Dibble said nothing; but walked slowly from the middle of the corral to the pole fence. He looked at the smoky horse, the mule and at Pete.

"What Dibble do?"

"What you're a-doin."

"You leave Dibble alone—with Cortez horses?"

"Sure. You afraid?" Pete laughed.

Dibble did not smile. "Aint no white man ever trust Dibble with nothin. Now, y'all . . . ."

"Out here, each man is free. All a man can do is trust his own judgment, mostly. Mostly, a fella trusts his judgment about a man and it works out fine."

"Posse maybe come. Maybe Dibble run some more with Cortez horses. You trust slave?"

"You aint my slave; nor any man's, I'm thinkin. And, there's somethin else."

Pete squinted at the black man, although the sun was not yet up.

"Aint a lot of the boys still livin as crossed a trustin man."

Pete picked up the mule's lead rope and swung into the saddle. He looked down at the black.

"About that there posse. They may not come down the Santa Fe Trail. It's a long, hard trip. Even if they do, it aint likely they'll come to The Cortez."

Pete waved and headed the horse and mule down to the trail. He heard Dibble call after him.

"Dibble, he come to The Cortez."

# 37

The right front axle of the loaded wagon lay across the steel-rimmed tire of the wagon wheel; and the large wagon wheel almost covered Red Hickman. The hub was in his chest, the rim cut his chin and spokes pressed his legs and arms and back to a huge boulder sunk deep in the sandy trail. Wiggle and squirm, he was pinned fair.

He heard the horse coming at a gallop. Halluck, he thought. When I pulled off the hub nut, I was a mite slow dodgin this here wheel. Now, here I am plumb stuck; and Halluck comin to ask, how come.

Hickman could move his right wrist and hand. Slowly, he pushed the large hub nut into the pocket of his jeans.

Just then a spray of dust flew over him as Blair Halluck pulled his horse up short and jumped from the saddle.

"Hickman. You hurt?" Halluck called as he knelt beside the wheel-pinned man.

"More stuck, Mister Halluck. God damn wheel just fell off, and me walkin right beside it. Son of a bitch, if'n it didn't."

"Pinned or not, Hickman. You know my rule. Cuss on my train and you draw your pay. Mistreat an animal, suffer the same mistreatment. And, besides. Walkin by this wheel is a long way from ridin drag where you're supposed to be."

"Please, Mister Halluck. Get me out from under."

Halluck called a halt to the wagons and waved a half dozen bullwhackers over to unload the heavy wagon. This took time; but, since Hickman was not hurting, they left him where he lay for half an hour or more. When the wagon was unloaded the men heaved the wagon axle off the wheel. They pulled Hickman out and jammed the wheel back onto the axle. One of the men brought a spare hub nut and the wheel was fixed.

"Looks like the nut just fell off," said Hardy, one of the bullwhackers. "By now, it's lost back there in the sand, I reckon. May have been off for hours before the wheel worked free."

Halluck looked to the southeast where the sun was cutting the morning in half. Just then, Hickman handed him a rawhide pigging string with some knots tied in it.

"Found it in the dust just now," he said. "Seen you had one like it."

Halluck nodded and took the pigging string and put it in his vest pocket.

"Lost more'n two hour. Let's reload the wagon. We'll push the stock so as to make the Canadian tonight."

Halluck mounted his Spanish bred Cortez horse and waved the men back to their wagons. He watched Hickman, struggling kind of stiff and lame, mount and head back to the cavvy of horses and mules that made up the drag, now spread out far and wide across the grassy plain. Hickman'll be clear to dark collectin that mess of animals from all over this good grama. He was the victim of the little accident. Pinned under that wheel like a rattlesnake skin nailed up on a barn door. Why do I fail to feel for the man?

Blair Halluck sat his Cortez horse as the six wagons went slowly by. He counted on his fingers the days on the trail and the days left to deliver the mail. *If we push her and have better luck than we been havin, I make Santa Fe in about fifteen, sixteen days. And sixteen days is what I got left to deliver the mail in.*

He counted on his fingers again to make sure. Then he pulled the rawhide pigging string from his vest pocket. He'd tied a knot for each of the days they'd been on the trail. Now he counted the knots. Fifteen. The knots tallied with his finger count. He put the pigging string back into his pocket.

*Seems accidents have crowded this trip. Ever since Hickman showed up, any how. Though before him, there was the stampede comin up to Lone Elm. And, Davis was killed before Hickman showed up; but it was Hickman who found him arrow stuck and bloated and brought him into camp.*

Blair Halluck wondered.

⸻

Fifteen tough-looking men had stood in front of the six wagons on the west side of the Missouri River opposite Independence. Blair Halluck rode the Cortez horse up to them.

"Men," he'd said. "We got thirty days to make her to Santa Fe and deliver the United States mail; or it won't matter to me or you whether we get there at all—or back here for that matter."

"It can be did," shouted a stocky man wearing a rakish bowler hat. "By God, Mister Halluck. Sure as nipples on a whore's tits."

"What's your name, son," asked Halluck quietly.

"Hardy's the name."

"You've not worked for me before?"

"No."

"Hardy, you know what it takes to work for me. No man's so new or stupid not to know my rules."

Hardy looked down at his boots and Halluck watched him dig a toe-hole in the dirt.

"For those few of you who are that new or stupid!" Halluck looked at Hardy until the man glanced up at the silence, then back at his boots. "I'll go over the rules again. Then, if you still want to work for Blair Halluck, you'll sign them or make your mark.

"While in my employ, you men'll not use profane language, nor cuss. You won't get drunk, nor let me catch you drinkin or gamblin. If'n you mistreat any of the stock, you'll get the same as you give out. In all other things, you'll act the gentle-man."

Halluck looked at the uplifted faces of the men. He saw he had their attention. A man smiled like belief was delayed. Halluck pointed at him.

"If'n you break any of my rules, you'll accept discharge without pay."

"Just one slip of the tongue and you'd fire us?" asked the disbelieving man named Jessup.

"True," said Halluck. "It's long been thought that bullwhackers must be vul-gar ruffians. Is that what you think, too? Well, in my four and more years of haulin freight down to Santa Fe, men who signed the rules and worked for me have worked better, got along better with each other and been happier than any others, then or now. Each man agrees to follow the rules; and understands that's part of what I pay him for. On my side, I treat my men fair, provide good grub and animals, warm blankets and the same pay or better as any other freighter. But I give the Sabbath off. Although, with the mail deadline starin me in the face, this trip you'll work most Sundays."

The men looked at each other. Halluck saw a sheepish face on Jessup as if belief had finally caught up.

"If'n I'm gonna become a gentleman," said Hardy. "I'm gonna need a better hat."

He threw a busted bowler hat at the water trough and watched it float. Sud-denly, he grabbed the sombrero off the head of the man next to him.

The man turned with balled fists.

"Don't cuss, now," said Hardy, raising a finger in the air. "Not so's the boss can hear."

"Aint said nary a word." The hatless man raised a hard fist.

"Knew you wouldn't," said Hardy. "Agin them rules."

He handed the sombrero back to the fisted man who took it and smiled.

Halluck chuckled in spite of himself.

"Best get at it," Hardy said.

He got his hat out of the horse trough, put it on and moved to the wagon. He signed the written rules with an X while his bowler dripped water on the tally book.

The other men followed. Most could write their own names and read the rules or, at least, sound out some of the words.

One, a gaunt black man, who made his X with the pencil held in a skillet hand, could read none of the words. Still, he ran his twisted index finger down the page, moved his lips and pretended hard.

Halluck nodded his head as each man signed or made his mark. When the last had signed, Halluck said, "I expect a pleasant trip. If we leave now, we can make New Santa Fe by dark, and Missus White's cookin'!"

The men shouted and started the stock for New Santa Fe, a small settlement and stage coach stop on the western border of Missouri where the trail jumps off into the land of the Shawnee Indians, the Caws and other tribes friendly to the white traveler.

It was after eight o'clock and dark before the men filled their plates at Missus White's hearth. After eating, they rolled in blankets next to or under the wagons. The black man slept apart.

Hoarfrost coated the morning ground as the men caught and hitched the stock to the wagons long before can-see. Before Missus White had stirred the breakfast fire, the six wagons were on their way again.

The mail wagon was the lightest and was pulled by four mules, two-by-two. The freight wagons were bigger and heavier. Six mules, two-by-two-by-two, hauled the five freight wagons, mostly with ease. Some of the men drove from a narrow perch at the front of the wagon, usually standing. Most, however, drove from the ground, alongside the stock, and walked the nine hundred and more miles to Santa Fe.

The train had its breakfast at the marred stump of Lone Elm, fifteen miles down the road. While the men ate, the stock was turned loose to feed on the rising grama grass.

Before the men knew it, the herd was off and running. No man saw the cause. Maybe a pack of wolves or sneaky Indians; but it took half a day to round up the stock. Some of the animals, they never found.

One of the drovers, a man named Davis, didn't come back. With the stock recovered, Halluck rode out to search for miles around for the missing man while the crew got the teams hitched and the wagons started.

"Plumb disappeared," said Halluck to the men as he joined the wagons. "The black man'll have to do double duty with the cavvy. Davis was a good man; but I can't wait on him any longer."

"Probably Indians got him," said Jessup looking all around with his hand on the butt of the pistol in his belt. "Still, we shouldn't ought-a leave him."

"You know the rules, Jessup. Out here each man takes his own fool chances." Halluck looked hard eyes around the group of men.

"If'n he's alive, he'll catch up," said Hardy. "If'n?"

The men mumbled. "Sure, if'n?"

"Let's move 'um out," cried Halluck. "Most of a day lost, some stock missin, and Davis; and more'n seven hundred mile to go. The luck of the trail—this time bad."

Day by day, they walked and drove and slept in sun and wind; in moonbeams and dark and under thunder-pulses of sudden rain. Bull Creek, Hickory Point, Rock Creek and One-Hundred-Ten. Brackish water and clear. Sand and grass and mud. Breakfast—sometimes. Dinner while the stock recruited on the ample grass. Supper after dark and sometimes under the slanting rain, seen in the flash of prairie electrics and felt clear through to the shivering skin. And, at Council Grove, a night of snow.

The men found shelter in the Astor House, so called because it had neither door nor window; but whose bare and dusty floor could sleep fifteen or twenty men, among the mice and fleas, warmed by a fire and out of the blowing cold.

In the gray morning, a Sunday, Halluck held a Bible reading for those willing to listen. Those who weren't willing could only retreat into the snow. Later, the men worked at harness or wagon repair. Some slept. Jessup and the black man worked all day reshoeing as many of the mules as they could get to.

Late in the day, the storm let up. Just as they were about to pull out, a rider came into the Grove and fell off his horse. He said between gulps of scalding coffee, he was the man chosen, and probably the last man alive, of a party of eleven.

More than three days ago, he said, their food gave out. Most of the boys was sick from bad water. Indians run the stock off. Probably all dead by now; but, just in case, send food. Then the man, his story told, up and died.

A mule was loaded with flour and bacon and, led by a local man, headed in the direction from which the dead man had come. Whether or not the party was found, alive or starved dead, the Halluck train never knew. The luck of the trail. Bad again. But this time, not for the Halluck bunch.

When each night ended another day, Halluck twisted a new knot in the pigging string.

The train drove seven miles of the six hundred and more miles remaining, to camp the night at Elm Creek. It began to snow again. Wet flakes hissed in the flames of the camp fires which burned late that night against the desert chill.

The dawn was wet with rain from the low-slung black ceiling. Red Hickman helloed the camp just at breakfast time. He took a cup of hot coffee and downed it before he rolled the dead man from his saddle. The body was some bloated in spite of the cold. An arrow stuck out of the man's back.

"Been dead a while when I come on him," said Hickman to Halluck.

Halluck looked at the swollen, dead face of the corpse.

"Davis. One of my drovers," said Halluck. "I thought maybe he'd cut and run. Black man over there is the other drover. And, against my better sense, you, Hickman, if you want to work."

Hickman felt the still swollen eye. "I do. Can't go either way without food, none of which I got. So, I'll sign your rules and work my way to Santa Fe."

"You'll work drag with the black man. Cut wood, haul water in camp. That suit?"

"It'll have to." Hickman smiled at the men who had come up to see what the fuss was and to look at the body of their former companion.

"First job, Hickman. Bury him." Halluck pointed to the body.

"Boy," Hickman called to the black man. "Bring a shovel."

The black man smiled; but did not move. "Dibble aint no 'boy' as y'all can plainly see. He Dibble by name."

"I know who you are, niggah. Bring the shovel."

"He can bring the shovel," said Halluck quietly. "But, Hickman. You do the diggin and the buryin, hear? When you're ready, call. I'll read words from the Book."

"You goin to let this niggah stay along. They say he's an escaped slave. Killed his master." Hickman grinned like he meant Halluck to lose another man by his own doin.

"The black does his work and more." Halluck looked at Dibble. "It's a man's now that counts. His yesterday is not my concern."

"Still, Mister Halluck," said Hickman. "I'd keep my eye peeled."

"I always do, Hickman. Always! Now get to diggin. We still got miles to cover this day."

From then on to just east of the Canadian, Hickman ate the choking dust clouds churned up from the cavvy's sharp hooves on dry desert. Hickman and the black man ate the dirt.

They passed clumps of buffalo; saw an occasional Indian in the distance; but lost no stock; smelled the far off smoke from a prairie wildfire, then saw the black cloud racing away within its own wind. Trail luck. This time, good.

The splits of daily travel varied. Seven miles, sixteen, twenty-nine, fifty. Mostly flat travel on firm to sandy soil; but dry. Always dry, and the animals thirsty.

The Cimarron, which they followed for several days, was mostly dry now, although the trail, known as the cut off, followed the river like a thirsty man follows hope, lapping at dream-water. Here and there, the river surfaced to form a pool, barely big enough to serve the needs of the men and stock. Then the river disappeared again into the sandy earth.

Dream food was buffalo. Hardy shot a bull near Sand Creek. The men feasted on the fat steaks. Jessup offered to toss Hardy for the tongue. He handed a silver coin to Hardy.

"You flip her and I'll call."

A look from Halluck reminded them both of the rule against gambling.

"Aint exactly gamblin," Jessup said to Hardy, who had agreed to share the tongue any way. Jessup showed Hardy the large silver coin.

"Same on both sides. I couldn't lose," said Jessup, laughing.

"Cheatin's against them rules, too." Hardy gave the coin a hard toss into the high grass.

"I'll still flip you," said Jessup, unperturbed. He snapped an identical coin between thumb and forefinger, let it turn in the air and caught it.

"How many of them coins you got?" said Hardy, grinning.

Hickman had been with the train for more than a week when the wheel had fallen on him. When he got back to the cavvy, he tossed the hub nut into the grass. Just then, the hairs on the back of his neck pulled his eyes up. He saw the black man sitting his horse like an Indian, staring right at him.

That night, Hickman told the story of the posse in Independence hunting a runaway slave. "Vowed to follow the black devil clear to Hell; or, at least, to Santa Fe. Tough men by the looks. The slave killed a powerful man over to Lebanon. His family'll pay well for this niggah's hide."

Hickman looked at the black man like he was meat on the table. So did the other men. So did Halluck.

"Posse's comin," said Hickman. "Right down this here trail, not more'n a day or so behind me."

Come morning the black man was gone. Halluck chose not to follow.

"The bacon and flour taken is less than the man's wages to date; but, now, I'm short another man. Hickman. You'll have to work some to keep the stock together. If'n you can't handle it?"

"Don't worry, Boss. I'm workin for my pay and the black's too."

Halluck nodded. "For twice the work, I'd pay a bonus." Halluck looked at Hickman; tossed him something.

"What's this?"

"Hub nut. Found it where the bacon was, bacon the black man took last night."

"How'd the niggah get this? It's from that wheel that damn, er, darn near killed me."

"The one you was walking next to when you should have been a-drovin?"

"Niggah must-a pulled this here nut a-purpose. To get me."

"I wonder," said Halluck quietly. He looked at Hickman. "I wonder why he left the hub nut for me to find. What do you think?"

"Crazy niggah."

"Some puzzlin."

In the next few days, a third of the loose stock disappeared.

"Indians," cried Hickman. "Must be, has to be. At night they are there in the rope corral. Come mornin, some are gone. The rope is tight. I don't hear nothin; but they're gone just the same."

"Mighty peculiar," said Halluck. "Only tracks I see around the corral are shod prints. Our stock or white men's mounts."

"Stolen by Indians," said Hickman, "From us or from others and rid by them. It's the only way."

Hickman twisted his hat in his hand. His face worked around from surprise past sorrow to convinced. In all of the workings of the man's face, Halluck noticed a hint of something else. Cunning maybe? More like the look of a mountain man comin into rendezvous trying to hide a winter of thirst.

Halluck circled wide; but found only two carcasses, arrow shot and carved up. Maybe proved up Hickman's idea, he thought. Indians.

Two day's later, at the crossing of a trickle of a stream known variously as Rock Creek or Coon Creek or Dead Man Creek, the trail luck went bad again.

Just as the mules pulling the mail wagon reached the steep bank of the creek, the entire cavvy of extra stock came thundering past, down the slope and across the creek with Hickman hide behind as if trying to stop the headlong rush.

The mules pulling the mail wagon jumped to follow. The wagon chased the team down the steep bank and jammed into their hind legs at the bottom. The mules broke leather and jerked free to join the cavvy, now in full stampede.

Over the wagon went. Side boards cracked; wheels spun at the sky. Bags and boxes of mail spilled from the wagon into the creek and over the dry prairie all around.

Between the rolled over wagon and the sharp, creek-bed rocks, a body lay pulpy and crushed. A silver coin stuck out of the sand next to the man's pocket.

As Halluck rode up to the fallen mail wagon, he looked toward the receding dust cloud caused by the stampede. He could just make out the figure of Red Hickman, waving his hat and following the cavvy at break neck speed.

"He tryin to turn them animals or run 'um out-a the country?"

A moan from the downed man cut Halluck's question in half.

The men worked as hard and as fast as they could; but, long before they got the wagon braced so they could pull Jessup out from under it, they could see that Jessup was dead.

Hardy picked the silver coin out of the sand. "Double sided or not, you still lost."

He put the coin into his own pocket and pulled a shovel from the next wagon to bury his friend.

"Two days lost, Davis and the black—and now Jessup," said Halluck to the men. Nervously, he pulled the knotted pigging string from his pocket and counted the knots. "Twelve days left to get this here spilled mail to Santa Fe."

"That's more'n two hundred mile yet," said one of the men, shaking his head. "It's a hard road twixed here and there. And we aint even seen a Comanche yet, or a Jicarilla Apache."

Hickman did not return with any stock until past noon the next day. When he finally came in, he was short almost half of the animals he'd chased. He didn't know what started the stock into runnin, he said. All he could do was follow; keep them in sight; keep Indians away. He was sorry about Jessup.

"Good man. A real shame. Trail luck, all bad, this time."

Halluck nodded, his mind decided.

"Too many coincidences, Hickman."

"Truth be told," said Hickman. Halluck saw what the man passed off for a smile, quick and sly.

"Let's see," said Halluck quietly. "If'n there's a way to stop this here coincidencin."

Halluck pointed a finger.

"Hardy! Put this man in the mail wagon. Tie him down good."

"Okay, Boss," said Hardy. He pulled a rope from the near wagon's box. If he were surprised, Halluck didn't see it on his placid face.

"Halluck!" Hickman yelled. "Aint no man goin to touch me."

"I'm goin to hog tie you till we get to Santa Fe."

Hickman's hand flashed to the pistol in his belt.

# 38

The early morning sunlight slipped off the tips of eagle feathers and blended with the blue sky as the three Indians trotted their horses from the hill down to the crippled buggy. One Indian rode directly to the grazing horses and, jumping from his pony, grabbed the halters of the grays and staked them to the ground.

Another of the Indians threw off the buffalo robe which had covered his shoulders and stepped into the back of the buggy.

Dressed now only in a buffalo hide loin cloth, he boldly straddled Beckey's sleeping form and sniffed her face and neck as if white women might smell different. He searched the few boxes and bundles around her. Beckey stirred but still slept through the vibration of the buggy. The Indian tossed a sack of flour and one of coffee beans to his companion. The latter held the rawhide reins of the three Indian ponies with one hand and caught the sacks of food with the other.

The Indian in the buggy spotted the fouling piece handy to the driver's seat and reached. He squatted and grunted as he grabbed the shotgun and waved it at his friend.

His crotch lump hung inches from Beckey's twitching nose.

Beckey screamed. All she could see was the hanging pouch of filthy buffalo hide. The stench filled her senses with disgust. Without will or knowledge of what she was doing, she jerked her head up into the hanging skin. She heard it yell and groan. With her eyes clenched shut, she felt it fall away from her and out of the back of the buggy; felt the buggy bounce up and down and then steady.

She heard laughter, guttural, but gleeful. She opened her eyes, too afraid not to see. The third Indian dropped the reins of the ponies. His toothless, laughing mouth filled Beckey's senses with terror. She screamed again.

She knew this nightmare was no dream.

The laughing Indian threw her blanket off and pulled her feet first from her buggy bed. She landed with a painful thump on the dew-wet grass. She tried to sit up; but a moccasined foot pounded her in the chest and pinned her down.

The Indian with the sore crotch was on his feet. One hand gripped his belly. In the other, he held a knife. As he was about to lunge at the prone figure, Laughing Indian grabbed his arm and held him up. He said something. The knife slid back into the sheath at Sore Crotch's belt. He cupped his crotch with his hand, shook his head and laughed painfully.

The Indian who had seized and staked out the horses motioned to the buggy. Sore Crotch and Laughing Indian unloaded it. Food, blankets, clothes and utensils were piled into one blanket.

While the loading was going on, Beckey was free as though the Indians had forgotten her. She got up and put out a protesting hand as everything she owned was being removed from the buggy.

Suddenly, the horse catching Indian turned to her. He looked her over fully, up and down. It was then she realized she was standing in front of the Indians dressed in long johns and nothing else.

Horse Catcher reached her in a single step and grabbed her arm. He pushed his face into hers. She smelled animal grease and exhaled constipation. She saw rape in his eyes. It was not the urgent, almost bashful look she had seen in Mister James' eyes as he eased her back on the schoolroom desk and reached under her dress. The Indian's look was fierce. A righteous look of burning triumph.

He ripped the long johns from her body. She had to fight him. To stop the disgrace. She hit him in the face with her free hand. She hit him again and again; but he seemed to ignore the blows of her small fists; even seemed to ignore the trickle of blood she had started from a split in his lip; or, maybe, she thought, he pleasured in it.

In an instant, she was spread-eagle naked on the soft grass of the prairie, held by powerful, groping hands. She knew her fight was over. Still she swung at Horse Catcher's face. She bit his arm as it crossed her mouth. She kicked his back with her heels. She felt her blows land and bounce. She felt nothing else; sensed everything.

One after the other, the Indians crushed air from her lungs as they rocked back and forth across her belly. She fought each one as hard as she could, although her strength was nearly exhausted. Still, through it all, she did not scream or even cry.

She knew she had been wetted by Indian rape; but was not stirred the way she had been with Mister James. She felt only cold, hard anger as each Indian ground her bare back into the grass and invaded her loins.

When the last Indian lay panting by her side, she knew she hated.

Laughing Indian grunted satisfaction. His discarded loin cloth lay by his side. A sheath and bone handled knife were tied to the cloth.

With a last spasm of strength, Beckey pulled the knife and plunged it into his ribs. The blade cut shallow and bounced off bone. With a surprised grunt, Laughing Indian rolled clear of her and sprang to his feet. Blood slid from the cut along a protruding rib and across his bare hip. He was not laughing now.

In a smooth motion, he pulled the knife from Beckey's hand, raised the knife over her head and plunged it downwards.

Beckey saw the descending blade bright in the sun with Indian blood. She tried to sink from it by exhaling. She shut her eyes and the blade disappeared. She felt no cutting penetration. Fear and surprise popped her eyes open.

Horse Catcher's hand had stopped the knife point at her breast.

The Indians argued and shoved each other and pointed at Beckey. Finally, with a flourish, Horse Catcher waved his arm and grunted. The discussion was over; the decision made. He picked up his loin cloth and wrapped it around his waist. The other Indians did the same.

Sore Crotch piled buffalo chips next to the buggy along with bits of cloth. In a minute, he had a small blaze going. Soon, the buggy was fully involved in fire.

Horse Catcher grabbed Beckey's wrist and pulled her to her feet. She tried to reach her long johns as she was raised; but, failed. She stood before the three Indians dressed only in rage.

The burning buggy crackled and hissed behind her. One of the grays rose on hind legs and backed off from the fire, pulling the picket pin from the ground. The Indians let the horse go, knowing they would catch it later.

Horse Catcher thumped Beckey on the chest and pointed toward the distant mountains. Then he made walking signs with his fingers. At first she did not understand because all she understood was the cool hate she felt. She did not think of death; but of killing.

Laughing Indian took a bow from his pony and nocked an arrow. He drew the bow and pointed the arrow at Beckey's breast. She turned to face the arrow, threw out her naked breasts.

"I welcome you," she said. When she said it, she smiled.

The Indians, even Laughing Indian, grunted and nodded their heads in approval. Horse Catcher pushed the taught bow aside; and, again, made the walking signs with his fingers. Then he pointed to the far mountains and gave Beckey a hard push in their direction.

She stumbled; stopped.

He shoved her again; then took her by the arm and ran with her until she was running on her own.

She understood then that the Indians were giving her a chance. She ran without looking back. She ran naked in the sun.

She felt the pain of rapid breathing, the cut of rocks on her bare feet and fury at having to run from rape. A sharp burning thumped her shoulder blade and made her stumble and fall; but she was up in an instant. Still, she ran. Hate was her engine.

She glanced back and something caught the corner of her eye in the slight wind of her own motion. With each movement of her glistening back as she ran, she felt the feathered shaft of Laughing Indian's arrow, deep in her shoulder, tease the empty sky with the promise of blood.

Without knowing, she'd run the Indian gauntlet reserved only for the honored brave among their enemies; and, though still running, she had lost.

Pete Cortez saw the black smoke rising almost vertically in the still air. Near the contrail, he saw a vulture, then another, circling.

"Indians!" he said to the smoky horse, digging heels into the horse's flanks. "Wagon burnin. Dead crew, I reckon. Not so far from here."

Pete had met the Halluck wagons two days before. He had bought supplies enough to load the mule. Just as he was about to head across the prairie toward home, Halluck asked a strange question.

"Seen any negroes about?"

"You lost any?" said Pete not wanting to lie to Halluck if he could help it.

He smiled at Halluck. Red Hickman stepped up.

"One," he said. "Took off in the night. Stole provisions and a mule."

"Hickman's right," said Halluck, pointing to the red headed man. "He's just come into camp from Independence. He brought news. A posse's chasin a black man. Say he killed his master over Lebanon way." Halluck pointed east, as if to mark the Missouri town almost a thousand miles behind him.

"The sheriff told me," said Hickman. "They goin to follow that niggah far as need be. To Santa Fe, anyways. Worth two, maybe three thousand dollars, dead or alive."

"Black'd be a surprise where I'm headed," said Pete. He turned to Halluck. "Thanks for the grub. You need stock, you send a rider to The Cortez."

That was two days ago. On the way west, Pete had seen tracks and had found a day-old camp. The horse prints and the camp smelled like Indians.

And, now the smoke. While he watched, the coil of smoke began to thin and pale as if the fire were nearly out. Pete swung the smoky horse and the pack mule toward the circling vultures.

"I can bury the dead, anyways." He looked all around, sniffed the air, studied each mound and depression clear to the horizon for sign of dust or the sudden jump of a quail or rabbit. "Easy, Smokey. Let's abide them Indians to get clean away. Can't bury the dead if'n I'm among 'um."

It took Pete nearly an hour to work his way carefully toward the smoke, now reduced to mere wisps of ember-dust. He sat the smoky horse and studied the scene. He saw the shards of Beckey's fire-gutted buggy; the nearly bare spot in the trampled grass. Looks as if several bodies squirmed and squirmed; and, maybe, a body died there, he thought, as he noticed the trace of blood on the grass. But where's the body?

The smoky horse whinnied and shied a step. "I smell it too, Smokey. Indians."

The Sharps was in his hand when he dismounted. He worked his way carefully around the charred buggy until he saw the dim trail of bent grass stems, heading west. He knelt to study the trail, saw part of a barefoot print.

"Small foot for a man, white or Indian."

He looked along the west-seeking trail; moved along it until it grew too faint to see. The rising breeze fluttered some of the bent grass blades beyond; and he saw a flash of color.

Carefully, he looked all around trying to scratch the itch at the back of his neck. He saw only heat waves rumpling the far away blue sky. He rubbed his neck with a rough, gloved hand; still felt the itch of hairs on end.

Slowly, he walked along the bent grass trail. The smoky horse followed him. He knelt again at the speck of color. He saw more specks, drops of red shinning in the sun.

"Blood! Looks like someone aint quite dead yet. By the strides, he's runnin and bleedin. Blood's some dry, some damp. If'n we move fast, but careful, we'll soon come up to him, dead or alive."

The smoky horse shook her head as Pete mounted and headed west. In the high of the blue sky, a dozen vultures swarmed.

Beckey thought she was still running, goaded by the pain in her back and the occasional blur in the corner of her eye as the feathered arrow shaft undulated with each swing of her arms. In truth, the running was all in her dazed imagination.

She lay twitching in a sand pocket at the roots of a juniper. Her breathing was short and sharp. Sweat rolled from fidgeting rump and thighs which glistened in the near-noon sun. The oncoming vultures heard her cries which she felt but did not hear.

At first Beckey had run from the Indians only because Horse Catcher had started her; but, almost immediately, prideful rage took command of her feet. She thought she flew away from torment. She felt the impact of the arrow; but not the pain of it; felt her feet stumble, her body fall and rise in flight again. Her breathing came hot and hard. Rocks cut her feet; and her skin was wet all over with the running.

She felt only the running and the rage and the rape. She did not know that the rape and the rage and the running were saving her for greater suffering.

On a knoll three hundred yards to the northeast, Sore Crotch poked Horse Catcher and pointed at the naked girl lying in the root-notch of juniper. Laughing Indian pointed too, and laughed. Then, Horse Catcher grabbed a hank of his own long, graying hair and gave a yank and a grunt. Laughing Indian pulled the scalping knife from its sheath at his belt and stopped laughing.

The Indians started their horses down the knoll toward the gleaming, shaking body. Each wondered if he would be the one to carry the scalp of long, red hair into camp that night. Each looked at the other out of an eye corner.

Suddenly, Horse Catcher dropped the lead ropes of the grays and heeled his pony into a run. Sore Crotch and Laughing Indian were a mere instant behind.

Horse Catcher leaped from his loping pony and somersaulted to Beckey's side. He pushed up to his knees with one hand and flashed his knife with the other. He saluted the noonday haze with a cry of triumph which froze in his throat.

As he reached down for a hunk of Beckey's flaming scalp-hair, his own black head shattered, showering Beckey with grease and hair and blood and bone.

Horse Catcher died before the sound of Pete's Sharps rifle reached the spot where he knelt in death.

Sore Crotch and Laughing Indian turned their horses toward the sound of the shot. Sore Crotch pulled his pony to a sliding halt and raised his rifle just as the Sharps spoke again.

The huge .54 caliber bullet split his breastbone. By accidental reflex, Sore Crotch pulled his own trigger and hung on to the rifle with both hands in a grip of death. As he sailed from the saddle, he felt floating for an instant and, then, felt nothing, forever. His discarded body crumpled across Beckey's back trail, thirty yards from where she lay.

Laughing Indian wheeled his own pony around and dug heels in flanks. He rode to out run the long-shooting rifle. He heard it speak and felt the whip of bullet wind pass his cheek. He was riding full out now, outrunning bullets. Speed pulled viciously at his long, stringy hair and the pony's tail.

Both flew and soared and waved as Pete's thunder roared again from farther away.

Pete found Beckey crying in mud of her own making in the sandy root notch of the juniper.

"Lord bless the lucky," he said. "An arrow-shot woman lying naked in the sun of this dry eastern slope; but still alive enough to cry. I'll just be damned."

Beckey was delirious. Her crying was raving. Without hesitation, Pete grasped the shaft of the arrow and tried to pull it from Beckey's shoulder blade. It would not come. He pulled again in spite of the girl's responsive groans.

"Mired in bone, I reckon," he said as if the girl could hear.

Finally, he snapped the shaft just above the swollen edge of the wound. He waved the broken shaft at the two inert Indian bodies and off at the distant hill where the third had disappeared. Shot? Pete didn't know; but he felt the itch of time pressing.

"The arrowhead will have to work its own way out, or stay."

He rolled her over on her side, careful to keep the wound from the dirt. Then, he tried to give her water from his canteen. Unconsciously, Beckey thrust swollen tongue and lips at the water spilling from the canteen. The taste of cool water opened her eyes. She coughed as water caught in her wrong throat. She sucked for more.

Suddenly, she stopped drinking and shut her eyes. Her body went limp.

"Hold on there little lady. Don't die on me now." Pete felt her chest for breathing and felt a heart beat. "Strong. And she's breathin kind-a regular. Maybe she'll make it."

Pete looked into the sky and shielded his eyes with his hat. A vulture cast a shadow on the wall of the sun; then another and another. The heat did not diminish.

"But not for long in this sun."

He covered her body with his blanket. Then, he mounted Smokey and went after the matched grays which still grazed a mile or so away. He led the horses back to the juniper. Carefully, he loaded Beckey into his own saddle and squeezed her hands around the horn until she gripped it on her own. Then he jumped aboard the near gray; and leading the horses and his own pack mule, he headed for the cottonwoods of the Canadian.

He tried to ride a rocky trail in case the third Indian made it home and thought to bring friends for vengence.

"Water and shade from the sun and a warmth against tonight's cold. That and luck, better'n you've had today. Hang on to the saddle horn little lady. It won't be long."

Pete watched as the cottonwoods grew nearer and wondered about this red-headed girl, naked and alone with just a buggy and arrow-shot in the midst of the desert and Indians about to part her from that red hair.

"Clear they had their way with her; and, from the look of her, and them Indians, she fought 'um knuckle and thumb. All the way. They set her runnin; stuck her with an arrow just to see her squirm; and sat back to watch the fun. When they thought she'd quit, they come for her hair."

Pete Cortez whistled to himself in amazement and patted the stock of the Sharps which stuck out from the saddle scabbard.

As the sun sank into the west, Pete pulled the brim of his hat down lower over his constantly searching eyes. Who is this girl? he asked himself. How come her to be alone in a buggy closer to Hell than anywhere? A lone girl. Arrow-bait on the Santa Fe trail. Damnedest thing. Well, I guess she'll tell me when she's able, if she lives.

Pete watched the girl lurching on the back of the smoky horse, head bouncing up and down, tight breasts jiggling in the opening of the blanket, white knuckles and red fingers around the saddle horn in a death grip. And, when the blanket slipped down from time to time, he saw the ooze of blood pulse from the jagged tip of the broken arrow shaft sticking out of the swollen red lump on the back of her left shoulder.

She's got sand, he thought. Might make it if the festering don't get too bad and poison her.

Pete knew the desert's daily cycle of orange, lemon and dusty plum from a lifetime of living in its light. In the morning the desert is a piercing clear orange as the sun climbs over the eastern horizon of dark buttes. By noon an undulating, lemon haze floats across the hot sky. At evening the desert's brush paints the sky with strokes of pastel purple streaked with magenta ribbons and, here and there, wisps of morning's orange and noon's lemon yellow nestled along the horizon of the dying day.

Pastel time in the desert is quiet time when quail settle into sand wallows under junipers and the coyote and wolf creep silently through the shadowy brush in search of supper.

At pastel time, it was Pete's habit, a survival drill, to stop, rest, eat, drink and recruit body and spirit and the stock for the inevitable cycle of the new desert day.

Pete lay Beckey in a blanket next to a cottonwood log fallen among the great trees on the west bank of the Canadian River. He pushed his hat to the back of his head and looked off to the mountains and saw the buttresses which held his valley, The Cortez, near now, and yet, still so far a ride for the wounded girl.

He heard Beckey moan in delirium and fever as he washed her sweat soaked and dirt stained body. When he came to the arrow wound, he gently washed the blood away from its swollen lips; and she cried out with each stroke of his hand.

"I know it hurts like hell; but we got to clean it, girl," he whispered. "The arrowhead is buried deep. Your wound seems to be pussin up some. An angry wound. I'll do what I can; but, in the end . . . ." He didn't know if she could hear.

It'll likely kill you just the same, he thought.

Pete sighed as he walked to the river to rinse the shirt he was using as a wash rag. Tendrils of old blood floated from the rag like legs of a jelly fish to mix with the sandy back water of the river.

When Beckey was as clean as the river water bath was going to make her, Pete let the warm night air dry her and cool the fever. Then he applied a poultice of chewed-wet tobacco, gun powder, and tree moss to the wound and wrapped the wet shirt-rag around her from front to back to hold the poultice tight against her torn shoulder.

Beckey lay on her belly moaning softly in rhythm with the desert wind of evening as pastel time went black with night. Her face was turned toward the cottonwood log. Pete covered her with the blanket. She whimpered as the rough wool floated onto her shoulder. Then she slept.

Pete built a small fire next to the log, careful to use the driest of twigs to keep the spiral of smoke one with the night. He boiled water in the coffee pot, added chunks of dried beef to make a broth. She needs sleep; but she needs food, too, to thicken her blood if she's goin to see mornin. He poured the broth into his tin cup and set it on the log.

While the broth was cooling, he scooped out a small depression in the sand to keep her wound from pressing on the ground and, slowly, gently, turned her on her back.

The movement woke Beckey. Pete saw her eyes in the fire-flicker, languid green at first opening, jump with fear. Beckey screamed and tried to rise. Pete fell back in surprise; then laughed softly.

"Whoa, little lady. It's all right now. You're safe here."

His rough hand betrayed a mother's love as he gently pushed her back down on the blanket. Still, she lashed out with a tiny, balled fist. It caught Pete on the left cheek with the force of the soft evening wind.

Pete laughed again. He watched the girl try again to windmill fists; but only her forearms came off the blanket; and only for a moment. Then they sagged across her breasts.

"Good. That's good. You've got some fight left in you."

She began to pant for breath until the heave of her breast brought a sharp bite of pain to her eyes. She slumped; and the breathing slowed.

"Use me as you will," she whispered, and closed her eyes.

"What?"

"You're a man aren't you." Her eyes were closed; but her body was rigid.

Pete thought at first that her body went rigid with fear; but the set of her cut mouth spelled anger, more like rage.

"Calm yourself, miss. You're safe."

Pete scooped his right arm under her head, careful not to touch the wounded shoulder. With his left hand, he picked up the tin cup and tasted the broth. With the touch of his arm, Beckey's eyes popped open and she tried to struggle from his grasp.

Pete held her with gentle firmness which she seemed to recognize.

"Here's some beef soup. Drink it."

Pete put the cup to her lips. Her body sagged into the crook of his arm. She sipped the broth, slowly at first. Suddenly, she sank her lips as deeply as she could into the cup and tried to inhale the soup. Soon she was coughing.

"Hold the pony, there," said Pete, laughing. "Easy does it. There's a-plenty."

Pete pulled the cup away from her mouth until she calmed. The splits in her lips had opened and droplets of blood puffed up and slid off her pout as she thrust cut lips at the cup.

"You've spilled most of this. I'll get you some more; but go easy on it."

He picked the coffee pot out of the coals and refilled the cup. The soup was still warm; and Beckey drank in controlled gulps. When the cup was empty, she looked up at Pete.

"Who are you?" she whispered.

Before Pete could answer, her eyes clicked shut and she was asleep. Pete lowered her head to the sand and snugged the blanket over and around her.

"Who are you?" he whispered back. "Who the hell are you!?"

Pete was up and at the small fire as the gray dawn was pushed aside by the piercing orange light of the new desert day. He had taken the Sharps and scouted their camp for a mile around looking for fresh Indian sign. He saw none; but knew, in Indian country, only the dead have perfect eyesight.

After a pot of coffee for himself, he made more beef broth in the pot. He fried some bacon in the pan. Then, he dropped a mush of atole, unbolted flour and water, to fry in the grease for biscuits.

He chewed on a piece of bacon while he stood and looked down on the girl. Her sleeping face was pale and drawn, and dry. Her breathing was steady and even. Might be a pretty girl under that pain and fear, he thought. He put a calloused palm to her forehead. It felt cool.

"Time to eat and ride," he said aloud.

Beckey stirred until her shoulder hit sand and she cried out and was awake.

"It'll hurt like hell today," Pete said. "A wound like that always does the day after." Unconsciously, he rubbed the side of his head where Garrard's ball had split his skull.

"I'll see to your wound after we eat."

He scraped a couple of atole biscuits from the pan into a tin plate and poured some broth from the pot into the tin cup. He put the food on the log and helped the girl to sit up amid a yelp or two of pain.

As Beckey sat up, the blanket slipped from her shoulders. Pete watched her shiver in the last of the cool dawn. He handed her the plate and held the cup to her lips. She drank deeply and moaned a little at what Pete guessed was the burn of the liquid on split lips. When the cup was empty, Beckey looked long at Pete.

He felt himself smile; and saw that she didn't seem to notice the fingers of air that bathed her all over and made tiny hairs stand erect. Pete could not help the roving of his eyes over flat belly and tight breasts whose nipples puckered hard in the coolness of the new morning. Mighty pretty, he thought without really thinking it.

Beckey glued her eyes to Pete's face and bit into one of the biscuits. She grimaced and spit.

"What is this? This paste?" she said, trying not to gag.

"Atole. Mestizo biscuits. Learned to eat them as a boy herdin horses on the desert with the Mexican and Indian crew. Taste aint much; but they'll keep your meatbag away from your backbone for most of a day."

"Meatbag? What kind of talk is that?" Still, her eyes had not left his face.

"Belly, stomach. Where the meat goes, you're lucky enough to have any." Pete chuckled. "Mountain man by the name of Long John Hatcher called his belly by no other name. For a time, me and Hatcher and old Louy Simonds partnered in New Mexico Territory and the California mines."

Pete took the plate and popped a biscuit in his mouth. Through spilling crumbs, he said, "eat the last one. We've still got a ride ahead of us. You'll need something in that meatbag of yours." He pointed at her belly. Her eyes followed his finger and she squealed.

"My Goodness! I'm naked." Quickly, she pulled the blanket around her. With the quick movement, the shoulder wound bit her hard and tears welled in her eyes.

"How I hate you!" she cried and the tears fell over the dam.

"Stand quiet, there. Naked's the way I found you. Way the Indians left you. My only shirt is your bandage." Pete couldn't help the smile and, then, a full-out grin.

"Aint seen many naked women, that's true." He felt the grin paint red into his cheeks. "Shockin though it is, seein you all naked, I'll get over it!"

He pulled his hat down to a rakish angle.

"Though, I appreciate your concern."

He turned on his heel and went for the stock. He called over his shoulder. "While the stock's waterin and gettin used to facin a new day, I'll dress your wound, miss . . . ."

He turned back. "What is your name? Mine's Pedro Cortez. Folks call me Pete."

Beckey cocked her head, hesitated. "I'm Beckey Goddard."

Still grinning, Pete touched the brim of his hat with a finger.

"Señorita Beckey, encantada."

He started to bow when she jerked him up to his full height.

"To Hell with you, Pedro Pete Cortez."

Pete felt the air go out of his balloon and he stared at her. Why is she so set on hellin me, I wonder? Just cause I've seen her naked body? Naked or clothed, I sure don't figure women. He turned to the stock. This time he didn't stop.

"Sure as shootin," he said so she could hear. "Hell must have a heap-a naked women."

Beckey clutched the blanket to her breast with her good hand and watched the tall, easy moving man walk into the sunlight. His stride was quick and sure. Now the hat sat square and business-like on his head. Her eyes, still wet from tears of pain, spelled out anger, shame and confusion.

"God give me the strength to fight him off me like I did the Indians so that he, no man, will ever touch me again." More tears wet Beckey's cheeks, this time from deeper pain.

Beckey scrunched her butt up against the cottonwood deadfall, careful not to hit the arrow shaft against the log. She wiped wet eyes with the back of her wrist, felt the twinge of pain as the sore flesh pulled at the shaft, winced. She watched Pete call in the stock, set the bridles and lead them to water.

As she watched, she searched through the delirium of the past days. Mostly, she remembered a dizzy haze, hot flesh, pain and feeling soothing hands and hearing soft, gentle words. She thought she remembered something else, more felt than remembered, a sense of asylum, cocoon-like, in the sure arms of this man.

She watched Pete kneel and inspect the hooves of each animal as it drank from the thin ribbon of giggling water.

Bad way to treat this man, she thought. This man who saved my life. Maybe he won't be like, like Pa. Surely not like Pa or the others, the boys who came to visit with hunger in their eyes. The savages. And Mister James. Mister James? His touch was, was dreadful. They all said I brought it on; but I was terrified at his touch, his hands. And, yet I felt something else. What? A yearning?

She watched Pete bring the stock into camp, fresh water dripping from eager muzzles. The smoky horse stood quietly while Pete saddled her. Beckey heard the soothing voice, like the voice she remembered from her haze, as Pete spoke to each animal in turn while he threw the Indians' saddles on the grays and the pack tree on the mule.

To this man, I'm just another horse or mule, she thought. I like the way he treats the animals with gentle kindness. Not like the bullwhackers of the wagon train with their whips and stones and cussing. This man is not like that.

What's this man to me? Savior, protector, healer? That much, maybe.

"We're packed up and ready to start out on the trail," said Pete smiling down at Beckey. "First, though, I'm goin to have to dress that there shoulder. It'll hurt some."

While Pete changed the poultice of tobacco, gunpowder and moss, neither spoke. When Pete pulled the shirt-bandage tight around the wound, Beckey cried out.

"Sorry," is all Pete said. Then, he pulled the blanket off her.

So, now it starts, she thought. She tried to struggle; but couldn't.

"Hold still, ma'am."

He cut a hole in the middle of the blanket and slipped her head through the hole. The rough wool hung around her serape-like. He tied it at her waist with a pigging string and bunched it up to keep it off the bandage.

"You look like a Mexican woman or a squaw, except for that red hair."

Pete helped her to her feet; helped her to stand on trembling legs; helped her to walk in halting steps to the gray. The horse turned his head and nuzzled Beckey. Before she knew it, Pete had boosted her into the saddle.

"That Indian saddle aint much," he said. "Just buffalo hide."

"It will have to do," said Beckey softly.

She looked down at Pete and tried to smile, felt the smile inside; but she knew her face was more a twisted grimace. She saw that Pete noticed. He turned away to gather the lead ropes of the pack mule and the other gray and mount the smoky horse.

Why can't I show him I'm grateful at least? thought Beckey. Why? Suddenly, she knew why.

He's a man!

Without a word or a look back, Pete led them out of the cottonwood grove, west toward The Cortez.

# 39

Soon after Red Hickman had left Independence with a sore eye to catch up with and sabotage Halluck's mail train, the man who gave Red his eye also rode down the Santa Fe Trail. Bobby Joe Potter had been deputized as sheriff in Lebanon, Missouri to catch and bring back the slave known as Dibble—for hanging. The reward was two thousand dollars, dead or alive, the grandest bounty he'd ever sought even after taking out two hundred dollars apiece for the three men who came with him.

Each of the four posse men rode a good loping horse and trailed a spare. In the early morning, the posse crossed the wide Missouri on a ferry man's barge; rode fast down the long day and camped past dark at Missus White's for the night.

After a good supper of pot roast and apple pie, Potter stood by the fire, his huge fists wrapped around a steaming cup of coffee.

"You boys think today was hard ridin, wait till you see what lies ahead. You aint never seen blisters like the one's that'll pucker your asses afore this chase is done."

Potter laughed and took a slug of the hot coffee, letting the excess slide along the creases of thick jowls and drip from the tips of his scraggly blond mustache.

"I'll pop a few blisters, bless me I will, for two hundred dollars and a dead niggah."

Potter's long time sidekick, Blessed Jones, spoke through a four-tooth gap in the front of his thin, flat smile. Potter and Jones had chased many an escaped slave through the Arkansas and Missouri hollows. Most were worth more alive than dead; so they brought them back to masters who paid well for the return of their property.

On occasion, when things were slow, Potter and Jones would sneak a slave or two out of their chains and through the woods. They would hide the men in a deserted cabin for a week or so and feed them better than they were used to. Then, they'd chain them up again and return them to grateful masters for the reward. The slaves gladly exchanged a whipping for the few dollars Potter and Jones shared with them for their effort and cooperation. It was a busy life, keeping slaves faithful to their masters.

The other two members of Potters' posse looked more doubtful. For each, two hundred dollars was a lot of money for a few weeks easy ride. Butt blisters were something else.

"What's the all-fired, god damn hurry, Boss," said Cussin Jim, looking up at Potter from his saddle pillow with his bad eye closed as it usually was, gummy from the constant puss eruption of a severe burn that wouldn't heal. "Shit don't smell up a privy as fast as your movin us."

Cussin Jim had gotten his eye burned a while back. He'd just bedded his neighbor's wife when Neighbor had come to fetch her home. Cussin Jim tried to shoot the man. His pistol back flashed into his right eye. The ball missed Neighbor by a whisker. Neighbor said to hell with his wife; aint worth gettin kilt over no woman. So, Cussin Jim was left with a puss-sore eye and Neighbor's wife.

When he joined up with Bobby Joe Potter, he dumped Neighbor's wife back on Neighbor's front stoop. "Aint no damned woman worth this pussy eye," he'd hollered and galloped out of there. Neighbor's bullet missed his head by a long hair.

"Aint no need to hurry," he said to Potter. "Get to Santa Fe late or soon, god damn niggah'll still be wherever he is when we get there."

Muddy Waters cupped his hand around the cigarette end that pasted a reddish glow to his nose. "Dumbest thing I ever heard you say; and I've heard a-plenty stupidness from you, Jim."

"What's god damn stupid is you," said Cussin Jim.

"Aint in Santa Fe yet," said Potter, running his thick fingers through a rat's nest of greasy, yellow hair and knocking his dirt-gray plantation hat off into the fire in the process. "That niggah is ridin with the Halluck mail train, I hear." Potter puffed out loud as he squeezed a ponderous gut to reach his smoldering hat. "We'll nail the niggah along the trail."

"What about that Halluck," said Muddy Waters, so called more for the dried and caked mud and dirt on his clothes and unwashed body than because Muddy fit with his surname. "Halluck aint goin to up and let us kill one of his men, niggah or no."

"We'll see about that. I got this here reward poster and Judge Lyle's order to bring back that slave dead or alive." Potter patted the pocket in his grease lined leather coat. "If Halluck still objects, well . . . ."

"God damn it, Potter," Cusssin Jim whined. "First it's ass-boilin blisters and now you want us to shoot it out with them freighter-bastards."

"Sheriff Potter to you, boy!" said Potter. The fire caught the ice in his piercing blue eyes as he looked down at Cussin Jim. Cussin Jim hadn't caught Potter's stubborn look.

"Sheriff, hell! You're as much sheriff as I'm a god-fearin preacher."

Cussin Jim was laughing when the pointed toe of Potter's boot clipped a quarter-inch of skin from the tip of his nose and the trailing spur cut his cheek.

Surprised, Cussin Jim's puss-eye opened wide. Blessed Jones and Muddy Waters let out a howl of laughter.

"You better start preachin, Jim. 'Cause I am the sheriff of this here outfit."

The other two laughed even harder. Cussin Jim rubbed the raw spot on his nose with one hand while the other hand went to the butt of the pistol in his belt.

"You son of a bitch!" cussed Cussin Jim.

"Pull that pistol and save me two hundred dollars," laughed Potter. His own Colt Dragoon was pointed at Cussin Jim's belly.

Cussin Jim slowly moved his hand away from the gun butt and wiped the blood from his cut cheek with one finger. The puss-eye slid shut again.

"Now say it," said Potter. "Sheriff Potter. Say it!" Potter's wintery eyes froze in the firelight. This time Cussin Jim didn't miss the killing message.

Cussin Jim smiled. "Sheriff Potter. SIR! Sheriff son of a bitch!"

Potter cocked the hammer of the Colt and held it steady for a moment. Then his puffy lips twitched and spread into a smile. The smile puckered into a fat laugh.

"You got that one plumb right, Cussin Jim. I'm a son of a bitchin, niggah killin, Missouri sheriff."

Potter did a little Arkansas shuffle with his feet and fired the pistol in the air.

"And don't you boys forget it."

Now they were all laughing.

"Bless my soul," said Blessed Jones. "I believe I feel like dancin."

With that Blessed Jones hopped up and linked arms with Potter. Around the fire they danced. Muddy Waters clapped his hands, not noticing the flakes of dirt that fell from his head as he wagged it in time to thumping boots. Cussin Jim laughed too, ignoring the trickle of blood that ran down his nose to wet his lips.

The next morning came early and wet with drizzle. Bobby Joe Potter walked heavily toward his horse as the others mounted. He stood with one hand on the saddle horn and looked west.

"Eight days hard ridin, maybe nine. We'll catch up with Halluck and that niggah. Money in our pockets, boys."

Unconsciously, he pulled his ponderous gut out of the way of his knees, jumped a foot in the stirrup and dove into the saddle before the gut could rebound. He pushed the cotton hat down over the grease-curls of his long yellow hair.

"Let's light a shuck," he said and sank the spikes of his spurs into already raw horsehide.

Cussin Jim yelled, "my god damn ass's sore already."

"It aint what it will be, bless the Lord," shouted Blessed Jones into the speed-made wind.

Muddy Waters gave a whoop and quirted his horse to catch up.

"God damn son of a bitch," said Cussin Jim to the same wind.

Out from Missus White's they rode. Bobby Joe Potter soon took the lead. He rode easy and smooth, ponderous belly steady in the saddle. Potter stared straight west at his just reward. Two thousand dollars for nothin but one dead slave.

Sheriff Potter's posse was headed hard and fast and deadly—down the Santa Fe Trail.

# 40

According to the knots on his pigging string, Blair Halluck had only five days left to reach Santa Fe on time. He was a full day, maybe more, behind schedule. And now, the Halluck train was stopped dead in its dusty tracks.

Halluck stood in the sun. His hat was pulled low and his right hand hung loosely by his side. He faced a man who needed killing.

If I'm a mite slow today, he thought, that man'll live to look down on the end of Blair Halluck, curled up bloody and shot dead in this desert. Halluck squared his shoulders to the task at hand. Well, so be it, he sighed to himself.

He squinted at Red Hickman a scant ten yards away.

Eyes clashed.

"No need for this, Mister Halluck," said Hickman. His hand was on the butt of his pistol. Wisps of red hair fluttered under the brim of his hat.

"Aint my fault your luck's been bad. I'm true blue for you and us all to make her to Santa Fe on time."

Halluck saw recklessness in the man's eyes; saw him lick dry lips.

"You need me," Halluck heard across the killing space. "And, besides. Aint no man goin to hog tie Red Hickman. No sir!"

Halluck saw red nuckles tense and turn white on the pistol butt.

Hardy stood near Halluck. "It's you been the bad luck of this outfit, Hickman. And, for Jessup and Davis, more'n luck, I'm thinkin."

Halluck watched the white nuckles. If'n they just twitch, he thought.

"You got a choice, Hickman," he heard himself say. "Pull the gun or drop it. Pull it and you'll be dead before it clears your belt. Drop it and you'll live. We get to Santa Fe, I'll turn you lose. No pay; but you'll be alive."

Halluck felt his own hand quiver over the butt of his new 1851 Navy Colt.

"I aint got all day. Make your pick!"

"He don't get you, Hickman, I will," said Hardy. "Jessup was my pard."

Suddenly, Halluck saw white nuckles flash in the sun.

He drew his Colt.

Hickman's hand flashed in the sun; but, away from the gun butt, palm out.

"No, Mister Halluck. No!"

Halluck leveled his pistol at Hickman's belt, thumb on the eared-back hammer. The hand was eager, but steady.

Now, Hickman stood with both palms facing out as if a gesture could stop bullets.

"You need me," he whispered.

"Shuck the gun," said Hardy. His own pistol was out and ready.

Hickman pulled the pistol from his belt, careful to use thumb and forefinger only, and let it drop into the sand at his feet.

Halluck felt the other bullwackers gather around; but he glued his eyes on Hickman.

"Gut shoot him, Mister Halluck," yelled Aymes.

"Y'all don't and I will," said Pole Hawkin. "This'll save the vultures the trouble of cuttin you up, Red."

Pole held a short barreled shotgun in his thin fingers, hammers of both tubes were cocked full-back. The other men murmured their approval.

"Now wait," said Hickman.

He looked around at the men and Halluck smelled his sweat and saw the fear.

"Wait. It was Alexander."

"Colonel Alexander put you up to the tricks you pulled?" Halluck said. He holstered his Colt and rubbed his clean jaw. "I been wonderin why you done them things. Now I know."

Halluck felt anger rising to replace the fear of death. He'd always lived by his word and expected others to do the same. He knew some didn't; but he was always surprised when it happened to him.

"I'll just have to disappoint the colonel," he said and felt the anger slide into a kind of sorrow of his own.

"Alexander says if you was delayed, you wouldn't get the mail to Santa Fe on time; and he'd get all you owned, your farm to boot. It was Alexander put me up to the idea of accidents, Mister Halluck. If'n I hadn't been so down on my luck . . . ." Hickman's eyes widened. "I'll work double, triple hard. I'll make it up."

"Hog tie him and throw him in with the mail," Halluck said and turned to walk away from the smell of his own dreadful sweat. "We'll untie him in Santa Fe."

The men gathered around. In seconds Hickman was tied arm and leg and tossed into the back of the mail wagon to ride and bounce on the uneven mounds of bags and boxes.

Hardy stood at the back of the wagon and looked up into Hickman's pleading face.

"We aint goin to watch to see that you stay put. You fall out of this here wagon, we'll let the vultures pick you up." Hardy winked. "If'n you get my meanin."

The wagon train moved out after noon. Less than five days now to cover six days of trail to deliver the mail on time, thought Halluck.

Alexander! That sneakin bastard! Halluck quickly looked around. My men know what I'm thinkin and my rules is done for. He smiled. Good rules. Hard to follow sometimes. Even for the boss. Lord forgive me my weakness; and, if it please You, squeeze Colonel Alexander like he's squeezin me, only more so. That bastard!

Halluck called the men together and looked them over with a hard and unforgiving eye.

"Time's short; and the days are long, boys. We push it, we can still make the deadline."

The men cheered and whipped up the stock. Faster now, the wheels rolled over rock and sand and time. The wheels ate miles out of the day. The faster rolling wheels slowed with the lateness of afternoon and tired mules.

Halluck sat his sweat stained horse and surveyed the day's run. He felt the horse breathing hard between his knees to match the mules. Faster aint fast enough, he reasoned. Would "faster" kill too many mules? Tired mules and exhausted men meant real accidents, he knew.

He tried to sense how far "faster" would take the heavy wagons in a day and at what cost. No matter how I slice it, "faster" aint goin to get us far enough. No, sir, it aint by a day, maybe more.

I've got to find a way to make up a full day, two for safety sake, thought Halluck, putting the lie to his encouragement of the men. If'n I don't . . . ?

<hr />

They pushed well past can't see. The stars had long ago risen to light a moondark sky. Now the milky way was paling into the late black of the pre-dawn morning. A mule stumbled in the dark. The wagon slowed. A mule fell; pulled his mates down with him. The wagon stopped.

"We'll rest here," yelled Halluck. "Sleep if you can. We move at first light."

He crawled down from his horse and sagged to the ground. The stock has been pullin for more hours than I can count. I got two spare teams left that Hickman didn't manage to run off. I've got to find a way; and killin what animals I got left aint it.

What is?

Before he could answer himself, he slept where he sat. His horse wandered off to graze. Still he sat enveloped within a stupor born of long anxiety as trail days dragged; a stupor reared by the urgent need to beat time with plodding mules too dry and tired to plod much further; a stupor, abruptly shattered by discovery.

"By Heaven, that's how we'll do her!" Halluck shouted, half in and half out of his sleep.

He barely heard some of the men respond with a murmur, some with an unconscious, "yes, boss," most with snores in stupors that had no ideas.

Halluck looked around the makeshift camp. Men slept where they had fallen. Animals slept where they stood; or grazed aimlessly. The dawn still held a few dark moments before it lit off a new day.

Give them another hour, he thought. Then it's off to Santa Fe with a vengeance. He slumped again to rest his head on the wheel of the mail wagon.

There was not enough light in the eastern sky to call it pastel time; but he was up rousing the men just the same.

"Unload this here mail wagon," he shouted. "The supplies, the baggage, everything except the mail."

"What about Hickman," called Red from the rear of the mail wagon. "You goin to dump me with the rest of the baggage?"

"Bet your sweet as . . . er . . . you bet we will."

Pole Hawkin pulled the pins and the tailgate fell down; and Red Hickman rolled out onto the point of his head as it bounced in the sand.

"Damn you, Pole," yelled Hickman.

"Tied or free, my rules bind here," said Halluck. "Lay quiet where you are; and we may remember to pick you up before the vultures do. Now, boys. Here's what I got in mind."

Ignoring Hickman's complaints, the men gathered around. Aymes had started a fire and was standing near the big coffee pot waiting for the sound and smell of the boil. He looked on with the rest as Halluck unrolled his plan.

Soon, two sets of four mules, in full harness were roped to the back of the mail wagon. The best team was hitched to the front. That left not more than a dozen mules and half a dozen horses for the other five wagons.

"Pole and Aymes. Saddle up. I'll need you to help push the team, care for the extra teams and keep me awake."

"Not to mention," said Pole Hawkin, "helpin you to keep your scalp, Boss. And, ours too. C'mon Aymes. Coffee."

"Last coffee you gents'll taste for many a day," said Hardy. "If'n I've guessed what the boss is up to doin."

"I aim to run this mail to Santa Fe. One team gets frazzled, we hitch up a fresh team. That one tires, we hitch the third. We work the teams turn and turn about. Two men awake at all times while the third sleeps; or tries to. We won't stop runnin till we get her to Santa Fe, or die a-tryin. Carry enough water for yourself Aymes. You, too Pole. The stock'll have to make do as we go along. Some biscuits and fried bacon in your pockets mite set well. We aint carryin supplies and we aint stoppin to eat."

He looked at the men and saw the sleep slide from their eyes.

"Well?"

Aymes looked at Pole Hawkin. "Best I fry up some bacon and biscuits," he said. He looked at Halluck. "How many days you reckon it'll take?"

"Three. Maybe four. Why Aymes? Why do you ask?"

"Need to know how many biscuits, how much bacon to fry up. Wouldn't want to miss a meal on this here trip."

Tired as the men were, they laughed.

"Pole's so skinny, he miss a meal or two and you won't be able to see him sideways," said Hardy. "Can't hardly see him that-a way now."

Pole Hawkin turned sideways to Hardy and wagged his skinny butt. "You see this?" he said while the men chuckled.

"Hardy. You and the rest of the men'll have to move on as best you can; or stay here and wait for me to bring you fresh animals. Either way you'll be somewhere between slow and stop most of the time."

Halluck was backing the four-mule team into the traces of the mail wagon.

"Short as we are of animals, we'll still make headway," said Hardy. "Even if we can move only two or three of the wagons at a time. We'll haul two or three wagons for five miles; unhitch the stock and go back for the other two. We'll meet you in Santa Fe, Boss."

The men nodded and murmured.

"Maybe," said one.

"Maybe not," said another.

Halluck stepped out from under the necks of the lead mules. "Look for Indians. Five wagons movin slow; or not at all. Temptin pickins, not to mention the stock and a good many white men's scalps."

This time one or two men laughed. Halluck did not.

"Pole! Make sure those spare teams are in full harness. Tied with lead ropes to the wagon. Until they get the hang of things, you'll have to ride drag on 'um, see they don't get mixed and twisted, all bunched up at the back end of the wagon."

"Okay, Boss. They're tied so's they won't no way come lose."

Pole Hawkin came from around the rear of the wagon. Behind him, mules squealed and stomped and squealed. Pastel light shot orange through the dust clouds they raised. Pole took the coffee pot from the fire and poured a cup. "Boss?" He held out the pot to Halluck who let him pour.

Aymes dumped a mixture of hot biscuits and greasy bacon from the frying pan into an empty flour sack and tied the sack to his saddle horn. On the side opposite from the food sack, he hung a full water skin. Halluck and Pole did the same.

Each of the men rode his personal horse. They would not walk anymore or ride in the wagon. They would haze the mules from the plunging back of a horse, urging them to pull the mail at a lope for three, maybe four days, unless they dropped along the way.

Pastel time was still cool with early morning wetness when they pulled out. Halluck and Aymes rode on each side of the team as it broke into a slow run. Pole Hawkin trailed the wagon and the extra teams.

In minutes, it seemed to the remaining men, they were gone.

Before noon, drawn at first by the dust cloud raised by the mail wagon, a single Indian sat his horse on the finger of plateau. He watched the five wagons crawl and stop, crawl and stop, across the desert floor. He watched too tired men rotate too few, too tired teams of animals between wagons. He saw that the wagons could not run.

Could those men still fight? he wondered.

At the sun's zenith for the day, the Indian turned his horse and headed off the mesa. Below, he could just make out the details of his camp across five miles of heat shimmer. His chest swelled with pride.

While my brothers hunt rabbits and quail with string traps, I bring news of great wealth free for the taking.

He put hard heels into his pony's side and enjoyed the frantic slide down the steep slope.

Free for the taking!

# 41

By the time Pete Cortez had climbed the buttress to the lip of the valley, the sun was driving broad golden spokes through the lower branches of the aspen trees; the doves were coming alive in their hundreds; the black-backed crows, cawing over the night's adventures, walked back and forth in twos and threes from carrion to carrion, almost under the horses' feet; and the shufflings and scufflings in the branches of the trees showed that the bats were ready to give up night-picket to pastel time and the day beyond.

Swiftly, the light gathered itself together, painted for an instant the faces of Pete and Beckey, his dark eyes alert; hers washed out, as vacant as space. Then the day crowded the mountainside, pulling down the nightshadow like a slow smile vanishes gloom. A touch of air drew sharpness where a low, even haze had hung like blue dizziness across the face of the country. Sharp air brought out, keen and distinct, the smell of woodsmoke and cattle and the good scent of bacon frying in its own grease.

Pete pushed the horses who needed no urging now. They smelled the scent of cut grass and home droppings.

Beckey moaned at the pick up in pace; and Pete had to reach over and hold her up on the big, gray horse.

He could see the cabin and the corral. Dew shown on the roof like melting ice in the sun. The melting dew misted and rolled like cotton across the shakes.

Four shaggy haired horses in the corral lifted heads and perked ears at him. One called out. In the echo's instant, he knew that the bedraggled horses in the corral were not Cortez horses.

He pulled the smoky horse to a stop and eased Beckey's gray up slowly so as not to dump her on the hard ground.

He drew the Sharps from the scabbard and eyed the cabin.

The patrol of flies hurried out from the porch; smoke swam into the blue sky from the chimney; coughing and orders rang from the dark interior of the cabin. Pete's eye mechanically watched the flicker of the sun on the swing of a rifle barrel poking out of the open window to herd him closer.

"Ho! The cabin. I'm comin in," Pete called out.

The rifle barrel held steady. A loud voice, clear as the note of a bugle, carried across the morning air.

"Reminds this coon of the first time he put rifle sights on a Cortez," came the song. "Near blowed his head clean off while he was a-spyin on our camp."

Pete jumped from the saddle. "Hatcher!" he shouted. "Long John Hatcher!"

Pete ran toward the porch and leaped up to the door. There he was greeted by a tall hunk of a man standing floor to ceiling in greasy buckskin pants; bare from the waist up to his bushy, blond hair. The man's blue-eyed face beamed like crystal through a droopy, blond mustache. Straight, white teeth flashed with the word, "Pedro;" and fell behind dry lips that grimaced as Pete hit him head on and tumbled him to the floor of the porch.

A short, dark-faced man wearing a wool cap came to the door and watched for a moment as the two men rolled in the dust and cuffed each other.

"Sacre damn childrens," said the little man.

Suddenly, the dark man looked up in time to see Beckey fall from the buffalo saddle. As she fell, the modesty of her serape-blanket floated up around her ears. She landed, bare skin sliding on sand, and lay still. The little man with the wool cap saw the red mound on Beckey's shoulder as new blood began to seep from under the bandage of Pete's shirt.

The man jumped at the two who now lay laughing on their backs.

"Sacre damn, Hatcher. There is a naked . . . ."

"Louy," yelled Pete.

Struggle though he might, in an instant, the small man was in the middle of the other two.

"Louy Simonds," yelled Pete. "You grease soaked little French bastard."

"Smell your ownself," said the Frenchman hugging Pete. "No smell worse than a sacre damn Mestizo."

The three men laughed and rolled and slapped and insulted each other in the joy of renewal and ignored the girl who moaned in the dusty yard.

Dibble came to the door. He was about to smile at the antics of these white men when he saw Beckey. Moving quickly, he picked her up and carried her into the cabin. When the men, still panting, looked over Dibble's shoulder, he was swabbing the girl down from foot to head with a wet flour sack.

"What have you found, Pete?" said Louy Simonds.

While Dibble cared for Beckey, Pete told what he knew of the girl, the Indians, her wound and the strange way she had thanked him for saving her life. As he talked, the men ate the freshly cooked bacon and drank the strong, black coffee.

From time to time, Long John Hatcher looked over at the bunk where Beckey lay moaning and, occasionally, writhing in pain. Dibble had covered her with a blanket; and was, himself, eating his ration of the bacon while he studied the three white men. Unlikely pards, his wide, white-ringed eyes said.

Pete saw the look and gave Dibble a brief history until Dibble said he'd heard it more'n once from Hatcher: how Hatcher and Louy had, quite by accident, become Pete's mentors after Garrard had shot Pete in the side of the head on a dark and scary night in the Sangra De Cristo Mountains; and how they'd partnered the Taos war, Indian fightin, grizzly bear baitin and seen the elephant all the way to California just before the almighty rush for gold.

"How'd you finally come out?" asked Pete, remembering how Hatcher had been cleaned by the monte man just before Pete had pulled out to come home.

"Gold minin," said Hatcher. "This hoss aint played a better hand for a longer time, 'less'n it was that first year with Sublette at Jackson Lake and on up the Snake and the land of the boilin springs. All summer and fall, beaver so thick a man could whistle 'um in his sack."

"Gold, she is like the beaver," said Louy. "To catch both, you must spend your days up to armpits in freezin water; both is heavy to haul; and both slip through your fingers like a squaw's affections."

"Naw, Louy. Gold don't smell so bad as beaver," said Hatcher, stabbing the last of the bacon with the tip of his Green River knife.

"The man who catch her, gold or beaver, he smell all the same." Louy wrinkled his nose.

" 'Bout the way you smell," said Hatcher as he pushed Louy out of his seat with a huge hand.

Louy jumped up and put a hand on the knife he wore at his belt. Suddenly, a black, skillet hand grabbed his arm and held it.

"Y'all. Little man. Fetch more water," said Dibble. "The white girl be hot with fever. Dibble think the arrowhead done sunk deeper. Maybe it have holed her wind. She's a-suckin hard just to take air."

"Arryhead?" said Hatcher. "Louy, get up that hot water like the man says. This coon knows a thing or two about arryheads in the windbag. Aint good. Usual fatal, if'n it aint cut out. Usual fatal, if'n it is."

Hatcher went over to look at the girl who lay on her side, face to the wall, shivering under the blanket Dibble had laid over her. Hatcher pulled the blanket back. Dibble had removed Pete's shirt and had washed the wound. Blood trails slid down from the red mound which was her left shoulder. Hatcher flicked his knife blade at the puss which ringed the tip of the arrow shaft.

"Got to come out," he said. "Louy! Where in the devil is that lazy Frenchy?"

"Dibble bring," said Dibble as he handed a pot of still rolling water to the mountain man.

Pete came up behind Hatcher and looked down at the wound.

"Red with fever and white with puss." He put a hand on Beckey's neck. "Hot as noon," he said quietly.

Hatcher stuck the blade of the Green River knife in the hot water.

"Boil this here knife in the water," he said to Dibble.

Dibble looked doubtful.

"She need help now," Dibble said.

"Seen a Crow medicine man boil this knife a-fore he cut at a arry wound. In thirty nine, it was. We'd been havin a runnin fight with the Blackfeet. Thought we was free of them pests when, along about evenin, they ambushed us. Kilt two of our'n afore we fought 'um off.

"This Crow had some wounded to cure or let die. Took this same here Green River and boiled it like a potato. With herbs and such. Made out as if there was some magic to it. Didn't seem like much to this old hoss. Gut shot is gut shot. Boil a man's whole meat bag, he'll die ever' time, if'n he's gut shot.

"What herbs?" said Pete.

"Tobacco'll do," said Hatcher; and he flipped a two ounce chaw into the boiling water.

"What I bound her with just after I found her," said Pete.

"Rather chew it or smoke it; but, sometimes a panther gives up a mouse to catch him a deer."

Hatcher looked down at the girl, bit into the rest of his chaw and offered it around. Louy pulled off a hunk and ground it in his hands. Then he stuffed his pipe. The others declined the offered tobacco.

" 'Course, often as not, the cat misses both baits." Hatcher spit toward the fire. "Where was I?"

"Lyin about that Crow medicine man," said Louy.

Hatcher didn't bat an eye. "Well, that there medicine man, he cut that arryhead out with this same here parboiled knife." Hatcher pointed as Dibble returned the pot to him with the knife handle sticking out of the steam. "Like this here."

Hatcher took the knife and made a cut across the angry flesh mound on Beckey's shoulder. She cried out. Puss and blood squirted from the incision.

He squeezed with thick, calloused fingers. More blood and puss and Beckey screaming. She rolled and turned, fighting the pain; but Pete held her arms and Louy held her legs. Her torso twisted until Hatcher stood up and sat down hard on her heaving hip.

After another squeeze or two, Hatcher took the pot and scalded the wound with the near boiling water. The red mound of flesh turned white, then pink, then red again as skin burned. The writhing figure sagged and lay still.

"Out cold, I reckon," said Pete, letting loose of Beckey's arms.

She groaned when Hatcher pulled hard on the tip of the arrow shaft. It didn't move. He pulled again. Beckey's breath was cut short as if she were struggling to keep the arrowhead next to her lung.

"Let her go, girl," panted Hatcher as he tugged on the shaft. He wiggled it back and forth in the wound, trying to work it free.

"Weren't like this with the gut shot man. Arry come right out." He pulled again. "Wipe the blood. My fingers is a-slippin."

Dibble applied a wet rag trying to dry the arrow shaft before seeping blood lapped and climbed all around it.

Suddenly, Hatcher yelled. "Got her, by god!" He had almost fallen off of the girl's hip with the hard pull. He waved six inches of bloody stick in the air. "By god," he breathed.

"Wash the cut and tie her tight. Then we'll see if this here little lady has grit."

"Grit or no, this lady, she will die by morning," said Louy.

"Ten prime plews says this coon has cured her," said Hatcher.

"You aint got no sacre damn beaver," said Louy, the white of his teeth showing.

"Ten pinches of dust, then."

"Gold? All you had, you left with the Mexican monte dealers and their whores, like the damn fool you are." Louy lay back on his bunk. "Hatcher, you don't got nothin but the talk. Still, I bet. Your bacon and coffee against mine in the mornin. Loser don't eat till dinnertime."

"Hell, Louy. That's Pete's bacon and coffee, and the black man's."

"What's ours is yours," said Pete.

"And, the gut shot man?" asked Dibble. "Did he live?"

Hatcher took the huge knife out of the pot. Pete washed the wound with the flour sack rag soaked in water growing tepid.

"Did he live?" asked Hatcher back. He wiped the knife on his greasy shirt and stuck it away in the deerskin sheath. Then he pulled up his shirt and exposed a washboard belly ribbed by a large red scar.

"I'm here to tell you he did."

Dibble looked at the scar and shook his head.

Hatcher took the tobacco chaw from his mouth and spit. Then he packed the well chewed tobacco all around Beckey's wound.

Beckey whimpered and sighed. Pete flattened the flour sack tight on the wound and wrapped his shirt around her and tied it tight.

"She's breathin some easier," he said.

"Pete, Pete," said Hatcher. "This old hoss recollects you talkin about your Cortez horses, a grand valley like this here for raisin them horses and a dream girl to share with. She that girl?"

Pete looked up at Hatcher, his eyelids flicking. The lids steadied, bent down to cover the dark eyes.

" 'Course not," he said quietly, looking at the now sleeping girl. "I'd kinda forgot that part of it."

"This girl," interrupted Louy. "She's not so lucky as the gut shot man."

Louy had picked up the arrow shaft from the floor where Hatcher had thrown it; and was waving it.

"The head of the arrow," he said, "be she flint or steel, she is still in this girl."
There was no arrowhead on the end of the bloody shaft.

A sharp pain woke Beckey from her dream of death. From death to life in an instant. She exhaled and the pain hit her again.

"Oh," she sighed.

Her eyes sprang open to the night song of cricket fiddles. With her eyes wide open, she saw nothing except the faint glow of almost dead coals strained through a haze of pain, far, far across the small room. She looked around her. Sheer black.

Suddenly, she caught a shine from the far corner. Sheer white. China white. Then another. Albino agate. Moving in tandem, rolling together to lag her where she lay. She watched the approaching whites, aware of the sharp pain of each breath and, more remotely, of the crickets' leggy song.

"Y'all awake, miss," a voice said. The voice came from the white ovals which she now knew were eyes.

"Water," she whispered. Her throat felt dry, constricted. "Water," she repeated.

The man said nothing; but the whites disappeared. She heard a clank in the far corner. The whites reappeared. She felt cool water on her lips; let it trickle down her throat, then let it fall, cascade, until she choked. She choked and coughed and cried down the whole valley with the pain of it.

In a moment of clatter, a lamp was lit; and she saw three white men and a black above her looking down. Even with her shallow breathing, she could smell them, standing in sweat stained long johns, faces brushed with new beard pushing old, eyes bright with wondering.

One man, a short, dark man, bent lower. Beckey cringed in spite of herself and the pain. He had no scalp. The top of his head was a mass of ridges of red scar tissue.

He noticed her look almost immediately.

"Pardon, Cherie."

He put a hand over the pulp and backed away. In a moment he was back, a wool cap covered his head.

The black man knelt by the bunk, a tin cup in his hand.

"Here be water. But, drink it slow. By 'n by you get enough." His voice was raspy, but soft. "Time you drink this, Dibble have beef stew mashed up and hot. You drink stew. Need strength." He held the cup to her lips, motioned for her to take it with her hand.

"Grit. This coon says she's got grit."

Hatcher took his hands from his knees, spit into the palms and rubbed them together. "By god!"

Dibble was across the room at the fire. "This coon, he say she got 'um guts and y'all listen to Dibble."

Beckey saw what passed for a smile come to the mountain man's face. "Louy, Pete. The little lady's got grit."

"Sacre damn. Louy know that when he first see her. What take you so sacre damn long? Eh? Long John Hatcher?"

"Frenchman, you bet agin the cure. You don't know grit from deer pills." Hatcher laughed. "Now, go back to sleep. Be a cold day in the hollar of Hell if'n me and Pete and Dibble, here, needs us a Frenchman to tell us about grit. And, come mornin, I'll have your bacon and biscuits and coffee."

Beckey saw another face up close. Not a new face. She'd seen that face. She knew it well; but, from where? Then she remembered. She remembered lying naked under a loose blanket along side the fallen cottonwood.

"Biscuits," she whispered. "Taste like, like, well, what he just said. Only from the back end of a hog." She didn't smile. She felt like hurting. "Hog dropping biscuits!"

Pete smiled down at her.

"Yes, ma'am. Glad to see you aint feelin any the worse for them hog droppins." He turned serious. "Hatcher cut out the shaft of the arrow. The head didn't come with it. Sharp pain you feel with each breath? Could be the head of that arrow pressin or cuttin into your lung."

She let his words sink in; felt the pain with each breath; felt the arrowhead deep inside her.

"Cut it out." Her voice was a whisper. The tone was a command.

"Can't," said Pete. "Too deep. You'll need a doctor for that kind of cuttin. Even then . . . ."

She heard his voice trail off to die in the cricket chorus that filled the late night silence.

"Stew. Mashed and hot." Dibble knelt next to the bunk, pot in one hand and spoon in the other.

"I'll feed her," said Pete. "She likes my fixins."

She saw him take the spoon from the black man.

"Slow and easy, Pete. Slow and easy."

The black man stood and passed from Beckey's sight. The other men, Hatcher and Louy, were no longer visible to her. She saw the spoon coming toward her and puckered with hunger in spite of the pain. She sucked stew from the spoon. It burned her mouth. She felt the sting; but didn't care. When the spoon was slow in coming, she grabbed Pete's arm and tried to force him to spoon more stew faster.

"Easy does it, Beckey Goddard. Stew's hot. Your meatbag has shrunk some. Can't have you pukin this good stew all over my cabin."

He put another spoonful of the liquid stew to her lips. She drank, coughed; cried out, puckered.

"More," she said, her whisper loud now, almost a voice.

"I told you boys she liked my cookin," Pete laughed.

Hatcher and Louy snored back at him from the other bunks. Dibble sat slumped in the chair, skillet hands draped like piles of rope on his skinny lap.

Pete turned back to Beckey and edged another spoonful of stew toward her lips.

"Tastes like," she sucked hungrily at the spoon, swallowed, whimpered. "Hog droppings," she finished.

Before Pete could argue back, she slept.

He took a spoonful of last night's mashed up stew. It was nearly cold now. He turned and spit it into the last of the coals.

"She aint as sick as she makes out," he said to the sleeping room.

Beckey Goddard sat rigid on the bunk, her arms across her bare breasts. She watched in the dim light of morning as Pete cut a wide slit in the new, red, trade goods blanket. It hurt when he pulled the slit over her head and let the blanket fall around her.

"Took your own sweet time about covering my nakedness." Her tone was truly nasty.

"Didn't notice," said Pete.

It hurt as Pete cut a slit in the blanket for each arm. The right arm was pulled through. Slowly, the left. She cried out. The pain passed. The arm fell outside the blanket.

"Best we can do for clothes till you're healed some." Pete smiled down at her. "There's a latrine out back, if'n you, well . . . ." Pete's face shied up at that. "We'll help you walk."

It hurt to hate. Hate scrunched her neck and shoulders. Man-hate hurt; but, she couldn't help it. The sharp arrow-pain had eclipsed the ache deep down inside her torn crotch. But she remembered. Soft-hard manshafts had ripped her and her soul felt stained. These men are no different, she said to herself. They want me for their pleasure. Never mind my grief.

"Take what you will, you bastards!" She shouted out loud, not knowing she was shouting out loud. "Bastards! Bastards! Bastards!" She swept them all, green eyes blazing.

Pete took a quick step backwards. Then he stood and stared.

"Suit yourself, lady," he said finally. "We got work to get done." With that he wheeled out of the cabin. Hatcher and Louy and Dibble followed.

Beckey stood. She felt weak all over; and her legs wobbled. She stumbled over to the fire and poured coffee into a tin cup. Her hand shook. She took a sip of the coffee and felt her teeth grow sudden moss. She spit out what she could.

She hobbled to the door and around the porch to the railing at the end of the cabin. The cut-board out house looked far away. Still, she'd walked many a mile before this. It took her more than half an hour to make it to the privy and back to the cabin door.

She could see the men down by the corral. She watched as the black man flew off the backside of a bucking horse to plow up dust and manure in the middle of the corral. In spite of herself, she laughed. The pain of it sent her to her bunk.

After what seemed like most of the morning, Beckey went to the fire. The frying pan held Louy's strips of bacon. There were a couple of cold biscuits left in a plate on the hearth. She ate a slice of the bacon; tried a biscuit; ate that and the other. Bolted flour, she thought. Makes all the difference.

The coffee pot was still in the coals. Now, if I can stand to swallow that hot mud they pass off as coffee. She poured more into the tin cup and got down a sip or two and threw the rest into the ashes.

"God! That's beyond strong," she said aloud.

"Y'sum. It on the fire day and night. Just add water and coffee, time to time."

"Oh!" Beckey jumped and turned. "Oh!" She looked into the whites of the black man's eyes.

"Dibble, he name, ma'am." He pulled off his hat. "Dibble see you's feelin some better. Let Dibble fry you up some beef and potatoes."

Dibble smiled and a picket fence of white teeth added to the eyes and seemed to fill the dark cabin with light.

Beckey started to yell at the black man; hesitated, then said quietly. "Thank you, Dibble. I could eat more. And, maybe its time to thin this coffee some."

"Y'sum."

Eagerly, the black man added cold, fresh water to the pot; lay newly cut piñon logs on smoldering coals; and sliced beef into the frying pan along with cut up potatoes.

Beckey sat on the bunk. "Who are you men?" she asked.

She felt the rough wool of the blanket coat scratch her nakedness underneath. Around these men, the blanket didn't feel much like clothes.

"How'd I come here? My back feels like Hell's own fire. What is it?"

"Pete can tell you most of it. Pete!" Dibble yelled out the door. "Lady wants y'all!"

"I don't either."

Beckey shouted at Dibble as he grinned back at her. Then his face got long and serious.

"Dibble aint no 'count; but these men. Hatcher, Louy and Pete. They's good men. Aint Indians; though they sometimes acts like they is."

He looked hard at Beckey and screwed up his forehead.

"Dibble aint used to talkin to white girls. Still, he's seen most ways a girl can be used. White man, Indian, niggah. Beast in a man aint colored. Any color. You been used by them Indians. When Dibble cleaned you . . . ."

"You what?"

"Washed the dirt and blood off'n you."

Beckey wrapped her arms around her breasts and shuddered at the sharp bite in her shoulder.

"You washed me?"

"Y'sum."

"All over?"

"Don't fret none. Dibble wash blood off more'n one woman. He don't mind the washin."

"'He don't mind the washin?' What about me?"

"You was too sick to mind."

Dibble turned to the sputtering pan and raked the meat and potatoes around in the hot grease.

"Pete!" he called out the door. "Pete Cortez. Miss Beckey want y'all."

"I do not!" Beckey shouted.

"Dinner's ready, ma'am." Dibble spooned the meat and potatoes onto a plate. "Come sit at the table. Fresh coffee's at the boil. Soon ready, too."

She felt weak from her excursion to the outhouse; but made the slow steps to the table without falling. As she sat down to eat, Dibble put skillet hands knuckle down on the table and tried to catch her eyes. For a moment she dodged; then, she let his eyes grab her. What the hell, she thought. He's seen everything else there is to see. Still, she veiled her eyes against the black man's probing look.

He spoke to her quickly, softly. He told her about the oxen he had slaughtered to survive, the bear, and a job, grub and a white man's bunk under roof. His sentence for stealing from this Cortez man was to feel the whip of his kindness and the dignity of free man's sweat.

He told her what he knew of Hatcher and Louy. And, he told her about Pete's dream of a great rancho, this, The Cortez.

"Pete Cortez be a good man." Dibble smiled. "The others be like children. But, their hearts aint small. All of them. Good folk. They only want you well. So, you can hate the Indians for what they done. Hate them as left you alone on the trail. Hate your pa, them other yankees."

"What!?"

"How do Dibble know?"

Beckey wagged her head. "It seems there is not much you don't know about me."

"Y'all spoke up some with the fever."

Dibble smiled and put a huge, rough hand on her forehead.

"Hum. Cool now."

He withdrew his hand. For an instant, Beckey missed its gentle touch.

"Hate them others all you want. But, these boys? You won't find no better. And, Pete? He's the best man among us."

Dibble's face paled with embarrassment.

"Dibble, he talk too much."

At that moment, Pete came into the cabin. Dibble turned quickly back to the fire. He sliced more beef and potatoes into the hot grease.

Beckey ate. Pete stared at her a long time. She finished her meal quickly; but she had to let the coffee cool. While she waited, she wiped the grease from the plate with a hard biscuit. She wrestled the biscuit with her teeth until it crunched and crumbled. She didn't look up.

"Soak it in the coffee," said Pete. "Help save your teeth. Biscuits don't stay soft in this dry air."

Beckey raised her eyes to him. The veil fell away for a moment. For that moment, she saw Pete as Dibble had described him; and she remembered his soft voice, his gentle touch.

Just as quickly, she rebelled and settled the veil over her eyes again. The momentary image blurred; then it faded.

"There is nothing soft about this place; or my, my jailers. And it is not the dry air."

Quickly, Dibble looked around from the fire. "Ma'am!" he said. Beckey ignored him.

"Mister Cortez? What do you intend to do with me? After you've had your way."

"My way? Oh, yeah. That."

She felt her own fierce pout and saw him smile at her anyway; thought the smile looked a little sad and wondered why.

"Hadn't given you much thought past havin my way."

He turned to the fire and picked up the coffee pot. He poured a cup and offered it to Dibble. He refilled Beckey's cup and poured one for himself. He stood looking down at the girl; took a gulp of coffee, gagged and spit it into the fire.

"Lord, Lord," he called after he finished coughing. "This aint coffee."

He threw the rest of the liquid into the fire.

"Dibble, I don't mind you a-bringin this here girl into the cabin, gettin my bedroll all blood-soaked, cuttin holes in my good blanket, sittin in the cool of the cabin of a mornin when there's horses to be broke, cookin and nursemaidin and wastin good biscuits on this here woman.

"No, sir, Dibble. I don't mind that! But, by god!" he shouted. "I'll not have horse piss for coffee. And this here is worse than piss."

He kicked the pot into the fire.

"Woman's coffee. I mind woman's coffee. I won't stand . . . ."

"That is entirely enough, Mister Cortez," said Beckey. "Your coffee is worse than your biscuits, if that is at all possible. Speaking of, well, piss. I ordered your man to make coffee a girl could drink without tasting privy with every sip."

"Miss," said Pete. She saw the sweat on his forhead. "You got part of that right. It's my coffee. Drink it or not, I don't care; but don't change it.

"As for Dibble. He aint anyone's man, except his own."

Beckey looked at Dibble, saw the sly smile.

"And, he knows how I take my coffee. Thick as mud. Hot as the wrath of God. Black as the soul of a bad horse—or woman."

"This old hoss aint heard coffee blessed that-a-way in a coon's age and a half," said Hatcher at the door.

Beckey turned to look at the mountain man. She felt the pull on her shoulder; but still marveled at the greasy buckskins, the smell of the man, his peach fuzz beard and the twigs in his scraggly blond hair.

"Boy's right, though, ma'am," he said. "Louy, step in here and make some real coffee. Seems the black man has forgot how."

Louy followed Hatcher into the cabin. He looked at Beckey and she remembered he was the scalped man and shuddered.

"I'll pour yours before she gets boiled to scum," he said quietly to her.

"Thank you, Mister Louy." Beckey smiled and stuck her chin out at Pete. "And, when the coffee's drunk, what do you intend doing to, eh, about me?" She winced with a sharp pain.

"We been talkin about that down to the corral." Pete's voice took on a deeper tone.

"I didn't think you'd had a thought about me."

"The arrowhead is still inside your shoulder. Maybe cuttin into your lung with each breath. You need a doctor to dig way in there."

"Arryhead cuts your windbag," said Hatcher. "All the air you suck in will leak out the hole. Slow or fast, you'll die."

Beckey looked from face to serious face. "Can you fetch me a doctor?" she said quietly.

"Ridin hard," said Pete, "take five, six days from here to Santa Fe. Same back, or slower, dependin on if the doc can ride. Or will. And, maybe the doctor aint there. Too long to wait, I'm thinkin."

Pete pushed his hat to the back of his head letting black curls fall across his forehead.

"On the other side, if we take you there, same six days goin; but the ride might do more damage than waitin quietly here twice that long."

They stood together in the small cabin. Boiling coffee and buzzing flies made the noise, and tight breathing. Beckey coughed. She could not help a small cry as the arrowhead seemed to bight deeper.

Louy poured the coffee all around. No one drank.

"I don't think I can ride and live," Beckey said finally. "Each time I cough or breath too heavily, I feel as if it moves a tiny bit deeper." She put a hand to her left breast. "I couldn't sit a horse for six days."

"Hair's off the bear," said Hatcher. "But it aint spring." He rubbed his chin. "Seems like if'n we take her, she dies sooner; we don't, she dies later. Maybe dies before the doc can get here. Even then . . . ."

"Travois," said Pete. "Indian travois. The gray horses of hers are even gaited and used to haulin. A bed of blankets would keep her quiet about as good as her stayin here. Six days. Maybe faster."

Beckey saw the shine in Pete's eyes and wondered, what the hell does he care?

"The country, she is mighty rough. The travois bounce pretty good over rocks and . . . ." Louy looked doubtful.

"We can fix she a sling," said Dibble. "Hang it between the two gray horses. Dibble see it done. Man ride on each side of the gray horses so they stay together. Buggy horses be used to that, anyways. A sling."

"A sling?" Pete asked.

In an hour it was done. The frame from one of the bunks with its rope strung mattress was lashed between pack trees mounted on each of the grays as they stood side by side. Dibble took the first ride around the corral. The grays worked well together and settled in quickly. He lay back with skillet hands under his head. The bed frame, slung between the gray horses, hardly swayed. The ride was smooth.

"We'll take her to Santa Fe in style," said Pete. "Me and Hatch and Louy."

"What about Dibble. It be he sling. Dibble come too." He looked long and hard at Pete.

"Naw. You got to stay and take care of The Cortez."

Pete looked off into the desert and kicked dirt with the toe of his boot.

"We by god meet some of them Jicarillo Apaches, another rifle'd be handy." Hatcher gave Pete a funny look. "This here rancho will take care of itself like it done for a few years afore you got here, son."

Pete looked from Hatcher to Dibble. "Well in a way you're right, Hatch. In a way, not."

"How not?"

"Seems there's a posse out to get Dibble. Halluck told me. Said they'd ride to Hell or Santa Fe, if need be. For two thousand dollars reward. Dead or alive."

"Well, if that don't beat the stink of beaver bait," said Hatcher. "What'd the black man do. Kill a white man?" Hatcher started to laugh; saw Pete's face. "I'll be damned."

"Dead is how," said Louy. "This far from home, dead's easy. Alive'd be crazy. They'll just shoot him and take back his head."

Louy ruffled the tight black curls of Dibble's top knot. "Not that we care a sacre damn about this boy; but dead blacks smell up a place."

"Headless, dead blacks do," said Hatcher.

"Dibble stays!" said Pete.

"Dibble don't want to stink up your place. No sir!"

Dibble smiled and winked at Beckey.

"You white mans don't need no another rifle. You got the Frenchman. Aint no Apaches stand his smell."

Dibble turned and walked to the corral where several unbroken horses milled in the dust.

Hatcher took one of the grays, Pete the other. They rode just outside of each horse, a lead rope tied to a headstall in hand. Beckey lay on blankets in the sling. Louy brought up the rear, leading a pack mule loaded with water, bacon, flour and cartridges.

They were nearly to the desert end of the valley when Dibble rode up on one of the fresh broke horses, the reins in his teeth and a long rifle cradled in skillet hands.

Pete turned at the sound of the up-trotting horse.

"Dibble," cried Beckey. "Go back. The posse."

Pete smiled. "He knows. If a man works for me, he does what I say. I told him to stay."

"Well, Pete Cortez, make him stay, then."

"Can't."

"Why? You just said . . . ."

"He quit! He don't work for me no more. He's a free man and goes where a free man goes out here."

"Where?"

"Out here? Wherever he wants."

"To be killed? Gunned down by money hungry scum posing as the law?"

Beckey was sitting up in the sling. Pete looked down at her.

"Maybe."

"You can't let him . . . ."

A cough shot sharp pain across her shoulder. She sagged back on the sling-pallet. One of the grays shifted legs. She bounced and cried out. "Can't let him—quit."

"Can't stop him. His choice. A man's choice. To live or die as befits him."

"Can, but won't stop him," she said. "Cruel. Men. All of you alike. Cruel with beast or man—or woman."

"Let's ride," said Pete, as if he did not hear her.

He turned away to lead the grays off the lip of the valley down the steep, winding trail to the desert below.

Beckey caught a fleeting look at Dibble sitting the Cortez horse at the top of the trail. He sat tall and thin and straight like a bronze, cast forever against the back light of the western sky. Just before Beckey dipped down the trail and out of sight of him, she saw a flash of proud eyes shinning.

It was evening and pastel time. Sheriff Bobby Joe Potter sat his horse and looked around the deserted camp. The horse stood spraddle legged, breathing hard from the ride just finished. Potter's ample gut crowded the saddle horn as it rose and fell; but Potter didn't notice. He was where he was second most comfortable, in the saddle. First most was any barroom.

The other members of Potter's posse pulled their sweating horses up. Each man sat his saddle frozen for a moment as if each feared he would shatter without the day long motion to hold him together. Then, in unison, a gust of air fled from pent up lungs as each man huffed and puffed in rhythm with the panting of his spent horse.

Potter did not wait for his horse to settle down. He pointed down at the cold fire ring.

"Check it out, Jones."

Blessed Jones crawled off his horse and stood for a moment rubbing his sore, wet rump. Then he hobbled over to the fire ring. Grunting with the effort, he got down on his knees. He felt the ashes, sniffed them, poked his finger clear to the dirt underneath. He looked up at Potter.

"This blessed fire aint more than a day old," he said. "I'd say yesterday mornin."

He tossed a handful of ashes into the gusting wind and watched the wind mix ashes with the gathering of evening dust.

"How the hell can you tell," said Cussin Jim. He stood by the side of his horse where he was in the process of making water. "One day, two, a week. Ashes, once cold, are all the same."

Blessed Jones walked around the camp, his head down. Near a juniper, larger than the others, he stopped to study the sand.

"Looks like a blessed contest."

He knelt again and ran his finger along the edges of several shallow furrows. Then he stood up and looked out along the stretch of trail to the west.

"Yesterday morn, for sure."

"Just as god damn likely, yesterday week," said Jim. His water-making was ending in a few final spurts. "Who the hell'd have a contest of any kind way out here in this god damned desert?"

Jones ignored the remark just like he ignored most of what Cussin Jim had to say.

Muddy Waters got down from his horse and went to watering the sand beside the spot where Jim had just finished. The light wind blew bits of saliva-made mud from his bristly cheeks. He looked back at Blessed Jones.

"Contest? Way out here? What kind of contest, Blessed."

Waters wrinkled his nose in doubt as he shook off the last three drops.

"Just like you and Jim there," said Jones pointing. "Whether you know it or not, you're in a pissin contest with Jim; and him with you. It's the same way with these freighter fellers."

"Pissin contest," said Potter, still in the saddle. "Aint any of you can piss past your buttons." He got down and stood next to Waters.

"Them freighters stood here," said Jones. "Maybe half a dozen. Pissed all over the place. This here feller won by a mile." He pointed down at one of the shallow furrows which marched out across the desert like a miniature riverbed.

Potter grunted; leaned back with both hands inside the front of his pants.

"It's all in knowing the elevation," he said laughing.

A long, yellow stream shot out from between his hands. It arched into the blue of the desert sky—and into a gust of wind. Quick as it had shot out, the wind was quicker.

"Son of a bitch, Potter," yelled Cussin Jim, jumping back. "You're pissin all over me."

"Sure enough," said Waters, laughing. A dead fly fell from Waters long hair.

Jones joined in the laugh, until Cussin Jim turned with his hand on the butt of his pistol.

"God damn it! Gettin pissed on aint funny." He had the gun half out of his belt.

"Hell it aint," said Potter. He landed a huge fist on the back of Jim's neck driving him to his knees.

After a moment of neck rubbing, Jim stood up. "I see what you mean, Bobby Joe," he said to Potter.

Jim had a thin smile on his lips; his puss eye was open wide along with his good eye. Potter read fear in the eyes; but, in truth, they spelled out stealthy death.

"Cussin Jim. If I smell you tomorrow or the next day," said Jones. "I'll know from the smell of you and the tracks across your vest, you was pissed on this evenin. That's ever-blessed trackin."

"You seen it. You seen him piss on me. God damn it! That's how you'll know!"

"That's part of scoutin, too."

Jones looked Cussin Jim in the eye and never cracked his own serious look.

"We'll camp here tonight," said Potter. "Let the animals recruit."

"And my sore ass," said Waters. He rubbed his butt and dislodged another dead fly from under his hat.

Potter motioned Waters toward the pack animals.

"Take us a day and a half, two more days at most."

He squinted into the last rays of the setting sun.

"Then we kill us a two thousand dollar niggah."

Hardy squinted at the pastel haze trying to make out what he saw slowly winding toward him out of the low foothills. Riders, he thought. But, what's that contraption between them horses? Aint no rig ever I seen.

"Heads up boys," he called softly to the other men. "Riders a-comin; and they don't look right to me."

Bob Ellis moved beside Hardy and handed him a rifle. Ellis held his own rifle at the ready.

"I count three," said Ellis. "And, looky there. Seems another man is followin some behind the others."

"Let 'um come," said Hardy.

The other men moved away from the fire and into the shadows.

"Maybe we'll meet the fellers been makin the dust along our back trail for the last two days," said Ellis.

A half hour passed. Pastel time faded into night. Suddenly, Hardy caught the quiet sounds of horses walking slowly. One of his own mules trumpeted. Surprisingly nearby, the call was answered with a snort and a whinny.

"Hello the camp!"

In spite of himself, Hardy jumped.

"Who be you?" said Hardy. "White man by the sound of him," Hardy whispered to Ellis.

"Pete Cortez and friends. We're comin in."

"Cortez! Come on; but make her slow and easy." Hardy smiled and let his gun drop to the crook of his arm. "Come on, and welcome."

Beckey slept near the dying fire. She still lay on the bunk frame on which she had ridden all day slung between her faithful grays.

Pete stood nursing a cup of coffee and looking down on her. Strange actin girl, he thought. Bitter, yes. Indian rape would gall anyone. Galls me for that matter. But, seems she makes more of it than it deserves now that she's safe. It's like she hates me. Why me? Hates all men? Maybe she does.

After cleaning her wound while the men busied their eyes elsewhere, Pete had fed Beckey and covered her with extra blankets against the cold desert night. In front of the men, she had yelled him away from her.

"Keep you're free hands off of me. Let me be. Indian!"

Just as quickly, she had fallen asleep.

The freighters had shifted their eyes away from Pete, embarrassed for him. They weren't embarrassed to see Dibble again; just surprised!

"Man, you're takin a chance. There's a posse right behind us and chasin your ass."

Hardy looked at Dibble as if half expecting him to jump on his horse and bolt out into the shelter of the night.

Dibble only smiled. "I recollect what Mister Hickman told y'all about Dibble. That's why he lit out before."

"Then why are you back?"

"Mr. Hardy. Before, Dibble had no friend. Never had him no friend. Now!" He pointed toward Pete and Beckey. "Dibble got friend." He held up three fingers.

"That's only three?"

Hardy pointed at the edge of the fire where Hatcher and Louy stood smoking and watching the night.

Dibble shook the three fingers at Hardy and pointed to the stump of the missing finger.

"All four are your new friends. Is that it?"

"Sure enough, Mister Hardy."

"I hope they're your friends when that posse gets here," said Ellis.

Dibble smiled a wide, bright smile, his high cheeks puffed higher by the fire's shadow light. He showed the three fingers around the fire.

"They Dibble friend."

A couple of the men shook heads as if in doubt. The men did not see the empty space at the end of the skillet hand where the little finger, the fourth finger, should have been.

Now the camp slept except for two of the freighters who clutched rifles in white knuckles and stood or sat or wandered out in the black night among the grazing stock.

⸻

The pastel time of the new morning was tinged with blood.

"Been scalped for fair," said Hatcher looking down at the two night guards.

"Aint a animal in sight," said Hardy. "How could they have made off with every head of stock and make no noise doin it."

"My fault," said Hatcher. "This hoss always says: any coon what allows another man to stand his guard is likely to lose his stock and his own hair. Well, this hoss slept a mite too sound last night. Louy, too."

Hatcher scratched an arm pit.

"Must be gettin old," he said quietly.

He began carefully to scout the area around the dead guards; then farther out where the animals had been grazing.

He came back into camp after an hour.

"Indians. Six of 'um. Come out of the night on foot. Walked the stock away one or two at a time. That-a way." He pointed west toward a sloping ridge and beyond. "Took near thirty head of stock. They're hold up somewheres for the day or we'd see the dust."

"This far south and west," said Hardy, "Apaches. Jicarillos most likely. Mean when they can profit by another man's stock. I reckon we been seein their dust behind yonder ridge for the last couple of days."

Hatcher walked to his bed roll and picked up his rifle and his possibles sack. Then he walked out of camp in the direction of yonder ridge and the western hills.

Pete and Louy grabbed up their weapons and started to follow. Hatcher turned to face them.

"Stay in camp. Fort up the wagons. Take care of the girl. I'll be back by noon with the stock."

"But a half a dozen Indians?" said Pete.

"Aint many for old Long John Hatcher. You'll just make dust. May be them Indians took the animals to draw a bunch of us away from the wagons. As it stands now, we're too many for six Indians. But they must be a-itchin to make off with your plunder." Hatcher wrinkled his nose and winked. "Besides, a Indian can smell Louy from a mile off." Smiling, Hatcher turned and continued on his way.

"Sacre damn Hatcher, she wear the same smell as Louy." Louy smiled and leaned on his rifle. "It is Hatch's turn to be scalped." Louy rubbed his own scalp under the wool cap. "Louy, she already been," he said.

With that Hatcher stopped, turned again. "This coon aint so much a fool as to get hisself scalped like a Frenchman. You boys stay with the wagons and the girl. And, say. That posse rides in, you side the black man. He aint a half bad cook."

Then, he pointed toward the western hills with his rifle and began to walk.

" 'Bout noon," he called over his shoulder, "walk on over that ridge to help with the animals." He smiled to himself. "If'n you don't see me nor no animals, come a runnin!"

Hatcher topped the far ridge and disappeared.

⁙

The early morning sun was just arrived on the desert floor. Above the sun's slanted rays, a pair of young hawks lay motionless in the sky, as if forever mounted on the pedestal of a warming updraft. Except for an occasional squirrel, the ground creatures, the quail and the rabbit and the wolf, had deserted their trails in the sand to hide away the day in holes under thick brush.

The night trail made by the stolen stock cut the pristine desert crust into fresh ribbons, curling here and there; but mostly smooth and straight ahead.

Looks like them Indians knew a-fore hand where to take them critters to grass and water, Hatcher thought. Won't be far. Maybe they're plannin on holdin them for a while and then bringin 'um back to collect a re-ward. Maybe?

Hatcher tread with the moccasin quiet of a man who had spent a lifetime walking with danger; and still lived. A sunning rattlesnake saw him pass close by like the breeze; and was not afraid.

Quickly, the rising sun grew hot on Hatcher's back. The heat melted the night's reservoir of body moisture which wafted through his skin to soak the buckskin shirt. Swirls of gentle breeze turned the sweat to gas as he walked; and the process kept him cooler than the sun meant him to be.

He carried the Jake Hawkin made rifle in the crook of his left arm. In between the fingers of his left hand, he squeezed three paper cartridges a .58 caliber ball tied into the end of each. The rifle had been born a flintlock; but, with the advent of the mercury cap, Hatcher fit the lock with a nipple. He carried three caps between thumb and fingers of the same left hand. He checked the percussion cap on the nipple of the gun. It was tight and ready. With the load in the rifle and the cartridges and caps in hand, he could fire, load and fire the muzzle loading Hawkin four times in less than a minute.

By midmorning a dust haze rode the desert's washes and scrubbed the hills. From just under the top of a ridge, Hatcher studied the distant mountains. He could make out the swale which marked the lip of The Cortez. Rather be up there than here, he thought. He stepped his gaze down the mountain from far to near, stopping at intervals like a gunner walks an artillery barrage.

In a matter of minutes, he bracketed the thicker dust coming from a depression not more than a mile away. Got them animals feedin on grass in a meadow, I reckon.

Hatcher began to walk the last mile. He moved quickly from juniper to rock outcrop, up the round mounds of brush covered hillocks, down the sand slopes into gullies. Soon he could smell the animals, and, he thought, the Indians. Louy's right about me smellin like him. I'll just stay down wind till I can sidle up to them Indians and talk 'um out of their stock. He smiled up the last slope, a bent and cruel smile.

He crawled the last few yards to the top of the incline and looked through a clump of greasewood into a small meadow of knee high grass and grazing animals. Part of the meadow was wet with the flow from some hidden spring, almost a marsh. Hatcher hunted among the stock until he found his own shaggy, mountain Palomino. It still trailed a lead rope from its jaw.

He saw the Indians beyond the herd. Quickly, he surveyed the enemy. Six braves around a smoldering fire. Nearby, the fly bloated carcass of a mule. Kilt them a mule for breakfast. Them Indians have et well. Indians do love mule meat.

Four of them redskins are laid out; appear to be sleepin the day away. Two sittin up, heads bowed. Sleepin away a gorgin of mule? I don't wonder. There's a rifle on the ground and a bow and quiver of arrows. And, another rifle. I count six rifles. All but one is a muzzle loader. T'other? She's a fast loadin Sharps. Armed mighty well for peaceable Indians. No horses nearby the camp. Turned their own in with ours, looks like. Well, noon aint a-far off.

Hatcher began the long, slow crawl down the slope and into the herd. He came off his belly for the first time at the fore feet of his own horse. His shirt front and pants were soaked from the marshy wet of the natural pasture. He took the lead rope and got to his knees. He pulled the horse's head down and made a halter of the rope around the horse's muzzle. Then, slowly, he climbed up the horse's near front leg. He took the rope halter in his left hand without spilling cartridge or cap. He took a hunk of shaggy main in his right hand along with the rifle.

The horse shivered as if he'd just awakened to what the man was doing; but, too late. With a bounce, Hatcher was a-straddle. The horse pranced a step or two then settled under the accustomed weight.

Instantly, Hatcher swung his eyes around the herd. The animals cropped grass, undisturbed. He looked across the backs of the animals to the hostiles' camp. The Indians still slept; although one of the two sitting up, wrinkled his nose as if he smelled the mountain man.

For an instant, Hatcher froze. Then he dug heels into his horse and burst to the upwind side of the herd. He gave a wild yell that never stopped and danced the horse back and forth at the very rumps of the mules and horses. Heads popped up. A mule kicked out at Hatcher. A horse snorted and bolted away from the yell that never stopped. Then, the stock was running, running back along the ribbon of trail they had cut the night before.

Hatcher rode in among them yelling the yell that never stopped. Next to him, a mule screamed and fell. Hatcher did not hear the Indian shot that had killed it; but he knew. He didn't look back.

He knew the Indians would be up now and running to catch the herd; to catch a straggling mule or horse; a-foot or horseback, to catch him. Out of the corner of his eye, he saw a horse pull away from the stampede and begin to slow; then another; and a third.

The memory of sweet grass is stronger than fear, he thought. He tried to circle over to pick up the hungry horses. A bullet sang by his ear. Instinctively, he kneed the Palomino back into the running herd.

His yell never stopped; and the prance of his shaggy horse kept most of the stock in a panic down the trail toward the wagons and the hour of noon.

The herd plowed over the last ridge and into the arms of eleven men with rifles and yells of their own. As the animals raced past the men, one man jumped up on a mule. Another grabbed a halter and let himself be dragged along until the horse got bored with the weight and stopped over the familiar grass of the night before.

Pete Cortez whistled; and the smoky horse cut away from the lead of the pack and circled around to skid to a stop at Pete's side.

Almost as fast as the herd had bolted at the mountain man's yell, it slowed, began to mill, became individual animals cropping grass, with here and there, a snort and a blow. Within minutes, several of the mules were rolling in the dusty grass. Others remembered the small spring fed pond beside the wagon camp and were drinking.

Hatcher's yell stopped. He rolled off the side of his horse, panting as if he too had run the miles on foot. Pete led the smoky horse and walked up to Hatcher. After a moment, he squinted into the sky.

"It was noon an hour ago," he said.

Hatcher caught a last bit of breath. He turned toward Pete with slab hands on hips. Then he looked back down the trail off to the west. On the far ridge a lone Indian sat his horse, a black cut-out in stone against the sky. Slowly, he raised his arm and shoved his rifle high above his head.

Hatcher raised his own rifle in return salute.

"Here where you been a-sittin, it may be a mite past noon," he said to Pete. "Over there where I come from, it aint noon quite yet!"

The freight men let the animals recruit for an hour before hitching them into the harnesses.

"Two less mules," said Hardy. "And the rest aint much. We'll maybe get fresh stock at Fort Union, Las Vegas or Tecolote. We're less than one hundred and fifty mile from Santa Fe." He looked into Pete's anxious eyes. "We're enough to keep them Indians off; and with you boys, we could fight a hundred. We'll get along, slow but sure."

"Thanks, Hardy," said Pete. "But the girl is breathin hard and plumb feverish. I think we better make a run for Santa Fe."

"Them Indians catch you out there and alone, it could go bad. And, them not over fond of Mister Hatcher after what he done to shame them."

"Have to chance it. I'm thinkin a day or two, one side or the other, may be the difference for her."

"She sets mighty high with you."

Hardy paused for a response. None came, except for a slight flush to Pete's dark face. Hardy smiled to himself.

"I don't blame you for settin store by her."

Hardy kept his eyes on the ridges ahead. Suddenly, he stiffened.

"But you're tradin a maybe thing for a sure one. Look."

Pete followed the freighter's finger down the trail. A mile along, three Indians sat their horses on one side of the trail, three more on the other. After a moment, the Indians turned into the trail where it cut into the sides of vertical cliffs and were gone.

"Beyond that ridge is the Wagon Mound," said Hardy. "Good ground for an ambush."

Hatcher and Louy walked up to Pete and Hardy.

"The girl's slung between the grays," said Hatcher, "and the black man is holdin our horses."

"Did you see," Pete pointed to the cut in the ridge.

"This coon seen many a Indian; come on 'um a time or five waitin in ambush; still got his hair, this coon has."

Hatcher puffed his chest and patted the Hawkin nestled in the crook of his arm.

"This old hoss lets each man go his own way. His choice, how he lives and how he dies; but that girl, now. She aint able to choose."

He spit a stream of yellow-brown tobacco juice at a tarantula just disappearing into its hole in the dirt.

"Won't matter much, one way or the other, if'n we don't get that arryhead out pretty quick-like."

"Just last winter," said Hardy. "Ten men lost at the Wagon Mound."

"These men, she do not have the fearsome Long John Hatcher to put the scare into the sacre damn Indians." Louy sounded as worried as he looked.

"After a day long fight against a small band of Apaches, and none the worse for wear, those men thought they was saved. But, during the night, a larger bunch of Utes joined the Apaches. At dawn, the Indians rushed the wagons; and it was over in minutes. Men and mules found dead, stuck with more arrows than a cactus has spines. Men must have put up a hell of a fight, though."

"How so?" said Pete.

"Not a one was scalped."

"No figurin a Indian," said Hatcher, keeping the spider in its hole with another rain of tobacco and spit.

"We'll keep an eye out," said Pete.

He mounted the smoky horse and motioned to Dibble to lead the grays.

Hardy stood a long time with his hand shading his eyes against the afternoon sun until the small group of riders with the funny looking rig disappeared into the narrow passage between the vertical cliffs.

# 42

Five days to make six, maybe seven. When Blair Halluck left his wagons to run the mail to Santa Fe, that was the time that pressed in on him. He and Aymes and Pole Hawkin had ridden the clock around and around.

They ran past Wagon Mounds. At Fort Union, Halluck traded six near-dead mules for six that had some run still left in them. It was after midnight when they galloped through the dirty, mud town of Tecolote. A few dogs barked. A woman cried out in pain or ecstasy. They took no notice.

Before dawn, they stopped for a long drink at the Pecos River. They noticed the thirst and the blur of vision as the orange dawn turned to lemon day. On the west bank of the Pecos, a mule died from too much water sucked in too fast. They barely took notice.

As they began to pull the wagon out of the river, Aymes fell from his horse. He lay feet first in the water, his chest on the shore, his cheek resting on one arm.

Halluck noticed.

"Sleepin," said Pole kneeling beside the fallen man. Pole's voice sounded like wind blown sand against a hollow log. "Peaceful as you please. Sleepin."

"Well, wake him," rasped Halluck from the seat of a water bloated horse.

Pole shook Aymes; tossed water on his face; finally, kicked him none too gently in the ribs. He grunted with that and began to snore.

"No use." Pole sat back on his rump. His chin hit his collarbone, bounced up a little.

"We'll dump him in the wagon," said Halluck, dismounting.

More slowly than he was aware, Halluck walked to the men.

"Help me lift him."

Halluck put his hands into Ayme's armpits.

Pole neither moved nor spoke. He sat on his rump in the mud of the river bank and looked straight at Halluck with eyes half open; and, he too, snored. Halluck let go of Aymes' arm pits and slumped down to sit by the sleeping men. He tried to count the days left on his fingers but never got passed one.

Vaguely, he heard a mule sputter softly, then another, like sleeping mules snore.

He slumped and slept the rise of the new day's sun, shading into lemon yellow, on the banks of the Pecos River.

They were less than a day's hard gallop from the United States Post Office in Santa Fe.

Muddy Waters rolled a cigarette. He struck the match along the side of his pants and cupped his hand against the wind. Smoke billowed from the cupped hand. He exhaled and sagged across arms folded atop the rounded pommel of the saddle. He and Cussin Jim and Blessed Jones sat their saddles and waited for Sheriff Potter to finish saddling his horse.

Potter stood beside the horse, one of the spares, and tugged at the cinch strap. Each time he tugged, the horse just naturally sucked in a desert full of air which puffed chest and belly way out. After Potter had begun to tie up the strap, the horse exhaled. The belly shrunk; and the cinch hung loose and useless.

"God damn it, Potter. Put a knee into his side and kick that wind out'n his god damn belly." Cussin Jim sat the saddle with one boot across the pommel and a hand resting against the raised cantel behind.

Potter's posse had just changed from run-ragged horses to horses not quite so tired; although, as spares, they, too, had made the fast trip from Missouri. With this change, they were down to the last of their extra horses. The rest, which had run the course, were turned loose to recruit on the spring grass.

"Blessed Indian bait, I'm thinkin," said Jones, looking at the cast offs as they rolled or lay in the desert sand.

"Buzzard bait, more'n likely." Waters tossed the butt of his cigarette at one of the rolling horses. "We run the hide right off'n them mounts."

The rolling horse ignored the slight sting as the butt flamed out on its flank.

Potter pulled the cinch strap as hard as he could. The cinch hugged the horse's swollen belly. Potter swung a boot at the horse's rib cage. The toe of the boot dug into the taught ribs. The horse exhaled. Potter exhaled as his own knee gouged his own belly hanging over his belt and started a tidal wave which stopped in his wind. Potter fell over backward, twisting and lurching. He clutched the cinch strap and his fall pulled it tight over a shrunken horse belly.

It took Potter until the men stopped laughing to catch his own breath; but when he got up, he tied the cinch strap and couldn't get his finger between the cinch and the taught skin of the horse's belly.

"Bless me," said Jones. "It aint pretty; but that's one way to lick that pesky horse, all right." Jones' eyes shown bright mischief from a serious, appraising face.

With a puff and a grunt, Potter climbed into the saddle. The tight cinched horse tried to buck; felt Potter's weight; thought better of the idea and went to grazing until Potter pulled its head up.

"Horse don't eat till I do," he said.

They rode out of camp. Wind came more slowly to tired lungs, stiffness clung and blisters popped on numb butts.

Muddy Waters was the first to see the dust. He had ridden ahead to scout the trail. He pulled up on a rise and shaded his eyes against the afternoon sun.

"I make out five wagons and damn little stock movin like bugs. Could be Halluck."

The others had ridden up beside Waters to take their own look.

"Movin slow, all right," said Potter. "Had trouble. Indians, maybe." He scanned the desert all around them. "Catch up a-fore dark."

"Like as not they'll still have victuals what can be et," said Waters, spitting into the sand. They had eaten very little in the last four days. Nothing hot.

"God damn, I'd give my share of that niggah for some hot coffee," said Cussin Jim.

As they watched, the wagons suddenly disappeared into a narrow tunnel of dark shadow cut between the vertical sides of rocky hills. The dust lingered behind in the soft wind.

"If'n you all want coffee and that niggah, we better ride."

Potter said it quietly; then dug spurs into the side of the cinched up horse. He took the jump with the inside of his thighs and settled his ample rump into the roll of the saddle under him. The rest followed.

"Coffee! God damn, hot coffee."

"Blessed coffee, you all mean."

"Hi yee!" yelled Waters.

Far behind, the abandoned horses still rolled in the sand or stood and watched the day slide by. One horse tried to gambol, ran a few yards and quit. High in the sky a turkey vulture circled in the afternoon thermals. A quarter of a mile away, a head popped over the top of a rocky outcrop, then another and another.

The wolves watched the horses and waited for pastel time.

Almost a day's ride west, beyond the shadow tunnel, in sight of the Wagon Mounds, the Apaches waited in pastel time.

On a rock high in the sky, the Apache with the Sharps rifle sat in purple shadows and watched the small party set up camp for the night. The sick woman's sling was lowered from the gray horses. He saw that the woman had become sicker during the day. In the first moments of stopping, she drank more water than the Apache would drink in a sun.

The animals' feet were tightly hobbled; and they were allowed to graze only as far as the end of a rope would let them.

The small man with the round, wool cap got a tiny fire started and began to cook. The big man, who had taken back their hard-stolen stock, stood, like the

Indian, in the shadows on a high rock. The Hawkin rifle was cradled in his arm. The Indian could not see into the eyes of the mountain man; but he knew that, just as he watched, he was seen.

Pastel passed to dusk and dusk to dark. The Apache went down from the rock to his camp. Dawn will be soon enough, he thought.

Hatcher came down from the high rock and knelt by the fire while Louy poured coffee into his tin cup.

"Mile and a bit more. Indian a-watchin Louy here, admirin that cap of his," said Hatcher.

"Think they'll hit us," said Pete.

"Reckon they aint forgot this mornin; but they know her condition. They'll feel comfortable waitin till dawn."

Hatcher sipped the hot coffee, knowing there was only a cup apiece until the Pecos.

"Then the sacre damn hell, she break loose."

The small fire lit the scar tissue of Louy's forehead where he had pulled the wool cap back.

In the darkness just outside of the ring of fire light, Dibble stood looking off to the west. His skillet hand rested on the butt of the long knife at his belt.

"Will them Indians have a fire like us," Dibble whispered.

"If'n they got mule meat left, they'll be a-cookin it, I reckon," said Hatcher squatting on his haunches. "Why? You got a idea?"

"Water," Beckey panted. As fast as she drank, beads of sweat burst from her forehead and rolled salt into her eyes.

"You've drunk it all up, Beckey," said Pete. "Hardly enough water to get us and the beasts to the Pecos."

"Water. Water."

"She's burnin up with fever," said Hatcher, his huge hand on her face. "Best rest her here for the night. See if the fever dies—or she does."

"It's what them redskins expect," said Dibble. "Movin or lyin still won't make no difference to her fever, no how."

They fed her a beef broth and waited. Waited for the end of bat flying time and the true dark of night. They cut shirts to muffle the horses' feet. By midnight, they were on a creep down the trail.

Just ahead, the Apache and his tribal brothers tossed and turned through the true dark time and dreamed of the riches in scalps and horse flesh the dawn would bring.

Halluck awoke with a start. It was the pitch black of night; and he didn't know what had wakened him or where he was. His head felt thick inside and he couldn't think. Then he felt it again, a swift kick to the ribs.

"I'm awake. That you, Pole?"

"Aymes, Boss. Pole's seein to the mules. Way we got her figured, we run tonight and tomorrow, we'll be at that post office in Santa Fe before evenin. That leaves most of a day to spare."

"I almost lost count; but, I think your right. Tomorrow is the twenty ninth day."

Halluck's head was clearing; and he bent his stiff fingers over and over as he felt the knots in the piggin string he carried in his jacket. He counted twenty seven knots. He tied another.

"If'n we aint slept a whole day through, this marks the twenty eighth day."

"What mules I could find is hitched," called Pole Hawkin through the night. "Four is all that is left. And, a horse apiece."

"Won't need more," said Halluck. "We got time now. We'll stop every hour for five or ten minutes. May still find some fresh animals along the way, now that we're this close. Though we've all had plenty of sleep, might use tomorrow to rest, if need be, since we got us an extra day."

He looked at the stars which told him they had slept maybe five or six hours in the last forty eight or more.

"I'll go on over to San Jose for some tortillas and beans," said Pole. "In the last three, four days, we may have slept ample; but, I been off my feed some. I'll catch up."

"Let's move 'um out," called Halluck.

Again, Halluck counted twenty eight days in the pigging string knots. For sure, he thought, tomorrow is day twenty nine. We have time and a day to spare.

He shoved the pigging string with the twenty eight knots back into his vest pocket. He didn't remember that Hickman had found his pigging string in the dirt after the broken wagon wheel had been pulled off him. Now, his fingers were tired along with the rest of his used body. When he tied yesterday's knot, his tired fingers failed to notice the curled gap in the middle of the string.

"Hi yee!" Halluck started the mules and they began to pull the mail wagon up the western bank of the Pecos. Time and to spare, he thought, and smiled into the dark.

"Hi yee! Mules! Hi yee!"

It was high noon. They were past the Wagon Mound and entering a small valley, wet with spring fed marshes, when the off gray went down. The gray squealed as blood spurted dark red around the arrow shaft buried deep behind its right fore-leg. Beckey screamed as the unslung bunk frame crashed into the ground at an angle.

Pete grabbed the halter of the other gray to keep it from bolting and cut the bed away.

"Apaches!" yelled Hatcher.

He fired the Hawkin from across the saddle in the same motion it took to dismount. He did not look to see if his shot had hit anyone; but seized the reins in his teeth and reloaded behind the protection of the horse. The Palomino snorted at the smell of horse blood; but stood fast according to Hatcher's training.

Louy was also on the ground fanning the low brush with the muzzle of his musket. Nothing showed.

Dibble jumped from his horse and knelt beside the fallen gray which lay snort-ing and squirming between Beckey and attack. He untied the bunk frame and lay her pallet in the tall, wet grass next to the downed horse.

He felt Pete take the other gray away. With the big knife in his hand, he covered Beckey with his body.

Pete rode the smoky horse to a shallow bowl formed by the low lying tips of several rocks. He part jumped and part fell into the scant protection of the outcrop. Still, the Sharps and a saddle bag came with him. The horses ran on a ways, stopped and began to dig into the sweet, wet grass.

Pete rolled over in the bowl formed by the low lying clump of rock heads. He checked the side pan just in front of the Sharps drop-block to make sure the auto-matic capping wheel was full of percussion caps. He eared the hammer and stuck the rifle around a pointed rock and scanned the northern slope. Clumps of piñon pine marched up the half mile of hill to wrinkle the horizon.

He looked to the right where the trail over which they had just come squirmed down the ridge to the east. To his left he saw the tall grass bend to a light breeze for two miles where it thinned and quit at the foot of the western ridge. There, a narrow trace of wheel ruts lifted from the grass to wind around boulders to the top of the next hill and on to Santa Fe.

Inches above Pete's head, a chunk of rock split off and showered him with gravel to the tune of gun thunder from the northern slope. He saw a puff of powder smoke rise from the low branches of a piñon and snapped a return shot. He ducked back behind his rock without waiting to see the fall of his shot and levered the block open to chamber another cartridge.

"Hatch, Louy, Dibble. Sing out! What do you see?" Pete called soft and low.

"Bleedin belly of this here horse," said Dibble, his voice slow and soft in spite of the gravel in it.

"Beckey? How's the girl?" said Pete.

"Breathin and scared," called Dibble.

" 'Bout how I am." Pete heard Louy off to his left. The voice was quiet and steady.

"Hatch?" Pete called out again. "You all right?"

"This old hoss is belly deep in water and skeeters," Hatcher whispered a few feet from Pete's rock bowl. "Best keep quiet. They say a redskin aint much with a rifle. Aint so. And many a smart old coon's been shot by a redskin with no more target than the sound of his own voice."

A shot rang out from the slope. Pete heard the ball cut grass and plop in the water just to his right.

"Damn. This talkity old coon near prophesied his ownself over the edge."

The gray took an hour to pump his blood into the grass and die. Except for the snorts of the wounded horse and the buzz of a million insects, the hour was quiet.

Slowly, Hatcher and Louy had bellied over to Pete's rock bowl. Careful to remove canteens, powder and shot, they had turned the horses loose. Beckey and Dibble were hidden by the bloating carcass of the dead horse; but, it also marked their approximate location. In all, only one arrow had been fired during the dying hour. It fell short of the rocks and hid in the tall grass.

The hot sun bled them of moisture which they could not replace from the nearly empty canteens. Each tick of time cut their chances. Yet, the Indians waited.

Suddenly, an arrow thudded into the gray carcass, then another and a third. Pete watched the quivering shafts break up the heat waves. He raised the barrel of the Sharps. A huge hand seized his shoulder and pushed him down.

"Easy. Nothin to shoot at. Them devils is just tryin to draw our fire."

Hatcher's face was so close to Pete's that Pete could smell the grease on the cartridge Hatcher clenched in his teeth.

"What're we goin to do? Just lay here all day?"

"Maybe," said Hatcher. "They think they got time on their side because of the girl."

"Sacre damn truth, that," said Louy.

"Well," said Hatcher. "Let's hurry things up some. Pete, here's what we'll do."

The speech was short. Pete nodded a time or two. Then he raised the long range, vernier tang sight folded just behind the hammer of the Sharps. Slowly, Hatcher crawled from the cover of the rocks until he came to a stunted juniper thirty yards away. He lay in the tall grass behind the juniper for a long minute.

Pete heard flies buzzing around his head and Louy breathing. His eyes froze on the juniper, waiting.

Suddenly, Hatcher stood full up and gobbled like a turkey. Pete jerked his eyes away from Hatcher and looked out across the dead horse to the piñon studded slope beyond.

A hundred yards up the hill, he saw an Indian jump up from behind a pine. The Indian's musket was leveled toward the gobbling turkey-man to his right.

Pete fired before the Indian. Instantly, the gobbling stopped. Pete heard a plop in the grass to his right. He saw the Indian pitch forward into the sand of the gentle slope from which he had risen to take Pete's round.

"One less to worry us," said Hatcher from the juniper.

Just then a musket smoked from some boulders on the slope near the fallen Indian. Pete ducked down behind the rocks. The ball tumbled into the rock with a dead thump just the other side of his head.

"You was a mite slow in duckin," called Hatcher.

"See him?" said Pete.

"In them piñons. To the left of the boy you plugged."

Hatcher's Hawkin exploded from a low branch of the juniper. Pete saw him wiggle away from the small tree as the smoke from his shot began to spread and drift across the grass.

"Louy?" called Hatcher.

"The ball, she hit the sacre damn tree. Hatch, he is gettin blind in his old age."

Louy fired at the same spot. An instant later, a shot rang out from the Indian's hiding place. Pete ducked. Louy ducked.

Hatcher laughed. "Why, you French son of a de-balled beaver. Damned if you didn't make a lucky shot with that old trade goods musket."

Pete looked across at the Indian's tree and saw a rifle slide out from between the rocks below, followed by the red hand that held it. The hand convulsed, spasmed again; relaxed, released the rifle which rolled twice, scattering a few pebbles down the slope, and lay still.

"Dibble," Pete called softly. "How is she?"

"How she is, is how she was: hot and safe."

The black man's gravelly voice played counterpoint to the constant, smooth buzz of a million tiny wings.

"And how am Dibble, y'all ask? Dibble need a Indian whose hide to carve. How am Dibble? That's how!"

The tall grass quivered with the slow eruption of the gravel throated laugh of the black man.

Four shots, as one, laughed back. Four balls pounded the carcass of the dead horse. Black powder smoke mushroomed from the slope.

As one, Pete, Louy and Hatcher fired into the low branches wreathed by the smoke. Pete dropped the block, reloaded and fired again. Almost as fast, Hatcher fed a paper cartridge of powder and ball into the mouth of the Hawkin, gave it a tap with the ramrod, fit a fresh cap on the nipple and fired. Louy was not far behind. His shot was last, but best. A cry spilled its surprise from the root of the piñon tree.

"Louy, I do believe you got the eye of the eagle today," said Hatcher to the tune of the tap, tap of his ramrod.

"Eye of the Frenchman," said Louy with a soft laugh. "She see the Indian better than the eagle see the mouse."

An Indian jumped from the tree where another Indian had cried just moments ago and ran from left to right across Pete's eyes.

Hatcher fired at the running figure. Pete saw the Indian's leg snap like a lightning bolt in the same instant that the flashing leg had reached out for the earth. The running man collapsed where the leg had been running. He fell flat and skidded inches from the safe mask of low slung piñon branches. He raised his head and pawed for the missing inches.

Pete killed him there in the sandy open.

"Long John Hatcher, she shoot a mite low, today," said Louy.

"Nothin of the sort," said Hatcher. "I had him plumb center. Just then a skeeter, big as a buffalo, lit on my front sight. All I could see was that there flashin leg—and skeeter balls."

"Look," said Pete. "They're runnin."

Two Indians broke from the cover of the trees. Between them, they carried a third, and weaved and ran and fell and crawled toward the top of the slope.

Pete slid the aperture up a notch on the tang sight and raised the Sharps. He stuck an elbow in the ground to steady the eleven pound rifle. He thumbed the hammer back with a loud click.

"Let them be, old son," said Hatcher quietly. "They're done."

Hatcher crawled to his knees and, stiffly, got to his feet.

"Let's get the girl loaded and be gone." He slapped at a mosquito sucking blood from his neck. "Dibble. It's over."

Silence.

"Dibble," called Pete, standing.

Silence.

Pete rushed over to the dead horse. He saw Beckey snugged tight under the overhang of the dead horse's belly. Dibble stretched across the body of the girl. The point of the great knife was fixed to his temple. In the girl's small hand it looked huge and more deadly.

"What the hell," said Pete.

"I said I'd kill the next man that tried to use me," she said in a small, sick voice. "And, I aim to."

"Beckey. He aint just a man. He's Dibble."

Pete reached down and pulled the knife out of her hand. A trickle of blood ran from Dibble's temple to color the white of his eye.

"Dibble, he get them horses," he said.

He jumped up and walked away. His gravelly voice sounded throaty, a little like a man crying.

"You damn fool."

Pete knelt down and put his face next to Beckey's.

"Dibble was shielding you from Indian arrows and balls with his own body. Look!"

Four feathered shafts stuck into the ribs of the dead horse less than inches from where Beckey lay.

"Look, damn it!"

"Indian arrows? Indians? Indians laid like that on me."

"That Dibble aint no Indian."

Hatcher had walked up. He looked down on Beckey's tear stained face as Pete fixed the blanket over her.

Louy stood to the side and shook his head. "That Dibble, he a sacre damn good friend to put his back to the fallin arrows." He waved a hand at the four shafts that stuck out from the ribs of the carcass.

Pete helped Beckey sit up. She put a hand to her mouth as she saw the arrow shafts.

"Oh!" she cried. Again, she wept; but this time the anger seemed to be turned inward.

"Horses is catched," said Dibble.

He had wiped the blood from his temple; but a splotch wrinkled in the crow feet of his eye as he smiled.

"Lady was scared and brave all at once."

It took them an hour to reload the animals so that the red horse, almost as big as the remaining gray horse, was freed up and gentled down to side the surviving gray, with Beckey slung in between.

Pete scanned the battle slope where three sandy mounds marked the sun god's dilly-dally day in sad mourning. He could not control the slight shudder of his body wrought by memory of the fight. A near thing, like Hardy said, he thought.

Pete pointed to the mounds. "Hell of a way to make a living, the Indian way," he said.

Pete let in the western sky through squinted eyes. A painter, perhaps skilled in the color of blood, seemed to have brushed the sun-disc setting round on the horizon, now artfully formal after its silly-dilly run. As Pete watched, the sun god bowed, inch by inch, beneath the curly tops of the far hills, etching the miracle of earth's fandango into the deep blue sky.

They moved out into the bat time of thick desert dusk when the day-shy creatures come out of hiding into the night to kill each other for a living.

"Make Fort Union by midnight," said Pete. "Shelter and food."

Beckey raised up in the swaying sling and waved a small, pink hand at the black man who followed behind.

"And, safety," she said, softly; and her eyes cried out at Dibble: "so sorry."

"Y'sum," said Dibble, white teeth and eyes shinning in last light. "Safety for sho 'nuff."

# 43

Pete led the red horse. Hatcher led the gray. Louy rode point and Dibble drag. Beckey rocked and bumped in between. They crawled through the moonless night. Snow, sometimes three or four inches deep, capped the high sides of the mountain trail and crunched under the horses' feet. Occasionally, Beckey cried out, mostly in fear, as they crossed over a sharp ridge or abruptly descended into a small valley.

A midnight sentry challenged them before they saw the pine log huts clustered in dim outline along right-angle streets. Fort Union had no stockade or breastworks. Except for the discipline of the young sentry, it seemed no different from any Mestizo village along the trail.

At the sentry's direction, they led the stock to water and feed in a corral behind the suttler's store. They stripped the animals and left the gear where it fell, except for their rifles and Beckey.

Pete carried Beckey to the store. The sentry opened the door. A soft glow from the evening coals painted gaunt faces. Pete and Beckey a pale orange, Hatcher light lemon, Louy ashen gray, and Dibble coal black. For an instant, the sentry froze his eyes on Dibble. Dibble grinned. The boy's eyes thawed.

"You're the first ni-ni—African! I've ever seen," he stammered.

"Glad to oblige, Corporal," said Dibble, the gravel voice quiet-tired.

The young corporal woke the suttler who grumbled and swore while he rolled out quilt pallets on the floor of his store. Hatcher and Louy fell where the pallets lay and were asleep in an instant. Dibble moved his bed into a corner. One eye closed, he half watched as Pete lay Beckey on the hearth.

The suttler grumbled and swore and went back to bed in the far room.

As if by magic, a plump Mexican woman shuffled barefoot into the room. She wore a serape over her night dress. Without being told, she stirred up the coals and heated water. Pete pulled Beckey's blanket off her; and, pointing, whispered to the woman in Spanish. She bathed Beckey before the fire and dressed her shoulder wound. Through the bath and the bandaging, Beckey slept. Neither Pete nor the woman seemed to notice Beckey's wet nakedness.

They let the fire dry and warm the sleeping girl. The woman left the storeroom. In a few moments, the woman returned with a white peasant blouse and skirt of cotton and a many-colored serape woven from sheep's wool. The woman dressed the girl as she slept. The clothes fit Beckey more than twice on every side; but, the woman fixed the overdrape with a wide rebosa which she wrapped around and around the slim girl's waist.

Pete offered the woman a coin which she disdained with a toothless grin.

"De nada, de nada," she whispered. She backed out the door to rejoin the suttler's snores which floated in from the next room.

Pete covered Beckey with the heavy serape and slumped down on the floor beside her. In an instant the fire-flicker danced up the adobe chimney arm in arm with the sound of his own heavy breathing.

Five o'clock reveille jarred the sleeping desert town. The sun had not yet climbed the other side of the eastern rim. Soldiers stumbled from low, pine-log cabins, yawning and slipping gallouses over sagging shoulders in the dawn light.

Here a Mestizo woman, there an Indian man, another woman beyond, other natives peeked from doorways to sniff the day; then stumbled behind their huts to urinate in the sand. Smoke began to trickle from first one and then another of the cabins.

The suttler's wife came into the store. She still wore the once white night dress, which hung, sweat stained and dirt streaked, from huge breasts to sweep the unswept floor. In spite of the early morning chill, she wore no serape.

Bending over Beckey, the woman watched for a moment. Reassured by the girl's gentle breathing, the woman grinned her toothless grin and kindled a fire from the coals that never died. Then, stepping over Pete and around Hatcher and Louy, she waddled to the sideboard where she kept dry tortillas and soaking frijoles. She measured each of the strangers sleeping on the floor as she ladled the beans into a pot. These strangers would be hungry when they woke; and her husband, the suttler, was always hungry.

As the woman was putting the coffee pot into the coals, Pete cried out softly. "Papa, Papa."

The woman was startled until she saw that Pete still slept. Beckey did not stir.

Dibble slept sitting up in a corner with his back nestled against a sack of beans. His great knife was gripped in a skillet hand. For the first time, the woman saw that the black man was black.

Hatcher and Louy lay on the floor with arms draped across chests like slowly breathing corpses. Neither had moved an inch from the late night before. The woman nodded her understanding. She too had fought the Apache.

In the square between the suttler's store and officers' quarters, an American flag fluttered at the top of a tree trunk as the last brassy notes of the bugle drifted on the morning breeze. The small contingent of soldiers ordered arms, broke ranks and headed to their quarters for breakfast before the day's boredom at Fort Union, New Mexico Territory.

The sun sailed over the eastern hills on the breeze and lit the village fort with momentary newness. Four men rode slowly out of the sun and into the square.

A sentry, a young man with corporal's stripes on his sleeve, ran beside the lead horse.

"Halt!" he yelled. "Halt!"

Command or no, each horse stopped where he wanted and drooped his head. Each man in his own time fell or slid from his horse to sit in the dirt on numb buttocks or stand with shaking legs.

A soldier, in officer's dress, adjusted the brim of his forage cap to the low morning sun and walked over to meet the new arrivals.

"I am Colonel Cook, commanding at Fort Union. And welcome."

The corporal snapped to attention and saluted. The men did not look up or reply.

Just then one of the horses fell to its knees and rolled over on its side. Legs dangled out. The horse began to gallop in the air. Instantly, a sharp breath heaved its chest; and its chest heaved with the gallop. Once, the horse cried out. Suddenly, the breathing stopped. The legs stopped galloping. The horse quivered all over and shrugged. The horse shrugged once and lay still.

"My god, man!" said the colonel. "You've run this horse to death."

"Clear from Missouri," whispered the stocky man with the over hanging belly. "In under nine days. And the asses won the bet."

"What?"

"Not by god damn much," said the man with the pussy eye. He ventured a hand to his rump, rubbed; felt nothing in butt or fingers. "Son of a bitch. I aint so damn sure which won."

The colonel waved a hand at the cussing man and pushed his nose into the stocky rider's face.

"What may I ask is so urgent?"

"Sleep," said the stocky man. "Been saddle poundin most of the last two days without stoppin."

Colonel Cook called some soldiers over.

"Take their horses," he ordered. "Walk them a little. Then feed and water. Not too much. See these men to some beans and a bunk."

The young corporal pointed to the man with the overhanging belly.

"Badge, Colonel. Looks like some kinda peace officer."

"Huh? Oh," the stocky man mumbled. "I'm Bobby Joe Potter, by name. Sheriff from Lebanon, Missouri. Chasin a niggah. Killed his master back to home."

"Well, Sheriff. Potter is it? We have Mexicans, Mestizos, some Indians. But, Fort Union has not seen a Negro in my memory, Sir."

The young corporal standing next to the colonel glanced toward the suttler's store, started to say something.

"Corporal. Bed these men down before they fall down like that horse. And, son. Clear this ground of that dead animal. But, don't waste the meat."

The young corporal hesitated for a moment. "Sir, I . . . last night, I . . . ."

"Corporal!"

"Yes Sir!"

The corporal saluted his colonel and, taking Potter by the arm, led Potter's posse to bed in soldiers' bunks.

Potter and his men had come on Hardy and the remainder of Halluck's freight wagons the night before. From Hardy they learned of Pete Cortez and his party and the wounded girl with the red hair. Hardy said nothing about Dibble.

When Potter asked about the black, Hardy told him Dibble had been with the train early on for several days; but stole some food and pulled out when he heard that a posse was coming down the trail looking for an escaped slave. Hadn't seen hide nor hair of the black man since. Some of the men shifted their gaze at this last; and a couple coughed too hard. One laughed. Too quickly, Hardy told the laughing man to shut up and look to the stock.

Although Hardy invited Potter and his men to share what was left of their rations, Potter said they'd move on through the night. Cussin Jim cussed. Blessed Jones blessed Potter until Potter let his hand fall to his gun butt. Muddy Waters rolled a cigarette and crawled up on his horse.

After riding all day, they started out to ride the night.

"That bullwhacker was a-lyin about the niggah," said Potter when they were on the run again. "I could see it in his eyes, the way them others hemmed and hawed, the way that feller laughed and was shut up a-sudden. That niggah is just ahead. With them what's takin the hurt woman to the doc in Santa Fe. I'll bet my ass on it."

"Son of a bitch," said Cussin Jim. "That's what I been a-doin all the way from Missouri."

"What? Doin what?" said Potter.

"Bettin. Will my god damn ass wear shut a-fore my god damn horse dies in the crack?"

Waters, who never said much, said, "better be right, Potter. My ass don't ride past tomorrow mornin."

"Lord bless all our achin asses," said Jones reverently into the whistling night wind.

They had ridden the night out to catch up with the Pete Cortez party and the slave. They rode butt-numb before midnight; finger-numb at three; and unfeeling by morning. Insensible bodies embraced like-kind souls in the last pounding saddle hours of dawn.

Now, Potter's posse was snoring in the rising heat of late morning. In the close soldiers' cabin, flies, attracted by the steaming aroma, buzzed hungrily around the sleeping men and supped at will from twitching faces and hands and succulent arm pits.

In the rising heat of late morning, while the flies fed on Potter's sleeping posse, Dibble stumbled out behind the suttler's store to take his turn in the one-hole privy. He wrinkled his nose at the pungent smell. He ripped a couple of pages from an old book; and, while idly waiting for nature, he scanned the pages which he could not read.

He sighed as he thought of the coming afternoon when, again, they would hit the trail to Santa Fe. He wondered if the rumored posse would catch them on the trail or in Santa Fe—or not at all. He smiled to himself as he sat and squirmed on the hand carved privy seat.

If'n it come to it, will these white friends of Dibble fight for him?

"Dibble don't rightly know," he sighed.

The falling sun painted a light pink skin on the underbellies of high flying clouds. It was almost pastel time again.

Blair Halluck bent low in the saddle. Looped around his saddle horn was the end of a lariat. The other end was noosed around the neck of the lead mule. Halluck pulled on the lariat; the lariat pulled on the mule; the mule and his three mates hauled the mail wagon across San Francisco street and into the plaza at Santa Fe.

Halluck stopped in front of the Governor's Palace. Aymes, who had been pulling the off mule in like manner, slid off his horse and eyed the Palace. It was dark and foreboding under the portico that shaded the front of the squat adobe from end to end.

Halluck swayed in the saddle. A Spaniard walked by, crossing the plaza.

"Where's the post office?" Halluck yelled at him. "The United States Post Office? I brung the mail."

Startled at first, the Spaniard raised his flat-top sombrero and pointed to the Palace.

"In there, Señor."

Halluck felt like he was leaping from his horse. In fact, he fell. He thought he was running into the government building. Actually, he barely walked. Inside, he came to a door marked Postmaster. He stopped. He thought he stood straight and tall; but slumped against the thick door. He thought he knocked; knocked again.

Instead, it was his heart pounding against the thick door. Finally, he pounded with his fist; felt the pounding and heard a light, thumpity-thump on the thick door.

No one answered.

Windows adjacent to the door were dark. The hallway was dark. Other offices were empty. It was five in the afternoon and Halluck had ridden right into city time.

Pole Hawkin came onto the porch carrying a sack of mail.

"Post office is closed," said Halluck.

Pole dumped the sack on the wood plank floor, rested a boot on top of the sack and his elbow on his knee. He cupped his chin in his hand and yawned.

"Mornin be soon enough, Boss," said Pole through the yawn.

Halluck leaned his back against the whitewashed wall.

"I guess."

He pulled the pigging string from his pocket and counted the knots. He tied one more; counted again.

"Twenty nine. Tomorrow's the last day, at close of business."

"Let's get us a room, a bath, some victuals and sleep," said Pole.

"I'm for that," said Aymes.

"I guess," said Halluck.

They went back into the plaza. Across the square, store windows were dark with closing; saloons were ablaze with light and the tinkle of life. Pole loaded the mail sack back into the wagon.

"Need a stable for these animals," said Aymes. "I'll find one." He took the leads of the mules and the three saddle horses and sniffed the evening air. He nodded his head and moved toward the smell.

Blair Halluck and Pole Hawkin were half way across the plaza. Aymes and the mail wagon were around the corner and out of sight. Halluck heard a man yelling before he saw him hoppity-hopping across the square.

"Wait! Wait!" an Anglo man yelled. He limped as he tried to run. The lower end of his right leg made a wooden sound in the dirt.

Halluck stopped and watched the peg-leg man limp closer.

"Who, Sir, are you?" he said when the man thumped to a stop in front of him.

Although there was still light in the blue sky, torches were being lighted at the corners of the square. The clinkity-plink of a saloon piano was playing something that sounded like time to quit work and dance the night away.

"Me? Why, I'm the man you're lookin for. That is if you're Halluck and you brought the mail from Missouri in thirty days?"

"I'm Halluck, all right." Halluck held out his hand, then pulled it quickly back and removed the glove.

"Bemis. Fred Bemis. United States Postmaster for the entire Territory of New Mexico."

They shook hands.

"I can't tell you how happy folks'll be to hear the mail's in; but I'm afraid you've missed the deadline."

"Missed? Why, man. I've still got tomorrow." Halluck laughed. He pulled out the pigging string with twenty nine knots in it and dangled it in Bemis' face.

"Tomorrow's the thirtieth day from the day I left Independence."

Bemis put fingers to his chin.

"I got word when you was to leave by the terms of the contract," said Bemis. "And when you was to get here with the mail. Today is the thirtieth day of your deal with the post office. Close of business today."

Bemis looked toward the dark windows on either side of the closed post office door.

Halluck studied the string with all of the knots so carefully tied in it. His face paled and his chest fluttered. For a moment, he could not breath. He saw the curl where day eighteen should have been knotted in.

Bemis turned back from the closed post office and looked concerned.

"Fatigue?" he said. "The hard, fast ride."

Halluck looked into the dark past of the long trail he had covered. He saw Red Hickman. Saw Red pick up the pigging string from the trail dust. Saw him twist and turn it; hand it back to him.

"Here's your tote-string, Boss. Seen you drop it," he heard Red say and saw him smiling.

"Hickman! Rule or no, he's a dirty bastard!" Halluck said.

"Huh? Who's Hickman?" Bemis took a stomp closer to Halluck with his peg-foot.

Halluck recovered quickly. "Oh! Feller I hired. No matter. Listen, Mister Bemis. I aint a-goin to argue with you. If'n you're ready to receive the United States mail from Missouri, I'm ready to deliver it—in thirty days—on the nose!"

Bemis pointed to the dark shadows under the overhang of the Governors Palace. "I already closed her up about an hour ago," he said.

Halluck nearly fell and Bemis grabbed him. Halluck steadied up.

"Say," said Bemis. "The feller that brought me news of your start date and deadline, brought me a letter. From a Colonel Alexander. Says if you don't deliver the mail by close of business on the thirtieth day, I'm to lock you out and not issue a receipt to you for the mail. Says that's part of your contract."

"Aint closin time yet," Halluck said.

"See for yourself" Bemis said. He clumped onto the wooden porch and pointed into the dark. "Who's this Alexander, anyways?"

"Man I borrowed money from to finance the mail train."

"More's the fool, then. No mail receipt, you don't get paid. You don't get paid and Alexander don't either, unless your richer than you look."

"He needn't worry," said Halluck, his slow, low voice like many-mile thunder. "I'll pay him back. With interest. Plenty of interest."

"Splendid, splendid!" Bemis clapped Halluck on the shoulder. "C'mon. Sometimes the United States Post Office stays open late—about every thirty days."

"I figured somethin like that," said Halluck and felt his legs go mushy on him. He turned his head to Pole Hawkin so he wouldn't have to move anything else.

"Please go get Aymes and the mail wagon," he said and thought he sounded steady enough.

"Mister Halluck," said Bemis. He opened the door and lit a lamp. "We'll be seein lots of you from now on. Monthly, I expect, with the mail from Independence and points east."

Halluck turned to the stumpy postmaster and took his arm. "Believe me, Mister Bemis. My great pleasure."

Halluck tossed the knotted pigging string over his shoulder into the loose dust of the plaza and allowed Bemis slowly to pull him inside.

"Next year, Mister Bemis. Eight, even twelve mules pullin a Concord stage coach. We'll beat thirty days regular and bring passengers to boot."

"Shake on it," said Bemis.

Hand in hand, they stood inside the United States Post Office, Territory of New Mexico, open for business.

It was late afternoon at Fort Union. Beckey's fever had passed on in sweat as she lay away the morning by the fire. But, every time she moved, a sharp pain seared her left lung. On occasion, she thought she tasted blood in her wind.

Pete had traded for fresh animals to complete the trip to Santa Fe and a doctor for Beckey. Now, Dibble and Pete were out behind the store saddling the horses and loading their mules. Pete still rode Smokey and the remaining gray was able to travel in tandem with the red horse. The mules were new and frisky. Hatcher and Louy had traded horses.

Louy's fresh horse was Army; and, like the soldiers, had spent weeks feeding on the mesa boredom in the wild. When Louy stepped into the saddle, the horse laid his ears back. Louy plopped into the leather and just as fast went sailing like the eagle. Only, unlike the eagle, Louy tumbled awkwardly and landed on his head. His wool cap flew like a tail feather; and his scalped scalp scooped up a trough of manure laden dust.

"I seen horsemen," said Hatcher slapping his thigh with his hat. "And I seen bronc busters; and a few Indians what could ride; but, Louy. I never seen a rider could fly—till you."

"Sacre damn horse, she is worse than an Army mule, or sergeant." He spit straw, dust and manure strands as he hollered.

It took three such flights before the Army horse decided to let Louy ride along.

Dibble led the horses from the corral and around to the front of the suttler's store; and bumped smack into Bobby Joe Potter and his posse.

"Niggah! It's the niggah," said Cussin Jim, not cussing.

"Bless my soul!" Jones whipped a pistol from his belt.

Muddy Waters rolled a cigarette and eyed Pete, Hatcher and Louy who followed Dibble and the horses around the corner of the building.

Potter pushed his belly against Dibble's washboard stomach and put his red-bulb nose into Dibble's face.

"You the niggah from around Lebanon they call the Devil?"

Dibble stiffened and dropped the reins of the stock. Instinctively, a skillet hand reached for the great knife at his belt; but Potter's belly, which usually hung down over his belt, got hard as rock on a whim. It was hard pressed against the knife. If Potter noticed the skillet hand reaching, he didn't let on.

"Boy. You killed the man who raised you and fed you; and you're goin back to pay." Potter turned to Waters. "Muddy, get the bracelets."

Waters took a pull on the cigarette and pushed it from his mouth with his tongue. "There's some fellers here, Potter. They may say you nay." Waters smiled, but did not move.

"Nay?" yelled Potter. "Muddy? What the hell is 'nay?'"

"Aint your black, mister," said Pete, the Colt Dragoon level-steady in his hand. "Been with me on The Cortez all winter and spring. Bustin horses."

Pete waited for the words to sink in. In the corner of his eyes, he could see Hatcher and Louy moving to his side. He sensed the glint of sunlight on the blade of Hatcher's Green River knife.

"Met up with a coon once," said Hatcher, "smart as this here Muddy feller. Coon sees the sun on the edge of this here blade and stands real still at thirty yards. He eyes me; and me him. We stand that-a way for maybe a hour. Finally, the coon gets a smart idea. I see him a-thinkin. Only a knife. Thirty yards. He jumps and runs."

Hatcher smiled at Waters. Waters said nothing. Flies rode the rising dust in the silence between them.

"Well, Long John Hatcher. What the sacre damn hell happen?"

"Louy, I'm glad you asked. Let's see if this Muddy feller has the same idea. Then, this old hoss'll show you."

Waters waved a gloved hand, palm down. "Aint jumpin nowheres," he said quietly.

While Potter and Dibble stood belly to belly and breathed each others breath, Pete and Blessed Jones leveled pistols at each other, hammers eared back. The rising dust froze in the afternoon sunlight. Flies hovered. Horses stood with heads bowed. Killing eyes glowed.

"Pete, I'm ready." It was Beckey Goddard. She stood in the doorway. The multicolored serape was in her left hand. Shadows cut lines in the low-cut peasant blouse and the light breeze tickled the hem of her cotton skirt. "I can ride upright. Oh!".

"Get inside, Beckey. There'll be shootin."

Pete stood rock-like. He spoke in a hard voice, hard as the words. Beckey ducked inside the store. In a moment she was back, Pete's Sharps rifle in her hands.

"Who'll I shoot first," she said, aiming the rifle at Potter. "That big belly ought to thin right down with a Sharps rifle ball through it."

"Now, miss."

Potter stepped away from Dibble and put up a hand, palm out to Beckey.

"Boys, and little lady. There don't have to be no shootin. I'm a duly appointed sheriff. There's a warrant out for this hellion. For murder. I'll take him off'n your hands and there'll be no trouble."

Potter wiped the palm of his hand on the thigh of his pants and hooked a thumb in his belt next to his pistol.

A shot cut the silence. Dust leaped at Potter's boot toe. In the doorway, he heard the click of block dropping and the click of it rising. He heard the hammer ear back. His hands flew wide. His eyes opened as big as the open palms of his empty hands.

"Hold on, miss. You all got no call to . . . ."

"Drop it," said Pete to Blessed. "My finger is tired."

Jones looked over at Beckey in the doorway of the store. He saw the Sharps, a steady extension of her shoulder. Cussin Jim and Muddy Waters were statues. Jones lowered the barrel of his pistol. Let it hang. Shoved it into his belt.

"Blessed peace to the strong, I says."

"Corporal of the guard and ten men. Follow me." The voice of command came from across the square as Colonel Cook ducked under the low door of his headquarters and ran at them, pistol in hand.

"Drop your weapons," he shouted as he ran.

Beckey lowered the Sharps from her shoulder to let the stock rest under her armpit. Pete did not move. Hatcher faced Waters, a smile on his face, the great knife gleaming in his hand. Louy took two steps to the balky Army horse and drew down his musket, checked the pan and cocked it.

"This here's the niggah I come for, Colonel." Potter pointed at Dibble as he spoke. Dibble pointed back with the point of his huge knife.

The colonel slid to a stop. He pointed his revolver first at Pete, then at Hatcher, then at Beckey almost behind him. The corporal came rushing up with three armed men behind him.

"Put your weapons away; or I shall be forced to order my men to fire on you." The colonel looked Pete in the eye. "Now!" he ordered.

"You soldiers. You shoot. The general, he be the first to die."

All eyes went to the accented voice of the little Frenchman. He stood beside the Army horse. His musket lay across the saddle and pointed at the colonel's heart.

"Tell this so-called posse to leave us alone."

Pete spoke quietly. His pistol still covered Jones.

"He aint their black man. Been with me all winter and spring. He's just easy pickins, easy blood money. They leave east; we leave west. No one gets shot. If'n they or you try to take this man. Well . . . ."

"Now, Colonel. This here's the right niggah. See? I got the warrant. This is his picture." Potter showed the warrant and a reward poster with a line drawing of a Negro.

"Looks like any Negro or all of them," said the colonel. "Let's all put our weapons away and talk this over."

"Not hardly," said Hatcher. He had moved to his horse and now held the Hawkin rifle at the ready.

The corporal and his men stood rock-steady with cocked rifles and grim faces pointed, one each at Pete, Hatcher, Louy and Dibble.

"Then, my men will open fire. Corporal . . . !"

Men with guns faced each other, each a frozen sculpture of death, waiting.

"Now just see hear," Dibble said. "Don't nobody have to get killed on account-a Dibble. Dibble is him. The niggah what killed he master."

"There you all see?" said Potter, pushing his belly back into Dibble's and taking the great knife.

Dibble looked over at Pete. "Now, y'all go on. Get the girl to the doctor. Dibble be all right. Go on, Pete."

His eyes were wide, white moons. "It be enough that y'all would fight for old Dibble." He looked at Pete, smiled up at Beckey.

Suddenly, ears tingled with the hum of flies around steaming horse apples in the sun of late afternoon. As quickly as it had started, the gun fight at Fort Union, that never really got started, was over.

Waters brought manacles. As if he had given up, Dibble stood with head bowed as Waters hitched Dibble to the chains. The soldiers leaned on their rifles at order arms. Colonel Cook smiled as he holstered his pistol.

Waters turned to Hatcher. "That coon. What ever happened to that coon?"

"I ate him for my dinner. Traded his skin to a Mandan Indian for a pouch of pemican."

"You shoot him when he jumped and ran?"

"Shoot him? Hell, no. Cut his head clean off with this here Green River. To give him a fair shake, I threw at forty yards."

"Forty?"

"That aint a question, is it? Like you doubt?" Hatcher put his hand on the handle of the knife at his belt.

"Call it surprise," said Muddy Waters; and he pulled the makings from his shirt. "Surprise," he chuckled.

Up the trail from the fort, a bullwhip cracked and a shouted "hi yee!" floated into the square on the wind. Hardy and the rest of Halluck's men had finally made the sanctuary of Fort Union.

Pete told the story to Hardy as he worked to unhitch the nearly dead animals from their traces.

"We'll take the posse along with us to Santa Fe," said Hardy. "See no harm comes to your black man along the way. That suit you Potter?"

"Suits fine." Potter shrugged fat lips into a smile.

"Obliged," said Pete.

He was mounted on Smokey. Beckey sat a fresh horse beside him. The anxious horse pranced in the square; and Beckey whimpered in pain.

"Arrowhead's got to come out soon," said Pete, extending a hand to the freighter. "When that's done, we'll see if Dibble don't somehow . . . ."

"Don't get no ideas, Cortez," said Potter through the fat-lipped smile. "You was lucky today."

Pete ignored the sheriff.

"See you in Santa Fe," said Hardy, winking.

"See you," said Pete.

He spoke to Hardy; but he looked over at Dibble.

"Dibble. I've left the Cortez horse for you. Potter! That horse is Dibble's own. Wouldn't want to catch anyone else ridin or sellin him." Pete smiled. "Need be, that horse knows the way home."

"I'll send him back to you from Missouri," said Potter. "After we hang this here niggah."

"You do that," said Pete. His smile did not change.

Pete and Beckey, Hatcher and Louy rode the falling sun out of Fort Union. At the first ridge, Pete looked over his shoulder. Dibble stood distant in the middle of the square. Pete could see the chains hanging from his shoulders. His head was up. His forehead gleamed with sweat in the setting sun. Pete could just make out the play of a smile, black lips over white teeth. Pete waved. Dibble lifted his head higher. Pete heard the distant rattle of chains as the black man raised a skillet hand.

Beckey followed Pete's gaze. As she too raised her small hand, her horse stumbled. She cried out in pain and bent over the saddle horn. Pete reached out to hold her.

"We can rig the sling," he said.

"No Pete, I can ride. It's faster by a mile." She pursed her lips against the pain in the middle of her chest. "I'm thinking I may need that mile. How far to Santa Fe?"

"About a hundred and ten of them miles. Two days and we keep movin."

"I can make it. I think." She smiled at Pete. He saw the pain in her eyes. He thought he saw warmth where once there had only been ice.

"Sure you can, Beckey," he said, and gently took her hand in his.

# 44

Beckey slept on the ground wrapped tight in the serape. Louy pulled a chaw from the last of his plug and squatted beside Pete who was sprawled next to the wall. Hatcher stood over them smoking his pipe.

"This hoss am a true mountain man what never lost a black man to no fat sheriff," sang Hatcher.

It was nearly midnight. They had pushed hard. Circling the large adobe establishment at Barclay's Fort, they came into the dirty, mud town of Las Vegas. Here in the public square, which resembled more a muddy field, they watered and rested the stock to the doleful clap-clap of the church bell.

"We wait," said Louy. "Behind the melted down walls of this ruin of a town, we wait for the sun and the fat sheriff."

"Seems right to this coon," said Hatcher. "By god, we'll scatter that there posse past graves and straight into Hell. Free up Dibble and get on to Santa Fe afore breakfast."

Beckey moaned in her sleep; suddenly cried out.

"Dibble's on his own," said Pete. "We'll be close to Santa Fe afore breakfast. I think Beckey's string is nearly played out and we don't get her to some fancy doctorin right quick."

Hatcher lit some tinder, held it to his pipe. "Damn me for a sneakin weasel. Everywheres you look, there's someone needs savin." He crucified himself against the wall with outstretched arms. "I aint no Jesus Christ; but damned if I want to see that black man with them bounty killers nor the girl here, with that arryhead creepin closer to her windbag, neither."

"Hardy and them will see to Dibble," said Pete. "Beckey's most needful." Pete got Beckey up and into the saddle, though she hardly woke.

"Let's ride," he said.

Just out of Las Vegas, they felt the trail dip into a narrow valley, black with night; and further on, a deep canyon of cold, vertical walls. Night's dark curtain was just beginning to lift as they rode into Tecolote. The town mirrored the squalor of Las Vegas; but here they ate and, again, watered and fed the stock.

"We'll sleep till sun up," whispered Pete through bone-dry lips. "Make Santa Fe afore nightfall."

Blair Halluck pulled the brim of his hat low over his eyes to cut the glare of the afternoon sun. He stood in the plaza. His attention was drawn to the trail worn quartet which was just then plodding into the square. Pete Cortez, he thought. And a woman.

"Can I help you, Pete," called Halluck moving to the party. "You don't appear to be as fresh as when we last met."

"Plumb beat this time Halluck. Obliged if you could direct us to the best doctor in Santa Fe."

Pete pointed to Beckey. To Halluck, she looked nearly dead. Her head hung down beside the neck of the gray horse and an arm dangled along the leg.

"Here, ma'am let me . . . ."

Just as Halluck approached to help, Beckey slid from the horse into his arms. "Well, I'll be. Follow me, boys. Doc Stafford is the best we got for man or beast."

"Thanks, Halluck," said Pete. "Glad to see you made it all right. Kinda wondered when I saw Hardy and some of your outfit at Fort Union."

"Hardy? Clear to Fort Union? Good." Halluck walked quickly across the plaza carrying Beckey like a featherbed.

"He'll be along directly," said Pete. "Hold up. I can't feel anything below my belt. Don't know if'n I'm sittin or standin."

Pete dropped awkwardly from Smokey's back and followed Halluck. Hatcher and Louy took the animals.

"I can smell the stable from here," said Louy. "Unless it's you."

"Smell me? Why, Louy this coon smells like the high Rockies in the cool of a spring morn, all pine and bird's nests and spring-fed water gushin fresh and pure up from the earth. 'Course if'n you smell somethin, Frenchman, you're down wind of your ownself."

"Sacre damn Hatcher!"

Outside Doc Stafford's small surgery, the plaza was alive with commerce. Freight wagons were being loaded with goods destined for the east. Women scurried here and there with huge stacks of fresh baked tortillas balanced in gaily colored rebosoas on their heads. Dogs barked and played among the hooves of oxen and mules a-stomp in the thick dust and dung of the square. Hard looking men stood quietly talking beside the wagons while they adjusted harness and load for the long trip over the Santa Fe Trail. Some would head north and east back to the States; others were pointed south toward Chihuahua where a brisk trade with old Mexico began.

Doc Stafford's surgery was located in Burro Alley, a block east of the plaza. Inside the low, mud hut there was a small sitting room and beyond that a larger room occupied by three beds, a cabinet filled with medicine bottles and, in the center of the room, a long, wooden table, just body length. Dark stains blotched the white slabs of the freshly washed pine.

One of the beds was empty. In the next a fat Mexican groaned and coughed. When he coughed the knife wound in his belly opened and wet a blood soaked belly bandage.

Beckey lay in the third bed where Doc Stafford examined her wound. Pete leaned against a wall and watched as the doctor palpated and probed around the swollen lump next to her left shoulder blade where scar tissue had grown in a vain attempt at healing. With each touch, Beckey moaned through clenched teeth.

"If the arrowhead were still attached to the shaft," said the doctor, as if speaking to himself, "and the shaft was where I could grab it, I could remove shaft and arrowhead easy. But, here, the arrowhead is sunk deep. There's no shaft to get a hold on. I'll have to cut and probe."

He turned to Pete as if just remembering he was not alone.

"You look all in, son. Go outside and rid yourself of that dust and you can sleep on the empty bed yonder while I work."

"I'll not sleep till I know she's saved," said Pete. "I can help; hold her while you, eh, work."

"Suit yourself and I could use your strength. I aint got but brandy to ease the pain." Doc Stafford poured about a pint of brandy into a clay mug.

"Here, little lady, drink this."

Beckey turned and raised up on an elbow and took the mug. She looked over the rim of the mug and smiled at Pete. "You won't be rid of me so soon, Pete Cortez."

Pete forced a tired grin.

"I don't aim to be rid of you, ever, Miss Beckey Goddard." His grin faded. "Drink your brandy and get roarin drunk."

Beckey tipped the mug to her lips and downed the hot liquor in coughing gulps.

Next to her, the Mexican with the knife wound in his belly heaved up on the bed, cried out and filled the wide bandage wrapped around his ample middle with more bright blood. Doc Stafford moved quickly to his side and pushed him gently back down on the bed. The Mexican moaned as he put a hand over the blood-wet dressing; the moan was cut short by a sudden intake of wind; the wind rattled in his throat; and he died under Doc Stafford's comforting hand.

"Accused a man of cheatin at three card monte. Got well stuck for his pains. Played the wrong hand and lost." Doc Stafford wiped the blood on his smock.

"Felix, Juan," he called through the window. "Your brother's just died. I am sorry."

While the dead Mexican's body was hauled from the surgery with brotherly love and sadness and kissing of thumbs, Doc Stafford turned back to Beckey.

"How you feelin," he asked.

"Better'n I've felt for some time; but dizzy."

The doctor straddled the bed and sat in the small of her back. Roughly he probed the wound with his fingers.

"That hurt?"

"Yes," said Beckey. "Sure it hurts—but I can't hardly feel it." She giggled into the pillow.

"Cortez, take her arms."

Doc Stafford picked up a scalpel-like instrument and wiped it across his blood smeared smock. He looked up at Pete and down at Beckey's naked back.

"Got her?"

"I got her," Pete said, a grim edge to his tired voice. "Get it over and done!"

"Reminds me of a mule I worked on just last week. Ran into a pitchfork. Pierced the lung. Had a hell of a time cuttin that fork out."

Doc Stafford inhaled deeply. "Mule died."

With that he plunged the scalpel deep into Beckey's wound.

Blair Halluck leaned his back into the hitching rail in front of the Union Hotel. He liked the feel of clean clothes and the breeze on a shaven face. Hatcher sat on a flour barrel. Louy squatted on his heals in the dusty plaza drinking pulque from an earthen mug.

"Sacre damn heathen drink," Louy said as he drained the mug.

"I don't touch liquor, myself," said Halluck. "Against the Lord's will."

"Me neither," said Hatcher rubbing his belly where two mugs of pulque sloshed around like liquid embers.

"Cortez seems hard set on that girl livin," said Halluck. "She his woman?"

"First love, I think," said Louy.

"When we met up with Pete," said Hatcher, "he often talked of his dreams. A good horse, a special valley he had never seen and a woman what would partner him through such life as he would have comin to him."

Hatcher smiled, remembering the early days with Pete.

"He put himself out somethin awful to get her here. Didn't seem natural; so I asks him one night on the trail. 'Pete,' I says. 'You're real stuck on that little gal, aint you?' And he says, 'Hatch. She's the one.' His face kinda got red when he said it. 'She's the girl of my dream. Ever since I first saw her all naked and bloody, scared and angry, I knew. I knew,' he says, like he really did know."

"Cortez is a good man," said Halluck. "I surely hope she makes it."

"We'll know soon enough," said Hatcher.

"Even if the doctor, he pull that arrowhead out," said Louy. "She die, I think."

"Hi yee! Hi yee!" The plaza echoed with Hardy's whoop. Halluck jumped up from the hitching rail and ran to meet him and the rest of his men and wagons. Trailing behind the wagons was Potter's posse with Dibble sitting his Cortez horse tall and sad and draped in chains.

"Where the hell is the jail," yelled Potter to Halluck.

"Yonder," said Halluck with a toss of his head while he pumped Hardy's hand. Then, he looked up at Dibble.

"You the one?" he asked. "Red Hickman said a posse was comin after you." Dibble only shrugged in his chains. "By the way," said Halluck to Hardy, "where is old Red?"

"In the back of yonder wagon," said Hardy. "Tied up neat as spring hay."

"He needs some jailin," said Halluck.

"I'll see to it, Mister Halluck," said Hardy.

"Say, Sheriff," called Hardy to Potter. "Let's fetch that redheaded back shooter along with the black."

Hardy walked to the rear of the wagon and jerked Red into the plaza dust; picked him up and shoved him toward the posse.

"C'mon, niggah," said Potter. "It's jail for you; and a gallon of beer for us."

"God damn right," said Cussin Jim.

"I'll drink a blessed gallon and more, my ownself," said Jones.

Muddy Waters pulled the lead rope on Dibble's horse in the direction indicated by Halluck.

"Be piss trails in the sand tonight," he said.

Potter hazed Red Hickman like he was cutting a calf from its mother. Red stumbled after Muddy Waters and Dibble.

Dibble looked over at Hatcher and Louy. His long, skinny face was blank and empty. He licked a swollen, bloody lip.

Hatcher and Louy stared back at Dibble. Neither waved, neither smiled.

———

In the days that followed, Pete slept on a bed in the surgery when one was empty; or on the floor next to Beckey's bed when all beds were full. Hatcher and Louy brought him food. He mopped Beckey's brow with a wet rag and did bed pan duty; and he fed her water and beef broth, a sip at a time.

"I've got a Mexican woman to do all that," said Doc Stafford.

"I've nursed cows and horses, sick miners and dyin Indians; and I've nursed this here girl for weeks, it seems. One's like another. 'Cept she's, well, more needful somehow. It's somethin I got to do, got to see to the finish!"

He only left Beckey to use the little house out back.

At first, just after the arrowhead had come out, it seemed to Pete that Beckey would leave him at any moment. She lay pale and quiet. Pete had to put his ear to her mouth to know she was still breathing. The flint arrowhead lay in a pan of bloody water by Beckey's bed. Doc Stafford went to throw it out.

"Leave it," Pete said. "She'll want to keep that when she's well; or take it with her, if'n . . . ."

Then the fever came.

"Infection," said Doc Stafford. "Got to expect it. Fever is the real test. If she passes the fever, she'll likely live. If not . . . ."

Pete went up and down with the rise and fall and resurrection of the fever. Hot, taught skin was followed by gallons of sweat and tears. Sweat dried instantly, fired by the searing updraft from the fierce battle raging within. The tears never left Beckey's swollen cheeks.

In her fits of fever, she cried, "Father, Father," and "Pete, Pete" and "No! No! No!" again and again, as if, Pete thought, she were under siege again and again by the Comanche braves who had used her and buried the arrowhead next to her lung.

For three days and four nights, the fever burned dry and tight and wet and hot and dry again. Again and again, Pete bathed her from head to toe with cool water and brandy while she cooked and shivered and cried out.

Before dawn of the forth day, Pete suddenly awoke in the dark. In his long night's doze, he'd missed Beckey's cries and the thumpy-thump of her body as she rolled and shivered in the bed. He jumped up and took her face in his hands. It was cool as death.

"Oh my god," he cried. Clumsily, he took a taper and lit it in the coals of the small kiva-fire. He lit the lamp. He looked hard at Beckey's face, expecting twisted death.

Her sweet face was dry and cool, her chest gently rising and falling under the thin blanket. He heard her breath flowing in and out, soft as peace. Her breath smelled clean and fresh.

Pete's knees buckled under him. He slumped to the floor.

"It's over," he sighed. "And, we won."

Instantly, he slept. He slept a deep sleep. He dreamed a deep dream. His dream. The smoky horse. The green valley of The Cortez. This girl. He dreamed his dream of freedom, home, mate.

At midday, Pete climbed out of his dream. His eyes opened to Beckey's gentle face. She lay on her side, one hand under her cheek. She was just looking at him and smiling. He put a hand to her cheek.

"Cool as a spring house apple," he sighed.

Beckey blinked her eyes, said nothing. She reached figertips to his cheek.

"In a few days," he whispered, "when you're strong enough, we'll go home to The Cortez."

He felt the pulse of life flow through her hand on his cheek and drew strength from it.

Beckey wore the arrowhead on a silver chain around her neck. She felt it bounce from one breast to the other as the gray horse climbed the up-thrusting trail out of the desert. Just ahead, her friends leaned into the necks of their plodding horses to compensate for the steep grade.

Her rump was sore from sudden use after idleness. The afternoon sun tore at the brim of her hat, spilling dust laden beams into squinting eyes. Squinting eyes searched past the heaving rumps of the horses ahead and across the switchback ribbon of trail as it squirmed up another mile or so to the top.

Not far, she thought. Not far.

Eagerly, she spurred the gray horse over the canyon lip into the valley of The Cortez. She saw Pete atop the smoky horse. Smokey stood with legs a-quiver sucking new wind into bellowing lungs. Hatcher and Louy pulled up along side Pete and let their horses blow and sweat out the effort of the long climb.

After the fever had broken, just two weeks past, she'd agreed to come back to The Cortez to recuperate. She had no real choice, no friends except these men, no money, no place else to go until she was strong again.

And she felt compelled to come back to The Cortez.

As one, they surveyed the valley. Far off, up the long slope to the mountain, they watched a herd of horses make for the creek at a gallop. Oxen raised their heads from the grama grass as the horses flew by. A covey of fat, mountain quail exploded from the dust and beat wings to a close clump of junipers. From the same clump of junipers, a bull elk jumped out as if to join the streaming horses. Suddenly, the great bull shied away at a run, raking mossy antlers across the blue sky.

"Louy and me, we been too long in the city," said Hatcher.

Like the horses, he too sucked in the high mountain air.

"You're home," Pete said. "We're all home now."

He moved Smokey closer to the gray. Hatcher motioned to Louy and they started the tired horses toward the corral and cabin on the buttress hill a mile away.

"You're home, Beckey."

Beckey sat motionless on the gray. She was examining the splendor of the valley he seemed to be offering her. Her eyes suddenly searched inward. Home? she thought. I have no rightful home. My only home is the shame my father pronounced upon me. In the oven of my fever or this cool mountain high. That's where I live. Will always live. In my house of shame.

"Beckey? Do you hear?"

"I hear."

She turned the gray horse to follow after Hatcher and Louy; so that Pete could not see the agony in her eyes.

Hatcher and Louy were at the corral, their horses pulled up, stiff legged at the gate. They stared into the corral, looked at each other. They did not dismount. Hatcher eased the Hawkin from its saddle scabbard.

Beckey rode up to the cabin. She felt sore and weak from the long days on the trail from Santa Fe to The Cortez.

At the cabin, Beckey pulled the gray horse to a sudden stop and slid to the ground at its shifting feet. Only a firm grip on the saddle horn kept her from crumpling in the dust. Slowly, she looked up at the cabin.

She heard Pete holler behind her; but all she saw was the shadow of a figure crouched in the cabin door and the muzzle of the long rifle pointed down at her.

# 45

Beckey followed the rifle muzzle up the rusty, octagonal barrel to the feature-less face hidden in shadow behind. Suddenly, the dark face behind the rifle flickered with spots of egg shell white. The muzzle lifted.

Beckey felt trapped air burst from her lungs. She let go of the saddle horn and the gray horse wandered off to crop tufts of grass. Beckey stared at the ghostly figure as it emerged from the dim-lit doorway and onto the sunlit porch.

"Dibble," she whispered.

Then she called to Pete. "Look it's Dibble." She waved at Hatcher and Louy down by the corral.

"Dibble's back—from the dead."

⁕

"This coon could smell a black man all the way from the corral," said Hatcher smiling over a hot cup of coffee.

"You smell no such a sacre damn thing," said Louy, holding the coffee pot over Beckey's cup. "That there lathered up horse in the corral, she was the Cortez horse Pete give Dibble. We both saw him in the corral and knew." Louy poured for Beckey and set the pot down on the table.

"We was fixin to meet you and that there posse down on the trail," said Hatcher. "Kinda surprise you like."

"Me and Hatcher and Pete, we'd-a plucked you from that stuffed sheriff like me and Hatch steal the beaver from sacre damn Englishers' traps. Smooth, easy, quiet."

"Indian-like." Hatcher winked at Louy. Then he looked at Pete. "Cortez here put the quit on that; and he was right. Another day . . . ." He thumbed at Beckey and shook his head.

"Dibble know. 'Course Pete right, 'cause here be Dibble."

"How'd you manage it, Dibble?" said Pete. "Last we saw, you was hobbled for fair in them chains and surrounded by Missouri bounty hunters."

"Yes, how?" said Beckey.

The black man turned his back to the fire. He pushed skillet hands out to ward off the questions. Then he smiled. His eyes and pointed teeth sparkled white in the fire's glow.

"Old Dibble, he just walk away from that Mexican jail." The black man chuckled. "Deep in the night, he hear a key rattle in the lock of that jailhouse; hear the creak of that iron door swingin open on them rusty hinge-pins. He feel the chains come off. Then he just walk out into that deep night. The horse be standin right there, saddle and all. So Dibble come here to bring he home."

"Who was it set you free?" said Beckey.

"Dibble don't know for sure; but it seem to me like two men. Smelt clean like wet soap. It so dark, Dibble can't see no faces. One man taller than the other. No one say nothin."

"Halluck and Hardy, maybe," said Pete.

"Maybe," said Dibble. "Them posse men been drinkin hard since you all left Santa Fe. To a man, they smell like a month of stink. It weren't one of them."

"Sounds like Halluck and Hardy," said Pete.

"That same day, Dibble look out the jailhouse window, see Mister Halluck and he crew. Wagons is loaded. Mister Hardy come over to the jail to say so long. He say they is headed up the trail, leavin that very day, for Missouri; say he reckon the posse catch up in a day or two. He shake Dibble's hand."

Dibble looked down at his huge right hand as if it were a trophy.

"That night Dibble's jail door open. Dibble free."

"Musta stopped outside Santa Fe. San Jose or Tecolote, maybe," said Hatcher. "And come on back Indian-like in the night."

"Funny thing," said Dibble. "That Hickman feller, he was locked up with me in that one room jail. Chained to an iron ring in the wall. Mister Hardy done that."

"What's funny?" said Pete.

"When Dibble walk away from that jail, Hickman still in there chained to that ring. He sleep right through it all. And, them rescuer fellers, they don't wake him."

"Halluck for sure," said Pete.

They sat quietly looking at each other, drinking coffee and smiling.

Suddenly, Hatcher pushed his chair back and grabbed the Hawkin. "Guess I'll take a look around," he said. "Them posse men'll know soon enough where to start lookin for you."

Hatcher ducked out the door.

"They won't come here?" said Beckey, looking over at Pete.

"They come," said Dibble, pointing to a large sack by the door. "Dibble fixin to move on. To California. He borrow some possibles. Lead, powder, grub and things. And the horse, too. For now, Dibble aint got nothin 'cept, well, friends. In California he make he pile, pay back what he owe."

"Like hell," said Pete. "The horse is yours. I give him to you. And possibles? Why, I owe you plenty wages for the horses you broke and more."

Pete got to his feet and went to his bed along the far wall of the cabin. In a moment, he was back. "Here's wages. Enough to get you to California."

Dibble's eyes got big and shinning white.

"This here's more money than Dibble ever see in a black hand or white."

He shook his hand and they heard the gold coins rattle.

"How much money's here, you reckon?" he asked.

"Two hundred dollars."

"Dibble earn that much just bustin a few horses?"

"Cortez horses. Broke gentle. And, fightin Indians." Pete looked at Beckey. "Helpin save the life . . . ."

"My life," said Beckey.

She got up and took Dibble's skillet hand in her tiny pink hands and wrapped the coins up hard in his fingers.

"It's Pete's money; but it's my love."

She gave the scrawny black man a hug and a tear wiped his cheek.

"Dibble better go," he said softly.

It was getting on to pastel time as Pete and Beckey watched Dibble ride the Cortez horse down toward the stream, and California. Louy stood near them on the wide porch, his musket barrel under his chin. Beckey waved at Dibble's back.

Hatcher was nowhere to be seen.

Pete felt a thickness in his throat and reached for Beckey's hand. She gave his hand a squeeze, then pulled her hand away.

"I'll miss him," said Pete. He watched purple shadows play with the dust puffing up from the horse's feet as Dibble rode on, stiff in the saddle, not looking back.

From behind, up on the side of the buttress, thunder clapped and echoed down the slope. Instantly, Pete was off the porch, looking up the hill. Beckey screamed.

"Dibble," she screamed and started to run to the Cortez horse. The horse stood now, wearing an empty saddle.

Pete ran after Beckey. Beckey knelt beside the quivering body of the black man. Dibble lay in the dirt. Blood seeped through his shirt to cover his heaving chest.

"Beckey," said Pete. "The cabin." He picked her up and carried her. She pounded small fists on his face and chest.

"Dibble. Save Dibble," she cried.

In a stride, Pete was inside the cabin. He heard Louy from the porch.

"Three, maybe four men slidin horses down the slope. Sacre damn. They all have rifles."

Pete put Beckey on the floor by the fireplace. "Stay put. This aint girl's play. It's them posse fellers."

He grabbed the Sharps and his cartridge pouch from above the fireplace.

"Dibble!" Beckey cried; but Pete was gone.

Outside, Pete crouched and ran to Dibble. The black man lay sprawled in the dust. His bloody chest was still. His eyes were closed. His jaw hung slack and skull-like across his shoulder. Pete took one look and turned to face the sloping buttress.

Four men rode and slid their horses down the hill. In the evening purple, each rider was a vague shape, one shape no different from the others.

"Best shot ever I made," called one shape to his friends.

"God damn lucky shot, Potter," said another shape.

"Bless my soul," said another. "There's a man with a rifle, looks like, standin right over the body of that niggah."

One by one the shapes pulled in their horses. The horses danced on stiff front legs wanting down off the steep grade. The one behind Potter slid up the rump of Potter's horse before he stopped.

"Damn and be damned."

Cussin Jim tried to turn his horse, failed. His horse stood nose to tail with the sheriff's horse.

"Reckon that man wants to fight," said Muddy Waters, raising his rifle. The other three shapes followed the point of his rifle, their own rifles at the ready.

"Boy!" yelled Potter. "You're standin in the way of official business—and four rifles."

Pete stood his ground and slowly raised his Sharps to his shoulder. He picked out the fattest of the purple shapes in the tang of his rear sight and ringed the fat man in the ring of the front sight. Slowly, the puffy, middle joint of his right, index finger began to squeeze the trigger.

Loud and sudden, Pete heard Hatcher from behind the fence rails of the nearby corral. "Reminds me of the time, up on the Snake River!"

Pete's finger held.

"Me'n Louy, that's Louy Simonds. He's the one got a bead on you boys from the cover of yonder cabin."

"Comin from the corral," one of the shapes yelled. "Can you see him?"

"Bless me!" said another shape. "There's two, maybe three guns pointed up this hill."

"Who the hell's down there? This is Sheriff Potter."

"This hoss guessed who you was right off," said the voice by the corral. "That's what brought back that time up on the Snake."

"What the damn, sam hell you talkin about?" came another voice from behind the fat-man shape on the hill.

"Well, sir. Me and Louy is surrounded by four Indians. Each has a rifle. All pointed at us. Between us we musters just two shots. We looks at each other. Well, Louy moves slowly to his left, me to the right. Just like now."

Just then a shadow moved from the porch. "Just like the man say, Louy, he move to his left. Be sacre damn sure. Got Papa's old fusil all lined up. Which one of you sheriff boys, is Louy gonna kill?"

"Louy. Shut your yap. You'll scare them lawmen." Hatcher laughed. "Now, them Indians figures they has us dead to rights and they's curious about what we is a-doin. They just sits their horses, like you boys, knowing they out gun us and all."

"What happens next? Well, I'll tell you. Bein he's a Frenchman and some impulsive, Louy fires. Just as quick, I shoot. Four Indians fall dead."

The purple shapes on the hill sat frozen horses.

"The way we moved, Louy lined two up and I did the same. At close range, one bullet, two Indians. Louy has already moved. This coon don't have to. You boys are lined up just fine."

"One good shot deserves another," said Potter.

Cussin Jim spurred his horse from behind Potter's and jumped to get out of the line of fire—just as Potter fired.

Pebbles splattered Pete's boots. His finger finished its squeeze on the trigger of the Sharps. He saw Potter jerk up from the saddle, puppet-like, yanked by bullet strings tied to devil fingers; saw his saddle empty; heard the Hawkin and the musket like one thunder; saw flame spit uphill.

In the lightning-flash, Pete saw one of the shapes fire; heard another rifle thunder, saw the flash. Heard Hatcher's Hawkin fire again.

Three purple shapes rolled and jerked down the uneven slope. Hatcher and Louy reloaded in unison.

Cussin Jim skidded against a corral post, lay still.

"Sorry, son. You jumped your horse and my trigger finger just naturally jumped with him."

Muddy Waters came to a stop near the cabin porch. At first he did not move. Then with a groan, he sat up. Louy shoved the muzzle of his musket in Muddy's face.

Slowly, Waters reached into his shirt pocket and pulled out the makings by the tobacco pouch string. With a shaking hand he spilled tobacco into the paper, rolled the cigarette, licked it and looked up at Louy.

"Got a light?"

His hand shook and blood pumped from the wound in his thigh.

Blessed Jones never made the bottom of the hill. His boot hung in the stirrup and he hung from the boot; and, while his horse cropped tender shoots of grama grass, he coughed up blood and died.

Potter lay where he fell, a Sharps ball splintered deep in his gut. He moaned loudly for a while. Then the rocky slope lay quiet in the night.

Pete paid no attention to the fallen men. Gently, he picked Dibble up and carried him to the cabin and laid him on the floor by the fire. Beckey saw his right chest was covered in blood. She knelt beside Pete and pushed her cheek against Dibble's lips. A long time she felt for the caress of wind on her cheek.

"Oh, Pete! He's, he's dead."

Hatcher came into the cabin. "Three dead including the fat sheriff. One calls himself Muddy Waters wants fire for a smoke a-fore I scalps him alive." The last said loud; then quietly, "and, Dibble?"

"Done and gone," said Pete.

"Damn," said Hatcher. "Reminds me of the time . . . awe, hell!"

Hatcher went to the door. "Louy. Bring that skunk in here for his smoke." He pulled out the Green River and danced the blade across his thumb.

Waters limped through the door, the sterile cigarette dangling from pale lips. Blood had poured through a hole in his pants just above the right knee. His jeans were wet to the boot top. With the short walk, more blood wet his leg in spurts.

"Smoke," said Hatcher, waving the huge knife toward the fire. Killing light danced along the steel to hide in the shadow of the concave blood trough which ran almost to the point of the blade.

Waters hobbled to the fire and lit his smoke with a flaming twig. He looked down at the spraddle-legged body of the black man. Then, he saw Beckey.

"Didn't know there was a woman in here."

He exhaled half the cigarette as his wounded leg gave way. Blood spurted from the hole in his pants to paint the floor along side Dibble's own paint.

After a moment of silent suffering, Waters said, "the niggah dead?"

"Yes," said Beckey. "You murdering bastard, he's dead."

She sank onto Pete's shoulder and sobbed out her grief.

"Too bad," said Waters. "Worth a heap-a money back in Missouri, alive or dead. You let me take him back, I'll split the money . . . ."

The Green River flashed at the words on Muddy's lip. A cut off slice of Muddy's lip flew into the fire, the butt of the cigarette still clinging, a-dangle.

"Now for your hair," grunted Hatcher.

Muddy put a hand up to his severed lip; brought it down; saw the blood on his fingers. He looked down at the blood still pumping from his leg. Then he stared up at Hatcher.

"Better get to it, you want live hair, Mister."

Hatcher raised the knife; swung; missed.

"Damn!"

Muddy Waters had keeled over on his face; and, just under the arc of the knife, he died.

They carried Waters outside and dumped his body by the corral next to Cussin Jim.

Back in the cabin, they gathered around Dibble.

"I'll get the shovel," said Pete.

Hatcher put hands under Dibble's armpits. Louy lifted the bony legs. Pete led them from the cabin, head down like a shrouded priest leading bearers of the sacred pall. Beckey walked along beside him.

"We'll bury him there just above the corral. Near the Cortez horses."

They stopped on a small knoll. In daylight, it overlooked the cabin and the corral and, far beyond, the tips of cottonwood tree tops frosted by first light and sunset beams above the Canadian River.

Hatcher and Louy put the inert body down. Pete stabbed the shovel into the soft sand, put a boot on the shovel to sink it deep. Beckey sobbed quietly.

Cicadas and crickets played taps to the bass drum beat of a hundred bull frogs. High on the mountain a solo coyote sang his lonely dirge. The steel-bladed shovel crunched in the sand.

In mid-lament, a new note crept into the night-song of death. A shudder like the slitting of a throat. A groan like bowels moving. The hack-hack-hacking of fresh puking.

Pete caught Beckey in a half-sob. He stopped pushing the shovel. One by one, the insect pipers in the grass quit the song.

"Beckey, go on back to the cabin. We can't have you doin that. Not on Dibble's grave."

"Pete," sobbed Beckey. "Th-th-that's not me!"

"Louy? That you a-pukin?" said Hatcher.

# 46

From the dark ground came a cough, a spit and another groan.

"Oh, my god," cried Beckey as she knelt in the dark.

"It be Dibble!" said a tiny voice. "Dibble pukin."

"Naw, it aint Dibble," said Hatcher.

"No!" said Louy. "Sacre black man's dead!"

"And the dead don't puke." Hatcher grabbed Pete's arm.

" 'Less'n dead blacks do."

"Oh, Hatcher," cried Beckey. "Quit clowning. Dibble's alive. Alive! Take him to the cabin."

Hatcher and Louy picked up the groaning black man. Pete put his arm around Beckey and hugged her hard as they followed the funeral procession, in reverse, down the slope of the high knoll toward the cabin and life.

"Where you white men takin this here Dibble. Dibble can walk good as any man."

⚬

The bullet had severed Dibble's collarbone going in and set it coming out. He spent a week in and out of shock and fever. They took turns at his side, day and night. Bone knit and bacteria slowly died inside him. He ate when fed without knowing and slept in fits of frenzied dreams.

In delirium, he felt the white man's cutting whip, felt his skin rip, the deep sting, salt in the wound of birth; felt the white man's pain-tax, the degradation of his shackled will.

In delirum, he thought his own free thoughts. He sensed the touch of gentle healing; laughed it off down the tunnel of his dream; laughed off the foreign touch; but cried for it.

His delirium accepted the feel of the whip and salt-sting as real; supposed the healing touch a dream's dream, fantasy to be denied. And, he denied it.

Still, the gentle touch and the free thoughts mingled with denial in his hot fancy, confusing the small part of his suffering that remained sane.

Finally, one day, he opened eyes long shut and saw Beckey's smiling face. He felt her white hands softly washing his black brow. He felt the touch of gentle healing and knew the gentle touch was real. Dibble am truly crazy now, he thought—or he be truly free.

For a long time, Pete had planned a garden on the east side of the cabin, near the spring. They had buried Potter's posse on the east side of the cabin near the spring where the boys from Missouri would do the most good for the garden.

On his race back to Missouri with the Santa Fe mails, Halluck sent Hardy to The Cortez to contract for the stock needed to keep the mails on flying wheels rolling to Santa Fe and back home every thirty days.

Hawks hung on a thermal sky as morning crept across The Cortez. Pete and Beckey sat on the porch, lazy like the circling hawks. They'd had coffee and breakfast. Now, they waited for the strength of the day to catch them up.

"Won't break no horses," said Pete, "'till Dibble's up to doin it."

"He won't be up to that kind of work for a while yet. If you want horses gentled, you better think about doing it yourself."

"Me? Why, I paid that man two hundred dollars to do the horse bustin for me."

Pete saw Beckey's sharp look; but kept a straight face.

"Pete Cortez!" Beckey jumped up from her bench. "Dibble busts horses when I say so. Not one minute . . . ." She caught herself; whispered, "before."

Here I am, she thought, suddenly giving orders like I belong to this place—to him.

Pete's laughter brought her back.

"Oh, Pete." She put a hand on his arm for a moment; withdrew it.

Pete noticed the touching and its sudden withdrawal; but didn't let on. He got off the log end he used as a seat and waved his hand across the expanse of the valley from south around the compass to south again.

Beckey watched Pete's hand as it defined his vast domain: the tall grass, the gurgling stream, the herds, the junipers and aspen, the rocky buttresses which seemed to support the upthrust tilt of the high mountains beyond.

"I've had dreams," said Pete, "since boyhood. A rancho, my rancho. Now I have The Cortez. Spanish horses was always part of my dream—and you."

"Me?"

"You, Beckey."

The strength of the day's coming had caught them up just as the revving thermals carried the lazing hawks swooping to the urgency of the hunt.

"No man's dream of woman," she blurted out in a kind of cry, "could have fixed on me, seen the shame I possess—and lingered."

Pete sensed her suffering. He saw her lips pucker and pout, not knowing whether they were poised to speak or to cry. Tears wet undecided lips. She seemed to be looking at events that rushed up from the shuttered door of her soul. He heard mumbled words of a raped woman's shame and the shunning.

"What? What did you say?" He strained to hear.

"I cried out to my father, 'I tried to resist. I was raped;' but he did not believe me."

"Beckey. You don't have to tell anything on my account."

She was shaking. But it was the tremor of rage. Her voice sounded hard like her eyes. Pete put a hand up to still her. Tight breath squeezed her words around his sign to stop them.

"And then the Indians. I fought them by god. When you found me naked as Eve and nearer death than life, still, I wanted to live. Thrice raped, I wanted to live." Her breast was heaving now; but not with breathing.

"So now you see. I can not be the woman of any man's dream."

Pete felt his eyes grow wet. He gripped Beckey, one strong hand on each shoulder. She pushed him away and, for an instant, he felt betrayed. Why?

"I have been used!"

He crushed her to him. The feeling of betrayal was gone, replaced by his need to fight for her, to win her from herself.

"Aint no greater virtue, I'm thinkin, than fightin for life against Hell, itself, and the savage nature in men. To keep on livin. That's what's needful in this hard land; and you done that."

Tight in the clutch of his arms, she slowly relaxed. Her head eased down to rest under his chin. She wrapped her arms around him.

She could feel the tenderness in him, remembered the way he'd cared for her. Gentle. Never more intimate than necessary. Nurturing confidence from which she drew the strength to be saved. And now she felt the longing of this man. It's in his eyes, in the touch of his hand, the tone of his soft voice.

My god, she thought. I feel like I did with Mister James. I was sick and afraid. But Pa was right. I liked what he did to me. And now, Pete wants me; and I want him. God, I do. But there is so much shame in the wanting.

"With you I've had feelings," she said at last. "At first, mostly fear and orneriness. You were just another Indian. With time and healing, other feelings have come over me. Feelings I've never had before. But, the new ones are mixed up with the old. Always will be, I guess."

"About all I can promise you, Beckey, is my love and the time you need to solve your mind-made puzzle here on The Cortez."

"In Santa Fe," she said, "Doc Stafford put me onto a job."

Pete shook his head and put a hand up the way a surprised man does to stop an avalanche; but on it came.

"Teaching school. I applied."

She gave Pete a hug, felt him start to melt, then stiffen. Quickly, she unwrapped herself and stepped back to look out over The Cortez and the lip of the valley into infinite desert haze.

"It is a dreamland," she said quietly. "But, is it mine?"

She turned to face Pete. Again, he put his hands on her shoulders; but his eyes were far off like the stars, she thought, watching a man's dream dissolve like the tissue of night in melty sunrise.

"Dibble's well enough after all, I guess," she said. "I'll leave in the morning. I can teach the children in Santa Fe as I did at home."

"I'll take you."

Pete dropped his hands from her shoulders as she pulled back. She moved to lean against the railing, wanting to feel far away. His shoulders sank into dangling arms.

"I'm sorry," she said.

He took in air and puffed his chest. He smiled, a little at first, then wider, the way a proud man smiles lopsided to hide the rump sores.

"Sorry?" he said. "No, ma'am. There aint no sorry. There's just doin. Bein done to."

He picked a bridle off the wall peg; looked it over like it needed fixing. He stubbed a boot toe at a loose knot and turned to face Beckey.

She saw a new, full-grown look to him.

"Santa Fe?" he said. "Hell. It aint so far a man can't visit from time to time. Specially, if he comes to court his dream."

The smile danced like mischief across his lips.

"I hope you will, often."

"Maybe in time, you'll come to dream about The Cortez." He waved his hand again around the compass of his world. "And love me some."

They stood there on the porch, separate souls melted together in understanding, and yet, apart, rocking to the beat of chancy desert winds.

Pete felt the windy kisses pull warmth from his cheeks, and his yearning.

Beckey was both chilled and warmed by the gusts spawned by spawning gales which had, themselves, circled the world long before she was born.

"Maybe," she whispered into the uncertain desert winds.

www.ingramcontent.com/pod-product-compliance
Lightning Source LLC
Chambersburg PA
CBHW020429030726
47495CB00006B/1730